Carol Wensby-Scott
educated at Farring
becoming a full-time
bookshop. She now li
in Northumberland, where she researched and largely
wrote her acclaimed Percy saga: LION OF
ALNWICK; LION DORMANT; and LION
INVINCIBLE. She is now at work on a new novel
set in the North-East.

COAL BARON

CAROL WENSBY-SCOTT

Futura

FOR GEOFFREY

A Futura Book

Copyright © 1988 by Karel Wensby-Scott

First published in Great Britain in 1988 by
Macdonald & Co (Publishers) Ltd
London & Sydney

This edition published in 1989 by Futura Publications,
a Division of Macdonald & Co (Publishers) Ltd

ISBN 0 7088 4064 7

Reproduced, printed and bound in Great Britain by
Hazell Watson & Viney Limited
Member of BPCC plc
Aylesbury, Bucks, England

Futura Publications
A Division of
Macdonald & Co (Publishers) Ltd
66–73 Shoe Lane
London EC4P 4AB
A member of Maxwell Pergamon Publishing Corporation plc

The Lambton, Hetton and Joicey Collieries

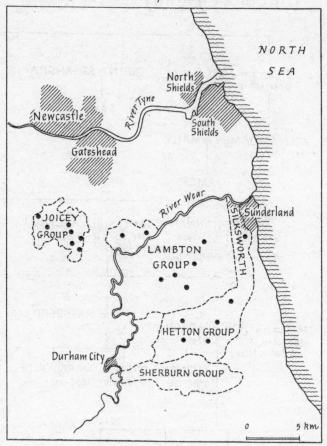

The Joicey Family

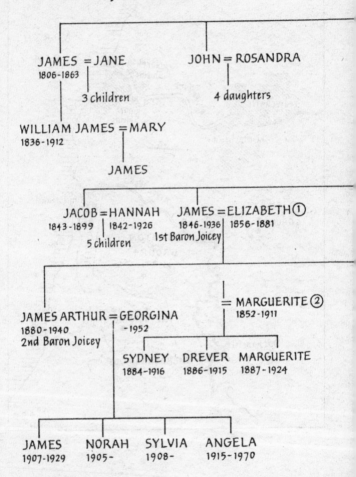

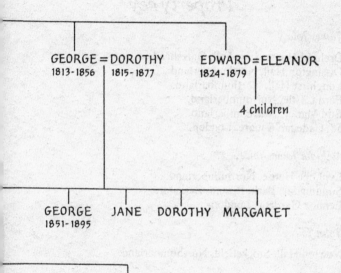

GEORGE = DOROTHY   EDWARD = ELEANOR
1813-1856 | 1815-1877   1824-1879 |
                                    4 children

GEORGE   JANE   DOROTHY   MARGARET
1851-1895

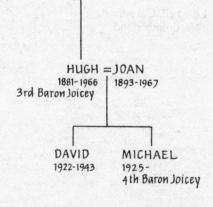

HUGH = JOAN
1881-1966 | 1893-1967
3rd Baron Joicey

DAVID   MICHAEL
1922-1943   1925-
            4th Baron Joicey

Property key

James Joicey

Orchard House, Low Fell, Gateshead.
Dissington Hall, Northumberland.
Longhirst Hall, Northumberland.
Ford Castle, Northumberland.
Etal Manor, Northumberland.
58, Cadogan Square, London.

William James Joicey

Lynhope House, Northumberland.
Sunningdale Park, Epsom, Berkshire.
Lennox Gardens, London.

John Joicey

Newton Hall, Stocksfield, Northumberland.

Edward Joicey

Whinney House, Low Fell, Gateshead.
Blenkinsopp Hall, Northumberland.

Author's Acknowledgement

My grateful thanks to Lord and Lady Joicey for their hospitality and kindness in allowing me access to their family papers. Also to John Bell and Bob Whips of the Beamish Museum for getting me below ground, and to the safety men of Woodside Colliery, for ensuring that I came up again. My thanks also to Mr Eric Forster for his book, *The Death Pit*, on which I relied heavily for the details of the West Stanley explosion; to Mr Tom Hewitson of the Northumberland Fusiliers Museum for the information on the 7th Battalion at the Battle of Ypres; to the staff of the Northumberland and Durham Record Offices, the Durham Miners' Association; to Mr Barry Metcalf for his invaluable instruction in mining technology — and to Jane Prytherch for 'Elizabeth', and James and Agnes de Courcy Wheeler for their help in the preparation of the manuscript.

PROLOGUE

Was there ever so slaving and slashing a trade,
Such a trade as this terrible hewing.

May 7th, 1863
— Gateshead, County Durham

The old man lay motionless in the ornate brass bed. His skull glistened pinkly through his thin grey hair, the engorged tributaries of his veins bulged through his skin. His hands were clenched rigidly on the fine linen sheets, and it was his hands that gave him away — big hands, pitman's hands, tattooed with ragged blue marks from splinters of flying coal; hard and calloused even after thirty years of soft living. Then James Joicey opened his eyes and turned them painfully toward the light. He was dying. He knew he was dying. The paralysis that rigidly imprisoned his left side was gradually creeping over the whole of his body. Not dead yet, though, he thought savagely. He still had his faculties, he still had the power of speech, though his normally harsh and powerful voice was now slurred and indistinct. And his eyes showed that he was still dreadfully alive; brilliant, intensely blue, remorseless and cruel, they moved resentfully around the high-ceilinged room of his house in Walker Terrace. They'd brought him here against his will, the first time in their lives that they'd ever defied him. He'd wanted to die at his Newcastle offices. It had seemed more fitting that he should. It was the only place he'd ever felt comfortable and at his ease. His eyes blazed with sudden fury. It was a hard thing dying before you'd even begun to live, before you'd known any real happiness or pleasure. A stroke, so that fool of a doctor had said — his mouth turned in a lopsided smile — a stroke of luck for the family, those dim figures

11

that moved and whispered on the periphery of his vision. They were waiting, he knew. Waiting, waiting, as they had all their lives to get their hands upon his brass. He eyed their expectant faces with wry amusement; Jane, the young wife he'd married just three years ago, sniffing dutifully beside the bed. His amusement increased. He couldn't say he hadn't had his money's worth out of Jane, bearing him two children in as many years and now heavily pregnant with a third. And she wouldn't come out of it too badly either. She'd be a rich widow soon. Not a bad reward for three years of grudging duty — and thinking about it, she'd been overpaid.

He sighed faintly and couldn't help feeling a momentary regret that he wouldn't see his boys grow to manhood. Probably just as well. Children had a habit of proving a disappointment. Then resentfully his eyes dwelt upon his eldest son, his bastard son, William James. His mother hadn't been important. He couldn't even recall her face. Her name had been Rachael, just a girl who'd fleetingly alleviated his lonely life and had died giving birth to his son. He'd brought the boy home. It had been his duty. He couldn't have borne the thought of his kin in the workhouse. My God, that had given them all something to think about, and he recalled the moment with malicious pleasure, himself standing there with a screaming brat in his arms and telling them straight to their astounded faces that this was his bastard son. A long time ago now, twenty-seven years, twenty-seven years of frustrated hopes and bitter disappointment, culminating in the knowledge that he detested William James almost as much as William James detested him.

His eyes moved on; Dorothy, his brother George's widow, thin, bitter and vengeful. Fleetingly, remembering the smiling vivacious girl that had married George, he felt a moment's pity. Dolly had never had much luck. George had died young, just turned forty, leaving her saddled with six bairns under fifteen and her belly full with a seventh. She hadn't had much luck with her children either; three girls as plain as pikestaffs; Jacob the eldest boy, stolid and dull; George, the youngest, a sickly cripple. Only James, his namesake, was worth consideration. Only James had ever showed him any liking or respect. Yes, he was fond of young James. He had meant to do more for

12

him only he hadn't reckoned on dying so soon. His scathing glance rested finally on his two younger brothers; John, big, bluff, false and jovial; Edward with his gentle and cunning ways. Hypocrites, he thought. Bloody parasites. He had no illusions left about his brothers. He knew they were ashamed of him, that he embarrassed them with his blunt forthright speech, his ability to see into their hearts. They resented his energy, his obsession with work, the fact he couldn't compromise on what he was. And most unforgivable of all, he reminded them too forcibly of where they came from, of where they'd still be if it wasn't for him.

And yet he was proud of that, to have come from nothing. A pitman and proud of it, he'd been down Longbenton pit before he was nine and fourteen hour shifts it had been in those days. Dark when he went down, dark when he came up and nowt but darkness in between. He'd worked his way up; trapper boy, putter, hewer, deputy, clawing his way up through the hierarchy of the mines, and then, no doubt, because he'd been able to wring every ounce of sweat from his fellow workmen, he'd been appointed overman and eventually colliery viewer. And all the time, scrimping and scraping, starving and sacrificing, till he'd hoarded enough to buy a ramshackle old brig and started running coals to London.

That had been the beginning. That had been the start. Two years later he had leased his first pit at Tanfield and within three months had struck a seam of prime gas coal. Oh, he'd made money right enough, hand over fist. It had been a boom time then. Everyone had wanted coals for gas. And he'd put the money to work. Every spare farthing had been ploughed into some new venture; gasworks, brickworks, engineering and steel. He hadn't frittered it away on fancy living. Of course, they'd all thought him an old skinflint, not open handed enough. Well, perhaps he had been, though in the end he'd always meant to be generous — as soon as he'd felt safe, as soon as he'd felt the company secure — except that he'd never felt safe, he'd never felt secure. The shadow of the pit had always hung over him, and the greater the distance he'd put between himself and the old life, the greater his fear of it grew. He'd never been able to forget that all that separated him from that wretched existence was money.

His mouth turned painfully into the semblance of a smile. That was the saddest thing. It had all been done for them; for John and Edward, for George if he'd lived. To get them out of the pits, to keep them out, to give them a better life. Oh, he'd given them that all right. He'd given them soft pink hands and brains to match: he'd made them shallow and envious and greedy. He could sense their impatience. Already they were speculating, spending his money, wondering how much they'd be getting. Not as much as they thought. He'd seen to that. The bulk of his money was to be held in trust for his legitimate children, their mother received only the income. For Dorothy, there was nothing beyond the pension she already received, though there were annuities for her daughters by way of dowry, and a thousand pounds each for her boys. He hadn't had any choice but to leave the company to his brothers — eighty per cent to be divided between Edward and John, twenty per cent to that good for nothing, William James — but all tied up in such a way that they couldn't sell out. If they wanted the money then they'd still have to work for it. His heart sank at the prospect. For all the codicils and provisos of his complicated will, he couldn't safeguard against bungling and mismanagement, he couldn't bequeath his ambition and strength of purpose. That grieved him the most, the thought of the firm in his brothers' incompetent hands. My God, he thought, they'll be like bairns with a shilling in a ha'penny store. They wouldn't be able to get rid of the money quick enough. The thought sent a surge of strength through his tired heart. Well, he wasn't dead yet. He might last for weeks. He gave a low malicious laugh, a strange gurgling noise that drew them all to the bed. He smiled at them happily and closed his eyes. They'd waited twenty years. They could wait a bit longer yet.

Dorothy sat by the bed, her eyes downcast. She would not look at him. She did not have to look at him; that cruel arrogant face would be etched forever in her mind. She was glad he was dying. She rejoiced that at least that harsh sneering voice would be stilled, those cold brilliant eyes forever quenched. She thought with sudden anguish of her dead husband; sweet gentle George, his fine body wasted and thin, consumed by

14

that whispering insidious cough. She lifted her eyes slowly to James Joicey's face. And it was this man that had killed him, old James with his greed and ambition and inhuman demands. George had been delicate. He'd needed rest and clean air. Instead he'd slaved day after day in that hell of a foundry, his lungs shrivelled by the scorching air, choked by dust and fumes and smoke. It had taken him a long time to die. She'd watched him die, slowly choking on his own blood and phlegm. Eight years ago now, dead from consumption in his fortieth year. It had been more than the loss of the man she'd loved. It had been the loss of pride and hope and all her hard won independence. Once again James Joicey had ruled her life.

Her expression grew hard, vindictively bitter. Of course, James had never approved of them wanting to marry. In James' opinion a man didn't take a wife till he was well set up in the world and could afford it. Pleasure must be paid for, he'd always said and, dear God, she'd paid for it; a life of near poverty, birthing children, watching them die and struggling to make a decent life for those that had survived. And then years of caring for George, for their small crippled son . . . She glared defiantly at the old man in the bed. She'd managed though. She'd kept her pride. Never once had she asked him for a penny. Imperceptibly her thin shoulders slumped. It was hard to look back, to believe that she'd ever been young and hopeful.

At the time she'd thought she'd done very well for herself by marrying James Joicey's brother. James had been the up and coming man on the Tyne and she'd imagined an easy and comfortable life. But that was before she had known the kind of man James Joicey was; a ruthless exploiter, remorseless and cruel. He'd made slaves of his own family so that his ambition could prosper, dangling the idea of eventual wealth before them as a means of keeping them to heel. And for her prosperity had never come at all. George had died, and at less than forty she'd been thrown back on James Joicey's charity, going cap in hand to him every month to excuse any small extravagance in her accounts. 'But Dolly, lass,' — the thick calloused finger prodding the sheaf of bills, the deep voice rising incredulously — 'Ten shillings for a hat?' Thus, grudgingly, he had paid her bills, for her two eldest sons to attend a decent school, for her daughters to learn French and the pianoforte — and with every penny he'd spent she had hated him more. Every day she'd prayed that it would be his last.

She rose to her feet and went to stand by the window, pulling the heavy lace curtain aside. It had rained earlier in the day, a brief cleansing shower that had sluiced the houses of their coating of grime and laid the perpetual haze of ash and soot. But not for long. It swirled against the glass, a palpable fog, belched from the tall chimneys that rose like a forest along the banks of the Tyne; blown from mountainous slag heaps — a nauseous, acrid dust seeping up from the shafts plunging fathoms deep to the rich coal seams beneath County Durham. Even behind closed doors you could smell it; you could taste it; feel it, abrasive as sand against the skin. It stung the eyes, it deadened the palate, it transformed all of the landscape into a hideous monochrome world where sun and sky were forever obscured by a pall of pewter cloud. Everywhere there was ugliness and squalor, everywhere there was dirt and noise. She heard the shriek and rattle of a train hauling the coals from pithead to staith. A plume of white smoke marked its passage, past brickworks and gasworks, foundries and coke ovens, ugly conglomerations of pitheads and slag heaps — steel monsters on great iron legs straddling oozing slopes of mud and slime, and crouched at their feet, meek and subservient, row upon row of mean, dirty houses, like supplicants before some mighty god. She smiled inwardly at the mildly blasphemous thought. Coal was their god. Like God it ruled and ordered their lives. They worshipped it and paid it homage, even to the sacrifice of innocent men's lives. It was their life's blood, running through the earth in thick, black, clotted veins ... It was coal that had made James Joicey a rich man.

She turned her head. Her brother-in-law John stood at her elbow. 'Doctor Cummings doesn't think he'll last the night,' he whispered.

Dorothy smiled grimly. 'He might,' she observed. 'It would be just like him to keep us waiting as long as he could. I wouldn't be surprised if he lasted for days.'

John affected to look shocked. 'Dorothy, really ...' He broke off and flushed at Dorothy's knowing look.

'It's all right, Johnny,' she said softly. 'You don't have to

16

pretend anymore. None of us do. He's dying. Soon we'll all be free.'

'Free?' John Joicey repeated the word softly under his breath. Free — the word didn't have any meaning for him. Free. Free. Free to do what? He wasn't a young man any more.

He moved away and went to stand by the bed, watching his brother's shallow breathing. Free — he couldn't get the word out of his mind — after twenty years of blind obedience, of being no more than his brother's clerk. Twenty years of, yes James, no James, well, of course if you really think so James ... Suddenly he felt a curious elation, a growing sense of power. No more James sneering at what he called his 'foppish' ways, no more James criticizing his clothes and his friends. But then James had always sneered at anything he didn't understand. He'd always taken great pleasure in squashing his social aspirations, forever harking back to their humble origins, proud of them in a perverse and cantankerous way. 'Brass is brass, Johnny, and won't ever pass for gold!' He flushed beneath his luxuriant moustache. He could see now how James had held him back. He could have made something of himself if it hadn't been for him. He'd always rather fancied himself as a military man. He felt he had a natural ability for command.

And he'd have married for another thing. There'd been a girl once but it hadn't come to anything. But then nothing that James disapproved of ever did. And so here he was, still celibate after forty-seven years, all his youth and passion lost. The flush deepened to a dull angry red. Bloody hypocrite, that's what James had been, imposing upon them a strict moral code to be followed by everyone but himself. And he hadn't even had the decency to be discreet about it. William James, the old lecher's bastard was here for all to see. His mouth drew down into a sullen line. My God, but it galled him even after all these years — all that preaching about moral strength — all that cant about lust and fornication. And then, bold as you like, to calmly present them with the proof of his own lust, his own fornication ...

He eased his thick neck from the stranglehold of his high collar. He must, he really must, stop thinking about the past. Dolly was right. Soon it would be over. Soon, for the first time, he'd be his own man. A faint smile lightened his heavy

17

features. He was going to make something of himself before it was too late, before life completely passed him by. He had it all planned out; the purchase of a small estate away from the stink of Durham. And of course he would marry as soon as decency allowed. His prominent eyes glistened moistly. A wife, a family, solid respectability, that was all he'd ever really wanted. And it wasn't too late. Forty-seven wasn't really old. And certainly he didn't think he looked his age. A little paunchy of late, he didn't deny that. Even so ... His manicured hand caressed his full moustaches. He was free now. Indeed, they were all free now, to live what was left of their lives.

'Not because we have not power, but to make ourselves an example to you to follow us. For even when we were among you, we gave you this commandment. If a man will not work, neither shall he eat ...' Edward Joicey was reading from an open Bible, although he knew all of the text by heart: Thessalonians II, verses nine to ten. It was James' favourite, heard countless times in this very house where every Sunday the family had gathered. In the evenings he would read to them, the great brass bound Bible open before him. In his rough and heavily accented voice he would extol the virtues of industry and hard work. Oh yes, work had been the thing as far as James was concerned. Work, work, work until you dropped. Edward smiled. And James had, just five hours ago in his Newcastle office, with quill and ledger beneath his hand.

He sighed pleasurably and gave himself over to thinking of the funeral. Even in this, James had made his wishes clear. The hymns, the epitaph, all chosen by himself, even the very spot of ground in which he was to be buried. Not in St Andrew's at Lamesley beside their brother George as he and John had thought fitting. James had insisted on being buried at Tanfield, within sight and sound of his filthy pits. There would be a stone later when the ground had settled, a fine altar tomb quarried out from Gateshead Fell. Nothing elaborate. James wouldn't have cared for anything elaborate. Plain and durable and simply inscribed — that was how he wished it. Edward's smile broadened as it occurred to him that really, James's wishes no longer mattered. Even he couldn't rule them from the grave.

He glanced around the room with wide childlike eyes. It was

a curious feeling, to be his own master after all these years. Again he smiled, a sly, almost cunning smile that sat oddly upon his cherubic features. He wasn't even resentful like the others were. In a way he felt almost grateful. Through James he'd been able to prove himself, to show God that he was worthy of His love. It had been God's way of testing him, a mild and painless martyrdom. And he'd borne all without complaint; James' impatience at his perpetual poor health, his scorn at his piety and natural compassion. James had despised him for being soft, yet even now, it seemed to him an awful blasphemy; to send a man to rip out the bowels of the earth, hour after hour, day after day spent in that filthy suffocating blackness. And not just men, but boys, little lads who grew up into dwarfish, misshapen old men for lack of room to stand. Sometimes the shame of it had been more than he could bear — to think that the very bread that he put into his mouth was paid for by a fellow creature's suffering. He'd always done what he could and given generously to the poor, or as much as James had allowed him. James had not approved of charity or handouts — 'Let them that wants it, work for it.' And so, quietly, joyfully, Edward had suffered. Like Christ he had borne the lash; James complaining when he was too sick and feverish to leave his bed, accusing him cruelly of malingering; James sneering at his sincere and cherished religious beliefs, at what he called his Popish leanings. James, of course, had been an ardent and fiery Methodist, all hell fire and brimstone. Such an aggressive faith, Edward always thought. His own idea of God was gentler, more beatific ... He sighed. Yes, indeed, James had been his cross and he thought, without vanity that he had borne it well. Never, either by word or deed, had he betrayed how much he had loathed his brother.

Behind him, William James fidgeted openly. He would have liked a drink, a good stiff brandy, though he didn't suppose there was any such thing in his father's house. The old man hadn't approved of drink. 'Strong drink like strong emotion turns a man from his purpose,' and so his father had never indulged in either.

He leant forward and nudged Edward. 'How much longer do you think? Shouldn't we get Cummings to have another look?'

Edward made a shocked noise deep in his throat and gave him a censorious look. William James smiled under cover of his blond moustache. He was used to that look; painful embarrassment, disdainful surprise, as if he were something unpleasant discovered on the drawing room carpet. And yes, he could quite see how difficult it had been for them. Plenty of men had moral lapses but very few of them brought their bastards home. For years they'd speculated, wondering who his mother had been. He wondered himself when he was young. On good days it would be a lady of gentle blood, a woman of breeding whose name his father was honour bound to protect. He had a natural arrogance of manner that surely gave the lie to his being wholly of common stock. And he had a gentleman's disdain for money, the earning of it anyway. The spending of it was another matter, for which again he found he had a natural flair. On bad days it had been a whore or even worse, some half witted girl his father had casually seduced on one of his regular trips to London. But not to know, not ever being really sure had bred in him a colossal insecurity, an instability of mood that was sometimes frightening.

Of course, he knew now, all the sordid and shameful details. He gnawed savagely at his upper lip, a habit he had when he was disturbed. And the thought of his bastardy always disturbed him, always made him feel small, second rate, insignificant. He supposed he should have been grateful — not that being James Joicey's son, illegitimate or otherwise, had given him any special privileges. He'd still had to work, and not a nice warm corner in a cosy office as he had envisaged. His father had insisted that he go into colliery management. And so of course he had. His pale eyes dwelt balefully upon his father's face and he calculated his share of the old man's wealth that wouldn't be tied up in the Company. Not so much as he once had hoped, his stepmother and her brats had seen to that, but there'd be something, enough perhaps to enable him to get away, to start a fresh life somewhere else ... Then suddenly the old man's eyes opened and fastened on his face.

'Gettin' impatient are ye, lad?' the old man called from the bed, and his voice, though thin and laboured, was quite audible. He grinned malevolently at the shocked silence. He could almost feel their fear and hatred. 'Get out,' he cried feebly. 'All of ye get out. Aye, an' ye an' all,' he added as Cummings came toward him. He sank back on the pillows. 'Just leave the bairn. Just leave young James. He'll come for ye if y're needed.'

He waited till the door had closed behind them and then beckoned the boy to sit by the bed. He gave his oblique, malicious smile. 'Well, ye might as well know, I've left ye nowt, or next to nowt. A thousand pounds is all ye'll be gettin'.'

'Thank you, sir,' said James politely. 'It's more than I expected.'

'Aye. An' more than ye deserve. A man should make his own way in the world.' He stared in silence at his nephew's dark strong face. He didn't take after his father, thank God. George had always been puny and weak. Strangely the boy looked more like him. They had the same intensely blue eyes. 'How old are ye now, lad?' he asked him gruffly.

'I was seventeen three weeks ago, sir.'

The old man nodded. He liked his voice, soft but strong. 'Y're a man, then, young James. In my day you were a man at ten, the first time ye brought home the pay.' He lifted his head and the muscles of his neck stood out taut and hard. 'And hev ye got yoursel' a lassie yet?'

'No, sir,' said James.

'Good. That's good. Women are trouble, ye'll find that out. Leave them alone if ye can and if ye cannot, make sure ye pick one that's got some brass.' He grinned. 'But divvn't leave it till y're past it like I did, lad, and then kill yoursel' off gettin' bairns.'

James smiled. 'No, sir,' he answered again.

'And what are ye going to do with yoursel'? Ye'll still be going into the offices like we planned? Will that satisfy ye, young James? Clerking for those two old fools at twenty pounds a year, an office of your own perhaps by the time ye're thirty.'

James flushed faintly. 'No, sir,' he said. 'I hope to do better for myself than that.'

'How much better, lad? How much do you want out of life?'

James met the old man's eyes, so like his own. 'Everything,' he said quietly. 'Everything I can get.'

Old James smiled. The answer pleased him. He'd have said

21

the same thing himself at that age. Everything. Everything he could get, everything he could choke from a greedy and hostile world. He'd only had one real talent and that was for money, the winning of it, the working of it. Money had fascinated him. Money meant freedom, money meant power, the means to order and dominate other men's lives, and perhaps more important than the need to dominate had been the need not to be dominated himself. He gave a wry bitter smile. And now it was finished. Soon he'd be dead, imprisoned again in the cold dark earth that he'd struggled so long to escape. And not long now. Already he was aware of the darkness against his eyes, a vague coldness enveloping his body. For a moment he struggled furiously against it. The iron will that had dragged him up out of the pit, continued to maintain a fragile hold upon life. Then suddenly he felt his fingers clasped. The boy's warm strong hand, pulsing with life and boundless energy, gently covered his own. Suddenly he felt comforted. Suddenly he felt certain that all would be well, as if by the clasping of their hands, something momentous had passed between them. 'Y're a good lad, young James,' he whispered faintly. 'Aye, a good lad . . .' He smiled weakly and closed his eyes.

James felt the iron pressure of the old man's fingers relax, and gently, he withdrew his hand. He sat for a few moments staring intently at the finely boned face. It was a face ravaged by every human emotion; sorrow, pride, hatred and grief, and if he could have known it, it would be his own face in years to come.

PART I
1873–1881

September 21st, 1873
— Exchange Buildings, Newcastle

'Well, I'm sorry, James, but it's quite out of the question. It's a great deal of money you're talking about.' John, Colonel John, as he now liked to be called, paced his large and grandly appointed office.

'We've got to draw the line somewhere,' he went on in his clipped and military voice. 'There's got to be a limit on investment. We can't keep pouring money into new fangled schemes without even being sure of a return.'

'Yes, I appreciate that, sir,' James said evenly. 'But our investment budget is particularly low — compared to what it was in Uncle James' day.'

The Colonel flushed. 'Well, that's because things aren't the same as they were in his day. Times have changed, my boy — and not for the better. For one thing my brother never had the unions to contend with. And now there's all this government legislation — Whitehall busybodies poking their noses in. It's already costing us a pretty penny just keeping up with their demands.'

'But that's my point, sir,' said James. 'By mechanizing the haulage system we increase efficiency and therefore output. If you'll just look at my figures again ...'

'Yes, well, I have looked, James,' the Colonel said testily, 'And I don't feel such an outlay is justified. It's all very new for one thing. Let's see how other people do with it, then we'll think about it again.' He beamed at James, the subject already forgotten. 'Well, I must be off. I'm late for my luncheon appointment already.' He picked up his hat and stick. 'I'll see you this evening then. You haven't forgotten we're all dining with Edward tonight?'

'No sir,' James avoided meeting his eyes. 'I hadn't forgotten.'

He opened the door for the Colonel and saw him out. Then quietly he closed it and stood with his back against it, glancing thoughtfully around him. The Colonel's office was the largest and most luxurious of the three partners' offices, though all were lavishly appointed. He also had an office of sorts, a cupboard sandwiched between colliery management and vending, even his name blocked in gold upon the door. But nothing like this. No red Turkey carpet or imposing mahogany desk, no plushly upholstered chairs. On the wall above the fire-place hung old James' portrait, painted in the last year of his life. The artist had depicted him with cold inanimate eyes but James found that the expression varied, depending on the strength and direction of the light. At times they regarded him with vast amusement, at others with mockery, sometimes even a grudging approval. Today they looked back at him with an expression of scorn, reminding him that at twenty-seven years old he was still nothing more than a glorified clerk.

James rose abruptly and paced thoughtfully to the window. At this hour of the day the Tyne seethed with life; the grey turgid water churned by the wakes of a hundred small craft; keel boats ploughing endlessly between staith and ship, steam packets ferrying passengers down to Shields. The larger vessels were anchored a little way downriver: sleek China tea clippers, square-rigged steel barques. Two of the ships moored there were the company's own, double-masted collier brigs laden with best house coal bound for London. And across the river on the Gateshead side; glue and blacking factories, glass and dye works, a frontage of grim ugly buildings, their grey uniformity broken here and there by garish hoardings proclaiming the virtues of Fry's Pure Cocoa and Eno's Salts. He glanced at the clock on the squat unlovely tower of St Mary's . . . Ten past . . . Another twenty minutes yet before the local mines inspector was due to arrive.

He crossed the room and seated himself behind the Colonel's desk. Thoughtfully he lit a cigar, the long West Indian cheroots that he favoured. He often used quiet moments like this to review his progress in the ten years since the old man had died. He'd started at the bottom naturally; messenger boy and runner at eight shillings a month, a year as a ledger clerk, another as assistant to old Clarkson in vending. When Clarkson had died he'd taken his place, working all hours to get the place back on its feet. Business had been bad then, orders falling off. It had taken him a year to get things up to scratch. Then gradually, more and more of the everyday business had fallen to him and he handled almost all the administrative work now, negotiating prices and contracts, purchasing equipment, everything but making the decisions. That was exclusively the preserve of the three partners. Technically, he was just an employee. Of course, a partnership was often hinted at. It was understood that in time he'd be offered a share in the firm. In time, at some vague and unfathomable point in the future. When he'd worked his ticket, proved his worth ... In the meantime, he'd continue to work fourteen hours a day, he'd continue to placate and wheedle, have his ideas and decisions questioned and haggled over ... He thought irritably of his recent interview with the Colonel. He'd set his heart on mechanizing the haulage this year. And it wasn't as if they couldn't afford it. In the last five years the firm's profits had doubled. The last three especially had been a boom time for the trade due to the protracted war between France and Germany. Anything black could be sold for coal these days, and the company had eight pits within a ten mile radius of Durham and Newcastle, all working double shifts, drawing coals twenty hours a day. Prices were astronomical; South Hetton and Lambton Steam fetching twenty-seven shillings a ton, their own Whitehall and Lady Windsor only fractionally less.

His expression for a moment became dark and brooding. Ordinarily he wasn't a patient man. These last few years had demanded iron control, complete subjugation of his arrogant nature. Only one thing had kept him hanging on. By the terms of Old James' will, only fifty per cent of any partner's share could be bequeathed outside the company. The remainder reverted to the surviving partners to be divided equally among them. Once he was a partner, no matter how small his share, when Edward and John eventually died, half of their joint eighty per cent holding would devolve upon himself and William James. It was for this reason he'd been so patient, why he'd allowed Edward and John their freedom without reproach. It was just a question of biding his time.

He left the office early that day, at least early for him, walking home as he always did across the High Level Bridge.

Anonymous carriages passed him. The six o'clock horse brake crammed with shop girls and clerks. At the Gateshead end of the bridge he stopped for a word with Blind Willie and dropped the usual ha'penny in his tin. They said the same thing to each other every night: 'Evenin', Mr James — Breezy the neet.' And he would answer. 'It is that, Willie. It is that.' Sometimes 'breezy' would be replaced by 'warm' or 'chilly' depending upon the season. But that was the only variation. He thought; I am a creature of habit, a machine. When I am thirty-seven I shall still be doing this.

He turned the corner into Walker Terrace and stood for a moment staring up at the lighted windows: Old James' house, his house now, bought with the money the old man had left him. Suddenly he was overcome by a feeling of utter dejection. The house was all he had to show for ten years hard work and the old man had even paid for that.

Upstairs in her room Dorothy stood by the window and watched him come in. For a moment. The sight of him had startled her. She wasn't used to him home so early. Usually it was dark. Often she was in bed. Then she remembered. The family were dining at Edward's tonight. Attendance was compulsory.

She moved away from the window, glancing around the pale walls of her bedroom. This had been old James' room, where he had died, and to her it would always be old James' room. Even after ten years she still sensed him here — aghast at the extravagant fire that roared in the grate, cringing at the cost of the new paint and paper with which she had tried to banish his presence. She'd learnt to live with him now and took a perverse pleasure in his imagined rage at seeing how lavishly his brothers were spending his money. And Jane, the old man's widow, she's taken herself off the minute they'd buried him, Married again by all accounts. They never saw anything of her now.

She prowled the room, an alien figure in its dainty femininity. It was a young girl's room, unsophisticated and fussy, all ruffled satin and frothy lace, crowded with knick knacks and ornament. It was a strange setting for such a harsh practical woman; this cheap sentimental prettiness, this sad attempt at luxury. Yet even now, at fifty-eight years old, she still harboured a secret nostalgia for youth; she still hankered after pleasure and gaiety. This room was her sanctuary, crowded with foolish little mementos of her dreary life. Here she dreamt of beauty and softness and remembered — not a time when there had been these things, but a time when she'd at least had hopes of them. But outside this room there were no dreams or hopes. Life went on, still trying to crush her with its cruel disappointments. Five years ago she'd lost her eldest daughter Jane, marrying and dying within the year, giving birth to a stillborn son. Of her two remaining daughters, neither were wed, though Dolly, the youngest was engaged. Jacob had married, though she didn't much care for Hannah, his wife. But at least he was married. It was more than she could ever hope for poor George. And perhaps she wouldn't have minded so much if it hadn't been for Edward and John, especially John, lording it up at Newton Hall with that supercilious wife of his, Rosandra. Edward too had married, a young girl half his age who now patronised her from that great extravagant house along the Durham Road. Tonight would be an ordeal for her; five full courses of Eleanor's genteel bragging, about how delighted she was with her newly installed bathroom and how much it had cost for the plumbing. Her mouth drew down. My, but it galled her to see the two of them taking their ease whilst James did all the work. Carriage folk they were now, with land and houses and servants galore — and all paid for out of the profits her son made for them. That was the worst thing, to know that they were exploiting him, using him, just as old James had exploited and used them. Yes, that was the worst thing, the way they managed to keep James on the outside. He should have had a partnership by now, a proper share in the firm. Ten years was a long enough apprenticeship.

She finished dressing; a plain gown without even the suggestion of a bustle and the prim lace collar high about her corded neck drew attention to her sagging jaw. She wore her hair with equally unflattering severity, drawn back from an exact centre parting that divided her head like a long white scar. But she was past vanity now, for nothing could have softened that iron mouth or eased the deep frowning cleft from between her eyes. The bitterness was still there, shadows that lurked in their clear blue depths — dark, stinking weeds beneath tranquil water.

She went downstairs and into the large and gloomy parlour. In a queer, perverted way, she was proud of this room though she detested almost everything in it. This was how the world saw her; solid, unimaginative, reeking of respectability and a decent Methodist upbringing. She stood for a moment in the centre of the room attempting to feel pleasure in her surroundings. There were some Indian brasses of which she was quite proud. She saw to these herself and polished them daily to a ferocious glare. The rest of the furniture was dark and ugly, the legs of her tables swathed chastely in chenille, the massive sofa and chairs upholstered in polished hide. At the windows heavy velvet curtains deadened the light. The same velvet draped the mantelpiece on which were crowded her set of Goss china, a black marble clock and a pair of ugly vases corroded with shells. And all this gloom and discomfort was approvingly observed by life-sized engravings of Charles and John Wesley, and a large oleograph of the reformer Calvin receiving the 'First Blast of the Trumpet against the Monstrous League of Women' from a sadistic looking John Knox. She smiled thinly, for she set great store by this display of pious respectability. It allowed her to frown on her family's lavish display, to openly disapprove of their ostentation. So she gave out that she abhorred extravagance and richness, and people who came here went away impressed by the spartan simplicity of her life. They never dreamt that it was a sham, all a pretence. They never dreamt how desperately she hungered for money.

She went through to the kitchen and cast a critical eye over the freshly scrubbed floor. They only had the one servant, a girl to do the heavy work who came in each day. All else Dorothy saw to herself. She preferred it that way. Hard work wasn't a habit that was easily abandoned.

She made the tea, good strong tea, not the pale scented stuff that Eleanor served. The bread, her own bread, she sliced and buttered thinly. And there was cake, heavy with fruit and sticky with sugar, just the way her son George liked it. Then erect and vigorous she carried the tray along the passage, knocking on the door before she entered.

George was reading, seated in a chair by the window. From the waist up he looked like any other young man, older perhaps than his twenty-two years, for the continual pain he had suffered for more than half of them had laid its mark upon his face. It was a handsome face, beautiful almost, like an exquisitely sculptured Grecian head, perfect of line and shape. His eyes were his finest feature, a deep intense blue, quiet, contemplative, perceptive yet tranquil; as if he saw all but felt nothing, as if he had detached himself from the physical ruin of his body and existed only in his mind. Over the years he had become something of a scholar. Books lined the walls of the large quiet room and were stacked in neat piles upon the floor. He was also a fair sculptor and several of his pieces stood about the room. She set the tray down by his bed and called to him to come and have his tea. Her manner toward him was brisk and matter-of-fact, though from the corner of her eye she watched with grim agony his progress across the room. She made no attempt to assist him. He would have resented that and she was always careful to show herself indifferent, to restrain her natural urge to coddle him. She always thought it ironic that with this son for whom she felt such love and compassion, she was the least able to show it.

She said, averting her eyes till he had manoeuvred himself into the chair beside her, 'I thought you wouldn't mind having your tea early seeing as James and I are going out. Dolly'll get your supper when she gets back from Shields. It's all ready. It just needs heating up.'

George sighed under his breath. His mother had always been preoccupied with his appetite, confirmed in the belief that the more she stuffed into him, the healthier he'd be. 'Is James home yet?' he asked.

'Aye, he is, which makes a change.' She piled his plate with bread and cake. 'But then I suppose he sees it as company business — dancing attendance on those two old fools.'

She looked up as James entered the room. He looked well in evening dress, the handsomest and best loved of all her sons, yet out of habit her look became stern, tinged with disapproval. 'Oh, it's you,' she said with heavy sarcasm. 'I'm not used to seeing you before dark.'

James smiled. He was used to her sharp tongue, used as a weapon to protect herself. He understood that. He understood her; that passionate nature so sternly repressed, that bitter and deep-seated anger. It wasn't an easy relationship though. Often

31

they quarrelled. He sensed that they would do so tonight.

He sat down and Dorothy surveyed him critically. He looked tired. There were lines of strain around his mouth and eyes. His face could have done with a little more flesh. Her mouth tightened. He was working too hard, slaving more like. It was time he spoke up about that partnership. She said bluntly, 'Why don't you ask them tonight? It's a good opportunity — about taking you into the firm, I mean.'

James frowned imperceptibly. 'No. Not tonight ...'

'Why not?' demanded Dorothy. 'It's time, long past time ...'

'But it's not the right time,' said James sharply.

'And you think there's going to be a right time, do you?' Dorothy looked scornful. 'If you're waiting for them to offer then you'll wait forever.' She slammed down her cup, choked with silent fury. 'My, but you're following in your father's footsteps right enough. Letting yourself be put on, treated like dirt, working yourself into the ground for nothing.'

'I thought you approved of industry, Mother,' James snapped.

'So I do, in reasonable quantities and when there's some point to it. But there isn't any point to it except to put more and more money into those two old skinflints' pockets, and that's good for nothing, William James.'

James was silent for a moment and then he smiled. 'It's all right, Mother. I know what I'm doing.'

'Do you? I wonder?' Dorothy looked grim. 'Your father used to say that. "Be patient, lass. Give it time." Only he didn't have any time. He was dead before he was forty.'

The dining room at Whinney House was a full forty feet long, a great vault of a room, brooding and massive, panelled in crimson moire silk and finest Honduras mahogany. Its dominant feature was a long table of carved black walnut, capable, by the clever insertion of extra leaves, of being extended to nearly the room's entire length. So useful, as Eleanor was fond of pointing out, for her more formal and extravagant dinners. But tonight they were only a small party, just the immediate family; Edward, plump and rosy as an ageing cherub; Eleanor, his young and pretty wife. The Colonel, resplendent in full dress uniform, his face heavy, assured, festooned with handsome side whiskers and an enormous moustache; Rosandra, his wife, massively pregnant, showing large white teeth when she smiled. And William James, blond, suave, eyelids drooping with boredom; the pale nervous creature beside him was Mary, his wife.

Dorothy laid down her knife and fork with a clatter. She had eaten hardly anything, refusing to be impressed by cold consommé and skinny grouse in a rich and sickly sauce. She would eat when she got home; a slice of cold pie baked by herself, some cheese and arrowroot biscuits. Her puritanical gaze swept round the room, despising everything. She felt like a servant, an object of charity. She could feel the other women's pitying glances. And she knew what they said behind her back, laughing at her, sneering ...

She dropped her eyes to her rough hands clenched together in her lap. Sometimes it was too much. This room, this house, these women in their finery ... She sipped at her water. The moment passed as it always did. She turned impassively toward Rosandra, who was enquiring if they'd set a date for Dolly's wedding yet as she and John were thinking of wintering abroad ...

'June.' said Dorothy, 'We thought the first week.'

'Very sensible. Once can usually rely on the weather in June — although last year, I remember, was unusually wet. I don't think we used the new victoria once ...' And so on and so on, chattering inanely about herself; her ailments, her condition: 'Of course, this time we're hoping desperately for a son. Not that John doesn't adore our three little maids. But of course, a daughter can't inherit, not in the same way ...'

And then after dinner, as they were leaving the men to enjoy their port, a fresh assault: 'You really must come up to Newton, Dorothy dear. It would do you good to get away from the town. And we have plenty of room, seventeen bedrooms ...'

Then into the drawing room; an explosion of crimson plush upholstery, black lacqueur cabinets and papier-maché chairs. Around the walls, ornate Buhl cabinets jostled with serpentine chests, each piece bursting with bric-a-brac and china, every surface cluttered and obscured with inlaid boxes, porcelain figurines, huge exhibits of exotic stuffed birds imprisoned beneath great glass domes.

Tea was served in eggshell thin cups. Rosandra, like a well-oiled machine, chattered on. 'Well, of course London's all very well during the season . . .'

Eleanor looked bored. She glanced at Dorothy. 'And how is George?' she asked, smiling. 'We don't seem to see very much of him these days.'

Dorothy's expression softened. 'Oh, he's well, thank you, Eleanor. He just doesn't get about very much, that's all.'

Rosandra interrupted in her shrill tactless voice 'I think you're so brave, Dorothy. It must be such a burden, a crippled son, although, of course, you still have the girls to help you. And James must be a comfort. My dear John tells me that he is doing very well in the firm.'

Dorothy eyed her with avid dislike. 'Very well for whom, Rosandra? Certainly not for himself.'

Rosandra's eyes widened. 'I don't know what you mean?'

'Perhaps you'd better ask your "dear John", then,' Dorothy's lip curled. 'He'll know what I'm talking about.'

Rosandra's eyes grew cold. 'If you have something to say, Dorothy, I suggest that you do so . . .'

Dorothy stood up. 'Yes,' she snapped. 'I've got something to say, though I doubt if you'll want to hear it.' she fixed Rosandra with a scathing eye. 'Don't you ever think, madam, where your money comes from? Don't you ever wonder who earns it for you? You must know it's not that husband of yours. It's years since he did a day's work.'

'John is a gentleman,' said Rosandra icily. 'He doesn't need to work.'

'Well, that's right enough,' Dorothy agreed. 'Because my son's fool enough to do it for him.'

'Dorothy,' said Eleanor sharply. 'What are you saying? That James is, in some way, being cheated?.'

'Yes. That's exactly what I'm saying. He was promised a partnership, a share in the firm, and all that he's had so far are promises and excuses. Every time it comes up, he's put off.'

Rosandra laughed unpleasantly. 'I'm afraid it's not quite so easy as that, Dorothy. One can't just walk into the company like that. It's usual to make some sort of contribution.'

'And you don't think ten years' hard work is some sort of contribution?'

'For which, I don't doubt, he's been fairly paid.'

Dorothy smiled grimly. 'Fair for one man's work, perhaps, Rosandra, but James has had to do the work of four.' She nodded her head. 'Aye, well, think about it, won't you. Just remember who's really doing the payin' before you start lookin' down your noses at me.'

She sat down in grim silence and picked up her cup. After a few moments the three other women started talking again, about their husbands, their children, their houses. Dorothy said nothing at all. She might as well not have been there.

In the adjoining room the four men sat together in pleasurable silence. Port had been placed upon the table — a Cockburn '51 — along with sherry and madeira. Cigars had been offered, good Havanas, and the Colonel settled back, wrapped in a haze of fragrant blue smoke. This to him was the most pleasurable part of any evening, an hour relaxing in the company of his fellows, for much as he loved his dear Rosandra, he still preferred the company of men. It was also a time for reflection and appraisal, when, his senses heightened by wine, his belly full, he took pleasure in looking back. A look of smugness and complacency settled upon his face. Amazing how quickly he had found his niche, how easily everything had fallen into place. Mind you, he hadn't got where he was without effort, cultivating the right people to get into the right places, greasing a palm here, giving a handout there. For years now he'd been a prominent benefactor, pouring money into any good cause that would get him noticed. And he'd done well, even if he said so himself; Colonel of the Volunteer Regiment, Justice of the Peace, Deputy Lieutenant for Durham. And his appointment as High Sheriff when old Radley popped off, he had been assured, was a foregone conclusion.

Then Edward said, touching his napkin fussily to his lips: 'I meant to ask you, John. What were your thoughts on these new mining regulations? James tells me it's caused quite a furore in the trade.'

The Colonel cleared his throat, preparatory to a long speech. There was nothing he liked better than the sound of his own voice and fortified as he was, with a bottle and a half of Edward's excellent Moselle ... 'Madness,' he said in his loud military voice. 'Complete and utter madness. If you want my honest opinion . . .'

William James groaned inwardly. Dear God, he thought, how that old fool could go on. He tilted his head back and stared up at the smoke wreathing above his head. He felt physically ill at the prospect of having to listen to that voice for another twenty years, or Edward's, or Mary's, on and on and on . . . He gulped at his port, draining his glass, waiting impatiently for the decanter to reach him. Christ! He'd go mad if he didn't get out of here soon. One day . . . But for how long had he been saying that? And here he still was, still bored, still trapped — except that they were different things that kept him now. He thought with fury and bitterness of his demure and colourless wife. Dear Mary, dear sweet virginal little Mary, the little grey mouse who'd unbelievably caught and swallowed the cat. Like father like son — except that Mary Clark had been the respectable daughter of one of the firm's engineers. He'd had no choice but to marry her, to tie himself up for the rest of his life to a woman he no longer desired and had never loved, and who had no assets either socially or financially. And then, as if to spite him further, she'd miscarried the child after just two months. She'd given him another since, the first and the last. For a long time now he hadn't shared her bed.

He yawned, bored by his own thoughts. The Colonel still rambled on, pontificating on the government's bungling of trade union reform and how much better he could have handled it. He writhed in his chair. He couldn't stand this for the rest of his life, being shackled to Mary, the company — and of course, his dear cousin James.

He slid a baleful glance along the table. The sharp lean profile was turned toward him, the cold eyes hooded as if deep in thought. Dear James, clever James, indispensable James. Without knowing why he averted his eyes. When he looked at James, when he really thought about him, an unpleasant sensation crept along his spine. He knew all kinds of men; scoundrels, rogues, hypocrites and fools — but he didn't know anyone quite like James. And not being able to know him, not being able to understand him had made him wary and distrustful. They'd never been friends, not even as boys. There were nearly ten years between them, but he never really thought of

James as being younger. There was nothing remotely youthful about him though he could understand that, saddled with a widowed mother, two sisters and an invalid brother to boot ... Then with a start he realised that James was speaking to him. 'I'm sorry,' he said, 'What did you say?'

'I said, there's wet in Main Coal at the Air Pit.'

'There's always wet in Main Coal.'

'Not so much as this. Five or six inches now I'm told.'

'Who told you?'

'Matt Henderson. I took the men's pay over this afternoon.'

'Ah! Deputy Henderson, your own personal spy. Wouldn't it have been better if he'd reported it to Keegan, the viewer.'

'He says he did. He says that he mentioned it to Keegan last week.'

'Well, then I'll wait until Keegan mentions it to me.'

'So you're not going to do anything about it?'

William James looked irritated. 'No, I'm not. If Keegan hasn't mentioned it, then he doesn't think it's worth mentioning. For God's sake! You expect a certain amount of water in shallow seams.'

'A certain amount. But not this amount. And Henderson reckons there shouldn't be water at all in that particular district. It's right up against the barrier.' James' voice hardened imperceptibly. 'I think you should look into it. Henderson knows what he's talking about.'

Open hostility suddenly flared between them. 'That remark, I presume,' said William James coldly, 'was meant to imply that I do not.'

'No. It wasn't,' James answered mildly. 'I was just stating a fact.'

'Well, let me state another fact.' William James leant toward him, anger thickening his voice. 'I know it's instinctive for you to want to do everyone else's job apart from your own — but management of the collieries is entirely my affair, and things would run a deal more smoothly if you'd allow me to do my job without constant interference.'

James smiled provokingly. 'I'd be perfectly happy to — if you did do it properly. I sometimes get the impression that work interferes with your social life.'

They stared at each other with polite enmity, for so long

that the tension between them was felt by the two other men.

Edward eyed them anxiously, sensing discord. 'Is anything wrong?' he enquired uneasily.

William James laughed shortly. 'No. Nothing's wrong, Uncle Edward. I was just putting James right on a point of company policy.' He gave his cousin a look of virulent dislike. 'Isn't that so, James?'

James merely smiled.

October 12th, 1873
— Beamish Colliery, County Durham

James waited for Henderson in the under-viewer's office, squeezed like an afterthought between screening sheds and weighs. The dingy painted walls were adorned with faded sepia photographs of the company's various pits: the Handen Hold and Alma at Pelton Fell, the Gate and the Burn Drift at Twizell. Here at Beamish, the Air and Second pits; the Jackie at Stanley. And over at Tanfield; the Whin, the Bute, the North and the Ann. Eleven pits in all.

He went and stood in the doorway, looking out for the deputy. It was fully dark — or as dark as it ever got in Durham for there was always the glow of a blast furnace somewhere, the reflection of gas lamps staining the sky.

'How then, Matt?' He stepped back to allow Henderson to enter the office.

'How again, Mr James.' Henderson spoke respectfully, but he made no other concession to James' position. They'd known each other since the old days at Stanley, when James had been just a scrap of a boy and he'd been a cocky young hewer. He wasn't so old now, not much past forty, but he had the crouched ageing stoop common to all pitmen, and when he spoke, his words were punctuated with little gasping sighs as he breathed through lungs corroded by dust. It was a queer relationship, reluctant on both sides. Neither would ever have admitted to friendship.

'What's the problem then, Matt?'

'Same as afore,' the deputy answered dourly. 'The wet in

Main Coal. Except I reckon I know what's causin' it now.'

'Have you spoken to Keegan?'

'Aye. I hev, but he still reckons I'm makin' a fuss about nowt.'

'Where is he now?'

'Over at the Second. I'll fetch him if ye like, but I don't reckon this is somethin' that can wait.'

James nodded. 'Go on.'

Henderson took a set of plans down from the shelf, unrolled them and carefully weighted the corners. 'If y'll look here, Mr James. I can show ye more easily on the plan.'

James stared down at the flimsy tracing, a plan of the underground workings in the Main Coal level. It resembled a gigantic spider's web, the travelling roads stretching out from the two main shafts, linked by the grid-like formation of the workings. Like most northern pits they worked bord and wall; pairs of bords or headings were driven some thirty yards into the seam then turned at right angles to form a cross holing or wall, thus isolating a pillar of coal which was left intact to support the pressure of the roof. These pillars were got out by a second working, either wholly or partially depending on the need for surface support.

'Now then, this section of the seam was worked out years ago.' Henderson pointed to an area on the perimeter of the workings. 'An' this is where the water is holin', all along this western section of the face, where our workings join up with South Derwent's pit. According to the plan there should be a good thirty yards of coal between the two pits.' He paused and looked at James significantly. 'Well, I'm tellin' ye, there's nivver thirty yards of coal there now. I reckon South Derwent hev broken the barrier and hev been workin' our coal.' Again he drew James' attention to the plan. 'Y'see. Just short of the barrier the seam dips down into a trough. The barrier coal should sit in that trough and carry on to the rise some twenty yards beyond. South Derwent must hev worked enough of our barrier coal to empty the trough, which has filled up with water from their old workings and is now putting pressure behind the face.'

James looked grave. 'It couldn't be an underground feeder?'

The deputy shook his head. 'It's dead water comin' through,

reeking of stythe.'

James was silent for a moment. Then he said; 'I think I'd like to take a look myself. Can we get down?'

'Aye. The hewers were up half an hour since. It'll be just the boys that are down.'

James changed into his pit suit: Norfolk jacket and breeches, thick stockings and boots, a leather skull cap to protect his head. Henderson was already at the shaft and waited for him on the upper decking level. He had to raise his voice above the noise, the continual roar of full tubs running over the metal floor to the weighs, the hollow rattle of empties returning. They had to wait for the cage. James glanced at the indicator set with the various levels of the pit; Beaumont, Shield Row, Five Quarter, Brass Thill — Main Coal at ninety fathoms. Then the warning bell sounded the approach of the cage. The sleek oily cable quivered with tension and began its swift and silent upward movement, flying up into the headgear a full seventy feet above their heads, over the pulleys, then sloping down to the tall brick tower that housed the four hundred horse power vertical winding engine. And all so smoothly and silently, so that when the cage with its twin decks abruptly leapt up out of the darkness, he was always faintly startled.

They waited for the cargo of tubs to be unloaded, from where they were run to the weighs before being discharged over the screens for grading and cleaning. James gritted his teeth as he stepped into the cage. He always hated the actual descent, that feeling of helplessness as the cage lifted and the restraining keeps were pulled away. He always had the same thought; two and a half ton suspended by a thin steel rope and a hundred fathoms of empty air beneath them. His muscles tensed, hearing the deep thrust of the engine, the whine of the steel rope scouring the wheel ... Then they were falling, plummeting down into darkness, the air rushing past, roaring in their ears. Neither man spoke. Neither could have been heard over the roar and clatter of the descent. Now and then the bars of the cage flashed into stark relief as they passed the upper seams. The air grew warm, harder to breath, pungent with the smell of wet earth, saltpetre, horse sweat and urine. Then suddenly his stomach lurched up into his mouth as the cage slammed down on its bed of rock. He was first out, his legs trembling from the force of the impact. It took him a few moments to get accustomed to the darkness. It was a different kind of darkness here, stubborn, unrelenting, heavy as lead. And the silence; separate and aloof so that all the noise and clatter of the pit was somehow outside it.

They collected lamps from the onsetter's cabin and moved off down the wide timber-baulked road. Though the height of the actual coal seam was a bare three foot, the going on the travelling roads was relatively easy, the roofs having been ripped down to make adequate headroom. On either side, deep caverns of darkness plunged between pillars of standing coal. Now and then a dark squat figure emerged, a flash of white eyes, a wet pink mouth, shadows that moved through the labyrinth of the workings with the ease of rabbits in a warren. James eyed everything with critical interest. They were working pillars in this seam — dangerously, laboriously and to James' mind entirely uneconomically, for more often than not the pillars deteriorated, becoming dead and winded in the interval between the workings, which sometimes could be years. Similarly, their haulage system was years out of date, hand tramming of the tubs between the face and the flats, then by pony haulage along the main roads to the shaft. He had hoped to install mechanical haulage this year; ropeways in tandem pulling the full tubs out and returning empties in a single operation. Now, of course, that would have to wait.

They turned off toward the waste. The timber stopping which diverted the air current had already been taken down. James gagged at the smell, a graveyard smell; cold stagnant air tinged with black damp that dimmed their lamps and settled like lead in their lungs.

They kept to the airways but even so they needed to stoop for the pressure of the overlying strata had crushed some of the pillars and thrown up the floor in several places. The silence of this place was vast and oppressive. Feeding upon the smallest sound so that their footsteps — stumbling over old rolley ways and heaps of stones, squelching through pools of oily mud — sounded like the marching of an army. They moved more slowly now, on their knees as the roof bore down and narrowed and headway to a mere two foot. The air grew heavier, harder to breathe. Now and again there was a whiff of stythe.

They were now a mile and a half from the downcast shaft with still another half mile to the western section of the face. Water was the major hazard now, dripping down from the porous roof, trickling through pack walls to swell the rivulets of oily stagnant water coming away from the barrier. Three inches now over the top of their boots. 'It's worse than I thought,' Henderson gasped. 'I'm not sure that we shouldn't turn back.'

James mopped his face. 'How far off are we now?'

'Not far. Just yards I reckon, from the slant of the heading.'

Then suddenly the ruptured wall of the coal face lurched into view; black, wet, glistening and evil, hissing softly as it breathed out gas. Henderson held up his lamp. Thin jets of water spurted through hairline cracks. The fractured coal groaned ominously. The deputy manoeuvred himself round so that he was facing James. His face was pale beneath his dirt. 'I reckon we'd best get back, if ye divvn't mind, Mr James. That bugger might give way at any minute and there's a powerful lot of water behind it.'

James nodded. He had seen all he needed to see.

Half an hour later, clad in dry clothes, James warmed himself by the fire in Keegan's office. He was thinking of Robert Dickinson, owner of the South Derwent Colliery Company — and how many tons of coal he'd had out of the barrier at their expense. It was an old game, and one at which Dickinson was particularly adept.

He turned his head as Henderson came into the office. 'I've sent over the Second for Mr Keegan,' the deputy said. 'He's bringin' extra pumping gear. There's more water coming into the haulage than our own pumps can manage.'

'Are all the men up?' James asked, making room by the fire.

'Aye. Up or coming up. We're lucky that both shifts of hewers had finished.'

James nodded and sat in silence for a while, tapping a pencil thoughtfully against his teeth. Then he said, 'What are our chances of proving the trespass conclusively, I mean as to actual amounts?'

'Not much. It'll be an old trespass. A lot'll depend on the state of their workings. They won't be up to much in all that wet. Happen there'll hev been falls. There's bound to be gas.

Ye'd nivver get a man down there to see.'

'It might be possible though, once we've pumped out and made safe, to make borings through the barrier to ascertain what breadth of coal remained and make a calculation that way?'

'Aye. Mevvies. But I cannot see Dickinson payin' much heed to that. Ye'd hev to go to law to prove it.'

James frowned. 'I suppose there's even less chance of proving that the trespass was deliberate?'

'Well, that'd depend on whether he had a plan of the seam which showed the boundary.'

'Would he have had a plan?' James asked.

Henderson shrugged. 'He might. We have. Although you didn't have to keep them in those days. An' even if he has, he'll not admit it.'

James smiled. 'He might, Matt. He just might if I go about it in a certain way.'

'Mr Joicey!' Robert Dickinson, owner of the South Derwent Colliery Company welcomed James into his Lombard Street office. He was a short, powerfully built middle-aged man with thinning hair which seemed to grow from a parting just above his left ear. He had a large mouth, rather brutal, which he minimised with a heavy waxed moustache. He also had a ready smile and small, very shrewd blue eyes.

James shook hands and was introduced to John Hale, viewer of the Shield Row Colliery, the pit responsible for the trespass. He was offered a chair, a cigar, a little something to keep out the cold. He accepted only the chair.

'Well now!' Dickinson leant back and smiled expansively. 'We'd best get this trespass business sorted out, I suppose.' His tone was off hand and mildly patronising, as if the filching of some thousands of tons of Joicey coal was nothing more than a clerical error. He leant forward and placed his large hands palms down upon the desk. The gesture seemed to say; See! I am an honest man. I have nothing up my sleeve. He went on. 'I hope we can settle the matter amicably, between ourselves, so to speak. After all the trespass occurred a great many years ago, possibly as many as twenty. It's usual in these cases to settle for the value of the coal taken, although, of course, it's unfortunate that the waste on our side has deteriorated to such an extent that your surveyor was unable to gain access.' Again the quick and easy smile. 'Nevertheless, I'm sure we can come to some mutually agreeable arrangement.'

James also smiled. 'I'm sure we can, Mr Dickinson.'

He withdrew some folded papers from his inside pocket. 'I presume you still have no explanation as to why the trespass should have occurred?'

Dickinson shrugged. 'As I said, Mr Joicey, it was some years ago. There are no actual plans of the workings in question. As you know we were not required to keep them then. I suppose to the workmen, one coal face looks pretty much like another.'

'I see,' said James. 'It's fortunate then that my company does have plans, and we have been able, by taking borings, to ascertain what breath of the barrier remained. In fact I already have some figures prepared.' He looked Dickinson full in the eye. 'By my estimation, we are talking about some ten thousand tons.'

Hale gave an involuntary exclamation. Dickinson flushed and gave an uneasy laugh. 'I think your calculations are a bit out there, old man. I wouldn't have thought it was half that.'

'Wouldn't you?' said James with an air of surprise. 'I wonder you can be so definite, Mr Dickinson, seeing as you have no plans.' He spread his hands in a regretful gesture. 'But of course, if the amount is going to be in dispute ...'

Dickinson flared up suddenly. 'Damned right it's in dispute at ten thousand tons.'

Hale cleared his throat nervously. 'No one can be certain. Mr Joicey. underground boundaries are almost impossible to define ...'

'Not if there are plans, Mr Hale.' James eyed him pleasurably. 'But then if there were plans that would make the trespass a deliberate action on South Derwent's part, which would put quite a different complexion on things.'

Hale glanced uneasily at his employer. 'There are no plans,' he repeated what Dickinson had said almost word for word ... 'The law didn't require us to keep them then.'

'But most coalowners did keep them,' James remarked quietly. He looked at Dickinson. 'You kept them, didn't you, Mr Dickinson? I know that, you see, because I have seen them.'

Dickinson and his viewer exchanged agitated glances.

'I'm afraid,' explained James, 'I took the liberty of telling the clerk in your tracing office that I had your consent to see them.'

'The hell you did,' shouted Dickinson. 'I've never heard of anything so underhand.'

'Have you not, Mr Dickinson? You don't think deliberate trespass, concealment of evidence, might fall into a similar category?'

They stared at each other for what seemed a long time. Dickinson was the first to let his eye fall. He flapped his hand in an impatient gesture. 'All right, Mr Joicey. Let's not waste any more of each other's time. What sort of money are we talking about?'

James consulted his papers. 'Well, bearing in mind your company have borne the cost of the hewing and transport from the face to the surface' — he made it all sound so very fair, as if he was giving him every concession — 'and calculating on a price at the pithead of four shillings and sixpence a ton. I would think seven thousand pounds would settle it very well.'

There was silence. Dickinson's face turned a purplish hue. Hale looked as if he would faint. 'Of course,' James added when the silence had gone on for a full minute. 'If you're really unhappy with my estimation, you may prefer to take the matter to law, which could involve both lengthy and expensive litigation. In fact, I've known cases like this drag on for years.' He smiled. 'And of course, if the court found against you, you would be liable for the costs as well. In retrospect. You might think seven thousand pounds a bargain.'

'Five thousand,' Dickinson snapped. 'I'll not pay a penny more — and you're bloody lucky to get that.'

Then James said, carefully and patiently. 'Perhaps you have misunderstood me, Mr Dickinson. There is no question of negotiation. Seven thousand pounds is the sum that will satisfy me and I shall give you exactly twenty-eight days in which to pay, after which interest will accrue at the standard rate.' James rose to his feet and bowed to both men politely. 'Good day, gentlemen. I can see myself out.'

December 20th, 1873 — Newcastle

Colonel John's boisterous laughter echoed round the room. 'Well done, my boy.' He slapped James heartily upon the back. 'My God, I'd liked to have seen old Dickinson's face. And to have paid up without a murmur.' He threw a scathing look at William James, as if to say; There! That's how it should be done. William James said nothing, already conscious that he had not come out of the affair at all well. No one had actually said anything yet but he knew that recriminations were bound to come.

Edward looked mildly unhappy. 'I can't help thinking you know, that it was — well, just a little unscrupulous on our part. After all, the value of the coal was only half that amount ...'

'Oh, come on, Edward,' shouted the Colonel. 'Dickinson's behaviour wasn't particularly scrupulous either. Business is business, you know. Dog eat dog. You've got to be practical. The company is seven thousand pounds better off and seven thousand pounds is a great deal of money.'

'Yes, it is,' said James suddenly.'A very great deal of money' — he paused — 'the price of a partnership, wouldn't you think?'

There was silence. The Colonel's smile faded. 'I'm not with you, m'boy. How do you mean?'

James looked at him without expression. 'As Uncle Edward said, the cost of the trespass to the company was only half that amount. The rest I earned for it. I think it entitles me to a stake in the company.'

'Now look here, young fella.' The Colonel glared at him. 'I'm not sure you know that I care for your tone. Naturally, in time you will be offered a partnership — but offered mind you. It's not a thing you can demand. My God, I worked for my brother James for nearly twenty years before I was taken into the firm. You wait your turn, young man, same as I had to.'

James' face was very white. 'I'm not prepared to wait any longer. I think I've waited long enough,' James said quietly. 'I want a five per cent share ...'

The Colonel's face turned purple with rage. 'Don't you damn well dictate terms to me!'

'I'm sorry that I have to ...'

William James interrupted. 'I agree with the Colonel.' He looked with smiling malice at James. 'These bullying tactics might have worked with Dickinson, but they won't work with us, you know. And quite frankly, three and a half thousand pounds is a pittance set against the company's assets ...'

'It's more than you've ever put in to it,' James threw back, 'and only a fraction of what you've taken out.'

'My God, you've got a nerve. Who the bloody hell do you think you are?'

'Silence, both of you.' The Colonel's strident voice restored some semblance of order. He looked at James. 'Now let's discuss the matter calmly.'

'There's nothing to discuss,' snapped James. 'If I am not to be a partner, if I am not to own some part of the company, however small ... Well, if I'm worth so little to you then you won't have any trouble in finding someone else to take my place.'

'He's bluffing,' said William James. 'You know damn well that he won't leave the company. He's put too much into it to get out now.'

'Shut up,' the Colonel yelled. 'You've already said enough.' He tugged uneasily at his handsome moustache. Then he glanced at his brother; 'Edward?'

Edward was looking at James, and he was reminded for some unknown reason of Faust. Yes, he could imagine James selling his soul for wealth and power, except that James would never have reneged on the bargain. James would have gone smilingly into hell. He lowered his eyes, examining his own pale and sensitive hands. Unlike his elder brother, who deluded himself that he was still in control, Edward was a realist. They needed James, and not just because of the hours and effort he put in. James had given them the freedom to do as they pleased and it was a privilege that he, for one, was reluctant to jeopardise. Perhaps James was bluffing but it wasn't a risk he cared to take. To him and his brother the company was just a source of wealth, but to James it was more, and though he had never really understood in what way it was more, he understood that to allow James to be defeated would not be in any of their interests. He might well back down from his threat of resignation. Perhaps on the surface nothing would be changed. James would carry on but his heart wouldn't be in it. And, more daunting still, he'd never forgive them. He for one, didn't care to be the object of his enmity. Then he said in his mild and conciliatory voice. 'Yes. I think, you know John, that it is really time. I think James should have his partnership.'

James flung Edward a look of gratitude. One for, one against. It all stood with the Colonel now. James looked at him and saw the different emotions pass across his face; astonishment, fury; dismay as he remembered how much they had come to depend on James, how out of touch he and Edward were with the trade. Then unease as he thought of James taking his remarkable talents elsewhere. And finally indecision, as he weighed the choices. It went against the grain to submit to blackmail, for that was exactly what this was. But on the other hand, when he thought of the inconvenience and loss to themselves, when he saw the look in James' eyes ... He was reminded for an instant of his dead brother James, and as he had always conceded to old James, he conceded now. 'Very well then,' he said grudgingly. 'I'll get Dodds to draw up the papers.'

'Thank you, sir.' James rose to his feet, almost sick with relief. For a moment he had envisaged himself walking from the room in defeat, out of the office, out of the company ... Then at the door William James caught at his arm and held him back.

'You won't always win, you know, James. By the law of averages your luck has to run out.'

James turned to look at him. 'You think I run my life like a game of chance?'

William James shrugged. 'You took a big risk just now. It might not have come off.' He smiled knowingly. 'I think we're both gamblers, you know, each in our own way.'

James looked at him. 'I am a gambler, William James,' he said. 'You are just a loser.'

Sunday tea at Walker Terrace: his brother Jacob reading lengthy passages from the Bible; his sister Margaret massacring Schubert on the tuneless piano. George hated these stilted family affairs, this public display of his pain and deformity. He was morbidly sensitive. He imagined that everyone looked at him with embarrassed pity or studiously avoided looking at him at all. Today there were eight of them gathered in the gloomy parlour; his mother and himself, Jacob and his wife Hannah; his sisters Margaret and Dolly, Dolly's fiancé, Nicholas Robinson and his sixteen year old sister, Elizabeth. James was absent, pleading urgent business at the collieries, which had provoked instant disapproval from his brother Jacob who was known for an ardent sabbatarian. But then Jacob had always disapproved of James. Much as he applauded the doctrine of self help, he found James' ambition nothing less than shocking. Thankfully, he was often heard to declare, he was untouched by such vice, quite content with his position as manager of the engine works, which left ample time for his devotional studies and the occasional Sunday's lay preaching.

'For we wrestle not against flesh and blood, but against principalities, against powers, against the rulers of the darkness ...' Jacob's gloomy voice, like a funeral dirge, resounded around the chilly room.

George moved his head slightly so that he could see the young girl seated between his sisters. It was the first time he'd seen her and though they hadn't yet been formally introduced, he knew who she was. Elizabeth; he liked her name, it had a soft and poetic ring, it suited her patrician beauty. He studied her face minutely with his cruel artist's eye. Her fairness was startling, her hair almost colourless, like fine ash wood. Excitement stirred in him as he saw the wonderful contour of cheek and jaw, the perfect line of her long slender neck. But what inspired him most, beyond her beauty and youth, was her expression of natural sweetness and simplicity, her look of joyous vivacity. One day, he thought, I shall want to sculpt that head, when she's older, when she's a woman ...

Then as if she felt his eyes upon her she turned and looked at him. She smiled and he saw the dimples hollowing her cheeks. The smile enchanted him. It was so warm and real and full of pleasure.

He wanted desperately to speak to her, to hear her voice. He knew exactly what it would be like; soft and light, full of joy and gaiety, warmth and laughter. He'd seen all of these things in her face.

Tea was served. The moment came — and if he'd been a

normal man he'd have got up and gone across to her, introducing himself with a confident smile. But he wasn't a normal man and so he sat, mute agonisingly conscious of the cumbersome wheelchair and his thin stunted legs.

In the end it was she who approached him, offering him cakes from the cheap plated stand. He waited. It always happened; the curious, furtive glance toward his legs, then their eyes jerking away in embarrassment. But her eyes remained steadily upon his face. She said, smiling, 'As it appears that nobody is going to bother to introduce us, perhaps we should do the honours ourselves.' She held out her hand. 'I'm Nicholas' sister, Elizabeth, and you must be Dolly's brother George.'

'How do you do, Miss Robinson. Forgive me for not getting up ...'

'Oh, please call me Elizabeth.' She sat down beside him. 'It seems rather silly to be so formal seeing as we're soon to be family. I hope I may call you George.'

'Yes. Yes, indeed.' Desperately George searched for something else to say, and hearing his sister Dolly's quick excitable voice discussing the annual Coalowners' Ball, he said, for lack of anything better. 'Shall you be going to the Coalowners' Ball?'

'Oh yes, I hope so,' She answered without thinking. 'Shall you?' Then she flushed as she realized what she had said.

'It's all right,' said George quickly. 'I don't mind as much as people think I do. In fact, I'm flattered that you forgot about it long enough to say that.' He smiled at her. 'I can get about still but I'm afraid dancing would be quite beyond me.'

Elizabeth smiled at him, knowing that his frankness was to put her at ease. She saw a young man, small of stature but with a pale and arresting face and very direct blue eyes. She said, knowing instinctively that honesty would always be the best way with him. 'Would it be very rude of me to ask what was wrong with you?'

George smiled. He wasn't offended. 'It's the same thing that my father had. Tuberculosis, except that I'm suffering from a different sort. It affects my spine it means that I can't walk very well.'

'You must get terribly bored, not being able to get about. What do you do all day?'

George shrugged. 'Sleep, read. Sometimes I paint. I also carve in wood.' He saw her glance around the room. 'I'm afraid there's nothing of mine here. My mother does not care to have them on display. She thinks they have a heathenish tone.'

She looked disappointed and after a moments hesitation he said tentatively: 'Would you care to see some of my work? My rooms are just across the hall.'

'Yes, I would,' she said eagerly. 'I'd like to very much.'

George flushed. Her eagerness was flattering. He hoped that she was not just being kind. He glanced wryly at the wheelchair. 'You'll have to push me, I'm afraid.'

He sat just inside the doorway of his room, watching her as she examined each piece. She made no comment even when she came to the study of an eagle savaging a new born lamb. Most people turned away in revulsion.

She moved on, pausing again before the study of a man's head. Sharp arrogant bones sprung out of the dark rich wood, a high bridged nose bore down on a long lipped mouth. 'How cruel he looks,' she commented softly. 'Almost frightening in a way.'

'He was frightening,' George answered quietly. 'It's my uncle James, or at least it was. He's dead now.'

She continued to look at the carving then remarked at length. 'You didn't like him, did you?' She turned to look at him. 'You don't really like any of these things. Why do you only portray things that are ugly and frightening?'

The question startled him. Nobody had ever looked so deeply into his work, so deeply into him. He shrugged. 'I don't known. Perhaps that's how life seems to me.'

She appeared to consider this. 'Yes, I can see how it might seem so. But it isn't, is it?'

George looked at her and smiled. 'No, it isn't. It's just that sometimes I need reminding.'

They went back to join the others and George talked and laughed as he never had before. He felt ridiculously happy, so much at his ease. Only when it was time for Nick and Elizabeth to leave did his restraint come creeping back. He took Elizabeth's hand regretfully. It was soft and warm and even after he had released it, a little of the warmth remained.

'I hope,' he said awkwardly, 'that I shall see you again soon.'

She smiled. 'Of course you shall. I shall often be here.'

George felt himself flushing with pleasure. 'I . . .'

Then abruptly, without announcement James walked into the room.

George glanced smilingly at Elizabeth. 'I don't think you've met . . .' His voice tailed off. Elizabeth was no longer looking at him; she wasn't even listening. All her attention was suddenly fixed on his brother, James.

Every alternate Sunday, Elizabeth came with her brother to tea at Walker Terrace. The routine never varied. They would arrive at three o'clock, at four they would sit down to a plain wholesome tea. Then there would be prayers and readings conducted by Jacob. Occasionally, when he was there, which wasn't often, James would be asked to take the reading. This was rare though. His amused voice was inclined to endow the words with a worldy quality to which his brother Jacob took exception. Afterwards Margaret sang, accompanied by Elizabeth on the piano and if she was asked, sometimes she played a solo piece. Then at six o'clock, chapel in the draughty Methodist Hall in Jackson Street. They always walked to chapel whatever the weather. Even in the rain, Jacob insisted that they go on foot.

George was excused attendance at chapel on account of his health. Usually he sat and read till they returned, but this evening he had seemed particularly unwell and Elizabeth had offered to sit with him.

'You needn't, you know.' His voice was peevish and mildly aggressive. 'I'm really quite all right.'

Elizabeth sat herself in the chair opposite him. 'Don't you care for my company then?'

'Yes, of course.' George gave a wry smile. 'I don't know that I care for you to see me as a pettish invalid.'

'Don't be pettish then.' She spoke to him as if they had known each other for years. And sometimes he felt that, so at ease were they in each other's company. Now, alone with her, he suddenly realised why. She's at ease with me as she would be with a decrepit old man. I am no threat to her. She thinks, like everyone else that my body is dead, that I am impotent, incapable, some sort of eunuch. She wasn't at her ease with

James though. He'd seen how her expression altered whenever James was there, how she avoided looking at him one minute and couldn't take her eyes off him the next. He didn't think that James noticed, though of course, you never really knew with James. That made it more unbearable somehow, that James should be indifferent when he ... A wave of intense hopelessness swept over him. His tremendous fortitude, his inner strength that had sustained him through years of pain suddenly deserted him. He shivered as if with the cold, and from beneath his half closed lids saw Elizabeth stoop to make up the fire. Abruptly he leant forward, though the movement sent pain screaming along his nerves. He grasped her wrist, 'I'm not so decrepit that you have to do that.'

Elizabeth looked at him. 'Why are you angry with me, George?'

He let go of her and slumped back in his chair. 'I'm not angry with you — just with life in general.'

'You mean you're feeling sorry for yourself?'

'If you like, yes.'

'Do you want me to feel sorry for you too?'

'Don't you already?'

'No.'

He flushed, detesting himself for this childish exhibition. He had never wanted compassion before but suddenly he wanted her compassion. He wanted her to pity him, comfort him. He said with unusual bitterness. 'That's because you don't know anything about pain. You don't know anything about life at all. You haven't yet discovered that the world is an ugly place.'

'Then why don't you put some beauty into it? Why do you fill it with more ugliness?' Her voice was impatient rather than angry and she came suddenly to kneel beside him. She took his hands in hers and looked at them. They were strong hands compared to the frailty of his body, muscular from constantly wielding a mallet, seamed with fine scars where the chisels nipped him. She looked up at him, her young face alight with tenderness. 'You have a fine talent and yet you abuse it by creating things people don't want to look at, in the same way as you think they don't want to look at you. But there are other things beside pain and ugliness in the world ...'

'Not in my world.'

'That isn't true.' She released his hands and moved away from him. 'At least you aren't alone. You have people who care for you ...'

'Do you care for me, Elizabeth?' His clear blue eyes, so like his brother's, rested on her lightly.

She met them steadily with a look of great gentleness. 'Yes, I do. Very much. You are, and always shall be, my dearest friend.'

George smiled above the pain of his heart which for once outweighed that of his body. Friend — not ever lover or husband, but always friend. He held out his hand to her. He understood. He was grateful to have even this much.

December 20th, 1873 — Newcastle

The Assembly Rooms in Westgate Street resounded with the noise of a full thirty piece orchestra. They were playing a polka, the loud strident rhythm whirling the dancers past where Dorothy sat. Disdainfully she observed the Colonel, lurching and bouncing around the floor, red faced and sweating with exertion. She frowned. Really, it was the most undignified thing. So violent, and all that whirling and stamping — so very bad for the heart. Nevertheless, under cover of her skirts, her foot beat furtively in time to the music. She had been a great dancer when she was young. Fast Viennese waltzes had been the thing then, the gentlemen in frilled shirts and cut away coats, the women in vast hooped crinolines. She didn't care for these bunched up gowns that were fashionable now — and those ugly puffed sleeves. She fanned herself vigorously to combat the heat. Her stern gaze ranged over the assembled faces, picking out the rich and famous; John Straker the younger, heir to the Brancepath Collieries of Straker and Love, and twelve thousand acres in Durham. The Priestmans too were here in force; old Jonathan and his sons, Francis and Lewis, all major shareholders in Ashington Coal and a host of other related companies. And William Armstrong, a cold little wisp of a man, whose ordinance works stretched for a full three miles on the Newcastle side of the Tyne. And at the far end of the room, as remote and untouchable as God in his Heaven,

George Frederick D'Arcy Lambton, Earl of Durham and the premier coalowner in all of the north, held imperious and exclusive court. Dorothy's eyes dwelt covertly on the select little gathering. The Earl at least, she knew by sight, darkly handsome with a long and haughty face. And the two young men with him must be his twin sons, John and Frederick, the eldest of the Earl's fourteen children. And at the edge of this august and intimate little circle the ambitious men hovered like courtiers. Men like the Colonel and William James, for whom wealth was no longer enough. Dorothy smirked, seeing their tense almost servile postures, alert for an opportunity to get their foot in the door. They never would, not on their own terms, never as equals. To men like Lambton, the Joiceys would always be upstarts, tainted with trade, always the crows among the peacocks.

In the relative peace of the smoking room, James sat, sipping tepid champagne. His companion, William Clark, the owner of a small, run down colliery adjoining his own, was already more than a little drunk and much flattered at the thought that James had sought him out and even seemed to be asking his advice.

'So, my boy. You've a mind to sink again at West Pelton?' Clark moved his head in negative gesture. 'Wouldn't have thought it the time to speculate myself. The boom's over for us now that France and Germany have made peace, and what with the damned Americans flooding the market with cheap coal.' He sucked in his cheeks gloomily. 'There's bound to be a fall in prices. Strikes, God knows what else. And there's no money about for investment, you know. I know that as far as my own pits are concerned — oh, thank you, my boy,' as James thrust another full glass into his hand. 'As a matter of fact, this last bout of legislation's put me in a bit of a fix. To be quite frank, I've just not got the resources.' He rambled on, encouraged by James' sympathetic expression ... Inadequate pumping system, problems with flooding, the upper seams as good as dammit worked out. And that was the worst of it. Good clean beds of coal just twenty fathoms below, and he hadn't got the wherewithal to get at it. And now this bloody government legislation. Pasty faced clerks telling a man what he could and couldn't do. No employment of boys under ten, a fifty-four hour week, and had the government any idea of the cost of sinking a second shaft? He patted James' shoulder. 'Not that I need to tell you all this. You'll be having the same problems yourself.'

'Well, as a matter of fact, it hasn't affected us all that much. We never use boys under ten except in very thin seams and most of our pits already have two shafts.'

'Well, you're lucky then, that's all I can say. Most coal-owners have it all to do.'

James was silent for a moment, then he said in his mild and amiable voice. 'You know, Mr Clark, have you thought that it might be a good thing to let someone else shoulder the burden of implementing the legislation. Collieries without a ready source of capital soon deteriorate. Faces crumble, seams flood, and there's always the risk of a build up of gas.' He smiled. 'I wonder if you wouldn't be wiser to sell out now, whilst the colliery is still a going concern.'

Clark stared at him blankly. It took a few minutes for the implication to sink in. Suddenly he saw himself, heard himself, prattling on, telling this man what he'd wanted to know. He licked his lips, trying desperately to clear his fuddled mind. 'What exactly are you getting at, Joicey?'

James shrugged. 'I'm just suggesting that you perhaps adopt a realistic approach. It's inevitable with this new legislation that some small pits will go under.'

'And what makes you so sure that mine will be one of them?'

'You've just admitted you haven't got the capital to implement the government legislation, and until you do implement it, you cannot continue to operate.'

'I could borrow ...'

'Mr Clark,' said James patiently. 'Even before we began speaking, I knew a certain amount about your financial position. And what I didn't know, you have just obligingly told me. Once that gets out, you know as well as I do, you won't be able to raise a penny piece inside Durham.' Clark smiled viciously. 'And of course, it would get out. You'd make damned sure of that. That sounds to me like blackmail.'

'That's a very ugly word, Mr Clark. I prefer to think of it as friendly persuasion toward something that could be to our mutual advantage. I am prepared to make you a decent offer. I can assure you of a very fair price.'

Clark swallowed. 'And what do you call a fair price, Mr Joicey? Half, no doubt, what the colliery's worth.'

'But twice what you'll get if you go to the wall. Bankrupt pits can be bought up for nothing.'

'Then why this eagerness to buy me out now? Why should your company be interested in a loss making pit?'

James answered him readily. 'I don't mind telling you that. As I said, most of our pits already have two shafts, in fact all except the Jackie which adjoins your own. The Jackie is a short term colliery with a life of perhaps another fifteen years. It doesn't warrant the major investment of sinking a second shaft. It's more economical for my company to buy your pit, and link the underground workings, thereby providing the Jackie with access to a second shaft. So you see, Mr Clark, your colliery is of little value to anyone except my company.' He smiled amiably. 'I really would advise that you sell to me whilst you still have something to sell.' He rose to his feet. 'Think about it, Mr Clark. I shall be in my office on Monday morning if you should want to see me.'

He went out, humming softly under his breath, avoiding the coterie of chaperons where his mother sat, knowing he would have to dance with his sister Margaret. He drifted into the supper room, crowded with couples sitting out. He saw his sister Dolly at a table by the window and went over in answer to her insistent wave. He nodded amicably at Nick who fetched him a chair and bowed politely to his sister, Elizabeth.

'Quite a crush,' said Nick in his loud cheerful voice.

'And everyone's here,' said Dolly avidly.

James nodded, a little bored, standing up again as Dolly and Nick got up to dance. He resumed his seat and smiled vaguely at Elizabeth. 'Would you like to dance?' James asked politely.

'No, I don't think so. Not just yet.'

'Perhaps I can get you some refreshment then?'

'Yes, thank you, that would be nice. A little of the fruit cup if I may.'

James dutifully fetched two cups of pale straw coloured liquid and silence fell between them again. Elizabeth glanced toward him, mildly intimidated by the haughty, patrician profile. She knew he was bored. She could see his fingers drumming restlessly upon his knee. She tried to think of something to say, something clever and sophiscated that would amuse him. But what did you say to a man ten years your senior who only bore your company under sufferance. Then she said, rather breathlessly. 'You don't have to, you know — sit with me, I mean. I really don't mind if there's something you'd rather do.'

'No,' James smiled politely. 'I'm perfectly happy,' But the remark intrigued him. He had the feeling that she didn't care for him very much. He glanced at her without admiration. He saw an awkward young girl on the verge of womanhood; a face remarkable only for its delicacy and expression. She rather reminded him of a fragile porcelain doll. He didn't care for fair women in any case. If he bothered about women at all, which wasn't often, he preferred them dark and voluptuous, intelligent and well bred. Even with women, he was ambitious. On the whole, though, he had a fairly cynical opinion of women. A good marriage seemed to be their single aim, pursued with varying degrees of desperation, depending on their looks and fortune. For that reason he was inclined to shy away from them. Not the women themselves, but the close, claustrophobic, commitment of marriage. He wasn't ready for that yet. Then he said, when the silence between them had gone on a little too long, 'Are you sure you wouldn't like to dance?'

She coloured faintly. 'No, not really. I'm quite all right as I am.'

James frowned. Her refusal irritated him. 'Why not?' he persisted. 'I thought dancing was what girls of your age liked to do.'

She turned and looked at him, flushing at his patronising tone. 'I wouldn't have thought you knew a great deal about girls my age.'

James looked amused, though he'd been obviously rebuffed. So she had spirit after all. He'd always thought of her as rather colourless. 'No, you're quite right, I don't.' He smiled at her. 'Tell me, then. What do girls of your age like to do? What do you like to do?'

She said, quite seriously. 'I like to make people happy.'

'Not make yourself happy.'

'It's the same thing, isn't it?' she answered, smiling.

James shrugged. He was disappointed. It seemed to him a rather negative ambition. More and more her outlook struck him as being naive. He leant toward her. 'Well, make me happy then. Get up and dance.'

She smiled, really smiled, showing her small white teeth. 'Well, I'm not very good.'

He stood up. 'Neither am I. We can practise on each other.'

She smelt of lavender water and soap, and her small, gloved hand seemed lost in his. He held her lightly, the statutory twelve inches apart. Their first few steps were hesitant for he had not lied when he'd said he was an inexperienced dancer. Carefully he pirouetted her into the reverse and emerged triumphant. He smiled down at her. 'There!' he said. 'We don't do so badly together, do we?'

Watching them together from the edge of the floor, Dorothy felt her heart contract. She saw the girl's radiant expression, her shining eyes. Her mouth tightened. She had so hoped it was going to be George.

George lay on his back, staring blindly at the ceiling. He had heard the carriage come back, the stealthy opening and shutting of doors. Then Dolly's high giggle, his mother's voice sharp in reprimand. And now footsteps, light feminine footsteps scurrying up the stairs. Then a man's — James' — pausing to turn out the gas in the hall, hesitating for a moment outside his door before moving on toward the stairs. He was glad James hadn't looked in. He wasn't in the mood for visitors, not even James whom he loved, had always loved ... He had to keep reminding himself of that. And he was tired, his fingers numb from holding a chisel, gritty and sore from sanding. But it was finished; the best thing he had ever done, the ugliest, the most frightening. He propped himself on his elbow and surveyed his creation. It was the crouched and twisted figure of a hewer at the face carved from a single piece of black oak. It was magnificent — and brutal and ugly, malevolent and evil, shocking in its expression of pain and despair. George smiled bitterly. He knew all about pain. He knew all about despair — and fear too, for only someone who had never suffered deep physical pain could contemplate it calmly and with courage. The first experience was a thing for the body alone to bear. Both the pain and one's ability to survive it were unknown quantities then. But the second time was coloured by memories of the first, and every experience diminished the mind's ability to survive the next. It was the prospect of pain that became unendurable. One waited, knowing that this was just a brief respite and it would all have to be endured again.

He moved the candle so that he could see it more clearly. In the grudging light the half naked figure looked almost alive. As the flame guttered, the man leapt from the shadows, the pale light washing over the long lines of stretched and tortured muscle. The back was bent, the shoulders wide and braced as if they supported some crushing weight. But it was the face that was so arresting — upturned, mutely and blindly questing for the light — the mouth slack and open — the lean emaciated features set in such an expression of hopelessness and despair and savage pain ... It was his own face, when he woke in the night racked with agony, when the weight of his useless and stricken limbs dragged him down into the darkness.

April 4th, 1874
— Walker Terrace, Gateshead

It was James' twenty-eighth birthday and Dorothy had opened up the big parlour for the occasion. He felt like a schoolboy — all his favourite dishes, the best china and glass, and beside his plate the gaily wrapped presents; a muffler and socks from his sisters, cigars from George, a Testament from Hannah and Jacob. His mother had given him finely knitted string gloves and from Elizabeth, a handsomely bound book, a copy of Browning's poems.

Elizabeth smiled at him shyly. 'I hope you like Browning.'

'Yes, I do. Very much. Thank you.'

It was a grand supper, wine on the table, everything he liked and yet somehow he wasn't able to enjoy it. His thoughts were constantly elsewhere; going over the mediocre half yearly returns, mulling over various schemes for increasing output.

Things just weren't moving fast enough. His progress seemed slow, and financially speaking, he wasn't a great deal better off. He had a share of the company, a very small share, and this fluctuated with the state of the trade. Of course, one day ... His expression grew sullen. All his life, it seemed he'd been waiting for something, dependent or being depended on. He glanced at his mother, at her proud stern face and a dull anger rose in him to see her, habitually frugal, gathering up left-overs from their plates. Waste not, want not, that's what she'd be thinking. But that wasn't true. His mother never wasted even a crumb but she'd wanted all her life.

They went through into the parlour. More people arrived, friends he hadn't seen for years, faces that he'd long forgotten. Suddenly he felt like a stranger, as if he didn't belong any more. The small crowded room became oppressive; Margaret banging the piano, Nick and Dolly, raucously singing, George smiling fatuously at Elizabeth ... His eyes rested thoughtfully on his brother's happy face. Slowly, it dawned on him. George and Elizabeth! Why hadn't he seen it before? George was so obviously in love with her. And Elizabeth? He glanced toward her. Suddenly it was important to know how she felt. As if she were aware of his gaze, Elizabeth turned her head. Their eyes met as they had a hundred times before, except that this time he wasn't able to look away. Slowly, he saw her expression change, the hot colour sweep over her face. He turned away, furious with himself. He didn't know why he was surprised. It was obvious when he thought of Elizabeth's frequent visits to the house, of how much time she and George were together. But he was surprised — and even more so that the knowledge should disturb him.

After that, it was an effort to keep up the pretence of enjoyment. He found himself longing for the evening to end, drinking a little more than he was used to.

Then at ten o'clock he escaped to the dining room for a cigar. The room had been restored to its usual polished splendour, the long windows thrown open to the chilly spring night. He paused, about to light a cigar. 'Elizabeth?'

She looked up, startled, and the light suddenly struck the perfect contours of her face.

He caught his breath, conscious, for the first time, of her

quiet beauty. He continued to look at her but stayed where he was. The thought of being close to her made him feel uneasy. He was suddenly restless, edgy, on his guard.

He said, politely, 'Will it bother you if I smoke?'

'No. Not at all.' She seemed relieved that their conversation was to be mundane. 'I rather enjoy the smell of a good cigar.'

'Well, you may change your mind. These aren't very good, I'm afraid my income doesn't run to Havanas.'

He glanced at her bare shoulders. 'Aren't you cold?' he asked.

'A little,' she replied. 'But it's worth it just for a breath of air. It's so hot and stuffy in the parlour.' She turned back to the window, staring out into the night. 'Don't you love the spring? It's the best part of the year, don't you think?'

James shrugged. 'I can't say that I've ever thought about it.'

She turned to face him. 'What do you think about then?'

He frowned, vaguely irritated. 'I don't think it would interest you.'

Elizabeth smiled. 'I think that was a snub. You're really telling me to mind my own business.'

'No. Not at all ...' His irritation increased. He didn't like being questioned. He liked even less having words put in his mouth.

'Anyway, I know what you think about,' Elizabeth said. 'Coal. Money. My father says that one say you'll be a rich and powerful man.'

'Well, let's hope that your father's right,' James said dryly. 'Perhaps then I'll have time to contemplate the seasons.'

Elizabeth stared at him gravely. 'But it'll be too late then. It won't matter then. You won't be able to feel things like that any more.'

James dropped his eyes. Under that gentle scrutiny, he felt old and cynical, aware of so much that had passed him by.

For a few moments they stood without speaking. 'Hadn't you better be getting back?' James said drily. 'George will be wondering where you are.'

'Yes, I suppose so,' she answered absently. She didn't notice the sarcastic tone of his voice, his aggressive look as he came toward her.

'You know, I suppose, that George is very fond of you?' said James.

'Yes, well I hope so. I'm very fond of him.'

'Fond enough to marry him?'

'No, of course not.' Elizabeth flushed. 'It isn't like that. There's never been any suggestion of that kind.'

'Well, if you've no intention of marrying him, don't you think it a little unfair to keep leading him on.'

'I'm not.' Her voice quivered indignantly. 'How dare you think that.'

'It's what anyone would think,' James snapped. 'If a woman spends as much time with a man as you spend with George, it's a fair assumption that she's in love with him.'

'And what would you know it,' Elizabeth cried hotly. 'You wouldn't recognise love if it stared you in the face.'

And suddenly it was staring him in the face. Beneath the anger and indignation, he caught a brief glimpse of the truth. For a moment he could not move. He was conscious of nothing but her nearness, her lovely face. On impulse he leant forward and kissed her; tenderly, gently, without passion or force. Just for an instant he felt young and carefree and reckless. The reality crowded in; the room with its hideous furniture, the raucous laughter from across the hall; the thought of George; waiting, wondering ...

He released her abruptly, almost pushed her away. 'I'm sorry,' he said. 'That was an unforgivable thing to do.'

Elizabeth stared at him for a moment. 'Yes, it was,' she said. 'Especially if you didn't mean it.' She waited for him to speak but he remained silent. Then quietly, she left the room.

He didn't sleep well that night, in fact, he hardly closed his eyes at all. He knew that something had happened to him, something that had momentarily lit up his sombre life. He didn't think of it as love. Love was something that grew between people over many years. What he felt was desire, infatuation, lust. Yes, it was easier to think of what had happened like that. Those kinds of feelings he could deal with.

He closed his eyes and instantly the image of Elizabeth came before him, his body grew weak at the remembrance of that

63

kiss. Restlessly, he turned in the narrow creaking bed. He was appalled at his weakness. He'd always thought of himself as being completely in control. He resented it bitterly, this intrusion, this distraction, this sudden disruption of his life in which love and marriage did not figure at all. Of course, in time he had planned to marry, preferably an alliance with another coal-owning family. But not yet. Not for a long time. He had enough responsibilities as it was; his mother and George would always need him. A wife would only be another burden, someone else to be considered, consulted, placated, someone else to make demands upon his time. And there'd be children of course, more responsibilities. Suddenly he saw himself, overwhelmed by domesticity; his ambition, all his grand schemes, come to nothing . . .

Abruptly, he flung back the covers and swung himself out of bed. Shivering, he lit the candle. He looked round the room, hating the drab furnishings; everything plain, serviceable, mediocre. Sometimes he felt he would have preferred stark poverty to this awful mediocrity that seemed reflected in his life, always to be on the threshold of something better, but never quite managing to get in. But he would get in, he was quite decided upon that. Somehow, someday, he'd manage it. He'd need to be strong though, he'd need to be ruthless. There were no prizes in life for runners-up. He smiled to himself. He felt vaguely triumphant, as if he had fought some gruelling battle and won. Nevertheless, he couldn't resist the temptation to pick up the book beside his bed. There on the flyleaf, in her small, round hand. 'To James, with love, Elizabeth.'

June 4th, 1874
— Whinney House, Low Fell, Gateshead

He was late for Dolly's wedding — a full two hours, arriving when the festivities were practically over. He made an attempt to explain. There had been an emergency — the pumping system at the Bute had failed . . . No one wanted to listen. Dolly glared at him, their mother refused to speak to him at all. In the end he gave up and took himself out onto the terrace.

It was a grand view, out over the Team Valley to the Ravensworth Woods and the sweep of moorland beyond. Not so clear as it was sometimes though. The heat of the June day had laid a mist over the landscape, veiling the factories and chimneys, the quarries and pits. One could almost imagine they weren't there.

He leant his elbows on the stone balustrade and screwed his eyes up against the sun. He'd forgotten what it was like to be out in the sun, to feel its warmth upon his face. But then he'd forgotten a lot of things lately; kindness, tenderness, the ability to laugh, all seemed to have been sacrificed in his desperate need to get on. And he was getting on, slowly but surely easing the Colonel and Edward out. And of course, they loved it, making money with no effort at all whilst he did all the work. But that suited him. That's what he wanted. Now it was he who made all the decisions.

Then he stiffened as he heard light footsteps behind him, the soft rustle of a woman's skirts. Instinctively, he knew it was Elizabeth. He took his time about facing her. He wasn't quite sure what to expect. Since that night he'd avoided her, deliberately keeping away when he knew she would be at the house. He couldn't avoid her for ever though. She was family now, his sister-in-law.

He turned toward her, his look defensive. He had expected to see an expression of reproach. But she smiled at him easily, pleased to see him.

'Hello James,' she said softly. 'We haven't seen much of you lately.'

'No. I've been busy. I've had a lot to do.' He added mockingly. 'I'm surprised you're still speaking to me. You must be the only one that is.'

'Well, can't you understand that? Weddings are very special occasions.'

'Only to the bride and groom I would have thought.'

She frowned slightly, hearing the sneer in his voice. 'You don't sound as if you approve of marriage.'

He shrugged. 'I don't disapprove. It wouldn't suit me, that's all. Women are a handicap when it comes to making money.

65

They have a natural tendency to want to spend it.' He saw her flush and added, 'I'm sorry. That was rude.'

'No. It's all right. I'd always rather that people were honest.'

'Would you?' He was genuinely surprised. Most women preferred a lie. To be told they were pretty when they were not, that they were loved when they were not. But yes, he should have known that Elizabeth would prefer honesty, because she was so honest herself. He said carefully, 'The truth, you know, is often cruel.'

'A lie is crueller, to allow people to delude themselves, to hope for something that cannot be.' She flushed painfully. 'You must know that I care about you, James.'

'You think you do,' he answered gently. 'But you wouldn't if you knew the sort of man I am.'

'That doesn't matter,' she said weakly.

'But it would ...' He broke off. He was getting out of his depth. She looked so young, so defenceless, so willing to accept him for what he was, that suddenly he was deeply ashamed. 'Elizabeth,' he tried to make his voice detached, matter-of-fact. 'What I'm trying to say is that for some men, a wife, a family is enough. But it wouldn't ever be enough for me. I want more out of life than that.'

'Why must a wife be a hindrance to what you want?'

'Because she would be a responsibility, someone to be considered. I need to be free to take my own risks.'

'Money is very important to you, then?'

'Isn't it to everybody?'

'No, I don't think so. It's not important to me.'

He flung her a scornful look. 'That's because you've always had it. It's easy to say you're not hungry when your mouth is full of cake.'

She said naively. 'Money doesn't bring happiness.'

'You think poverty does then?' His eyes hardened. 'In this life, Elizabeth, we have to live by the rules and all the rules are made by rich men. I want to be one of those men. I want to make my own rules.' He looked at her and his voice softened. 'Do you understand what I am saying, Elizabeth?'

She answered him only with a movement of her head. Yes, she understood. He was only telling her what she had always known, that there was no place for her in his life, no place for anyone or anything that might interfere with the vision he had of himself. Then she said lightly, as if nothing of any consequence had passed between them. 'Well, I must be getting back.'

'Yes. Of course.' He did not look at her. 'I'll be along later.'

It was seven o'clock that same evening before Dorothy broke her self-imposed silence, and only then because she could no longer contain her anger. She glowered around the parlour where her family were gathered. Margaret idly leafed through a book of patterns, George was stretched on the sofa feigning sleep. James was reading, pretending to read. He had not turned a page for the last half an hour.

'Well!' she burst out suddenly, glaring at him. 'Have you nothing to say for yourself, my lad?'

He looked up at her. 'What do you want me to say? I've already apologised — several times. I told you — I just couldn't get away.'

'Why not?' Dorothy demanded. 'What do you employ engineers and viewers for?' She stabbed at him with an accusing finger. 'The truth of it is that you didn't want to get away. You cannot believe a thing can be done unless you do it yourself. You didn't consider your sister's feelings, my feelings. You spoilt her day. You spoilt everyone's day.' His silence inflamed her all the more. 'I never thought I'd see the day when a son of mine would put that company before his own flesh and blood.'

James stared at her with growing anger. 'You think it more important then — for me to dance attendance on you at social gatherings than to prevent what might have run into thousands of pounds worth of damage?'

'Oh that's it. That's it. It's the money, isn't it. That's all you're worried about. Money! Money! Money! You get more like old James every day.' She gave him a look of contemptuous bitterness. 'That may give you some idea of my feelings, that I can compare you with that terrible old man.'

'On the contrary, I'm flattered.' A faint pulse showed beneath his jaw. 'I'd think myself lucky to be just half of what he was.'

He had never seen her so angry. 'You can say that when you know how badly he treated your father — treated me — all of us?'

'I know how badly you think he treated you. I know how you resented his money but it never stopped you wanting to spend it. I can remember ...' He broke off, moving his head in an angry impotent gesture.

'Yes? What do you remember?' She spoke through white and trembling lips. 'Come on. Let's hear it. Have your say.'

When he wouldn't answer her, she got up out of her chair and came to stand over him. 'So! Suddenly you have nothing to say. Well, when you have, when you've come to your senses enough to apologise, I'll be out in the back.'

She went from the room, ram-rod straight, and slammed the door behind her.

George looked at his brother unhappily. 'You were a bit hard on her, weren't you?'

'You seem to think so,' snapped James.

George eyed him curiously. He would have liked to ask about Elizabeth, to know what had happened at Whinney House. He had seen Elizabeth follow him out onto the terrace, seen the look on her face when she had returned. Knowing James he could guess — Elizabeth wouldn't have fitted in with James' plans. The thought should have angered him, that James could turn his back on that which he would have given anything to possess. But he was still human enough, fool enough to find in it a faint glimmer of hope. Perhaps in time she might turn to him. He was ready to be friend, confidant, anything at all, just so long as he could be near her. He would have settled for that. He was used to taking second place to James, physically, mentally, in their mother's affection ... His eyes grew sad as he thought of his mother. He understood — oh yes, he understood. He supposed that all of them, in a way, felt like that about James, a mingling of affection and dislike, anger and tenderness. He didn't allow you to love him absolutely.

Then he said in his quiet voice. 'Don't you think you had better go to her? She is our mother, after all.'

'That doesn't give her the right to treat me like as if I were ten years old.' James muttered.

George shook his head. 'You don't understand. She's only like this because she's afraid.'

James looked at him scornfully. 'Of what?'

'Of you — for you. She's afraid you're going to turn out like old James. And despite what you say, I think you're a little afraid of that yourself?'

'For God's sake, George. He's been dead eleven years. Can't any of you forget him?'

'I think it's you who can't forget him,' George observed quietly. 'You think that to get anywhere you've got to be like him, and so you put up this show of not caring. But he wasn't pretending, James. He really was like that. It was easy for him to get what he wanted. It won't be so easy for you.'

'Well, thank you for all that good advice, George. Now I know exactly how I should live my life.'

George flushed. 'I wasn't being critical. You know I wasn't.'

James sighed. 'Yes, I do know.' He ruffled his brother's hair affectionately. 'All right. I'll go and make my peace. After all, what's one more apology.'

She was scrubbing the table. She always scrubbed the kitchen table when she was angry or upset, whether or not it needed it. She'd put on a long white apron over her dress and her cuffs were unbuttoned, turned back to expose her thin veined wrists. A throb of compassion beat in him as he saw her wrists and he waited for her to look at him, ready to smile. But she wouldn't look at him and continued her furious assault on the table. In the end it was he who was forced to speak. 'I'm sorry,' he said.

She looked up then and glared at him. 'No, you're not.' She beat her wet clenched fist against her flat breast. 'Not in here you're not.'

James stiffened, the compassion fading from his face. 'Very well. If you say I'm not, then I'm not.'

She bent again to the table. 'I thought I had raised you better than that. I never thought you'd need to be reminded of your duty.'

'My duty!' He gave a short angry laugh. 'That's the last thing I need reminding of.'

The sneering laughter brought her eyes to his face. 'What's that supposed to mean?' She demanded. 'That your duty is a burden? That your family is a burden? Keeping you from getting on, are we? Keeping your pockets empty.' She wrung out the cloth as if it were his neck and finished swabbing the table.

Then she marched off to the back scullery, clattering the pail about in the sink. She came back wiping her hands on her apron. 'Oh, aye.' When she was angry her voice became heavily accented. 'I can see how it is. It cannot be easy for ye, saddled as ye are with me and your sisters and a crippled brother an' all. And I dare say you're glad enough to have Dolly off your hands.'

James shook his head. 'Why do you say these things? You know quite well they're not true.'

'Do I now? And how would I know? I know nowt about you except that all ye think about is workin' yoursel' into the ground. All you care about is making money.'

'Why do you have to make it sound so obscene?'

'Because it is obscene. Money corrupts. It turns folk, makes them change ...'

'So does lack of it. It changed you. I can remember a time when you wanted money.'

A faint colour showed in her sallow cheeks. 'Perhaps I did — A little more than we had. For your father's sake, I wanted it. But not money for money's sake, not to buy power, to buy people's lives. That's what you want it for.' She nodded her head rapidly, a vicious pecking movement. 'Aye, for your father's sake I wanted it, and you'd understand that if you were anything like him. But you're like that old Devil, you're like old James. He did for your father, you know. It was him that killed him, worked him to death.'

'Father had consumption. He'd had it for years. That was hardly the old man's fault.'

'I know what he had,' Dorothy said grimly. 'But he didn't live the longer for being old James' brother. He should have had treatment, proper medicine ...'

'And he would have had them if you hadn't been so proud and stubborn. If you'd asked ...'

'Asked? Asked?' Dorothy's voice rose shrilly. 'I shouldn't have had to ask. He had eyes in his head, didn't he?'

'But you didn't have to ask,' James shouted. 'Time and time again the old man offered to help. But you wouldn't have it. You didn't want his money. You could manage, you said. My God, if anyone did for Father, it was you.'

Dorothy's eyes dilated with pain and shock. Suddenly her

hand came up and struck him hard in the face. 'I'll never forgive you for that,' she breathed. 'Never. Never. Never.'

For a long time they looked at each other; violent blue eyes staring into violent blue eyes. His face was very white, the imprint of her hand flushing scarlet. She thought in sudden bewilderment; I do not know this man. This man is a stranger to me. Then as he turned and walked away from her, she realized that, indeed, she knew him very well, she'd known him for nearly all of her life — except that this James Joicey was her son.

June 28th 1877
— Orchard House, Low Fell,
Gateshead

It was June again. The height of a long, hot, sultry summer. Despite the heat, a fire burned in the drawing room of Dorothy's elegant new house. And yet she was cold, always cold, no matter how high she piled the coals. It was her age, she thought. Everything was slowing down, wearing out. She leant her thin body closer to the lamp. Even her eyesight was failing and not up to the fine stitching of which she'd always been proud. She was darning one of George's singlets. There was no need for her to darn it — they could easily have afforded a new one — any more than there was a need for her to clean her own brasses or make up her own bed. They had servants now; two kitchen girls and a cook, and a parlourmaid called Vickers who bristled through the house in starched apron and cap and obviously thought herself related to the Queen. Dorothy didn't get on with Vickers. She didn't get on with servants at all. There was never a job done that she didn't believe she could have done better herself. She spent a great deal of time prowling the house looking for dust, complaining that the vegetables were undercooked or overcooked, and the bread was never sliced just how she liked it.

She glanced around her. Yes, she supposed it was all very nice, all very tasteful; expensive. And it was what she'd always wanted, to be away from the town. No ropeworks or pitstocks spoiling the view, no factory soot upon her windows; but no memories either, no feeling of belonging, no sense of being wanted, loved or needed ... She bent her head to her stitching. How cruel life was. After all these years, after all the suffering, only now to discover where she belonged. She thought longingly of the crowded, familiar rooms of Walker Terrace. That was her world, small and comfortable, every face known. It occurred to her that in all her sixty years she'd never been the once past Durham.

She glanced with deep sadness across the room at her son. James sat in his usual chair, the evening newspaper spread on his lap. He hadn't changed much. His face thinner perhaps, his mouth harder, less ready to smile. He'd done very well for himself in the last three years. He'd lived up to all her expectations. A man to be reckoned with, she'd heard it said; successful, wealthy, respected, even feared. They used words like shrewd, far-sighted, ruthless and cunning. Words meant to be flattering, for by the standards of the men that used them, they were qualities to be admired. But she couldn't complain. They wanted for nothing, at least nothing that money could buy.

She finished the mending, snapping off the thread with her still strong teeth. Still she did not speak and the room seemed to throb and quake with her silence, undiminished by the slow ticking of the marble clock, the occasional rustle as he turned a page. This then, was the pattern of their evenings together, the very few that he spent at home. Silence like a wall between them, or the very least that needed to be said. — 'I'll never forgive you. Never. Never' — She gave a grim smile. Well, nobody could say that Dorothy Joicey didn't keep her word. Never once since she had openly acknowledged him as her son. And yet often she'd weakened. Sometimes when she saw him smile all the ache of her love returned. If he'd just said some word, made some gesture ... Once he had. Just after they'd quarrelled he'd tried to make amends but she'd been too full of anger then. He wouldn't try twice. He was like her in that, proud as Lucifer, stubborn and unrelenting. Hadn't she always taught him that? Pride was the last thing to be relinquished. And so it went on; the silence, the bitterness, the awful loneliness — and worst of all, the knowledge that she'd caused them all herself.

The clock struck the quarter. When it struck the hour she would announce her intention of seeking her bed. He would look up from his paper and seek her eyes. She never returned his look, acknowledging him only with a nod of her head. Then she'd leave the room, walking briskly and purposefully, as upright as if she had a board nailed to her back. Only when the door was between them would she let her body sag. Then slowly she'd drag herself upstairs and shut herself up in her room. She'd lie awake, sometimes for hours. She wasn't sleeping so well of late.

She folded her work neatly and laid it in the basket at her feet. 'I'm away then.'

He looked up at her. 'Goodnight then, mother. Sleep well.'

'Aye. Goodnight,' she bestowed upon him her usual unforgiving glance, letting him know that her heart was still closed against him.

James sat for a few moments staring at the door that had closed behind her, listening to the drag of her feet upon the stairs. Sometimes he had the urge to get up and go after her, to gather her skinny worn-out body up in his arms. He never did, though. She was a stubborn woman, his mother, hard and proud. She wouldn't give in as easy as that.

Then he folded his paper and laid it aside. The news was all bad — the worst trade depression in years, cuts in wages and hours, unemployment, the closure of yet another colliery. He passed a hand wearily over his eyes. He felt tired, drowsy, the result of the two large brandies that had followed his lunch. He had meant to make a start on the half yearly figures tonight and there was still this month's survey reports ... He needed to slow up, he told himself, ease the pressure a bit — except that he didn't believe he could do it now. The idea of success was too deeply ingrained, like being on a treadmill and unable to get off. No sooner was one thing accomplished than another was begun. He couldn't look at a man without wondering how he could use him, how, if he had a weakness, it might be exploited. He closed his eyes, thinking back to his meeting with Lewes Priestman that day. He considered he'd made the right decision, refusing to join the Coal Owners' Association. Few had to be asked. Even fewer would have refused. Priestman, quite clearly, had been taken aback.

'Well, I can't say that I'm not disappointed, Mr Joicey. I had hoped for a more enthusiastic response. All of the major coalowners in the county are members.' He smiled dryly. 'And there's no doubt that you are a major coalowner now with an output of some three quarters of a million tons. Maximum output, minimum price is your strategy, I believe, especially when there's a slump in the market and everyone else is struggling to keep prices up and production down.' He smiled. 'You see, I have done my homework.'

James returned the smile cautiously. 'My strategy, if I have one, is just to make a profit. Better to sell at five shillings a ton than not to sell at all. One has to be realistic. Times have changed. Customers are finding they can buy cheaper from America and Germany. I just make sure that they can't.'

'That doesn't answer my question, Mr Joicey. Why you're so reluctant to join us.'

James took his time about making an answer. He was rather enjoying this, being courted by the Chairman of Ashington Coal. He glanced appreciatively at his surroundings, the smoking room at the Northern Counties Club where the élite of Northumberland and Durham gathered. Quiet colours predominated, shades of brown and gold with highly polished doors of figured walnut leading to library, hall and the panelled dining room where they had just partaken of an excellent Dover sole and a faultless beefsteak pudding. Oh yes, he was being feted all right and he thought he knew the reason why. He could always gauge how well he was doing by the extent to which he worried his rivals. And Priestman was worried, enough to pay for an inordinately expensive lunch and to make a pretence of being charming.

He said at last, 'The short answer, Mr Priestman, is that I don't care for combinations of any sort, either of masters or men. Associations mean rules. I would have to abide by them whether I liked it or not. I would lose my independence over pay and conditions which my firm has always negotiated directly with the men. We'd have to accept whatever deal the Association made, whether it suited us or not. Besides, I think it would be a mite hypocritical for me to dissuade my men from joining a union and then join a similar movement myself.'

Priestman looked offended. 'I wouldn't have thought the

Coal Owners' Association had anything in common with the Federation.'

'You don't think so, Mr Priestman?' James flung him a cynical look. 'Wouldn't you say that both worked on the principle of grabbing as much as they can and giving as little?' He smiled at the other man's mildly shocked expression. 'You see? I'm not going to be any asset at all. I'd probably cause more problems than I'd solve. I'm afraid I'm not an "Aye" man by nature.'

Priestman gave a short laugh. 'So it would appear. But so far, you've only mentioned the disadvantages of becoming a member. There are advantages also, you know. One of the reasons the Coal Owners' Association has been formed is to counteract the union. They're growing stronger every day. Three years ago the Durham Miners' Federation had a membership of a mere three thousand. Now it's more like thirty thousand. Employers, sooner or later, are going to have to make a stand.'

'That depends what you mean by making a stand. If you mean lock-outs, candymen — gangs of coalowner hired ruffians turfing strikers from their homes ...'

Priestman flushed. 'Sometimes these things are necessary, Mr Joicey. These are hard times and often we need to use hard measures.'

'They're hard times for the men as well, Mr Priestman. In the last three years their pay has fallen by thirty per cent. Even pitmen, you know, have a right to live. To hear some owners, one could believe that we were fighting some sort of war and that the men who work our coal are the enemy.'

'Not the men, Mr Joicey, but the union. Fanatics, trouble-makers, men with chips on their shoulders ...'

James' eyes narrowed. He didn't like unions but neither did he like men like Priestman who believed it was the employers' God given right to bully and exploit their workforce. 'I still don't think bully boy tactics are the answer,' he said quietly. 'A far more effective way of keeping the unions powerless is to pay your workforce a reasonable wage. I have never needed to make slaves of my men to balance my books, and as a result, less than twenty per cent of them belong to the Federation.'

'I truly wish it was as simple as that, Mr Joicey. Frankly, I think you're living in the past when employers could make their own arrangements. Unity is strength — isn't that what the unions say? And the day is fast approaching when no employer will be able to stand in isolation.' He leant forward earnestly. 'That's why it's important that we stand together, that we act in concert on pay and conditions ...'

'You're being very persistent, Mr Priestman.' James remarked. 'I'm beginning to wonder why?'

Beneath the heavy moustache Priestman's mouth grew pinched. He had by now abandoned all pretence of amiability. 'Quite frankly, Mr Joicey, because we don't like outsiders. We don't care for your aggressive and somewhat piratical methods. Relatively speaking, you're still a new boy in the industry. You perhaps don't know that there is a code of practice ...'

'As in honour among thieves, Mr Priestman?'

'Mr Joicey.' Priestman spoke with careful restraint. 'There are two ways of doing this; amicably — inasmuch as you join the Association and adhere to its principles ...'

'Or?' James' eyes glittered dangerously.

Priestman smiled thinly. 'It isn't always a good thing being on the outside, Mr Joicey. Life can become difficult, especially for large exporters of coal like yourself. I have known the most abominable delays with customs; bills of lading misplaced and that sort of thing, shipments going astray. I once knew of a case where a cargo of some twenty thousand tons was lost, apparently vanished off the face of the earth, only to be discovered months later in an out-of-the-way railway siding. Of course by then it was too late. The contract was lost — and once a firm gets a reputation for not meeting delivery dates ...' He paused meaningfully. 'I think you will find that members of our Association rarely have these problems. One of our functions is to protect our members' interests.'

'I have taken your point, Mr Priestman.' James said coldly. 'And quite honestly, you couldn't have said anything more likely to dissuade me from joining.' He leant back in his chair and regarded him smilingly. 'Fortunately, I am inclined to be stimulated by threats, rather than intimidated. And I am not easily defeated, you know, Mr Priestman. In fact, there isn't really anything I wouldn't do, short of breaking the law, if I am severely enough provoked.' He stared for a moment into the contents of his glass. Then he raised it and smiled. 'Your good health, Mr Priestman. Here's to success.'

Success. Success. The magical word. Yet how was it measured? Was there ever an end? Would the day ever come when he could say — I am here. I have done it. It is enough. He had reason enough to be satisfied. Despite a falling market he had achieved a great deal. James Joicey & Company were now in the premier league, on a par with firms like Priestmans. For the past two years he'd had virtual control of the company's finances. Edward's poor health had forced him into semi-retirement and he spent most of his time at Blenkinsopp these days, the five thousand acre estate he had purchased in the Tyne valley, which he modestly entitled his 'summer residence'. The Colonel occasionally condescended to look in. He was totally involved in politics now, and had been nominated to stand at the next general election as the prospective member for North Durham. It was rare now for either of them to oppose him.

He smiled, thinking again of his encounter with Priestman. He hadn't taken his threats seriously and it wouldn't have made any difference if he had. That was part of his strength, that he never looked back. Once a decision was made he never questioned it. Sometimes, though, in moments of solitude, he thought about Elizabeth. The spark was still there, deliberately smothered but somehow he had never quite been able to put it out. He knew she still came to the house to see his brother George, but never when he was there. Naturally, he still saw her. She was, after all, his sister-in-law and they met occasionally at family parties. And he was always courteous and polite. She was always pleasant and gracious — she gave no sign that she wished they were other than friends. And he certainly had no regrets. He knew that he had done the right thing. He would never have achieved what he had unless he'd been free. No. He never doubted that he'd done the right thing. His life was running quite according to plan. Why then, he wondered, did he feel so desolate? Why sometimes did he feel so empty?

Matt Henderson eased himself down on a balk of timber. It always took him a minute after coming up — all that sharp, clean air rushing into his lungs. It was part of his evening ritual, these few minutes of solitude round the back of the sheds. A man had to have a minute to ponder, to gather up his thoughts for the morn.

He began to cough — another part of the ritual — a harsh racking sound from deep in his chest that brought blood and phlegm into his mouth. He spat, a thick black tarry substance, a legacy from his days as a hewer. Strangely enough, he still missed the hewing. There was skill in that, the working of the coal. It wasn't just a matter of hacking it out willy-nilly as some folks seemed to think. In his time he'd worked all sorts of coal in all sorts of seams and never two faces the same. Like women, some could be worked tenderly, others needed a good clout, and he'd known coal so soft that it fell away under its own weight and some so hard and stubborn that nowt would shift it but blasting. He'd working narrow bords and wide bords, panels and longwall. He'd worked on his belly and his back, wet and dry, sometimes up to his neck in clarts and water, sometimes roasting at temperatures of a hundred degrees. He'd suffered from almost every injury; split thumbs, twisted back, crushed fingers and feet. He'd been half drowned, buried by falls, singed and gassed — but still, he missed the hewin'. He missed the danger and excitement, the feeling of pride. He missed the humour, the crudeness, the rough easy talk. Not that you talked much when you were hewing — there wasn't breath left except to curse. You didn't think much either, except sometimes to remember the million tons of dirt and stone groaning above your head. And after a while you didn't even think about that. For the seven hours of your shift you ceased to be human. You were just a heaving machine of sweating flesh and tortured muscle ... And yet at the end of the day, even when you could hardly stand from exhaustion, when you stepped out of that cage still all in one piece you felt you'd beaten something, that you'd won some kind of battle. You didn't always win though. His own father had been blown to bits at Haswell in '44; three of his brothers had died entombed at Hartley. But it hadn't stopped him going down, and it wouldn't stop his bairns. Two of his boys were down already and Mark, the youngest, would start in when he was ten.

He sighed regretfully. Yes, he missed the hewing and if it

hadn't been for the dust taking his lungs so badly, he thought he might have gone back. He wasn't always comfortable being a deputy. He was an 'official', 'management', 'working for the company'. Inevitably it distanced him from the men. They resented being ordered by one of their own kind, though he couldn't see the logic in that. To his way of thinking, only one of their own kind could ever have done the job; a deputy had to know what he was doing. And nobody but one of their own kind could have had his nose for gas; to be able to detect its presence above the stink of his own sweat. To know the difference between those that you could live with and those that could kill you off. You had to know about air, too. How the furnace in the upcast first warmed the air and set it in motion, drawing it down into the main shaft and the intake airway where it was divided into a dozen different currents by stoppings and doors, then diverted along the roads to the various workings. It was a queer thing, air. Above ground it was invisible, odourless and colourless. But a hundred fathoms down it took on another dimension, so hot and heavy that a man felt he would drown in it, so light with gas that he thought he would float away ...

He turned his head at the clatter of pit boots across the yard, and saw his eldest son coming toward him. His face expressed mild disapproval. Cocky young bugger, his Matthew was. Always too much to say.

'How, then, father.'

'How again, Matthew.'

His son settled his back against the screeing shed wall. 'There's a Federation meetin' at the Institute the neet.'

'Oh aye,' Henderson responded without enthusiasm. Staunch Federation man his Matthew was. He wasn't a union man himself though he supposed they were a good thing. To him they just seemed another source of authority, more clever-dicks telling a man what he could and couldn't do. And half the time they stirred up more than they ever settled, always telling a man how badly he was done by. It unsettled the young 'uns. His Matthew now, always wingeing on about conditions and legislation. He wondered how you legislated against twelve ton of rock coming down on your head, or having your legs blown away from under you.

'Is that all y've to say, then?'

'What de ye want me te say. Ye know I'll not be gannin'.'

'Divvn't ye want te know what it's about?'

'I know what it's about. Y've been ranting on all week about it — ye divvn't think y're paid enough.' He gave his son a scathing look. 'Ye want te try doin' a bit of work, mon, instead of allus' talkin' about it. If ye worked as hard as ye talked, ye'd be the best paid hewer in County Durham.'

His son's thin face flamed. 'Well, I might hev known better than te think y'd stand wi' me, ye bein' a company man, an' all that.' He smiled slyly. 'Is that what y're stoppin' here for, Dad? Waitin' on the master, are ye?' His lip curled. 'Ye think y're pals, divvn't ye, ye and Mr James? Ye think he's different, that he listens te ye, that he's bothered about what's goin' on. Well, y're a bloddy fool, then. Y're useful te him, for the minute at any rate. But when y're not, he'll drop ye like a hot coal.' He nodded, sneering. 'Aye, the day'll come when y'll want summat from him — and then we'll see how different he is, then we'll see if y're pals or not.'

He stormed away, across the yard, kicking the door of the overman's office as he passed. Henderson sighed, knocked out his pipe, pushed himself to his feet and followed him out round into the yard. A man emerged from the viewer's office and he quickened his step. 'How then, Mr James.'

'How again, Matt.' James fell in beside the old man and slowed his long stride to the same leisurely pace.

Henderson glanced up at the flushed evening sky. 'Looks like it'll keep fair for the Big Meetin' the morn.' He glanced at James. 'Ye'll be gannin'?'

James grinned. 'Aye, I'll be gannin', Matt. I've not missed a one yet.'

July 5th, 1877 — Durham City

The streets of Durham City seethed with hot and sweating humanity; men with scrubbed and pallid faces in creaking boots and shiny suits; women in neat dark skirts and crisp flounced blouses, their faces flushed with heat and excitement

80

beneath cheap flowery hats. There were children everywhere, shouting, laughing, wriggling between the legs of their elders to get a better view. The crowd stretched all the way from Elvet Bridge to the racecourse but was thickest here outside the County Hotel from where the visiting dignitaries viewed the proceedings. They were already in their places on the flag-draped balcony; the two guest speakers, the Liberal MPs Alex MacDonald and Sir Arthur Middleton, both renowned for their sterling work for the trade. Union and lodge officials milled around; William Crawford and Thomas Cann, portentous looking men with heavy moustaches. Everyone, who had connections with the trade, seemed to be there.

Elizabeth, squeezed between Dolly and her brother Nick, watched from a first floor window. The colourful and noisy cavalcade passed directly beneath her; colliery bands playing loudly on instruments of dazzling brass, the great lodge banners — sheets of rippling silken colour, borne as proudly as battle honours. The silks were hand painted with various devices — peaceable emblems mostly urging unity and strength. Some were more savage, bitter reminders of how closely these men courted death; a pit belching orange flame into the night, a woman standing alone with her orphaned children. Then Monkwearmouth with its court room scene commemorating the miners who had first broken the yearly bond. Tursdale with its simple motif of two clasped hands; and Sacreston, Vane Tempest, Stanley and Seaham, like the sails of a mighty fleet of ships surging through a grey anonymous sea.

'There's Twizell! That's one of ours.' Proclaimed Dolly proudly, for in these things she still counted herself a Joicey. 'And Tanfield Moor — Can you see? Just following behind?'

Then silence, so sudden and absolute that Elizabeth was startled. A banner passed, its glowing colours dimmed by swags of black crepe. 'The widow drapes,' Dolly whispered. 'Seven men were drowned at Hetton last week.'

Elizabeth stared down at the silent crowd. The men had drawn their caps off and stood with heads bowed, a few of the women were quietly weeping. She swallowed hard, suddenly moved by these pale proud men with their emblems of death and disaster.

They followed the procession up to the racecourse. The air

was hot and heavy, pungent with the smell of trampled grass and food and sweating bodies. The noise was deafening. The Handenhold band played with gusto, drums thundered, cornets shrilled, children ran screaming across the turf and rolled boisterously down the bank. At the far end of the field where there was dog fighting and pitch and toss, the crowd set up a continuous roar. Some of the men had taken off their coats and lounged in their shirtsleeves, drinking warm beer from thick dark bottles.

Somehow, among the crowds, Elizabeth lost sight of Nick and Dolly. She browsed for a while amongst the stalls. Ribbons and lace, patchwork and cheap scent, rag dolls with flat faces and stiff woollen plaits. She bought one of the dolls, amused by its sadly comical face. She glanced round, and looked straight into familiar and cynical blue eyes.

'I've been sent to find you,' James said, smiling faintly. 'Dolly and Nick have gone down by the river ...' A band struck up — *Blaydon Races* — she couldn't hear what he was saying. He took her arm and steered her away from the bulk of the crowd. 'They've gone down to the river. I've been sent to escort you.'

Mockingly, he offered her his arm and she took it without embarrassment, as if he were just some casually encountered friend. On the whole, she thought she was bearing it rather well, just this faint little tightening around her heart.

They walked slowly in silence.

Then he said suddenly, as if he'd been thinking about it. 'You shouldn't wander off alone. It's not always safe ...'

'I should have thought myself safe enough among this great crowd.'

'That doesn't matter. You can't ever tell. People are not always what they seem.'

She wanted to laugh. She thought that a wonderful remark for him to make. 'You mean people pretend to be nice when they are not?'

He missed the note of amusement in her voice and answered seriously. 'Everyone pretends that to some degree.'

'Do you?'

James frowned. He'd forgotten how forthright Elizabeth could be. Her candour had always disconcerted him, demand-

82

ing a similar honesty from himself that he'd never felt able to give. 'Sometimes,' he admitted. 'It's not always wise to let everyone know what you're thinking.'

'That must make life difficult.'

'Life is difficult,' he observed with his invariable cynicism.

'It is for people like you. You're always looking for challenges, battles to fight.'

He looked at her. 'That's a rather sweeping statement to make about someone you can't possibly know that well.'

'Perhaps I know you better than you think. I know that you're ambitious, single-minded, quite determined you get what you want. After all, you told me that yourself.'

He didn't answer her and she bit her lip. She hadn't meant to bring it up, to recall their last real meeting. She blushed now, thinking how she must have embarrassed him then, with her naive declaration of love. But she had been naive then, at least, enough to think that a casual kiss would lead to a proposal of marriage. Of course, she knew better now. She knew James better ... She glanced toward him. He was thirty to her twenty, though to her he didn't seem any older. She often wondered if he was happy. She thought not somehow. Success, she felt, must be the result of an obsessive discontent, a vain, continual search for satisfaction.

They walked on, threading their way through the thinning crowd; men with their wives upon their arm, giggling young girls pursued by flushed young men. She saw how they looked at her, eyeing her plain but expensive clothes. 'You know,' she said, 'I can't help feeling an intruder here.'

'You are. We both are. This is their day. We're here on sufferance, as privileged guests.'

She turned to look at him, surprised by the caring note in his voice. 'These are your men?' she asked gesturing toward the field with its noise and colour and brazen music.

He laughed. 'Not all of them. I haven't yet achieved that measure of success.'

She looked at him gravely. 'But you are very successful?'

He glanced at her. 'Yes. I hope so.'

'You always meant to be though, didn't you? It didn't just happen by chance?'

'No. I don't think success is a matter of luck. Or life either for that matter. It's what each of us want to make of it.' He paused for a moment, then went on awkwardly. 'And you, Elizabeth? Are you well? Happy? I would have thought to see you married long before now.'

She smiled faintly. Yes, she'd often thought that herself, but the right husband never seemed to come along. She told herself it wasn't because of James. She was far too sensible to waste her life in useless longing, and she never thought of herself as waiting particularly for James. For someone like him perhaps, someone who could make her heart beat this much faster, who made the world an exciting and wonderful place. But no one ever had, so here she still was, trying to pretend he didn't matter any more, trying to keep the love from her eyes. 'Yes,' she answered him lightly, not looking at his face. 'I dare say I shall some day.' She shrugged. 'It doesn't seem important at the moment.'

James smiled. So there wasn't anyone in particular then. If there had been, she would surely have mentioned his name. He was surprised at how light-hearted the thought made him feel. From the corner of his eye he studied her face; her radiant expression, the shining translucence of hair and skin, the long fair lashes shadowing her cheeks. He couldn't help wondering whether she still thought about him at all. There was never anything in her manner to say that she did. Probably not. Probably, it had been just a girlish infatuation. At that age, girls thought they were in love with any man who looked at them.

Then Elizabeth turned her head and caught his glance. She smiled. Suddenly she felt absurdly happy; the glorious day, the sun on her face, and James, James ... She looked smilingly toward the old city set securely on its rock in a loop of the Wear. 'Don't you think Durham the most beautiful place? It has an air of sanctity about it. I always feel that if God lives anywhere it must be in Durham Cathedral.'

James followed her gaze. Steep narrow streets climbed up from the river, rows of grey roofs like a flight of steps. And on the summit, breathtaking, majestic, the towers and turrets of castle and cathedral soared over the smoke-stained landscape. It had for him quite a different appeal, an impression of enormous power and strength, of absolute impregnability. It struck him then how differently they saw things, how unalike they were in every way. Perhaps if they'd had more in common, if they'd been more obviously suited . . .

Gallantly, he offered his hand as they came to a steep part of the bank. Casually, she took it, looking down at her feet rather than at him. Then suddenly she stumbled and fell against him. Instinctively, his arm encircled her waist. For a moment neither moved, then slowly he released her. 'Are you all right?'

'Yes. Yes.' She made a great business of brushing her skirts then walked ahead of him toward the boathouse where Dolly and Nick sat waiting.

December 16th, 1877
— Stanley, County Durham

A week before Christmas it was already bitterly cold. There was ice underfoot, a glittering opaqueness that sheathed the cobbled slope leading up from the station and several times caused Dorothy to stumble. She leant against a wall to steady herself. The breath rasped in her throat, icy cold. The wind, such a wind, battered her from behind, flattening her skirts against her legs. At the top of the hill she paused again, sheltering in a doorway against the gale. She did not even know what had prompted her to this mad excursion; to undertake such a gruelling journey, to come back after all this time. Nothing had changed, at least not for the better. If anything it was even uglier and dirtier. The house was still there, the old pit house where George had brought her as a young and happy bride. It stared back at her, squat and malevolent, cheap gaudy curtains showing bravely through grimy panes. She'd hated that more than anything else — the constant dirt, the constant scouring and polishing to keep it at bay. It had always defeated her, rushing in at every opening of the door, sneaking insidiously through every crevice. From the first moment she'd set her foot across the door she'd disliked the house — its smallness, its meanness, its close proximity to the pits. She remembered the cramped dingy rooms quite clearly; two up and two down with a small paved yard at the rear where every spring she'd planted flower seeds in pots, and every summer watched in despair as soot and ash had burnt and smothered the young green buds. In the upper room that faced the street all three of her sons had been born — and a fourth, who had never uttered a sound although he had lived a full ten days. So why was she here? Because somewhere among the hateful memories there was a feeling of warmth, of belonging. Memories of children's laughter, of George sitting at his cluttered desk, a pencil between his teeth, of the two of them laying together in bed, his voice, soft, caressing, 'I love you, Dolly — forgive me for all this . . .'

She turned away, lowering her head against the buffeting wind, walking quickly toward Front Street. There were few people about; women with thin anxious faces, men on street corners, squatting on their haunches in the habitual pose of a pitman at his ease. She glanced at their faces — old men mostly, worn out, worked out, eyelids flickering with nystagmus. This to her was the paramount ugliness; these men, grey, dwarfish travesties of men, so used to crouching and crawling that even when they had the room to stand straight they still squatted out of habit.

She hurried on, averting her eyes from the squalid shopfronts, the steamy windows of beer houses. They were using the Methodist chapel as a soup kitchen and men queued outside; gaunt-eyed, hollow cheeked men with no work and no hope of work. These were bad times. There would always be bad times for men like these. Hadn't old James often said; 'Even in a hundred years from now it'll still be bad. Hewin' for coal'll always be the Devil's work.'

Outside the newly built Queen's Hotel she hailed a cab, quite unable to face the walk to the station. It was only a short distance, a matter of minutes and her feet and hands had not even begun to thaw before the driver pulled up outside. She had half risen from her seat when the first pain assailed her, doubling her slight body like the blow from a fist. She staggered, gasping, then fell back on the seat. She'd had this before, though not as bad; this pain, this great hand squeezing her heart. She clenched her teeth, steeling herself. And again — a second vicious onslaught that forced the breath out of her in a low whining scream. Then suddenly she found herself quite unable to move. A curious lethargy imprisoned her limbs

86

and only after the driver had called down a second time did she manage to thrust her head from the window and redirect him to Walker Terrace. She sank back, shivering into the corner seat. She felt quite feverish, as how now as she had previously been cold. Pulling down the window she admitted a blast of icy cold air, breathing deeply, dabbing at the perspiration that pearled her upper lip. She closed up the window, clutching at the edge of the seat as the cab braked for the descent of the hill.

The Team Valley spread before her; skeletal trees, smoke stacks, the long dark scar of the railway, factories spilling down the slope from Gateshead. She remembered she'd ridden this way with George once before, the day after they had been wed. A long time ago — forty years this October just past. He'd have been an old man now, older than her, though she couldn't remember by exactly how much. He'd been just forty when he had died. Not old, not young, though she always remembered him as being young. Even after all these years she could see him quite clearly; the lock of dark hair falling over his brow, his blue eyes smiling ... 'Come away, Dolly lass. Let's be close together the night ...' Then frowning as she'd insisted on finishing some trivial task. It wasn't that she hadn't loved him, hadn't wanted him ... It was the aftermath of that closeness and togetherness that she hadn't wanted — the long heaviness, the pain, another mouth to feed. Pleasure must be paid for, the old man had said ...

Margaret was weeping, a high-pitched keening sound that penetrated the haze of laudanum like the point of a knife. Dorothy's sunken lids flickered but she did not open her eyes. They were all here. She could hear Jacob sniffing, Hannah praying, the rattle of Dolly's beaded gown as she leant down to the bed. George was the little oasis of calm and quiet thought. And James — she knew that the hand that clasped hers with such fierce tenderness was his. Her parched lips moved soundlessly. There were so many things she wanted to say to him, things she should have said long ago. She wanted to look at him but it seemed such an effort, she no longer seemed to have control of her senses. She would have liked, just once, to have taken him in her arms, to have held him against her heart. She knew she was dying, for only death could have achieved in her this perfect peace, this shining and effortless calm. It was over. All the grief and anger, all the disappointment, were memories of some other time. She felt almost impatient to be gone. George would be waiting. He would, she knew, have kept a place for her. And old James? Her ailing heart leapt as his long dark shadow fell into her mind. Would he be there? Not if there was any justice, he wouldn't. By rights he'd be stoking the fires of Hell with Wallsend Steam. Then a faint smile turned her tired mouth. Even the deep well of her hatred was dry. Compassion, at last, softened her features. Poor old James, to have been so rich and died so poor. Life hadn't been kind to him either. And all things were equal now, all the pride and hatred and suffering of her life, dwindled down to these last desperate moments. There wasn't time for pride now, or enmity or anger. She wanted her last thoughts to be loving.

She smiled with rare and genuine content, aware of gentle hands smoothing her pillows and tucking the coverlet beneath her chin. The room seemed cold and chill despite the roar of coals in the grate. She heard George say that it was snowing and she shivered. She'd always hated the cold. How much nicer, she thought, to die in the spring, to be laid in warm and fecund earth, to be covered by new grass and budding flowers. Yes, how much better to die in the spring ... How much better not to die at all ...

Slowly she turned her head to look at James. 'Forgive me, son,' she whispered.

His eyes filled up, sparkling with tears. 'There's no need for that,' he told her fiercely. 'It's you who needs to forgive me.'

Dorothy smiled. Well, wasn't that just like them? The two of them bickering to the very last. But he understood. She knew he understood what was in her heart.

She moved her head restlessly, the pain, quiescent so long that she'd almost forgotten it, stirred at last from its long sleep. She felt it gathering itself within her, a last final effort. Her hand lying passively within his, made a sudden feeble movement. It was only this warm strong hand that held her anchored to the earth, that kept her clinging to life. She closed her eyes. 'Let me go, son,' she murmured faintly. 'Let me go now, son. I'm tired.' Then pain overwhelmed this, her last conscious thought, dull at first but gathering swift and savage momentum — and then when it seemed she could bear no more, a glorious lassitude enveloped her limbs, a stupefying languor ... 'George?' She heard her own voice, a faint crackle of sound. She felt his presence strongly, solid and reassuring as an encircling arm. She heard his voice. 'Come away, Dolly lass. Let's be close together the night.'

December 21st, 1877 — Orchard House, Gateshead

She was buried at Lamesley, beside her husband, her daughters and her baby son. The whole family attended, the Colonel driving the thirty miles from Stocksfield, despite a foot of snow. Even Edward was there, racked as he was by a feverish cough — and strictly against his personal physician's instructions, as he was often heard to declare. But on the whole their sorrow was real, if not for Dorothy herself, for times past, for the passage of the years. It seemed an end. None could remember a time when Dorothy hadn't been there.

After the interment they returned to Orchard House. Tea and sympathy and solemn hypocrisy. Edward prattling on about the will of God, Rosandra shrilly discussing the wreaths ... James moved away to stand by the window, the stiff line of his shoulders and deliberately turned back, as good as a closed door between them. He stared blankly at the pale colourless landscape, the valley shining with the radiance of fresh snow. He felt a burning sensation at the back of his eyes. The grief was slow in coming — or was it guilt? Remorse for all the things he hadn't said or done — for all those that he had. It was hard now to admit that he'd ever grudged her his time, that he hadn't always listened. He wasn't even aware yet of the extent of his loss, except to know that something irreplaceable had gone from his life.

Abruptly he left the room and went upstairs, pausing outside the door of his mother's room. He hesitated a moment before going in. It seemed an intrusion. Ridiculously, he still felt he should knock.

The room looked neglected already, all her cherished ornaments and fussy furniture filmed with dust. He went to stand by the hearth though it gave out no warmth. He gazed bleakly at the row of yellowed photographs in dull silver frames; one, very faded, of his father as a young man; one of himself and Jacob in knickerbockers ...

Then he stiffened as he heard light footsteps behind him, the soft rustle of a woman's skirts. Instinctively he knew it was Elizabeth.

'James?' She spoke to him from the doorway, her voice uncertain and sad. 'Would you rather be left alone?'

'No.' He turned to look at her. 'No. It's all right. Please come in.'

'I don't blame you wanting to get away. All those people ...'

'Yes. It's difficult to be sociable at a time like this, isn't it? Grief, to me, is a very private thing.'

Elizabeth flushed. 'Yes, I'm sorry. It was thoughtless of me to come ...'

'No. I didn't mean that ...' He shrugged. 'I never seem to be able to say the right thing to you, do I? I never could with her either. We always seemed to be quarrelling.' He thrust his hands in his pockets and stared down at his feet. 'I — I loved her, you know. Only somehow I was never able to show it. She always seemed to be embarrassed by affection. I never knew till it was too late, that it was all she wanted ...' His voice broke. 'She called me "son" just before she died. She hadn't called me that for years ...'

Elizabeth didn't speak, but she moved toward him, laid a comforting hand on his arm.

'I thought I knew her so well, you see. I thought I understood her, I thought I knew what she wanted. She was always so bitter, always saying how different things would have been if my father had lived, how she felt that she'd been cheated. I thought it was money she wanted — no, not money perhaps, but the security and ease that money could buy. And so I gave her what I thought she wanted — and the more I gave her, the further we seemed to grow apart.' Then he looked at Elizabeth, at her calm lovely face with its open expression, the tender sweetness of her smile. He thought suddenly how easy she was to love. There was no pride, no coquetry, no subtlety in her glance. Everything about her was natural and honest. His heart quickened. Suddenly he felt an overwhelming need for that honesty, for love and tenderness to be part of his life. He said hesitantly, 'It's true, you know. You don't realise how much people mean to you till they're out of your reach.' He stared at her gravely. 'I wouldn't ever want you to be out of my reach, Elizabeth.'

'But I'm not, James.' She gave him a look of undisguised joy. 'I'm here. I've always been here.'

He reached out then and drew her to him. And at the feel of her in his arms, all the pent-up longing of years broke out of him. 'Elizabeth,' he whispered as he sought her eager mouth. 'Elizabeth. Will you marry me?'

April 23rd, 1879
— Orchard House, Low Fell

They lay together in the drowsy aftermath of lovemaking. Her head was pillowed against his shoulder, her pale hair streamed over his naked chest. She had been his wife for just twelve hours.

James smiled into the darkness. He barely remembered the actual ceremony; the crowded church; himself, grim-faced and sweating with nerves. The minister's grave and sepulchral voice; his own, 'I, James, take thee, Elizabeth, to be my lawful wedded wife ...' Then the short carriage ride back to the Robinson's house at Shields; pearls of rice down the back of his neck, the clinging warmth of Elizabeth's hand. His own hand had been wrung, his back slapped, glasses of Veuve Cliquot thrust into his hand ... 'To James and Elizabeth. Happiness and long life.' James and Elizabeth. He liked the sound of that — like brandy and soda, pepper and salt, the one always lacking without the other. He turned his head to look at her. It was the strangest feeling, the sudden plunging of his heart whenever their eyes met, unpleasant yet pleasurable, a mingling of ecstasy and fear. Strangest of all was the sense of completeness, as if a great emptiness in him had suddenly been filled. Resentment too, a vague sense of failure, because in the end he hadn't been able to resist. Already, in some subtle way, he knew himself to be weakened. His very strength had been that he'd never looked too deeply into himself. He'd never questioned his own motives, made excuses for himself; even less did he do so for others. Now everything was changed. He was changed, and he mocked himself cynically. After all, he had been like other men, emotional, impulsive, dominated by his flesh. And yet there were no real regrets. He was happier than he'd ever been in his entire life. He smiled with sheer contentment. Elizabeth, his wife — for richer or poorer, for better or worse, to love and to cherish, till death do us part.

June 13th, 1879
— Stanley, County Durham

A woman was screaming, a harsh flat grinding sound without pitch or resonance. She looked grotesque, her eyes squeezed shut as if with some terrible pain, her mouth wide, her pregnant body slumped a dead weight between the two men who dragged her from the house. In the gutter, sitting among the smashed debris of their few possessions, a man cradled his broken face in his hands and the blood squeezed redly through his fingers.

'Oh my God!' Elizabeth pressed a stricken face against the carriage window. 'What are they doing? That poor woman . . .'

Eleanor leant forward and quietly drew down the blind. She patted Elizabeth's hand. 'There are some things it is better that we do not see. In fact, it was stupid of me to think of coming through Stanley at all whilst the strike is on. We should have taken the high road over the moor.'

'What . . .' Elizabeth flung the blind up again. 'What is happening? That man — there was blood . . .'

Eleanor fanned herself with a luridly painted chicken-skin fan. 'You musn't concern yourself, my dear. Those people are strikers and, quite rightly, are being evicted. Once they have given in their notices, they are no longer entitled to live in the colliery houses.'

'But where do they go? What happens to them?'

Eleanor shrugged. 'I don't know. I don't think about it and I advise you not to think about it either.'

'Not think about it!' Elizabeth stared at her. 'But that woman was ... She was to have a child.'

Eleanor lifted an elegant shoulder. 'It's really none of our affair, my dear. They're not even our workers. Those houses belong to South Moor.'

'And I suppose that makes it all right, does it?' demanded Elizabeth heatedly.

Eleanor looked bored. 'These people, you know, bring it upon themselves. No one forces them to give in their notices. They're always whining about starvation wages, but come down this street on pay night, my dear. The ale houses are full to overflowing. They've always got money for drink.'

'I don't blame them for that,' Elizabeth declared. 'I'd take to drink if I had their lives.' She continued to stare unhappily from the window. She saw glimpses of shut and squalid streets, rows of uniformly drab houses — and men; grey slumped amorphous creatures with gaunt and brutal faces and terrible eyes that stared at nothing. She looked away, tears of pity welling up in her throat. She'd seen poverty before, the rough, brazen and defiant poverty of the shipyards and docks. But never this stark and awful despair that assaulted the eye in every direction, that fastened so grimly and tenaciously upon the heart. There was no hope here, no light or laughter. It was a world where the inhabitants knew only darkness. They worked in darkness, breathed it into their lungs. It clung to their bodies and their mean little homes, penetrating even their spirit. And she was part of it now. It was this despair and darkness that clothed and fed her, that had paid for the mountain of packages piled on the carriage seat. She looked at Eleanor, at the pearls that encircled her long white throat and drooped palely from her ears. 'I don't agree with you, Eleanor, that it isn't our concern. Suffering like that must surely be everyone's concern.'

Eleanor smiled her dry astringent smile. 'What on earth do you think you can do?'

'I don't know.' Elizabeth shook her head. 'But I shall do something. For one thing I shall speak to James.'

Eleanor raised a tawny eyebrow and supressed her instinctively cynical retort. She eyed Elizabeth critically. Of course, as James' sister-in-law she'd found her quite charming; that blithe disposition, that appalling naivety, that impulsive and reckless generosity; all admirable qualities in their proper place. But in James' wife! Well, that was quite different. She'd always imagined James as marrying someone worldly, someone who would help him in furthering his career. She didn't think Elizabeth would be any help. Her sensitivity, for one thing, was an obvious drawback. Of course, she could quite understand why he had married her. She was quite a beauty in her way. It was a revelation seeing the two of them together, the way they looked at each other, the way they made excuses to touch. It had never been like that between her and Edward, even taking into account the fact he was twenty years her senior and almost an old man when she'd married him. Edward had never been passionate and their three children were the product of strenuous duty rather than any desire. They cared for each other in their own way, but not in the same way as James and Elizabeth ... Her gaze sharpened jealously. Edward adored her too, fawned over her in an almost sickening way and thought that she would be the making of James. Eleanor wasn't so sure. For a man like James to remain single-minded he needed to remain single. Marriage, purely for love, would be a handicap. Again her eyes flickered over that enviable face. She recognised that soft and squeamish streak. Edward had it too, except that Edward had learned to turn a blind eye. He assuaged his guilt by founding churches and soup kitchens. Elizabeth would assuage hers by nagging James.

She said at last. 'I wouldn't if I were you. Speak to James, I mean.'

Elizabeth looked at her. 'Not speak to him? Why not? Somebody has to.'

'Because he won't care for it, my dear. He'll see it as interference and men don't like that. And besides, you're looking at it from a purely sentimental point of view. James won't see it like that.'

'How will he see it then?'

'Probably as none of his business, seeing as it's not our men that are involved. That's all that will concern him. And really, you know, there's nothing he could do.'

'I don't believe that,' Elizabeth argued stubbornly. 'People always say that when they don't want to be bothered.'

'James won't want to be bothered,' Eleanor told her bluntly. 'He can't afford to be sentimental. He can't afford to concern himself with how other coalowners run their businesses. He has enough to worry about running his own.'

Elizabeth's mouth settled into a mutinous line. 'I'm still going to talk to him,' she said.

Eleanor shrugged. A pity, she thought. She'd always felt James would have made a wonderful scoundrel.

George watched from an open window as the carriage drew up. Elizabeth emerged, the wind ruffling the feathers on her frivolous hat, lifting her skirts in a whirl of silken colour. Then her light, clear voice sounded in the hall.

'Has Mr George had his tea yet, Vickers?'

'Not yet, madam. He said he would wait as you weren't back.'

'Then have it served in his rooms, would you, please — and some of those little sweet cakes he is fond of.'

George picked up a book, pretending to read, so that it wasn't so obvious he'd been waiting. Not till she was fully in the room did he look up.

Elizabeth dropped a light kiss on his brow and glanced at the book. 'Macaulay!' She pulled a face. 'I didn't know you liked Macaulay.'

'I don't. But he helps me sleep. Those long laborious phrases have a curious numbing effect. Much better than laudanum — and it's not habit forming either.'

She laughed. 'Did you want to rest then?'

'No. Not now.' He smiled at her with open affection. It had been easier than he had thought to reconcile himself to the fact that she was now his brother's wife. He'd always been prepared for it and in a way, it seemed the natural thing. He'd always lived his life through James. James was the substance to which he attached his shadow. Through James he had walked and run, laughed and cried, so that it followed, that when James loved, he would love also. And better James than a stranger. At least this way he could still be near her. He could continue to protect and guide her. That was his only possible role now; friend, companion, confidant, advisor. He had learned to be content with that.

He said; 'Do you feel like sitting for ten minutes or so. I'd like to do that profile sketch again.' He took up his pad and charcoal. He had been working for some time on a study of Elizabeth and his studio was littered with preliminary drawings.

Elizabeth talked while he sketched, telling him about the evictions, how beastly Eleanor had been about it all.

George said mildly, without looking up from what he was doing; 'I must say, my dear, I'm inclined to agree with Eleanor. I should think twice before worrying James.'

'Oh George!' Elizabeth cried. 'I would have thought you, of all people, would have had a little compassion.'

'I have. But compassion by itself doesn't change anything.'

'But surely compassion is the starting point for making people want to change.'

He looked up at her then. 'It isn't easy to change things in the coal trade, Elizabeth. It's a dirty and dangerous business, but there's nothing we can do about that except to minimise the risk where we can. But it's a risk for the coalowner too, you know. I've known men sink thousands into putting down a shaft without ever finding a workable seam.'

'George! How can you possible equate human life with money?'

'I'm not. I'm just pointing out that you should try to take a balanced view. You won't get anywhere with James unless you allow that there are two sides to the question. And if you're going to bring up the question of eviction, you should at least know what your talking about. I presume you're aware that free housing and free coal are part of the men's pay? It goes with the job and they expect it. But what happens when they no longer work for the colliery? If they strike or get sick or just get too old? If we let them stay on in their houses, where do we put the new workers coming in? If we can't provide houses then we don't get the men, therefore we can't produce the coal. You see,' he added, as Elizabeth remained silent. 'It's not so easy, is it?'

'No,' answered Elizabeth thoughtfully. 'It isn't easy. But that isn't going to put me off.'

In the fine evenings she and James always walked together in the old orchard behind the house. The air was warm, heavy with the scent of wild rose and elder; pale blossom drifted down from the gnarled old trees. They walked in silence, their fingers twined loosely together. James looked down at Elizabeth and smiled. Pale tendrils of hair blew about her face and her skin was flushed and damp with the heat. She looked thoughtful her brow creased with the beginnings of a frown. He squeezed her hand. 'What are you thinking about?'

She hesitated then said absently; 'A woman — I don't know who she was. I saw her when we came through Stanley. She was being evicted, forced to leave her house. And her husband — he had been beaten.' She glanced up at James. 'Is that sort of treatment usual? For people to be bullied that way?'

'No. It's not usual . . .'

'But it's not unusual either?'

James frowned. 'A lot depends on the individual coalowner, what his policy is. It's a difficult situation. The men and their families have the house rent free providing they work in the collieries. If they refuse to work then they must give them up.'

'Have you ever evicted anyone?'

'I have done, though not forcibly. Mainly they go of their own accord.' He glanced at her. 'Why all these questions?'

'I'm interested that's all. I was wondering why our collieries are still working when others are not?'

'Because it is only the union men, men that belong to the Durham Miners' Federation, that are on strike. Not all miners belong to the Federation, in our case less than twenty per cent.'

'These union men, then — why are they on strike?'

James shrugged. 'It's rather difficult to explain. I doubt if you would understand.'

'I would like to understand.' She looked at him gravely. 'In fact it's very important to me that I should understand.'

'Well, the simple explanation is money. The score price — the rate that the men are paid for every twenty tubs hewed — has for the last year been linked to the selling price of coal. It's called a sliding scale agreement and it means that in good times the men's pay is high, in bad times it is not. These past two years have been bad times with the price of coal on the open market falling and pay and profits with it. Consequently, the Coal Owners' Association have demanded a twenty per cent reduction in wages, which although it would bring pay into line with the selling price, would also take it below the agreed minimum. Naturally, the Federation have refused.' He glanced at her, smiling faintly. 'Do you understand all that?'

Elizabeth frowned. 'Yes, I understand. But what happens now. How will it end?'

'As it usually does, with the men going back on the owners' terms when all their resources are exhausted.' His mouth tightened. 'It's all so damned pointless. The men can't possibly win. They're striking against a receding market with a surplus of both men and coal. Most owners are more than happy to limit production for a while. Every colliery in Durham's been on short time for the past six months and there are stockpiles of coal and coke in every part of the county. We're only keeping going ourselves by virtue of the fact we have some good contracts.'

'Then why do they do it?'

He was a little while answering. 'I suppose because there comes a point when a man feels he has nothing to lose. When his life is so wretched that there seem to be no further depths of humiliation and degradation to which he cannot sink. He becomes angry then. He wants to lash out, to fight, even if by doing so he can only injure himself.' His voice was bland and expressionless but his eyes were bleak, for there was still some part of him that identified with these men, that distantly felt their pain.

Elizabeth halted. 'And you know all this? You understand all this — and yet you do nothing?'

He turned to look at her in mild surprise. 'What can I do?'

'Something. Anything. Couldn't you make some attempt to get the strike settled, to prevent further evictions?'

'That's up to the owners and the union executive to sort out.'

'But you are an owner.'

'Yes, I know.' He was becoming irritated. 'But I'm not a member of the Owners' Association whose business it is to handle these things.'

'Why not?'

'Because I choose not to be. I've always preferred not to get involved.'

'Like Pilate?'

James frowned. 'Let's drop it, shall we, Elizabeth? You really don't understand.'

'Oh yes I do,' she said hotly. 'I understand much more than you think. You speak of masters and employers as if you were not one of them. You seem to think that because you treat your own men fairly that you are absolved from any responsibility to the others. You say you care about them — but not, it seems, to the extent of standing up for them, of trying to persuade your fellow owners that what they are doing is cruel and unjust ...' She broke off. 'I'm sorry,' she said. 'It's wrong of me to make you feel guilty. Perhaps you are right, perhaps there really isn't anything you can do, but it's important to me to know that you tried.' She looked at him appealingly. 'Isn't there someone you could speak to? Someone who belongs to the Owners' Association? If you went to them, explained to them ...'

James looked thoughtful. Instinct told him not to get involved. That business with Priestman still rankled and even though his threats had come to nothing, there was still subtle pressure upon him to join. They still didn't like outsiders and once or twice Richard Lamb, the chairman of Cramlington Coal had brought the subject up. He liked Dick Lamb though and had respect for his views. Perhaps if he had a quiet word with him ... And yet he couldn't see his opinions influencing the committee unless he offered to join. In the face of Priestman's threats that seemed like capitulation ... He glanced at Elizabeth ... Perhaps she was right. Perhaps it was time he made some sort of open commitment. He slipped his arm round her waist. 'All right then. I'll see what I can do.'

July 1st, 1879
— Coal Trade Offices, Westgate Road, Newcastle

'I can't tell you how glad I am that you've agreed to join us.' Richard Lamb ushered James up the staircase of the Coal Trade Offices in Westgate Street. 'We're only six this evening;

old Cookson, John Straker, Lewes Priestman and Lindsay Wood. I expect you've heard that old Durham is sickly so we have his eldest son, Viscount Lambton instead.' He paused outside and smiled ruefully. 'It's going to be a bit sticky I'm afraid. I had a hell of a job getting the committee to agree to see you at such short notice, and out of hours, so to speak.'

James flung him a brief look of thanks, even though he was already bitterly regretting having allowed Elizabeth to persuade him to come. The circumstances were all wrong. Already he was on the defensive.

Silence fell immediately upon his entrance. He felt their hard appraising glances, their imperceptible drawing together. His heart sank, sensing their hostility. His hopes of persuading them to a settlement diminished further. If he achieved anything, it would be to prejudice them even further against the men.

Dick Lamb made the necessary introductions. 'I expect you more or less know everyone here — except perhaps his lordship ... Viscount Lambton — may I introduce our new member, Mr James Joicey?'

'Well of course,' his lordship murmured. 'We all know Mr Joicey — at least by reputation.'

James disliked him on sight. Dark eyes, pale skin, mean pursy mouth, his hair plastered down so sleekly with pomade that it appeared to be painted on his skull. Then Lindsay Wood said in a bored and languid voice: 'Could we get on, gentlemen? I have other appointments.' He looked coldly at James. 'It's not usual, you know, to see members privately.'

'No. I understand that.'

'Do you also understand, Mr Joicey,' said Lewes Priestman, 'that one of the conditions of membership of this Association is that you abide by the committee's decisions? You will no longer be free to make private arrangements regarding wage settlements as I understand you have done in the past.'

'Of course, I am aware of that — but conversely, membership surely also gives me a voice, a say in whatever decision the committee takes?' He saw a flicker of open hostility pass over Priestman's sallow face. He added smilingly, 'I presume members opinions are taken into account?'

He was answered coldly. 'Taken into account, of course —

but not wholly binding. The committee has full power to settle disputes as to conditions and pay — or not, as the case may be.'

'I see. Then . . .'

Lindsay Wood interrupted him. 'I understood Mr Lamb to say that your business was urgent, Mr Joicey.'

'Yes of course . . .' James glanced around the circle of impatient and derisive faces and came swiftly to the point. 'I understand that you will be meeting with the Federation executive tomorrow to discuss their new offer to concede ten per cent. Gentlemen, I urge you to accept.' (How lame it sounded. Hardly the fiery and passionate speech he had planned.)

There was silence, an exchange of glances. Then Lord Lambton said in his high London voice, 'On what grounds, Mr Joicey, do you make this request?'

'On the grounds of common humanity, my lord. The men are living in reduced circumstances as it is. To lower their wages by as much as you suggest would bring some families to the brink of starvation.'

'Quite frankly,' said Priestman, 'I don't see what else we can do. We're paying five per cent over the minimum rate as it is. We can't subsidize the industry for ever. And as it was at the union's insistence we adopted the sliding scale in the first place, they can't complain now merely because the times are against them.'

'The times are against all of us, Mr Priestman,' said James grimly. 'But we will survive them. A great many of these men and their families will not.'

'That's hardly our affair, Mr Joicey. We did not force the men to hand in their notices . . .'

'Didn't you?' They were startled by the sudden malevolence of his voice. 'It's an old game, you know. Demanding the impossible to provoke a situation that cannot help but result in a strike. We're all perfectly aware that the sliding scale agreement runs out at the end of the month. It's common knowledge that most employers do not want to renew it because it limits them as to how far they can cut pay. In my opinion, gentlemen, you made an inflated demand in order to force the men out and you're going to keep them out till the agreement is void. Then you'll be free to impose what terms you like, and after two or three weeks on strike with the resources of both the men and the union totally exhausted, they'll have no choice but to settle.'

There was silence. They all looked at him with open dislike. Then Lord Lambton gave a short, brittle laugh. 'I wonder, Mr Joicey, if you wouldn't be more at home becoming a member of the Miners' Federation than this Association. If you'll forgive my saying so, it's attitudes like yours that give the union ideas.'

'And if you'll forgive my saying so, my lord, it's attitudes like yours that created the union in the first place.'

Lambton's small eyes widened fractionally but he remained viciously polite. 'You seem to be much in awe of the union, Mr Joicey.' He smiled pleasantly. 'In my experience I have always found the working classes rather like sheep. They obey the dog with the loudest bark, the sharpest teeth . . .'

James turned to look at him, his eyes dark and violent. 'Those days are gone, my lord, when you could starve and humilate these men into submission. They are not beasts, animals, to be driven by blows. They are men, decent men, who have a right to decent treatment.'

Lambton regarded him with a fixed vicious stare. 'Well, I dare say, Mr Joicey, that with your background you think you know these things.'

There was an appalled silence. None of them even dared to look at James. The flesh around his mouth was lividly pale, the line of his jaw clenched and rigid. Then he rose to his feet unhurriedly, suddenly smiling with apparent pleasure into each embarrassed face. He looked at Lambton, and the smile grew even more affable, affectionate even. He said in his mild and pleasant voice. 'One day, my lord, I shall exact payment for that remark — and with a very great deal of interest.'

The sneer faded slowly from Lambton's face as he looked into James' eyes. He felt a curious weakness in his bowels, as if he were looking down the barrel of a loaded gun and this man's finger was on the trigger. He tried then to smile, to shake the feeling off, but the sensation persisted long after James had left the room. He glanced at his associates and saw their tense and apprehensive faces. He gave a nervous laugh. 'My God! Who does he think he is? The man's a nobody, a damned upstart.'

Then Lindsay Wood gave his laconic smile. 'I hope he is, my

lord. Indeed, for all our sakes, I hope he is.'

Anger always affected him like a physical illness and all the way home a sickly nausea burned in his throat; spots of violent colour danced before his eyes. Once inside the house he found relief in shouting; 'It's not what he said — It's the fact that he knew that he could say it, as if I were nothing, a nobody ...'

Elizabeth sat quietly, an island of calm buffetted by the storm of his rage. 'They're just words, James,' she said calmly. 'Nothing is really any different because they've been said.'

He rounded on her. 'Oh yes it is. Everything is different. I shan't ever forget tonight.' He gave her a grim look. 'Can't you see now what I'm up against? Can't you see now why I didn't want to get involved, why I didn't want to join the Association? I haven't done the men a blind bit of good, in fact, I've probably done them harm. And the worst thing is, I'm bound to that damn Association. Whatever they settle on, I'll have to agree.'

'All right,' said Elizabeth sharply. 'So you're bound to the Association, but that doesn't mean that you're bound by their principles. You're still the same man. You still have the same standards. You've joined the Coal Owners' Association, James, but you haven't joined *them*.'

She came towards him and laid a hand on his arm. 'Lambton was right. It is because of your background that you feel for the men. That's nothing to be ashamed of, treating them with compassion and decency ...'

He pulled away from her. 'That's just cheap, sentimental rubbish as far as I'm concerned. Feeling sorry for people doesn't do anything.'

Elizabeth flushed. 'What does, then? Money, I suppose.'

'Yes,' he snapped. 'For once, you're right. It all comes down to money in the end. That's what life is all about.'

'Not my life ...'

'Yes, even your life.' He interrupted her harshly. 'Because without money you wouldn't have time to feel sorry for people. You'd be too busy trying to scrape a living yourself.' He looked at her scathingly. 'And you don't even understand the people you're trying to help. They don't want compassion. They don't want pity. They want decent wages, decent conditions, and they'll only get that from strong and profitable concerns. That's what I've been trying to give them. But I can't do it without money; money for new equipment; modern machinery; decent houses for the men and their families. We need to double our output to keep up with the really big firms like Lambton and Londonderry. We need to produce massive amounts of coal and sell it cheaply to keep the foreign competition out. But we're not expanding quickly enough. We're still taking too much out and not putting enough back in ...' He broke off. 'I'm sorry. I hadn't meant to lecture you.'

'No, please go on. I'm interested,' she said eagerly. 'I want to know, James. I need to know. I don't just want to be an ornament, James. I want to share every part of your life. And I can't live surrounded by all this misery and hardship unless I know the reason behind it, the reason why it has to exist.'

James was silent. He wasn't really sure that he wanted her to know. She was the only thing of real beauty that there'd been in his life. He didn't want it spoilt. He said slowly, 'Elizabeth ... I'm not sure that I want you to get involved with all this ...'

'But I'm already involved, James,' Elizabeth said firmly. 'I became involved the day you married me.'

November 27th, 1879
— Lambton Castle, County Durham

The mourning bells tolled out over the valley of the Wear, monotonous, repetitive, the deep melancholy sound deadened by the stagnant November air. From the keep of Lambton Castle, the sable and argent pennant hung limply at half mast; the hatchment hung cornerwise over the door. George Frederick D'Arcy Lambton, Earl of Durham, was dead and all of the county had come to mourn him.

James stood bareheaded on the edge of the crowd gathered at the foot of the steep carriage drive. He watched stonily as the funeral cortège emerged from the gates; the hearse with its plumed horses, the bier draped with the dead man's coat of arms and surmounted by his earl's coronet. A fleet of mourning carriages followed behind; his widow and eleven of his fourteen children. More carriages; his fellow aristocrats, Londonderry and his son Viscount Castlereagh, the Liddells, the Greys, the Ridleys, the Peases. Then men on horseback; landowners and coalowners, Straker and the Priestmans, the pallid features of Lindsay Wood. And lastly, sidestepping the dung left by the horses, a small contingent of men in creaking boots and newly pressed suits, one man from each of Lambton's fourteen collieries. Then James looked long and hard at the man he had really come to see. Jack Lambton, Earl of Durham now, riding alongside his twin brother Frederick. James's eyes dwelt malevolently on the long aristocratic face, he heard again the shrill sneering voice ... He turned away, walking to where he had tethered his horse. He wore full mourning, but not for this man. Six weeks ago Edward had died and left him richer by the sum of five thousand pounds and a further ten per cent share of the company. He now held fifteen per cent against the Colonel's fifty and William James' twenty five. The remaining ten per cent was now held by Eleanor. He gave a wry little smile, thinking back to their rather curious conversation on the day after Edward's funeral. As one of the executors he'd been sorting through some of Edward's effects, when suddenly Eleanor had said: 'Are you going to wait a decent interval, James — or shall you ask me now?'

He'd looked at her, startled. 'Ask you what?'

'To sell you my share of the company.'

He'd met the shrewd amber eyes slowly and said with amusement. 'I was going to wait a decent interval.'

She said, still holding his amused gaze, 'Well then. How much will you give me for them?'

'What they're worth. Something in the region of seven or eight thousand pounds.'

'Yes, I know what they're worth, James. I meant rather, what they were worth to you.'

'Isn't it the same thing?'

'I don't think so, James.' She gave him a look of smiling cunning. 'I think it would be worth a great deal more to you than seven or eight thousand pounds to be on equal terms with William James. Ten thousand pounds at least.'

He dropped his eyes to conceal his surprise. He'd always thought of Eleanor as rather frivolous, empty-headed almost. Certainly he'd never thought of her as being able to drive such a shrewd bargain. He eyed her warily and with reluctant admiration. 'I haven't got ten thousand pounds,' he said carefully.

'Then I'll wait till you have. I'm not in any hurry.'

'Why do you want to sell at all?' he said curiously. 'You don't need the money.'

'No. I don't need the money. Indeed, as you know, Edward left me extremely well off. I'm a very rich woman but I don't have any objections to becoming richer. I thought it might be amusing to dabble in high finance. And besides, James, if I don't sell to you voluntarily, you'll only bully me unmercifully until you get them.' And he would, she had thought, charmingly, smilingly, but he'd have them in the end.

James smiled faintly. It was a proposition worth thinking about though it would be some time before he'd have that amount of money to spare. The trade was still stagnant, barely holding up. Last quarter's returns had been abysmal and though the strike had been settled at the end of July, the bitterness lingered on. And far from weakening the union as the employers had thought, it had strengthened them. Every day more and more men joined. They numbered nearly half of his work force now. And besides he had other responsibilities now. Elizabeth was expecting their first child in the Spring. He smiled at the prospect. A son. Yes, he hoped for a son ... Momentarily, his eyes darkened. He'd be glad when it was all over, though. Elizabeth wasn't strong, not physically at least. She wasn't carrying the child as well as she'd hoped. He worried about that in a confused masculine way, for she engrossed him so completely now that there was no moment of his life that was free of her. He didn't want there to be either. He'd never been happier in his life.

He rode down toward the river, swollen to spate by a week of rain; brown turgid water foaming between narrow banks, the rank smell of wet rotting leaves. He paused by the bridge and looked up. Lambton Castle towered above him; an extravaganza of mock battlements and fanciful turrets that had stood for little more than fifty years; a princely sham, a mammoth fake, a monument to greed.

He rode on, turning out by Bournemoor onto the Sunderland Road. He halted again at Penshaw, at the foot of the steep
hill crowned, incongruously with a mock Grecian temple.
Another Lambton fake; a monument to the first Earl of
Durham, that arrogant hot-tempered vainglorious individual
they had called Radical Jack.

He was curious suddenly to see it at close quarters, to see if
any shadow of the man lingered there. But there was nothing,
just a dead empty space contained between massive smoke
blackened pillars. He emerged again into the daylight and the
ugliness of the landscape burst upon him, a vista of almost
stupefying drabness. Sunderland astride the mouth of the
Wear with its shipyards and slipways and squalorous suburbs
of dirty roofs. And the river itself, slinking between banks
corroded by coal staiths, fed by dirty little streams that crept
out from the hills. And for as far as the eye could see, sprawling
colliery towns darkened the landscape; Silksworth, Ryhope,
the grimy snout of Seaham thrusting out into the sea. And
further inland; Hetton and Murton, little pockets of squalor
nestling in the folds of the hills. And here, at his feet; Lumley,
Herrington, Philadelphia and Houghton; twenty thousand
acres of Lambton coal ... But he didn't see the ugliness. He
saw only money and power; Jack Lambton's money, Jack
Lambton's power ... He smiled. Suddenly he knew it wasn't
just money he wanted, it wasn't just an empire. It was this
man's money, this man's empire. All that this man had he
wanted, and more.

September 6th, 1880
— Orchard House, Low Fell

Elizabeth's child was born on the 1st May, a boy, named James
for his father and Arthur after Mallory's hero king. It was a
difficult birth, three whole days of intense and painful labour,
and in the end, high forceps had to be used. She was sickly for
weeks afterwards. Nervous debility, Dr Fergus called it, and
only to be expected after such an ordeal. It would soon pass, he

assured her, and in the meantime he prescribed powders for her nerves and tonics for her blood. But she was slow mending, slow to put the experience out of her mind. Even now, in September, she was still not herself.

She stood at the morning room window considering the moist autumn day. The gardens were past their best, the tall beeches flanking the gates were losing their colour; the odd wayward leaf tumbled across the lawn. She was sad to see the summer gone. Summer had been the best time and she thought back happily to the three weeks she and James had spent together at Harrogate; long lazy days, soft warm nights, and James pleased as a schoolboy to have caught a five pound trout ... Yes, that had been the best time, James at his ease, content to do nothing ... It had made it hard to come back, to face the poverty and chronic despair. The trade was still depressed with a great many out of work, and lately, she'd taken against going up to the town. To see the men with their weary desperate eyes, the women with their quiet patience ... It preyed on her mind, the hopelessness, the despair. Nothing seemed to get any better. There was so little one could really do.

She returned to her contemplation of the garden again, the bedraggled trees already braced for the onslaught of winter. She looked forward to the Spring and seeing the results of her handiwork; the brassy splendour of daffodils, pale narcissus, and perhaps the lilac trees would bloom this time. She imagined their poignant and wistful scent. She saw herself carrying armfuls into the house and arranging them in tall vases. And in the summer there would be roses with their blatant perfume; clematis and wisteria clothing the front of the house. She smiled and felt a little more cheerful. Yes, things would look better in the spring, once the bleakness of winter was behind them.

She went out into the hall and along the passage to George's room. She knocked and waited for him to call out to her before she entered.

He was sitting by the fire, staring listlessly into the flames. She noticed that his breakfast tray was untouched.

Elizabeth looked at him reproachfully. 'You won't build your strength up if you don't eat, George. Let me get you something hot. It'll do you good, my dear.'

He answered her irritably. 'You should know by now, Elizabeth, that I have a natural aversion to anything that will "do me good". It's a phrase I seem to have been hearing all my life — eat your cabbage up, George. It'll do you good; take your medicine, George ...'

Elizabeth frowned. She could see he was in one of his queer moods today; gloomy and quarrelsome and morose. Usually she humoured him, sparring with him until she made him laugh, but today she was in rather a queer mood herself. She went and stood by the window, ignoring him.

George watched her silently, his passionate gaze intent upon her face, as if he were seeing her for the very first time. For weeks now he'd been labouring to perfectly reproduce that face, to capture the essence of her spirit. That was what eluded him, that was what made sculpture such a challenging art. Wood wasn't the easiest medium to work with. One could capture the substance, the flesh and bone, but character, expression — these were easily lost. And in Elizabeth, these things were constantly changing. The young girl whose innocence and beauty he had set out to capture had gone. She was a woman now. Marriage and childbirth had given depth to her expression. Her eyes held a new maturity, the shadow of remembered pain. His heart went out to her. He understood that look, he understood pain; the fear of having to face it again, of perhaps not having the courage to face it again. Physical pain passed quickly, the body recovers. But the fear of pain, the anticipation of pain, sometimes becomes a greater anguish than the pain itself. He would have liked to have told her that there was nothing to fear but fear itself. She was young, healthy. Her natural gaiety and resilience would soon assert itself. What seemed to him a greater danger was her sensitivity to her surroundings, her overwhelming compassion and the effect it was having on his brother. James had changed, so subtly and gradually that he wasn't aware of it yet. But George noticed. There wasn't much he didn't notice, watching and listening from his front row seat, an audience of one.

He transferred his gaze to the fire, thinking how once he would have laughed at the idea of his brother cocooned in blissful domesticity. Gone were the days of spending half the night at the office, gone were the mounds of paperwork that had once cluttered the house. He was a family man now, arriving home for dinner on time, spending the evenings with his wife, his family, his friends, careering off to Harrogate at the height of the Vend. He'd lost that wonderful arrogance, that supreme confidence that had made people think he was right even when he was not. He'd begun to question himself, question his motives, and already he was beginning to make mistakes. They'd lost the Norwegian contract that they'd held for years, and twice Priestmans had undercut them.

He looked at Elizabeth again. Her silence, her tenseness, suddenly alarmed him. 'You're very quiet,' he said. 'Is something wrong?'

'No,' she smiled wanly. 'I was just thinking that's all. How nice it would be to get away for a while, just a few weeks before the winter sets in.'

'I don't think James would be able to manage that. I think he's got rather a lot on.'

'He might,' she said, with that stubbornness in her voice. 'Just for a week even. A week won't make much difference.'

George was silent for a moment. Then he said, 'Did James mention to you that the firm had lost a major contract last month?'

'No. No, he didn't.' Elizabeth looked concerned. 'What happened?'

'What happened was that James took three weeks off at the height of the Vend, which is when contracts are negotiated and renewed.' He shrugged. 'At the last minute another firm put in a lower bid. James wasn't there that's all.'

Elizabeth stared at him, aware of the innuendo in his voice. 'What is it that you're trying to say, George?'

He avoided her direct gaze. 'I'm trying to say that James' work, the firm, is an important part of his life. He has responsibilities to other people as well as you. He isn't always able to please himself. He isn't always able to please you.'

'What you mean,' she said calmly. 'Is that I'm making too many demands upon him, that I'm taking his mind off his work?'

'Yes, in a way.'

'And you don't think that a good thing? For James to have

some pleasure in his life, to have some other interest beside the company?'

'Yes, but there should be a balance. He shouldn't be faced with the choice of neglecting the company or of neglecting his wife.'

'Well, that depends on which makes him happier,' Elizabeth cried. 'And besides why must the responsibility for the company always rest with James? What about the Colonel and William James? They seem to do as they like.'

'That was by James' own choice. He engineered that situation deliberately to give himself a free hand. He had nothing else to concern him then.' He looked at her gravely. 'Think about it, Elizabeth. Think about how much he has changed ...'

'Changed for the better though,' she broke in defensively. 'Or perhaps you don't think so. Perhaps you preferred him the way he was, always working, always worrying ...'

'He's still worrying,' George snapped. 'Except that now he's worrying about you.' He looked at her angrily. 'All his life he's been surrounded by people who've needed him, who've burdened him with their weaknesses and fears. And yes, before you say it, I'm one of them. But I always thought that in you he'd found someone to share the burden with. You used to be so strong, so supportive. You used to understand.'

'I still do understand, George,' Elizabeth said calmly. 'At least, I understand what you're trying to tell me. You're saying that I've killed his ambition, that I resent him wanting to get on. That isn't true. I'm not against ambition. Ambition in itself isn't an unhealthy thing. But James wasn't just ambitious, was he? He was obsessed with being a success. Obsessiveness isn't healthy, George; blindness to all but a single aim. When people feel like that, they will overcome every obstacle that gets in their way. And all right, if those obstacles are of a practical kind, then no harm is done. But if they are people, if they're friends and family ...' She fell silent for a while and then said quietly. 'Perhaps you're right, George. Perhaps I have changed him — but if I've saved him from turning into someone like that, then I'm glad and you should be glad too.'

George shook his head. 'Oh, Elizabeth, my dear, you're so wonderfully naive. If only life was as simple as that.'

111

They stood hand in hand looking down at the sleeping child.

'He's very like you, don't you think?' James said thoughtfully. He turned toward her. 'Blond and beautiful, I mean.'

Elizabeth laughed and saw how his face lightened at the sound. She squeezed his fingers lovingly. George's criticism of her had had more effect than she cared to admit and she'd made a special effort to be cheerful tonight, to think only positive and happy thoughts. She looked at him and smiled apologetically. 'Forgive me for being such a misery lately. It's not like me to indulge in self-pity.'

'That's all right,' he said softly. 'I understand. You had a bad time. Naturally, it's taken time for you to recover.' He looked at her with concern. 'You're feeling better now, then?'

'Yes. Much better — and very ashamed at having taken so long about it.' Then she added casually, 'By the way, you didn't tell me that the firm had lost a contract.'

'No, I didn't.' He looked annoyed. 'May I ask who did?'

'Does it matter?' she asked lightly. 'Was it a secret, then?'

'No, of course not. I just didn't want to bother you while you were feeling so down.' He shrugged. 'It isn't that important. It happens occasionally. I don't always win, you know.'

'You used to,' she reminded him quietly. 'Before you married me.'

He looked at her, frowning. 'What on earth makes you say an idiotic thing like that?'

'Because it's true. You'd never have made such a mistake before. You'd never have let yourself be persuaded to go off to Harrogate ...'

'I wasn't persuaded,' he interrupted her irritably. 'I wanted to go and you needed to go ...'

'That's what I mean. I needed to go, so you went because of me.' Her expression grew serious. 'I remember you once saying that a wife was an inconvenience ...'

'A responsibility is what I said ...' He took her face in his hands. 'But it's a responsibility I want. It's one that I chose. It wasn't ever forced upon me.'

'James,' she said earnestly. 'I wouldn't want to think you'd given anything up ...'

'I haven't given anything up,' he said gently. 'I've just replaced them with other things, things I wanted more.' He kissed her lightly. 'And just to prove to you that I'm still the ruthless, ambitious man that you married — I'm afraid I shall be late home tomorrow night, probably very late. I've got a pack of engineers breathing down my neck for some figures they should have had last week, as well as a rather difficult meeting with the Colonel and William James.'

'Oh,' she said curiously. 'Is there a problem then?'

'Only the usual one. Having at last persuaded them that we need to deepen the shaft at South Tanfield, I've now got to convince them it's a false economy to try and do it on the cheap.'

'Can't you insist? I thought you handled the money side of things.'

James frowned. 'Well, I do, up to a point. But for any expenditure over ten thousand pounds, all three partners must consent.' His eyes hardened fractionally. 'And I'm still very much the junior partner. Either one of them can overrule me, which is probably going to be the case. To put the sort of money I'm talking about into the South Tanfield project, would mean taking a hefty cut in profits next year.' He smiled cynically. 'They're both very touchy when it comes to taking a cut.'

'How will you manage it then?'

James grinned. 'How I always manage it. By exploiting their most obvious weakness, which is that neither are really interested in the long term future of the company. To them it's just a source of income, the means to pay for their high style of living. That's why they'll be against me, because the more that goes back into the firm by way of investment, the less they'll have to spend. But even more than money, they grudge their time, especially the Colonel, now he's an MP. That's their real weakness, and if I persist, if I keep them talking long enough, make things difficult enough ...' He nodded confidently. 'That's the first rule of business, go for the weak spot. Everyone has one. It's just a question of finding out what it is.'

'And what is yours, James?' Elizabeth enquired mockingly.

He looked at her, smiling. 'You.'

The Colonel — and Right Honourable Member for North Durham, as he never lost an opportunity of reminding everyone — fidgeted impatiently and looked at his watch for the third time. 'How much longer is he going to be? I'm dining with Lord Ravensworth tonight and I've got to get all the way to Eslington Park yet. It damned well better be important.'

'Mmmm,' William James made a noncommital noise and drew long and thoughtfully at his cigar. He didn't particularly care whether it was important or not. Whatever it was it upset his plans for the evening and like the Colonel he was anxious to get away. He and the Colonel were kindred spirits there; connoisseurs of good living although the Colonel's taste tended toward the mundane and respectable. But they both knew, as James would never know, the importance of having friends in high places, the art of cultivating the right people. In his opinion an invitation to shoot on the Colonel's grouse moor at Blanchland could get better results than all of James' financial wizardry. It was a fact of life. It wasn't what you knew but who. In consequence he lived well, dressed well, entertained lavishly and already there were rumours of him being asked to sit on the Bench. Of course, such a lifestyle needed some keeping up and quite frequently he overstretched himself. It irked him that his income wasn't more. In fact he'd had it in mind for some time now to propose an increase in the dividend. He fingered the luxurious nap of his coat, adjusted his Ascot tie with its discreet pearl pin. Smilingly he glanced up, about to make some remark to the Colonel — and stared into pale cold sneering eyes ... Quickly he averted his glance from his father's portrait. Why the hell did they even keep it here? It wasn't as if any of them needed reminding ...

'I'm sorry to have kept you.' His father's cold eyes were replaced by others not so very different. James smiled at him. 'I hope you haven't been waiting long.'

'Long enough,' William James answered shortly. 'I hope this business isn't going to take hours ...'

'It needn't,' said James easily. 'That depends on your reaction to what I have to say.'

The Colonel shifted uneasily in his chair. 'Can we get on, James. My time as you know, is at a premium.'

'Yes, of course.' James seated himself behind his desk. 'It's regarding the proposed deepening of the South Tanfield shaft. There're a few details I'd like to confirm.'

'Yes,' said William James, stubbing out his cigar. 'I've been giving that one some thought myself. I wonder you know if we're wise to go ahead. With the market so low, one wonders if it's really the time to expand. Especially seeing as you let the Norwegian contract slip through your fingers. I'm not sure that there's any justification now for opening out the lower seams.'

'There'll be other contracts,' said James. 'Bad times don't last for ever any more good ones do. We'll need that coking coal sooner or later. If we open out South Tanfield, we'll have access to the Beaumont, Tilley, Busty and Brockwell seams which will extend the life of the colliery by some thirty years.'

'They're all thin seams,' William James objected. 'The Busty especially is riddled with bands.'

'Yes, I know that. But even so, we're talking about some six hundred and fifty acres of workable coal. If we calculate on a minimum quantity of twelve hundred tons for every foot of thickness per acre we get a figure of some six and quarter million tons, a duration of thirty years working on an average output of eight hundred tons a day.'

William James looked bored. 'My, my, James. You do love to juggle with figures, don't you? Shall we get to the point. What sort of money are we talking about?'

'That depends on whether we do it your way or my way. As it stands, you're planning to deepen the downcast only, then divide the shaft to draw coals and ventilate up to Main Coal level.'

'That is the most economical way to do it. Otherwise it means thousands spent on deepening the upcast.'

'I don't agree. You're proposing to raise the coals worked in the Busty and Brockwell to Main Coal level, lead them to the upcast and draw them to bank there. It will necessitate double onsetting and double banking out in addition to the haulage. We'll be putting dead money of threepence on every ton raised. On a long term average of six and a quarter million tons ...'

'All right, James. We take your point.' The Colonel glanced again at his watch. He didn't really want to get involved. He couldn't spare the time for one thing. His parliamentary duties pressed upon him hard. He was chairing three committees as it was and what with all the dashing back and forth to London

... 'I'm sure you know what you're doing, my boy.' He threw a prompting glance at William James. 'Wouldn't you say so, old man?'

William James scowled. 'No, I wouldn't say so, as a matter of fact. It's getting to be a habit, letting James make all the decisions. I think it's time we made a stand.'

'Does it matter who makes the decisions, as long as they're the right ones for the company?'

'Who says they're the right ones?' William James argued.

'Are you questioning my judgement?' James asked coldly.

'Yes. Why not. You're questioning mine.'

James smiled. 'It's not your judgement that I'm questioning, rather the motive behind it. Your way is the cheapest way, I grant you that, but I get the feeling that cost is the major influence behind any judgement you make — above safety, above efficiency — just so long as it's cheap.'

'Now look here, James. It's a perfectly legitimate way of doing things ...' William James broke off, controlling his voice which had begun to rise. 'Anyway, I'm not going to get involved in a lengthy argument. I insist that we stick to the original plan.'

James was silent for a moment before he spoke. 'You're prepared, then, to take full responsibility for the project? Attending meetings with engineers; surveyors; being on hand for any emergency?'

'And you, sir?' He looked at the Colonel with limpid blue eyes. 'I know that you don't have a great deal of time to spare ...'

'Damned right, I haven't,' shouted the Colonel. 'And I'm telling you now, I'm not prepared to get involved in this. You must sort it out between yourselves.'

'There's no need for you to get involved, sir,' William James declared confidently. 'I'm perfectly capable of handling things myself.' He looked at James. 'As my share of the firm is the second largest, I can quite easily overrule you on my own.'

'Well, that isn't quite true,' James observed. 'If we're going to decide the issue on the strength of our stock, then I would suggest that Eleanor be consulted. She does after all hold ten per cent. And of course, if Eleanor voted with me against you ...' James gave the Colonel a hard meaningful look. 'It would be up to you then, sir, to decide.'

The Colonel flinched visibly. James was going to be difficult, he knew. He could see the whole business getting wildly out of hand; himself getting caught up in it; demands being made upon his valuable time. He licked his lips and glanced anxiously at his watch. 'Well, what I suggest,' he said, attempting to compromise, 'is that James gets some hard figures out. Then we'll compare the two estimates, and if the extra costs aren't too exorbitant . . .'

'I've already done that, sir.' James passed him a sheaf of papers covered in his neat, clerkly hand. 'The actual difference is some seven thousand pounds, which on a projected output of eight hundred thousand tons in the first year of operation, would give twice that return in the first six months.'

'Yes, well, that seems to be all right.' The Colonel looked pointedly at William James. 'It hardly seems worth falling out over.'

William James inclined his head, though his expression remained sullen and resistant. But he could see by the Colonel's face that it would be unwise to persist. He said, grudgingly. 'I dare say you're right.'

The Colonel slapped his thighs and got to his feet. 'Well, that's that then. No more business is there, James?' He slapped him cordially on the back. 'Forgive me dashing off, my boy, but you know how it is. You must come up to Newton for a days shooting some time. We've got some good birds this year. And bring that pretty wife of yours with you.'

He bustled out leaving his two nephews alone in the room.

William James drew on yellow wash leather gloves. 'Well, you've managed to pull it off again, James. And I must say I admire the way you handle the old boy. He'd agree to anything rather than get involved.' He smiled briefly. 'But that won't always be the case, will it, James? When the old boy pops off there'll be just two of us then — and I shall be the senior partner holding the majority of shares. We'll see about you making all the decisions then.' He tapped James smartly on the shoulder with his silver topped cane. 'Think about it, old chap, won't you?'

Left alone, James resumed his seat behind the Colonel's desk. He stared across at the old man's portrait. Indeed, he was thinking about it. He had been thinking about it for years.

He stayed on till late, working into the early hours of the morning. He had forgotten how much he enjoyed having the office to himself; the vast silence of the empty building, the muffled sounds of river traffic, the tinny chimes of the clock on the Customs House measuring out the hours. It was past two o'clock when he eventually left and he stood for a moment on the wide stone steps, staring out across the river. Mist rose like steam from the black oily water. Rooftops and chimneys crowded a flushed orange sky.

He shrugged himself deeper into his overcoat and set off on foot, intending to walk as far as the station and pick up a hackney from there. The telegraph office on the corner of Lombard Street splashed light onto the pavement. A small crowd was gathered outside and James paused. 'What's up?' he called out.

A man in a bowler hat turned a grim face toward him. 'Pit's fired at Seaham. Two hundred poor devils blown to Kingdom come.'

Elizabeth was crying, tears of compassion and pity sliding quietly down her face.

'I shouldn't have told you,' said James regretfully. 'I should have known you'd be upset.' He put his arm around her. He felt quite like crying himself. It had been a grim story. They knew all of the horrific details now. Of the two hundred odd men that had been underground at Seaham only sixty-seven had been brought out alive. The rest were dead; burnt, blown up, poisoned and suffocated by carbon monoxide gas. One hundred and sixty-four men and boys, five of them only fourteen years old.

He'd been over to Seaham that morning. It was expected for fellow coalowners to pay their respects. Disasters like this touched them all — Seaham today but perhaps Beamish or Tanfield tomorrow.

On the surface things hadn't seemed so very different; dirty grey town beneath a dirty grey sky, dirty grey sea beyond. He glanced up at the blackened headgear, stark as a gallows against the sky. Even from here he could smell the acrid carbonised breath of the burnt out pit — and, perhaps it was his fancy, another smell, sweet, distinct, the stench of charred human flesh.

He turned the corner toward the Londonderry Institute where the official enquiry was to be held. He was early and only one or two people waited outside. A policeman in uniform guarded the doors.

'Mr Joicey, isn't it?'

James turned and smiled in recognition. 'Mr Atkinson.' He held out his hand. 'I should have expected to find you here.'

John Bolam Atkinson, Her Majesty's Inspector of Mines for the North Eastern Division shook hands. He was a short, thick-set man of about James' age; hard faced with a permanent expression of bitter cynicism which was borne of a lifetime spent viewing the mangled and mutilated remains of his fellow men.

'It seems I'm early,' said James.

Atkinson nodded. 'Officially the enquiry doesn't begin till eleven but they're letting witnesses and officials in. You're welcome to come in on my ticket though. The powers that be have allocated me a cupboard under the stairs they very grandly call an office. You can wait in there, if you like.'

It was indeed a small room with the upper walls panelled in dirty frosted glass. 'Well at least they've given us a fire,' said Atkinson. He held his hands out to the flames for a moment then seated himself at a small bare desk. 'So!' He eyed James with an air of derision. 'You've come to see if you can profit from this sad experience, have you, Mr Joicey? Profit is the important thing with you coalowners, isn't it?'

He drew a flask from his inside pocket. 'Whisky! Care for a nip? Hardens the heart as well as the arteries.' He poured himself a generous measure. 'You must forgive my cynicism but coalowners aren't my favourite people today, having been required to view their latest handiwork.' He eyed James curiously. 'You're a queer breed, you know. Quite an unknown species as far as I'm concerned. I don't understand the way you think — if you think at all. Take the venerable Marquis now, the owner of this miserable pit. Do you know he's donated a thousand pounds toward the Relief Fund. And of course every-body's saying what a jolly good fellow he is. But if he'd spent that thousand pounds on keeping his pit up to scratch in the first place, there wouldn't have been any need for a fund. However, I don't suppose you came here to listen to me banging my drum.' He swallowed the remainder of his whisky in a single gulp. 'Just out of interest, why did you come?'

'To find out what happened — in the hope that I can prevent it happening to me.'

Atkinson regarded him gravely. 'Do you really want to know? The truth, I mean? Or would you prefer the watered down account you'll hear at the enquiry?'

'I've already said, Mr Atkinson. I want to know what caused the explosion.'

'Well, that's easy enough. Coal dust is what caused it. They were shotfiring to enlarge refuge holes just minutes before the explosion occurred. And you know how shots are fired. A hole drilled in the section of rock to be brought down and stuffed with explosive — then run for your life to the nearest bolt hole, kicking up clouds of coal dust on the way.'

'It's not as primitive as all that,' James objected. 'It's dangerous, I agree — but unless you can think of a better way ...'

'No, I can't. But until someone does, every precaution should be taken to minimize the danger, and that means keeping coal dust down which in turn means wetting it down or deadening it with stone dust. But that costs money, which is why of course it is never done.' He leant forward. 'I can tell you something that this enquiry won't. The deaths of those men were due to dirty and dusty workings. Deep pits like Seaham — you're talking about three hundred fathoms full depth — are notoriously dry and dusty by virtue of the massive air current needed to ventilate the workings.' He gave a short angry laugh. 'It's ironical, really. The better the ventilation the greater the danger. In the old days when ventilation was poor, you didn't have explosions of this magnitude. It was gas that was the main hazard then so we pushed and harried for better ventilation till owners were pushing tens of thousands of cubic feet of air through their workings. The current dries up any natural moisture, stirs up the dust and impregnates it with enough oxygen to turn it into an explosive mixture. A shot is fired and there you are. We have solved one problem only to create another.' He glanced at James. 'The problem now is to make owners recognize that it is a problem and get them to do something about it. Did you know, Mr Joicey, that the flame from a blown-out shot can travel almost a hundred feet when there's coal dust in the air?'

'Yes, I did,' answered James. 'I read your paper for the Mining Institute.'

Atkinson raised a brow. 'Well, you must have been the only coalowner that did.'

'You're quite sure then that dust was the cause? It couldn't have been gas?'

'Quite sure. Coal dust explosions follow a classic pattern; quiet combustion for the first seventy yards, then props blown out, heavy roof falls. All the bodies in this area exhibit broken backs and limbs. Then as the explosion gains speed and velocity, tubs smashed to matchwood, men literally blown apart.' He leant back in his chair. 'You know, Mr Joicey, for the last fifteen years I've been submitting reports on mining accidents. I've seen them disappear through the portals of Whitehall to emerge sometimes years later, whitewashed, watered down, full of ifs and buts and maybes. Even the government, it seems, think twice about offending men like Lambton and Londonderry. And in the meantime, I continue to make out my reports demanding action, legislation, all that kind of thing. I continue to deal with inundations and explosions and think to myself that perhaps if something had been done, some of these men might still be alive. I sometimes wonder how many dead men I've actually seen; men without arms and legs, without heads — it's one of the symptoms of blast, you know, it blows off the top of the skull clean as a breakfast egg ...' He broke off. 'I'm sorry. I'm getting morbid. My job is inclined to make one like that.'

'Have they recovered all the bodies yet?' asked James.

'No. It's a long job, I'm afraid, with both cages out of action and the workings still thick with stythe. Of course, if we hadn't had to send all the way to Newcastle for breathing apparatus we might have been able to save some of them. We've evidence that some men survived the explosion for at least twenty four hours.' He rose from the desk and went to a small cupboard set in the wall and took from it a battered tin bottle of the kind that pitmen carried their water in. It was covered with faint scratchy writing. 'This belonged to a man called Michael Smith. We found it beside his body,' Atkinson said. 'It's rather hard to decipher. It's been scratched on with an old nail or something of the kind. Shall I read it to you? I know it practically off by heart.'

He began to read, turning the bottle between his hands;

My dear Margaret. There was forty of us altogether at 7 a.m. Some was singing hymns, but my thoughts was on my little Michael that him and I would meet in heaven at the same time. Oh Dear wife God save you and the children, and pray for me . . . Dear wife Farewell. My last thoughts are about you and the children. Be sure and learn the children to pray for me. Oh what an awful position we are in. — Michael Smith. 54 Henry Street.

Atkinson had looked up at James, his eyes burning with quiet fury. 'How's that for a last will and testament?'

April 20th, 1881 — Orchard House, Low Fell

She was pregnant again, less than eight months since her last confinement, and mingled with the joy was a small niggling fear. But she'd vowed to be sensible. It wouldn't be so bad this time. The first time was always the worst. And at least she had the good weather to look forward to. Winter was behind them; a bleak January, cold and cruel, when for a few weeks the grimy landscape had been cleansed with snow. February had been worse; iron frosts and freezing temperatures had crippled trade; rail shipments marooned in ice bound sidings; export cargoes frozen up in port. March had brought the thaw; and a rash of pale buds had appeared on the frost bitten trees. It was April now; soft and green and bursting with new life. She laid her hand upon her still narrow waist and thought of the new life stirring within her. It would be all right, she told herself firmly. She was stronger now, both in mind and body, at least she knew now what to expect.

Then she went downstairs, humming softly under her breath. On the landing, she paused. From the drawing room, through the half open door she could hear clearly the sound of raised voices. James' was the loudest. She could hear distinctly every word he said:

'Well, I hope you know what you're doing. If there's any trouble, I'll hold you entirely responsible. We're already behindhand with Simpson's contract, which I might remind you is loaded with a massive penalty clause.'

'There won't be any trouble,' William James answered coolly. 'The men won't lose pay over a single man. Times are too hard for that. And I don't know what you're getting yourself so worked up about, James. I was perfectly justified in sacking Matthew Henderson. He's a shoddy worker and a troublemaker to boot. He accused Collins the viewer of rigging the cavils and demanded to be set on in a different place. When Collins refused he became abusive and violent and quite openly attempted to incite the men to strike.'

'And so you sacked him. Without even bothering to find out if what he said was true?'

'I don't see that it's relevant. As I said, he's a troublemaker. He spends more time on union business than he ever does on ours. He's perpetually getting the men worked up over some grievance or other and whilst I'm prepared to tolerate the enemy in the camp I draw the line at actual sabotage ...'

'The men will see it as victimization, and of course, they'll be quite right.'

'Frankly, I couldn't care less how they see it. If they don't like it they can hand in their notices. I can find you hundreds of men more than happy to take their place. I only mentioned this to you, James, as I understand you have some interest in the family. Something was said, so Collins tells me, about appealing to you. I thought I ought to make it clear at the outset that there can be no question of your interference. However much we may disagree in private, publically it's important that we present a united front. In fact, I've already had a word with the Colonel and he's in total agreement.' He smiled. 'I just thought I'd let you know, old boy. Wouldn't want you to make a fool of yourself without knowing how things stood.'

He went out, slamming the door behind him, and Elizabeth

came quickly down the stairs.

James was standing by the fire, kicking moodily at the fender. He looked round as Elizabeth entered the room. 'I suppose you heard?' he said bitterly.

'I heard you,' she said in mock reproach.

James frowned. 'I'm sorry. Was I shouting? Yes, I suppose I was.' He flung himself down in the chair opposite her and stared broodingly into the fire.

Elizabeth said, 'This man that's been sacked — Matthew Henderson. Is he important to you?'

He shrugged. 'No. But his father is. His father is ...' Why did he hesitate to use the word 'friend'? 'I ... I've known his father for a very long time.'

'I suppose he'll be turned out, then? Is he married? The son? Does he have children?'

James shrugged. 'He has a wife, I believe. I'm not sure if there are children.'

Elizabeth's eyes clouded. 'What will happen to him then? Will he be able to get work elsewhere?'

'Not locally he won't. There are hundreds of men out of work as it is. No coalowner in his right mind is going to take on a known union agitator. That's the very reason William James wants rid of him.'

She was silent for a while and then Elizabeth asked, 'What did he mean by rigging the cavils?'

'The men draw cavils or lots every quarter for the places they will work. Some headings are good, some are bad. Rigging them would make sure that Henderson always drew the wettest dirtiest place.'

Elizabeth's mouth tightened. 'What are you going to do?'

'There isn't much I can do. I can't overrule the Colonel and William James.'

'That's never stopped you before,' Elizabeth reminded him quietly. 'You stand up to them readily enough when it's a question of money.'

James' head jerked up. 'I stand up to them when the disagreement can be kept to ourselves. I have never, nor will I, quarrel publicly, over money or anything else.'

Elizabeth flushed. 'Yes. I'm sorry. That was a terrible thing to say.' She bit her lip. 'Only it seems so unjust. You said

124

yourself the man was being victimized. Couldn't you perhaps ... Couldn't you at least see that his family didn't suffer? Financially, I mean.'

James smiled bleakly. 'What are you suggesting — that I offer him a bribe?'

Elizabeth frowned. 'Compensation was the word I would have used.'

James nodded. 'Well, we'll see ...'

He was quiet for a long time and after several abortive attempts to read the paper, he got to his feet and said. 'Would you mind if I went out for a bit? I feel like a walk.'

'No, of course not, my dear.' Elizabeth smiled. It wasn't hard to guess where he was going.

He took the train to Beamish and walked into Stanley, long sure strides for though the road was rough and unlit, he knew it well. He passed the Jackie pit, deserted, silent, except for the dull throbbing of the pump, sounding like a massive palpitating heart. At the Burns Pit, nearer the town, the back shift had just come up. They moved ahead of him, shadows among shadows, all walking with the same stooped and shambling gait. Exhaustion emanated from them like a distinctive smell and he found himself slowing his pace till they had turned the corner into Front Street. At the crossroads he paused, glancing down the narrow dingy street; a few shops, a rash of pubs, Methodist and Wesleyan chapels, all in the shadow of South Moor's Louisa pit with attendant rows of miserable houses. On the other side of the crossroads there were similar dwellings, row upon row of his own company's houses, reaching from where he stood to as far as Kip Hill. In one of them, he had been born.

He passed down the first of the shut and squalid rows between grimy windows and lines of privies. Half way along he paused and raised his hand to knock. The door opened quickly. A small boy stared up at him and stepped back wordlessly to let him in.

It was the first time he'd ever been in the house. There was only a single downstairs room apart from a diminutive scullery. Three children, a man and a woman sat crammed into its steamy warmth, also a table, a sideboard, a bed concealed in a highly polished cabinet and an assortment of stools and chairs. The room had a strange but not offensive smell; a mingling of sweat and polish, fresh bread and damp washing. The black leaded range gleamed with brass and on the mantel above, standing guard over a collection of odd plates and jugs, a pair of ginger and white imitation Staffordshire dogs eyed their surroundings with smug approval.

'How then, Matt. Don't disturb yourself. I've only stopped by for a minute.'

The old man subsided in a fit of wheezing. 'Sit yoursel' down then, Mr James,' as James hovered uncertainly. 'Pull up a chair and hev a bit warm. Whatever else we divvn't hev, we allus hev a champion fire.' He proceeded to light and fill his pipe then said between alternate puffs and wheezes; 'Ye've come likely about wor Matthew then?'

James nodded. 'It's a bad business, Matt.'

'Aye. It's that right enough.'

James swallowed. He said quickly before they went to far. 'I'm sorry, Matt. I wish there was something I could do.'

Henderson looked at him slowly. It took him a few minutes for the implications of James' words to sink in. 'Ye'll not be taking him back then?'

'No. I'm afraid not, Matt.'

Henderson slowly transferred his gaze to the rag rug beneath his feet. He'd been so sure, even when his lad had sneered at him for a fool, yes, even then he'd been sure. The young master would sort it. Mr James would see that his Matthew got his rights ... He felt betrayed, foolish. He'd been deceived. He'd deceived himself that this was one man to whom fairness and justice mattered. He saw now that they were all the same, that when it came to it they were all of a piece. He looked up, anger contorting his placid features. 'Y'know the lad's been victimized. Y'know he was sacked on account ov bein' a Federation man?'

James avoided his eyes. 'Yes, I know that.'

The old man's accent thickened unintelligibly with anger. 'An' y're still gannin' te de nowt?'

'Aa tell't ye!' Matthew Henderson suddenly emerged from the scullery. 'Aa tell 't ye te expect nowt from him.' He glared at James belligerently. 'It's the Federation we've to look to. It's the Federation that'll see I get my rights.'

'You think so?' enquired James with a derisive smile. 'I'm afraid you're going to be as disappointed in the Federation as you are in me. In my experience, union officials are eminently sensible men. They won't risk hardship to the rest of their members on account of a man like you.'

'Aye, well, that's what ye think, maister. But the Federation, like the company, looks after its own. An' if ye remember, it's for bein' on union business that I'm sacked.'

'Again I must disagree with you. The Federation conducts its business after hours and above ground. You were on your own business, stirring the men up, looking for grievance, pursuing some private vendetta against the company.' James looked at the boy's father. 'And you know that's true, Matt. If he weren't your son, if he were in your section, you'd have wanted rid of him too.'

The older man flushed but he made no reply. His son stared at him bitterly. 'Aye, well, aa might hev known y'd agree wi' him, being a company man.' His lip curled scornfully. 'Well, aa've no need of ye — or of ye either,' he added, turning to James. 'Ye can stick y're bloddy company an y're bloddy job. Aa'd rather starve than work for ye.'

He slammed out of the house. James looked at Henderson's pale, sickly face. 'I'm sorry, Matt,' he said awkwardly. 'I wouldn't have come if I'd known he was here.' He hesitated. 'Look, Matt, if there's anything I can do in any other way. If it's a question of money ...'

The old man recoiled as if he'd been struck. 'Well, ye knaa what ye can do with y're brass, maister.'

'For God's sake, Matt. It wasn't meant like that. Surely you can see ...'

'Oh, I see. I see reet enought. When it comes to takin' sides, ye masters hev to stick together. Aye, well. Ye stick wi' your kin an' I'll stick wi' mine.' He stood up agressively. 'This is the company's house, maister, and I dare say ye're entitled to come and gan as ye please. But that chair ye're sitting on is mine, and I'll be pleased to hev' ye out of it.'

James rose slowly to his feet and for a moment they stared at each. Then James turned quickly and went out of the house.

He walked the seven miles back to Gateshead and it was

past midnight when he eventually arrived at Orchard House.

Elizabeth was still up. 'James, it's so late. I was worried.'

'Yes, I'm sorry,' he said distractedly. 'I should have taken a cab, but I needed time to think.'

'You went over to Stanley, then?'

'Yes.' He sighed. 'And made a mess of the whole thing. The son was there and we quarrelled. His father practically threw me out of the house.' His eyes clouded with anger and regret. It had been more than the end of that tentative friendship. It had been the end of the easiness he'd always felt with the men, the end of a familiarity he'd always cherished. He gave a harsh laugh. 'It's ironic, isn't it? The masters despise me for being a pitman and the pitmen despise me for being a master.' He shook his head. 'I never before realized how little I fitted in. I don't seem to belong to either side.'

'But that's your strength, James,' Elizabeth told him, gently. 'You're independent. You're unique. You're not bound by the prejudices of either side. That's why you'll survive and they won't.'

James smiled at her. 'I hope you're right.'

'Of course I'm right. I'm always right.' She leant down and kissed him. 'Now come to bed, dearest. It's late.'

George lay listening to the night sounds of the house. He could not sleep despite a massive dose of chloral. He was not in pain above the usual raw feeling of his nerves. But he was afraid, consumed with the chronic invalid's awareness of self; aware of the whisper of air in his lungs, the rush of blood through his veins. His pulse was rapid, beating up like a drum into his ears. And his heart — engorged, palpitating, feeling as if any moment it would burst ... He struggled up on his pillows. His breath came quickly; sweat cooled on his skin; spasms of cramp knotted his muscles. He thought of Elizabeth; Elizabeth and James ... He closed his eyes. That was a worse ordeal, thinking of her lying in his brother's arms, imagining their passion, their joy in each other. He thought morbidly that nothing in his life was ever without pain, of the body, of the mind, he didn't know which was worse. But always there was pain.

He flung back the covers and bodily heaved his legs over the side of the bed. He sat quiet for a moment. There was hardly any feeling in his left leg at all, just a heaviness to let him know it was there. He reached for his canes and lowered himself so that his feet were touching the floor. Pain surged through him and contracted his spine. He gritted his teeth and threw his weight upon the canes, flinging the lower half of his body forward in an ugly lurching movement. A pause while he regained his balance, then again, another step forward, his atrophied muscles screaming in protest. Sweat poured from him and soaked his nightshirt as step by laborious step he crossed the room, inching his way toward his workbench. In triumph he sank down upon the high backed stool. He glanced at the clock. Five minutes exactly. He was getting slower. Once he could have done it in three.

He lit the lamp with stiff trembling fingers and Elizabeth's lovely face suddenly filled the room. It was finished, apart from the final oiling and polishing of the wood. He had used palest ash for its delicate colour and lack of grain, portraying her as she had been when first they'd met. Shy, virginal, the head arrested in the sideways movement that was so peculiarly hers, the face upturned so that the light flowed down over the perfect bones and the long stretched line of her throat. Her mouth was turned in the familiar pensive smile. Her hair he had left loose, lifted back from her face as if by a light breeze. He knew, looking at it, that, apart from the hewer, it was the finest thing he'd ever done. And as the hewer had been created out of his frustration and rage, so this was borne out of love and adoration. This Elizabeth belonged to him, his own immaculate conception. He leant forward and touched the smiling innocent mouth with his own. 'Elizabeth,' he whispered. 'My love.'

August 21st, 1881 — Newton Hall, Northumberland

'I am the Resurrection and the Life. Whosoever believeth in Me shall never die.'

The interior of the chapel was cool and dim in contrast to

the heat of the August day. In the arch of the chancel the Colonel lay, magnificent to the last, coffined in polished oak and gleaming brass, weighted with a mountain of lilies. Both the *Journal* and the *Chronicle* had carried glowing obituaries. Even *The Times* had noted it: 'August 15th, 1881 — peacefully at his residence'. That would have gratified the old boy more than anything — to have died like a gentleman, decorously in his bed, surrounded by weeping relatives and friends. And he'd have been pleased with the turnout, James thought, discreetly observing his fellow mourners; Matthew White-Ridley, both the Priestmans and old Pease, and those of the county set who'd been unable to attend had all sent impressive wreaths. And the family — Hannah and Jacob, William James and Mary, Eleanor, her two daughters and fifteen year old son, Rosandra the widow and her four plump girls. He himself was alone as Elizabeth was considered too far advanced in her pregnancy to make the journey to Newton. And all of them diminished in more than the physical sense by the old Colonel's death. Even he would miss him, if only as a buffer between himself and William James.

They stood to sing the old boy's favourite hymn; 'Onward Christian Soldiers.' James raised his eyes and fastened them speculatively on his cousin's elegant broadcloth back. 'My dear. My dear.' He heard William James' solicitous whisper and saw the elegant arm encircle Rosandra's trembling shoulders. He looked down at his feet as it occurred to him that possessed of twenty per cent of the Colonel's share of the company, Rosandra now held the balance of power. Even if he eventually managed to buy Eleanor out, he could only ever equal William James' forty per cent. To overrule his cousin and partner in any major decision he would need Rosandra. And William James had obviously anticipated him there. As her late husband's dearest nephew and friend he was already well entrenched as Rosandra's advisor. James gnawed at his lip. He'd foreseen this a long time ago. He should have had some strategy prepared. But then he hadn't expected the old boy to die so soon. He'd thought that he had plenty of time ... A frown drew his brows together. Things weren't doing well, certainly not as he'd planned. He found it increasingly hard to concentrate these days, to keep himself from thinking about Elizabeth. As her pregnancy had advanced, his concern for her grew. She seemed to be suffering more than was usual. Not that she complained. On the surface she seemed cheerful, she laughed at his fears and yet he knew instinctively that she was fearful herself. That made it worse, the fact that she needed to hide it.

He started as Eleanor touched his arm. Suddenly it was over. The Colonel with full ceremony was being borne from the church. James followed the sombre procession out into the sunlight; sleek black horses, dropping melancholy plumes, the scent of decay and flowers. And William James, 'So, James.' He showed his teeth in an unpleasant smile. 'Now there are just the two of us.'

'I shall miss him, you know,' Elizabeth said sadly. 'Whatever his motives, he did a great deal of good and that's really what matters in the end.'

James smiled drily. 'The good that men do shall live after them?'

'Yes,' Elizabeth smiled wanly. 'Something like that.' She poured tea into fragile Rockingham cups. 'Will the Colonel's death make much difference to the firm?'

'It'll make a difference to me,' James answered quietly. 'William James is the senior partner now.'

'Do you still care so much?'

'Yes,' he admitted. 'I didn't realise quite how much until today.'

Elizabeth regarded him thoughtfully. 'What about Eleanor's offer to sell you her share? Could we afford to buy her out?'

'Well, yes, I suppose so, at a pinch, we could, but there wouldn't be any point in it at the moment. I don't need to buy her out all the time she's prepared to back me rather than William James. I'd be spending money I could use better elsewhere and I'd be gaining nothing in voting power at all. You see, the two of us together can only match William James. It's Rosandra's share that's important.'

'Do you think she'll want to sell?'

'She might, eventually. There are no sons to follow on, and knowing Rosandra, she'd be quite happy to break any links with the trade. No, the problem isn't going to be getting Rosandra to sell, but for me to be able to buy.' He frowned.

'And that's going to be a very long term prospect, the way trade is at the moment.'

'Are things so bad?'

'Well, they're not bad but they're not good either. Our profits this year will be well down.'

'But surely the market's bound to pick up soon? This slump seems to have gone on for years.'

'I don't know, Elizabeth.' James admitted frankly. 'Once I could have told you perhaps. I used to have a feeling for these things. I seemed to be able to sense the way the trade was going to go and make my plans accordingly. Once, you could never have taken me by surprise.' He shrugged. 'It doesn't happen like that anymore.'

Elizabeth flushed. 'You've lost your touch, you mean. Is that because of me?'

He looked at her curiously. 'You've said that before. Why should it be because of you?'

'Because nothing seems to have gone right for you since you married me. Everyone is always hinting that you've thrown away a brilliant career ...'

He looked at her steadily and his heart turned within him to see her pallor, her slight body distorted with the child. 'I only ever throw away things I don't want, Elizabeth,' he told her gently. 'If I've given anything up, it's because it's not important to me any more.' He sat down beside her and took her into his arms. He looked down into her face and thought that he could never love her more than he did now, he could never feel so tender and protective. 'Elizabeth,' he whispered 'I've got what I want. You're what I want. I love you, Elizabeth. You are my life.'

November 21st, 1881
— Orchard House, Low Fell

The third week in November, ten days past her time and still the child was not born. A daughter they all said. Only a female would keep them waiting so long. Elizabeth did not smile. With the waiting, the fear, the awful anticipation grew. Every day that passed increased her dread.

She woke late that morning. It was becoming increasingly her habit to do so. Vickers moved busily about the room, stirring up the fire, straightening cushions, drawing the curtains on the grey November day. Elizabeth turned her head away, the shaft of light on her face like the slap of a cold hand.

Vickers placed her breakfast tray on the table by the bed. 'I've set your wrapper and slippers by the fire to warm.' She plumped up the pillows at Elizabeth's back. 'Mrs Edward looked in. She said she'd call back again this afternoon.'

Elizabeth smiled. Mrs Edward. Mrs James. As if they had no personality of their own but were merely extensions of their husbands. And sometimes lately she felt like that, as if she were not a real person at all but a shadow dancing impatiently on the heels of this gross and ungainly stranger.

She picked at her breakfast; a mouthful of tea, a finger of toast. Vickers glared in disapproval at the uneaten food. Cook's good coddled eggs not even touched. The crisp toast cold and congealing.

'It's a poor stringy bairn you'll be havin', and that's a fact.' She treated Elizabeth as if she were a bairn herself, fussing around her, leading her like an invalid to the chair by the fire, positioning her conveniently close to the bell rope in case she needed to ring. Elizabeth received all this cosseting with submissive gratitude but nevertheless she was glad to be left alone. She glanced at the clock. Half past ten. Usually she was up and about by now, attending to such duties as were still permitted her. But it was an effort to move, to leave the fire's circle of warmth. She closed her eyes, aware of an immense langour stealing over her, a feeling of quietness and peace. It will be today, she thought suddenly. Her child would be born today. And another son despite all the predictions.

The room darkened. It had begun to snow, the first real fall of the year. She roused herself and went to stand by the window, the pale light reflecting on her face. It was covering quickly, the driveway already merged with the lawns. She felt a moment's anxiety for James coming home. And what if she should need Dr Fergus? She was suddenly cold, the hair on her body lifting her flesh into shivering peaks. There was something almost sinister in the way the snow clung wetly to the panes, obscuring her vision, shutting her in. She turned back into the room, suddenly needing the reassurance of its familiarity and warmth. She went back to the fire. Just those few minutes standing had brought a dull pain to her back. She sank down in the chair. The pain sharpened, curved inward from her spine, recognizable now as the onset of her labour. She waited calmly for the contraction to pass. It didn't pass. The pain grew, demanding, urgent. She breathed deeply, leant forward to grasp the bell rope with sweating hands. It was then she screamed, a high, thin piercing sound like the monstrous pain that suddenly divided her body.

December 1st, 1881
— Orchard House, Low Fell

Eleanor straightened the ruffled bed covers disturbed by the doctor's recent visit, smoothing them tenderly over Elizabeth's still body. She lay quietly now, sedated by a mild dose of laudanum that was to be repeated every four hours. The worst was over now, thank God, the fever abated after raging through that frail childlike body for the best part of a week. Strangely enough, it hadn't been such a difficult birth. The complications had set in afterwards. There was some small infection, Dr Fergus had told them delicately. He hadn't made it sound so very much. He hadn't told them that she was likely to die. But the worst was over. The crisis had passed. It was just a question now of getting her strength back.

Eleanor leant over the bed, smoothing the damp tangled hair upon Elizabeth's brow, tucking it neatly beneath the edge of the frivolous lace cap. The face beneath was ashen, bloodless, the eyes partially open and clouded with a milky glaucous film. But the panting breast of the previous nights was stilled, her breathing quiet and even for the first time since the birth.

She sank down again in the wicker chair. She was tired. She hadn't slept for days herself, just odd hours snatched here and there. Her skin felt soiled and gritty and the armpits of her gown were stiff with dried sweat. She closed her eyes, opening them again almost immediately, disturbed by a baby's loud wailing. She had almost forgotten the child, Elizabeth's new born son. Hugh Edward Joicey cried a great deal as they hadn't yet been able to find a wet nurse and he had to be fed with sweetened milk out of a bottle. Again she closed her eyes but only fleetingly. She heard the door of the room open, the long masculine step advancing toward her. James was dressed for the office; black broadcloth coat, grey striped trousers, Ascot tie elegantly knotted. He smelt of clean linen and soap, a strange intensely masculine smell in the cold sterility of the room. He looked thin and tired, jaw and cheek bones sharply defined, dark bluish shadows beneath his eyes. And his voice, quiet and even as it always was, had a brittle rawness that was painful to hear. 'How is she?' he asked quietly.

'Much better,' Eleanor said, smiling. 'She's sleeping quite peacefully now.'

James nodded. 'That's good,' he said. He seemed to have difficulty in speaking, in taking his eyes from the pale still figure in the bed. 'I have to go out,' he went on. 'There are a few things I need to attend to at the office.' He looked at Eleanor. 'She'll be all right, do you think?'

It was said with such an air of desperation that Eleanor's heart went out to him. Poor James. This was all quite beyond him. Men were so helpless when it came to these sort of things. 'Yes, of course she'll be all right,' she answered him gently. She patted his hand. 'Go on. Get yourself away. It'll do you good to get out in the air.'

She walked with him to the door and gave him a last reassuring smile. Then she walked across to the bed ... 'Now then, my dear.' She addressed the still figure briskly. 'We must make our plans for when you are well. We shall be quite rushed off our feet to get all done by Christmas ...'

Despite the bitter weather he walked from the station, the long way round, up Grainger Street to the markets, then down Grey Street, past Richard Grainger's lofty and elegant buildings faced with tall, severe Corinthian columns that blossomed abruptly into lush and leafy capitals. Smoke had already darkened the pale stonework and pigeons crowding the little ornamental galleries frequently spattered the walls with their droppings. At the end of Dean Street, classical elegance gave way to the Tudor squalor of the Side. Ramshackle buildings climbed the short steep hill, the lower stories given over to dingy shops, the upper floors, offices and cheap lodgings. On the Quayside he paused, standing in the shelter of a tall warehouse to watch the docking of a Norwegian lumberman, a day late he noticed, for the pit props she carried, all of best peeled larch were destined for the Company's own collieries. It was high water. Smooth oily waves lapped at the ship's hull, throwing up ridges of foaming scum. He heard the clock on the Custom House strike the half hour and out of habit took out his watch. Eleven o'clock. He had promised Joe Thompson he'd be there at ten. But he felt no urgency. Nothing seemed important any more. Nothing seemed real. Not the day with its yellow sulphurish sky, not this place, the noise and clamour of the crowded wharves drowned out by the sickly hammering of his heart. The cold sensation passed over him again. Elizabeth. Elizabeth. He couldn't seem to think of anything else.

He moved away, walking briskly along the Quayside and up the steps into the Exchange Buildings. The vestibule was cold as a tomb. The porter emerged from his chair, his breath like steam. 'Good morning, Mr Joicey, sir.' He climbed the stairs against the flow of hurrying clerks and runners. In his office, his chief clerk greeted him with a mound of papers.

'Just these few that really cannot wait, Mr James. I took the liberty of dealing with the bills of lading myself, and Richardson's were also pressing for a decision on the Marseult lamps so I reordered in the same quantities as last time.' He waited till James was seated at his desk. 'Perhaps I could just trouble you, Mr James ... these three or four letters ... I'd like them to catch the evening post.'

Out of habit James scanned each paragraph of uniform clerkly script before setting his name to the bottom.

The clerk maintained a flow of polite conversation. 'And how is Mrs James, sir?'

'Much improved, thank you, Joe.'

'Oh, I am pleased to hear that. We've all been that worried. Please give her my own and Mrs Thompson's regards.'

'Thank you, Joe.' James added his quick firm signature to the last of the letters. 'I'll tell her.'

He walked to the station and picked up a cab. It had begun

to snow as only it can snow in the north, suddenly, violently, the wind whipping it up into massive drifts. The driver refused to turn off from the main Durham Road and James was forced to walk the rest of the way. Within minutes the blood had ceased to flow in his feet and hands, his flesh ached and burned with the cold. It was almost a pleasurable state, total exhaustion of mind and body, not to be able to think or feel.

His hands were so numb that it took him a while to manage his key. Then inside the door he paused. The silence struck him like a physical blow.

He stood quite still, irresolute, uncertain. Then he heard music, a piano, growing louder and louder. Suddenly the whole house was filled by the violent, discordant sound. He hurried into the drawing room. George sat at the piano, his fingers pounding furiously at the keys.

James slammed down the lid. 'For God's sake, George!'

George bowed his head. He wouldn't look at him. 'You're late, James,' he said softly.

'Yes, I . . .'

Then George giggled suddenly, a queer hiccupping sound. 'Too late, James. You're much too late.' He looked at him then, his face ravaged and blotched by tears. 'She's dead, James. Elizabeth . . . Elizabeth is dead.'

PART II
1883–1896

It is a giant with one idea.

Coleridge

July 2nd, 1883 — Newcastle

The train was seven minutes late leaving Newcastle, though the stationmaster assured him that they would have made up the time long before they reached London. Nevertheless James was irritated and he checked his watch for the third time as they pulled out of the station. Not that he was in any particular hurry. His time was his own for the next three days except for a business appointment the following morning with the chairman of London Gas.

He leant out of the window of the First Class Pullman carriage as the train steamed slowly across the High Level Bridge. He saw the river below — flat steely water furrowed by ships, grey familiar buildings crowding down to the wharves — except that nothing was really familiar any more. Even after a year and a half everything in his life still seemed tinged with a vague sadness, distorted by memories of grief.

The train gathered a little speed as it crossed the viaduct. He peered down at Gateshead; more dirty houses huddled in the shadow of the railway arch, dingy little streets glimpsed through a fog of sulphur and steam. Swinging east now towards the South Shore, there the noxious fumes of the chemical works defied even a blade of grass to show. The line swung south again, the train lurching and swaying as it negotiated the turn. A dozen lines converged here, intersected by the wagonway from the Oakwellgate Pit running down to the coal drops at New Greenwich. Then past Ellison's Glass Works, the saw mill and ropery, past the great open wound of the grindstone quarry. Gradually the view changed. The buildings grew fewer, grander; pale stone houses glimpsed through trees. In the distance he could see the line of low hills, the wide green sweep of the Team Valley. He had always imagined life to be like that; the changes slow and gradual, so that he was always prepared, always sure of what was coming next. He knew now that it wasn't. One could never be prepared, one could never be sure. Sometimes it only took minutes.

The train plunged into a tunnel. He saw himself reflected in the darkened glass; his eyes, deep caverns beneath heavy drawn brows, his face thinned by the dark sleek beard. The image vanished as they emerged into the light. He closed his eyes against the sudden brightness. It still hurt to think of her though the first monstrous anguish had quietened. Grief to him had been just another challenge, another obstacle to be overcome. There was just an emptiness now; a void where his heart should have been, as if a limb had been amputated but his mind refused to acknowledge the loss; still registering sensation though there was nothing there. He knew Elizabeth was dead, but he still looked for her, he still reached out a hand in the night, he still listened for her laughter.

Outwardly his life moved along ordered lines. He lived a frugal, almost spartan existance, arriving punctually at the office at seven each morning, as he had done since he was seventeen. He lunched at the Queens' usually, again an old habit; then the brisk five minute walk and an hour spent at the Exchange, then back to the office to sign his letters. The only divergence was dining at his club and more often than not staying the night. He preferred the anonymity of the impersonal rooms to the memories of Orchard House which held so many memories and his brother George with his bitter pent-up grief. Even his sons, small poignant reminders of all he had lost; though he cared for them intensely, he tended to avoid them in a rather cowardly way. It had been a relief when Eleanor had offered to care for them. Oh yes, life went on. He went through the motions but without enthusiasm or purpose, just moving doggedly from day to day.

He still had his work. That was all he had, and since Elizabeth's death he had driven himself hard. Profits had doubled, annual production was up and they now held blocks of shares in every major industry: shipping; railways; banking and steel; options on coalfields as far flung as Australia; franchises in electricity and gas. He was by anybody's standards a wealthy man and he supposed he should have been satisfied. He was only thirty-seven, in the prime of life. He could have travelled, seen something of the world, enlarged his knowledge of art and music. Yet it had always been his weakness, never to find satisfaction in anything but constant achievement. And besides, the erratic state of the trade didn't allow a man to rest on his laurels. The brief boom of the last two years was already tailing off. Soon the whole industry would be fighting for markets.

He thought again of his meeting with David Paulson, the chairman of London Gas, mentally revising his calculations. By letter they'd discussed a contract price of four shillings a ton though he was prepared to drop another two per cent. He was already undercutting Lambton's, who'd held the contract for the last eight years, by as much as threepence a ton. This he knew since it had cost him fifty pounds to a clerk in Lambton's office to learn the exact price of their tender. He smiled faintly. He felt no compunction now about using mildly unscrupulous methods to get what he wanted. Since Elizabeth's death his cynicism had deepened, his ambition, if anything, had intensified. He lived for the company now, his only relaxation was a speculative interest in art, and he had begun a small collection of what were derisively termed 'modern' works, paintings by virtually unknown artists such as Monet and Cezanne. Even this he viewed in the light of investment for in time, he knew, they would be regarded as masterpieces and be worth a hundred times more than he'd paid. It was an example of his foresight, his quiet and deadly patience.

In the same way he moved toward absolute control of the company. He had bought out Eleanor months ago, putting himself on equal terms with William James. Now he considered the question of Rosandra. It was her twenty per cent that was the key issue and somehow he had to manoeuvre Rosandra into a position where she was ready to sell, and William James into one where he was unable to buy. The latter, he thought, wouldn't be so very difficult. William James moved in exalted circles now, rubbing shoulders with the nobility on his Epsom estate, entertaining his townie friends at his London house, fetching them up to shoot at Lynhope. All this took money, more money than the company could be expected to provide. He smiled his thin, subdued smile. He happened to know for a fact that two of his cousin's properties were mortgaged to the hilt.

It began to rain, a brief shower that struck the carriage window in vicious little gusts. It had been raining the day of

Elizabeth's funeral. Rain, rain, rain, streaming in cataracts from the roof of the hearse, bruising the petals of the wreaths. It dragged at their clothes, at the plumes of the horses, rattling like stones on the narrow coffin. '*Elizabeth Amy Joicey. 1856 — 1881. Beloved wife of James*'

He hadn't felt much. He hadn't really believed it was Elizabeth slipping down into the weeping earth. He had seen her just once more, swathed in swansdown and ruffled silk. She had looked very young, the child she had been when first he'd met her. He hadn't touched her except to slip once more the wedding ring upon her hand. At the back of his mind he had heard his own voice; 'With this ring I thee wed, with my body I thee worship ... for richer or poorer, for better or worse ... until death us do part ...'

The train stopped at York to take on water and he left the carriage to stretch his legs, taking two turns about the platform. When he returned, he saw with irritation that the carriage he had hoped to have to himself now had a further occupant. A woman sat in the far corner, wearing what he could only describe as the most extravagant of hats. He acknowledged her presence with a brief, courteous bow, seated himself in the opposite corner and pointedly opened his newspaper.

'Excuse me?' She had a deep voice; smooth, languid. He lowered the paper, looking decidedly hostile. He hoped she wasn't one of those silly garrulous women who would chatter for the entire journey.

'It's Mr Joicey, isn't it?' she enquired with a smile. 'I wasn't sure ... the beard, you know.' She held out her hand, 'Marguerite Drever. We met at one of Agnes de Courcy's dinners ... Oh, it must be nearly two years ago now.'

'Oh yes,' he said blankly, unable to recollect either the face or the name.

She smiled. 'I see you don't remember. I must admit it was only the briefest of encounters. We weren't officially introduced.'

'Oh yes,' he said again, glancing at her hands as she stripped off her gloves. She wasn't married, though she gave the impression of being quite worldly and completely at her ease with men. He cleared his throat. 'You travel unaccompanied?'

144

he asked rather stuffily. 'It's a great distance for a young woman alone.'

She looked amused. 'Well, I'm not really so young, Mr Joicey,' she said drily. 'And when one has travelled the length of India virtually alone, York to London does not seem so very daunting.'

'You live in London then, Miss Drever?' he asked.

'Yes and no. We keep a suite of rooms at the Dorchester for the season but we usually winter in France where we have a villa. In between times we importune a circle of rather generous friends and occasionally come north for the shooting. Normally, my father accompanies me but unfortunately, at the moment, his health doesn't permit him to travel.'

James said that he was sorry to hear that and for a while they lapsed into silence. He returned to his paper, glancing up now and then to observe her. She stared from the window, the strong profile turned toward him. As she'd said herself, she was not so young, about thirty he would have thought. Neither was she beautiful, though she possessed the most remarkable complexion, clear and pale as Italian marble. Her mouth was small but without meanness and softened by an expression of perpetual amusement. Her eyes were good too, wide spaced and of a strange opaque green. Her figure was fashionably full and voluptuous and he was reminded of a Rossetti drawing he had once seen in the house of a friend. But what struck him most was her impression of serenity and stillness, her air of vital calm and quietness. She seemed so at ease, so self assured. He wasn't sure whether he liked that or not. He'd always thought a certain air of fragility an added attraction in a woman. Yet for some reason he still continued to observe her; a lady, no doubt of that, despite her air of casual familiarity. And a rich one, he would have thought, judging by the expensive simplicity of her clothes. And the hat — he was quite overawed and faintly intimidated by the hat — a high crowned affair with the brim upswept on the left side of her face and decorated with a cockade of osprey feathers, and worn with such an air of supreme confidence that he was sure it must be the very latest thing.

He folded his paper, laying it neatly beside him upon the seat. He took out his watch — another three hours yet. Already he was bored. He cleared his throat. 'You mentioned India, Miss Drever. Do I take it that your father is perhaps a military man?'

'He was,' she turned her long slow gaze upon him. 'A Colonel in the Bengal Army. I'm afraid that since leaving India he's never quite been able to settle. He misses it still, very much.' She fell silent again, taking up a book, then after a few moments, as if unable to concentrate, she closed it and laid it aside. 'May I enquire, Mr Joicey, is it business or pleasure that brings you to London?'

He liked her voice; low, soothing without a trace of shrillness. 'Business in part. Though I have also a day or two's leisure.'

'And your wife does not accompany you? I seem to remember that you are married.'

He stiffened, averting his eyes from her tranquil gaze. 'I was,' he said shortly. 'My wife died some little time ago.'

'I see,' she murmured, 'I'm sorry, I didn't know. How very sad. She was quite young if I remember.'

'Yes, she was,' he said. 'Twenty-four.'

She let a few moments elapse before continuing the conversation. 'And what shall you do with your days of leisure, Mr Joicey. Do you have anything planned?'

'Not really,' he admitted. 'I'm afraid I don't know London at all.'

'Well, what can I recommend? Nothing very much at such short notice. Do you care for the theatre? There are some very good plays, though really it's too late in the season to get tickets for anything good. Of course, there are concerts, art galleries, museums, parks; houses for gaming and drinking, even houses of ill repute. London caters for all the vices.'

Ridiculously he found himself embarrassed. 'I hope I do not have any,' he said pompously.

She laughed softly. 'You make yourself sound very dull, Mr Joicey. An interesting man always has at least one.'

James shook his head, amusement suddenly welling up inside him. 'You know ...' He laughed out loud. '... I don't know how to answer that.'

'You don't have to. It was a statement not a question. It doesn't need a reply.' She smiled at him again, that curious,

146

intimate smile he found so intriguing. 'If my memory serves me, you are a coalowner, Mr Joicey? Would it bore you, I wonder, to tell me something of your work? I must admit myself quite ignorant.'

The rest of the journey passed quickly and pleasantly. She asked intelligent and searching questions and listened intently to the sometimes lengthy replies. He found that strange. Few woman of his acquaintance ever really listened. And it eased him to talk. After a while he found himself telling her all manner of things; about Elizabeth, his two boys, how he now found himself at a loss . . . If she was bored or embarrassed by his flood of confidences she gave no outward sign. She just listened quietly, offering neither comfort nor advice. He wondered afterwards how he could have been so indiscreet, to unburden himself to a virtual stranger. But perhaps that was the reason, because she was a stranger. He wasn't very likely to see her again.

They parted at the barrier, a little island of intimate stillness in a sea of strangers. She made, he thought, a small effort to detain him. 'I have a carriage to meet me. Are you sure that I cannot offer you a ride.'

'No. Really. I have imposed enough. Besides, I would rather find my own way about. I shall feel quite insecure till I have my bearings.'

She smiled and drew a card from a little silver case. 'Should you have the time during your stay, please call upon us. My father, I know would be delighted to meet you. Perhaps, if your business permits, you could join us for supper tomorrow evening? There is no need to give me your answer now,' she added as she saw him hesitate. 'Just come if you can. We keep virtually open house. It's one of the advantages of living at an hotel that extra guests prove no problem.'

'Thank you,' James said. 'You're very kind.' He held out his hand. 'Goodbye then, Miss Drever.'

Her grip was firm. 'Goodbye, Mr Joicey. I hope that we shall meet again.'

He smiled. 'Yes, indeed. I hope so too.'

He went because he was bored and because his habitual loneliness seemed harder to bear as a stranger in a strange town. He

147

sent up his card with mixed feelings. He didn't set much store on such a casual invitation. London people always said these things and then discovered they had better things to do, so that he was surprised and relieved when she came down to the lobby to greet him herself. He watched her approach, her movements slow and graceful, everything about her quiet and controlled. She wore a fashionable gown of maroon glacé silk and her skin, by gaslight, had a wonderful paleness, an almost transparent luminosity. Again he was struck by her complete self possession, her lack of deference to him as a man. She treated him as an equal, with casual amiability. Immediately he was at his ease.

'I'm so glad you could come,' she said, smiling. 'I was not sure that your business would allow it.'

James returned the smile. 'I was glad of the invitation,' he said frankly. 'My business was concluded rather more quickly than I had thought and to be honest, without your kind offer, I wouldn't have known what to do with myself.'

'Your business was successful, I hope?'

'Yes, indeed ...' James smiled. More successful than he could have hoped, the contract clinched at three and eleven-pence a ton, twopence up on his bottom line. His mood had been buoyant ever since, more at the thought of outdoing Lambtons than at any financial gain. He glanced covertly at the woman walking beside him. For some reason being in her presence enhanced that mood. He felt strangely exhilarated in her company. She was quite unlike any woman he had met: the full voluptuous figure, the obvious swell of her breasts above the low cut gown. Even the scent she wore, not the light flowery fragrances he was used to, but a dry, heavy sensual smell that made him feel almost light headed. She exuded sophistication and intelligence and he knew instinctively that her knowledge of literature and art would greatly surpass his own. And yet, strangely, it was her calmness that excited him, that provoked in him the urge to ruffle the surface of that immense serenity and see what lay beneath. A flicker of excitement and anticipation ran through him. This was the first time in almost ten years that he had thought of any woman but Elizabeth.

She showed him into a small hallway that gave access to a

suite of five rooms. He had the impression of silk panelled walls, pale Empire furnishings and an Aubusson carpet he could have drowned in. The drawing room was vast and brilliantly lit; seven gas jets in etched glass bowls blazing like a constellation above his head. There were more people than he had expected: men in velvet coats and extravagant satin waistcoats, expensively gowned and jewelled women. It was like an aviary of rare and exotic birds who sat around in chattering little groups, calling to each other with trills of laughter. He looked out of place, a sleek predatory crow in his dark and sombre clothes. And he was vaguely disappointed. He had expected something a little more intimate. Supper, she had said, but this was more like a small reception with champagne and a lavish buffet, and in an adjoining room there was dancing.

Marguerite introduced him and he spent a few minutes in brittle conversation with a brace of right honourables and a fledgling lord. She led him away to meet her father; an elderly vulture, James thought, with those dark syrupy eyes, that supercilious beak, all set in a jaundiced skull. And his voice, pitched to an invalid's note of eternal complaint. Politely James extended his hand. 'I'm very pleased to make your acquaintance, sir.'

Thomas Drever smiled his painful smile, greeting James as he greeted all of his daughter's possible suitors, with suspicion and reserve and hostility. The dark eyes swept over James in frank appraisal and he saw a man past his first youth, cold of eye and hard of mouth, a pale ascetic face that commanded attention, its expression controlled and formidable. His soft vowel sounds betrayed his northern origins though his voice was pleasant and well modulated. A financier perhaps? He had that air of quiet ruthlessness that went with making money. A clever man then, arrogant and inflexible, not the sort of man, he would have thought, to have attracted Marguerite. But she was attracted. He did not know this man but he knew his daughter. He glanced at her now and saw the faint colour sweeping her cheeks, her anxious scanning of his face to see if he approved. Well, he didn't approve. He knew the kind of man that would suit his daughter; one of their own kind, of impeccable background and social consequence. Without even knowing anything about James Joicey, he knew that he did not fit the bill.

Marguerite left them together, excusing herself to welcome new guests. Drever motioned James to take a chair beside him. 'So, Mr — er — Joicey, wasn't it? What tempts you down from the fastnesses of the north? Business. A coalowner. Oh yes, I see.' Trade then, and not to his mind a particularly savoury one. He knew the type. Every season they flooded down from the midlands and the north; boot manufacturers and button kings, pushing their way into decent society, thinking that money was a substitute for good blood. Thomas Drever was inordinately proud of his blood. His mother had been Marguerite de la Fontaine, daughter of the famous French general. And on his father's side were generations of high ranking military men. Never had his people stooped to trade.

'Have you known my daughter long, Mr Joicey?'

'No.' James answered frankly. 'We met yesterday on the train.'

Drever felt mingled relief and dismay. On the one hand no strong attachment could have been formed on so short an acquaintance, but on the other — for Marguerite to be enamoured after just a casual meeting ... Then he caught sight of the gold ring on James' left hand. 'Are you married, Mr Joicey?'

'I was. I have been a widower for nearly two years.'

'Children?'

James frowned. He was becoming a little irritated by this eternal catechism. 'I have two boys,' he answered shortly.

Drever pursed his lips. That circumstance put the fellow completely beyond the pale. The thought of Marguerite mothering another woman's children ...

Then he said, smiling to excuse his obvious discourtesy. 'You must forgive this inquisition, Mr Joicey. I'm afraid I'm inclined to be somewhat over-protective where my daughter's friends are concerned. She is my only child, you know. Her mother died when Marguerite was very young. In consequence she has had a liberal upbringing, a great deal of freedom in her choice of friends. Unfortunately, on occasion she doesn't always choose wisely — fortune hunters, you understand. That kind of thing; men who hope to elevate themselves socially by

150

marrying out of their class.' He watched James' face closely to judge the effect of his words and saw the long mouth curve into something between amusement and disdain. The cold eyes returned his look unflinchingly and in the end it was the old man who flushed and looked away. He said — another question but without his former impertinent tone. 'Do you play bridge at all, Mr Joicey.'

'No, I'm afraid I don't,' James answered coolly. 'I'm a very bad loser, even at something so trivial as cards.'

'You shouldn't apologize for it, Mr Joicey.' Marguerite had returned and stood beside him. 'Indeed, I think it a very admirable trait. People who don't mind losing usually do.' She smiled at her father. 'Will you excuse us, Papa? I haven't yet offered Mr Joicey any refreshment.'

Her smile and her obvious attention soothed his mounting annoyance. It was perfectly clear that the old man had been warning him off, that for some reason he thought of him as a grubby opportunist making up to his wealthy unmarried daughter. He was half inclined to laugh. Nothing could have been further from the truth.

'Will you take some champagne, Mr Joicey?' Her voice, low, pleasant, cool like the wine. She smiled up at him, that slight but intensely personal smile that was so at odds with her indifferent manner. 'Have you been able to see anything of London at all, Mr Joicey?'

'Nothing much,' James replied. 'In fact, I was rather hoping to be able to persuade you to act as my guide.'

'Why, yes. I should enjoy that.' She agreed readily without the least hesitation. It was one of the things he liked about her, the complete lack of coquetry in her manner.

They wandered through into the small improvised ballroom. Marguerite watched the dancing for a moment then said, 'Do you care for dancing at all, Mr Joicey?'

'I used to,' James said, 'Though I'm afraid nowadays I rarely have the time.'

There was a little pause. Marguerite gave him an amused glance. 'Do you have the time now, Mr Joicey?'

James laughed, more at himself than anything else. Dear God, he was making a prize fool of himself. Had he forgotten so quickly how to behave with a woman?

151

Of course she danced exquisitely and had a repertoire that ranged from a polka to a gavotte whereas he had never progressed much beyond the waltz. It was a pleasurable experience, the soft warmth of her body, the heady perfume that drifted up from her hair. It was a long time since he had been interested in a woman, a long time since a woman had been interested in him.

They danced once more, later on in the evening. He filled in the time making polite conversation having discovered a little banker with whom he trod some mutual ground. He left early, purely for the purpose of being able to speak to her alone.

'You haven't forgotten your promise to show me the sights?'

'No, I haven't forgotten.' She smiled at him. 'Would ten o'clock be too early for you to call?'

'Not at all.' He took her outstretched hand. 'Till tomorrow then, Miss Drever.'

He was impressed with London; Westminster and the City linked by the Strand; Mayfair, Belgravia, Kensington and St James', crescents and squares lined with tall elegant houses grouped around islands of clipped turf and pleached limes. The City especially impressed him; the grand scale of the buildings, the bustling streets, the fast exacting pace. Here he had felt was the real centre of wealth and power. Here at least he had felt at home.

It had been an exhilarating day. The morning spent touring in an open carriage, then oysters at Rules, lunch at the Café Royal. The afternoon they had spent browsing in Agnew's in Bond Street, and he had discovered that they shared a taste for modern art. She was openly envious of his possession of a Cezanne. Now as they walked together along the sunlit embankment he felt a reluctance for the day to end.

He glanced down at her, smiling. She was always faultlessly dressed, this time in rustling bronze silk trimmed with sable. 'You're very quiet,' he observed.

'Yes, I'm sorry.' She glanced up at him from beneath the wide brim of her hat. 'I was thinking what a delightful day it has been. It's a pity you haven't longer. You've only seen just a tiny part. I had hoped that we might have time for a visit to Westminster. In the afternoons one can sit in the Stranger's

152

Gallery and hear the debates. Next time you are in town you should make an effort to go.'

'Yes, I will,' said James. Next time he was in town — and he knew suddenly that there would be a next time. He wanted to see this woman again.

Then she said casually, 'Are you interested in politics at all, Mr Joicey?'

'Yes, I suppose I am. At least, I'm a great admirer of Mr Gladstone.'

'Yes, I thought you might be,' Marguerite commented drily.

He looked at her sharply. 'You say that in almost a derogatory tone. I must assume your politics are otherwise.'

'As a woman, Mr Joicey, the law does not allow me any political allegiance.'

'It may not allow you a vote but it allows you to have a point of view.'

She smiled. 'Well, let us just say then that my point of view does not incline to the Liberals. I find their policies a little too radical.'

'Don't you agree, though, that radical policies are necessary for the common good, that the Liberal party stands for the concept of freedom?'

'Freedom for whom, Mr Joicey?'

'For all men.'

'And women?'

'Yes,' he answered cautiously. 'At least to a certain extent.'

'To the extent of giving them control over their own lives, the right to vote for instance?'

He was silent for a moment then he said. 'Well, if you want my honest opinion, then no, I don't think it practical to go as far as that. I don't think women would understand the issues. They'll vote emotionally — or as their husbands tell them to.'

Marguerite raised her eyebrows. 'And does that rather damning assessment of female intellect apply also to me?'

'No,' he said honestly. 'I think probably you are an exception.'

She smiled and they walked on in silence for a while. Then James said, 'You've never married, Miss Drever?' Somehow the question wasn't impertinent with her.

Marguerite paused, standing by the wall to watch the

progress of a passing barge but otherwise she answered readily enough. 'No, I've never married — but only because I've never met a man I particularly wanted. It's always seemed to me something of a gamble, to put your life and happiness in somebody else's hands. But then on the other hand, I hold no particular brief for spinsterhood either. It has always seemed to me a rather negative state. To experience life, to live it to the full it seems one needs a partner.' Then she gave her low breathless laugh. 'I dare say that one day I shall pluck up the courage. I am an ambitious woman, you know, Mr Joicey, and as a woman can have no ambitions for herself then I shall have to have them for my husband and my children.'

They resumed their walk. It was only some little distance back to her hotel and though neither spoke for a while, the silence between them was easy and unconstrained. Then Marguerite said, 'So you return to the north tonight then, Mr Joicey?'

James hesitated fractionally before replying. 'Yes. Unfortunately I must. There is a meeting of the Coalowners' Association tomorrow I am duty bound to attend.'

'I am sorry,' she said honestly. 'I have enjoyed your company.'

'And I yours.' Then he added on impulse, a deliberate lie, 'I have to return to London at the end of the month. Perhaps you would do me the honour of allowing me to return your hospitality. Perhaps you and your father would dine with me?'

She accepted smilingly and though he listened for a note of eagerness in her voice it remained quite cool and matter of fact. He wondered why suddenly that should irritate him.

August 13th, 1883
— Exchange Buildings, Newcastle

Sunlight flooded the stuffy office and the gilded lettering upon the windows patterned the carpet with strange hieroglyphics. James slowly exhaled smoke from his second cigar, watching it drift across the room to be imprisoned in the thick shaft of light. He was waiting for William James and had been for some

154

forty-odd minutes. They rarely met now, once a month suffi-
cing to settle any Company business. Even so, their intolerance
of each other was still very real, except that James was better
at concealing it.

He glanced down at the papers arranged neatly upon his
desk; investment bonds and property holdings, securities,
stocks and shares. He had divided them into two distinct piles,
those that he intended to retain and those that were to be
despatched with an accompanying letter to his broker with
instructions for him to sell. There was also the letter from
Rosandra Joicey confirming her acceptance of his offer for her
share, and folded beneath it, out of sight, a list of William
James' debts and commitments that totalled some twenty
thousand pounds.

He extinguished his cigar, hearing the light affected voice
calling out greetings to the clerks in the outer office. 'Hello Joe.
How's the 'bago? And Mrs Joe? Good. Give her my best.'

Without knocking he opened the door of James' office.
'Sorry I'm late, old man. Only just got your message. You were
lucky to catch me as a matter of fact. I was just off to Lynhope.
Got some people coming for the weekend to shoot ...' He drew
off his gloves and flung them down on the desk. 'And how did
your sojourn in the metropolis go? I thought afterwards you
know, you could have stayed at Lennox Gardens instead of
some God-awful hotel.' He seated himself in the chair opposite
James and crossed his legs. He looked, as always, every inch
the gentleman; his thick fair hair sleeked back with pomade,
the heavy moustache lending a dubious strength to his weak
and feminine mouth. He was expensively dressed; a diamond
stickpin nestled in his silk Ascot tie and his waistcoat of pale
oyster satin was fastened with real pearls. He gave James a
quizzical look. 'What's up then, my dear fellow? What is so
urgent that it couldn't wait until Monday?'

James smiles disarmingly. 'Nothing so urgent really. I just
wanted to get a few loose ends tied up and discuss the matter of
Rosandra.'

'Rosandra?' A little of the good humour faded from William
James' face.

'Yes. Rosandra. She wants to sell.'

'Since when?'

155

'Since I made her an offer she couldn't refuse.'

'I see,' said William James slowly and his face took on a guarded look. 'I didn't know you saw anything of her these days.'

'Oh now and then. Now and then,' answered James evasively. 'We've always kept in touch.'

'So it would appear.'

James lifted his eyebrows at his cousin's cold tone. 'You don't seem to approve. I thought we'd decided some time ago on eventually buying Rosandra out. It's the sensible thing as far as the company is concerned. Rosandra is dead weight. She contributes nothing to the business. She's not even on the board, yet we are still required to pay her a dividend.' He shrugged. 'It seemed to me the obvious thing.'

William James licked his lips. 'Yes, I suppose so. It's just that I'm rather surprised. You do have rather a habit of springing things.'

James smiled blandly. 'Yes, I'm sorry. I assume that because these things are on my mind they are on everyone else's as well.' He glanced down at the papers upon his desk. 'Now — naturally, my offer to Rosandra was made on a joint basis, the twenty per cent to be divided equally between us as would be the purchase price of twenty-four thousand pounds.'

William James winced. Dear God, he couldn't even raise a quarter of that, let alone half. He'd had some heavy losses at the tables recently besides which his expenses were enormous; the upkeep of Lynhope, the house in Lennox Gardens, Sunningdale Park, his sprawling Berkshire estate. And then there were his mistresses, his horses, his discontented and demanding wife, his idle and extravagant son. And added to these, a quite ruinous rate of taxation and mounting interest on some rather indiscreet borrowings. Ridiculous really to be so short of ready cash when on paper one was worth tens of thousands. Covertly he eyed James; the full Imperial with its first sprinkling of coarse grey hair gave him the look of a Spanish grandee. Like his smile, it was deceptive, softening the arrogant line of his jaw, detracting from the cruel sarcastic mouth. He was quietly dressed, correctly, severely, somehow making his own fashionable clothes seem vulgar.

He cleared his throat nervously, reluctantly meeting the

cold, hooded eyes. 'It's a great deal of money, James,' he said. 'I don't know ...' Quickly he swallowed down the admission of his impecunious state. He needed time to think, to work this one out. James, he knew, was up to something ... And then he saw, in the smile that briefly touched the long impassive mouth, in the gleam of his eyes before he lowered them. James knew; probably right down to the small change in his pocket, he knew exactly how he was placed. It was all quite clear now, this rush to buy Rosandra out, knowing full well he couldn't meet the price. James obviously could, probably twice over. Once he had admitted that he was out of the running there was nothing to stop James acquiring all of Rosandra's share and control of the company as well. He stared down blankly at the glossy toes of his Oxfords. He felt physically sick, the urge to launch himself across the desk and sink his fist into that cold impassive face was almost overwhelming. He schooled his trembling mouth into immobility. Somehow, somewhere he must find the money. Twelve thousand pounds — not so very much when you thought of what his share of the company was worth. The banks were out, though. His assets were already encumbered up to the hilt. There wasn't anywhere that his credit wasn't stretched to the limit. He supposed he could sell something. He had pictures and furniture worth ten times that amount. Yes, that was the answer. He'd put a few good pieces up at the Rooms. But that would take time, a couple of months at least. Unless he could persuade Rosandra to hang on ... Yes, even better. He'd talk to Rosandra, at least make certain that she didn't sell to James until he'd had a chance to raise the money. He leant back in his chair, his smile expansive. He felt a certain elation at having caught James out, at the prospect of being able to thwart him.

'Yes, I suppose you're right, James,' he said casually and his elation grew as he saw the faint widening of James' eyes. Didn't expect that did you, you bastard?

Then he rose to his feet and his movements were confident. 'Let me know when you have the papers ready to sign.' He drew on his gloves, settled his hat at a jaunty angle, then went out, banging the door behind him.

James sat for a few moments, tapping a pencil thoughtfully against his teeth. Then he got to his feet and went to stand before the portrait of old James. 'Well,' he said. 'What do you make of all that? Perhaps there's a little bit of you in him after all.'

September 12th, 1883 — London

James stood in the dining room of William James' house in Lennox Gardens, his cold eyes appraising its contents. The long table of figured walnut laid with heavy silver and Waterford glass, the panelled walls crowded with paintings. He recognized a watercolour by Turner and two Rembrandt etchings, an elegant Gainsborough woman. And yet to James the room jarred, exhibiting all the brash flamboyance of the nouveau riche. Everything was positioned purely for effect, every picture and ornament was meant to be noticed. And everything valuable, acquired for its worth rather than its beauty, so that baroque clashed hideously with Venetian chinoiserie, Thomas Sheraton rubbed shoulders with Louis Quinze. He could see now how he had miscalculated. This quick and easy source of money he should have taken into account. The contents of this house alone were worth a fortune. He chewed broodingly at his lip. Yes, without doubt he'd miscalculated, both the value of his cousin's assets and his determination to keep him from getting the upper hand. It was a setback, of course, but one that he had anticipated in part. There was another way, more costly to himself financially and more certain to put himself and William James forever at odds. It was a pity, he thought. He always preferred these things to be concluded with at least the appearance of amity.

He began to pace the room, glancing occasionally at the clock. Seven o' clock he had said and it wasn't even yet the quarter to. He was cynically amused to find himself a little nervous. He wasn't normally intimidated by women, but then he'd never met one quite like Marguerite Drever. It was some three weeks since he had seen her, though he'd written to her twice; a letter thanking her for her kind hospitality followed a week later by a note to inform her that he would be in London on the 19th and reminding her of her promise to dine with him. He'd had in reply just a casually scribbled card saying that she was looking forward to seeing him. He'd thought of her though and often attempted to analyze his feelings. He wasn't in love with her, that at least was certain. She attracted him physically. He couldn't help but regard that cool surface composure as something of a challenge. It was that composure that drew him, that air of remoteness that seemed to promise so much. She seemed an enigma, for though she was neither reticent nor secretive she had revealed nothing to him of her private self. He was curious and mildly provoked by her ability to be familiar yet somehow manage always to keep him at arm's length.

Again he checked the time. Seven o' clock, five past, ten past — he had been so certain that she would be punctual. When it reached quarter past he went through into the drawing room and poured himself a small whisky. His nervousness had now increased to mild agitation mingled with a certain amount of pique. This wasn't a position he'd ever been in before, hanging about for a woman, speculating on whether or not she'd come.

Then to his intense relief he heard the sound of a carriage drawing up outside. He adjusted his tie, ran a quick hand over his freshly barbered hair, waiting till the servant had answered the bell before going out into the hall to greet her.

'I'm so sorry to be late.' She banished his irritation with her slow lazy smile. 'Only, Father cried off at the very last minute. I'm afraid he's not really up to dining out. I hope it doesn't put you out?'

He was taken aback, mildly shocked, that she should consider dining alone with him. And yet excited, elated ... She was, indeed, the most astonishing woman.

He helped her out of her furs, murmuring something conventional about it not mattering in the least. He showed her into the drawing room. 'Can I offer you a glass of sherry, Miss Drever?'

'Marguerite,' she said, smiling. 'Please call me Marguerite. It seems foolish to be so formal in the circumstances.'

'Yes ...' He frowned, feeling suddenly ill at ease. 'Isn't this going to be rather awkward for you?' he asked her bluntly.

Marguerite looked amused. 'Aren't you being rather provincial?'

'No. I don't think so. Even in London, I wouldn't have thought it was usual for a woman to dine with a man alone.'

'Is it my reputation you're concerned for, or your own?' She smiled at him mockingly. 'I'm not a raw young girl, you know. I'm perfectly aware of what I'm doing.'

'Are you? It's something you've done before then?'

'No.' She coloured faintly. 'No. It isn't something I've done before.' She smiled wryly. 'To be perfectly truthful, I've always led a strictly conventional life — a little dull, a little tedious, but always eminently respectable. But, do you know, just lately, I've grown rather tired of being conventional. I'm tired of being passive, of sitting back and seeing life pass me by. I'm tired of being a prisoner of my gender and class. It's rather sad, you know, to have reached my age without ever having experienced one single moment of real excitement.'

'And you think I can provide that?'

'Yes, I do.' She answered him frankly. 'That is why I am here.'

It set the mood for the evening. He was stimulated and aroused, intoxicated by her company. He laughed a great deal. She seemed to have a endless fund of amusing and lighthearted stories. He watched her as she spoke. She wasn't beautiful as Elizabeth had been beautiful, but listening to that rich and sensual voice, seeing the radiant animation of her face, the glow of her marvellous skin, he was persuaded that she was.

They ate little, preferring to talk. Under his prompting she told him something of her life. Her mother had died when she was just a year old and she'd been raised by a series of governesses and maids, travelling India with her father's regiment. James listened attentively. He could see now why she was so at her ease with men, having been surrounded by them all her life. Her interests too showed a predominantly masculine influence. She was greatly interested in politics, unusual for a woman, and she could argue any issue as fluently as a man.

They again fell into a lively discussion of the merits of the two political parties. 'The Liberal Party is the people's party,' argued James. 'All the people; rich, poor, lord and labourer. The Tories represent only a privileged minority.'

'But don't you think that's inevitable, James? How can the interests of rich and poor ever coincide?'

'Why not? Why must there be such rigid distincions drawn? The Liberals acknowledge the right of a poor man to become a rich man. The Tory policy is for the rich to get richer and the poor to get poorer.'

Marguerite gave him a provoking look. 'And how do you equate such radical views with being a capitalist yourself?'

'I am not against wealth, only against the hoarding of wealth by a small minority. All men should have the right to wealth. It is privilege I am against, the laws of privilege made by a minority to protect a minority.'

Marguerite smiled. 'You mean you want a slice of the cake as well.'

'Yes. All right, if you want to put it like that.'

'To me those are just Tory sentiments hiding behind a Liberal façade.'

'Why must the desire for beauty and freedom be exclusively a Tory preserve? Do you think that because a man is poor he has no appreciation of these things, that he doesn't want to better himself?'

'No, I don't think that — at least not now I don't.' She tilted back her head and regarded him gravely. 'You know, you'd make rather a passable politician yourself. Have you never thought of standing?'

James laughed. 'Good Lord. Are you serious?'

'Yes. Why not? You have all the qualifications: a good voice, a persuasive manner, an independent income — a necessity, for as you know politics do not pay. There are other rewards of course. Power, influence, a voice in affairs. Anything is possible in politics.'

Suddenly he was filled with a queer pounding excitement. All at once the future seemed to hold promise, a challenge. He glanced at her suddenly. Their eyes met, and the look was as intimate as if, physically, they had touched.

Then Marguerite rose to her feet. 'I really should be thinking about leaving. I arranged for the carriage to return for me at ten.'

He saw her out into the starless September night. She leant from the carriage window. 'Goodnight James. Thank you for a wonderful evening.'

Her perfume drifted toward him on the clear night air. 'I have till Sunday,' he said. 'Perhaps if you are free for lunch tomorrow ...'

Lunch, tea, dinner at the Savoy, for the evening he managed to get tickets for the opera. The next afternoon he accompanied her to Westminster to hear a debate. Politics had always seemed to him a fairly dull business before, but seeing it at first hand, actually hearing Gladstone speak ... He was impressed, exhilarated, amazed that he was still capable of such enthusiasm. But that was all part of Marguerite Drever's allure, the discovery of new passions, the glimpse of a world of wealth and power of which she seemed such an integral part.

He returned north with reluctance on the Sunday evening and even as the train drew out of King's Cross, he was thinking about the next time he would see her again.

September 20th, 1883
— Newcastle

For the second time in his life he felt a reluctance to enter the offices. The unchanging solidity of Exchange Buildings seemed to emphasize the monotony and regularity of his life. The same faces passing him as he mounted the stairs, the pungent smell of carbolic and polish. He walked through Vending, past the familiar sea of bent industrious heads raised briefly to greet him. 'Good Morning, Mr James,' like a chorus of parrots. It was the same in his office; everything familiar to the point of tedium, everything small, restricted, like a cage. He looked out of the window at the eternal greyness of smoke and steam. For once the naked ugliness of the view oppressed him. Its dirt and stark poverty was suddenly offensive. He thought of Marguerite but somehow he couldn't even conjure up her face. It was another world here, another dimension. London and Marguerite seemed a thousand miles away. Perhaps that was the attraction. Neither held any reminders of Elizabeth whereas here he could not escape from his sense of loss. It pursued him inexorably; the house, the children, even here at the office where so often she had smilingly coaxed him from his work.

He sat down at his desk and opened his case. The work had piled up in his absence. There were bundles of dockets to be gone through, ledgers to be checked. He was behind with the costings for the new sinking at Beamish. It took him three hours to clear his desk but he still had a few minutes until William James arrived. The transfer papers were ready. Rosandra's flowery signature in violet ink sprawled along the bottom. His own personal cheque made out in her favour was pinned neatly to the top. All that was needed to complete the transaction now was a similar amount from William James.

Then he heard the outer door of the office slam. On cue William James entered. He was in a confident mood, his expression triumphant, his manner smug. He flung his hat down, greeted James cheerfully and went to the cupboard where whisky and sherry were usually kept.

'Will you join me? Yes, I know — just a small one with plenty of water. Shades of your Methodist upbringing, my dear James. "Woe unto them that rise up early in the morning, that they may follow strong drink." He handed James a half filled glass. 'The book of Isaiah, I believe.'

He sat down, still talking. 'My God, it's been a hellish morning. I don't know that I'm really cut out for the Bench. Had to give some poor wretch six months hard just for raiding the Hon Pease's orchard. Seems a bit excessive, don't you think? No, you probably wouldn't, James, having the pluto-crat's inborn respect for money.' He regarded James mockingly over the rim of his glass, secure in the knowledge of a banker's draft burning a hole in his inside pocket. It had taken some doing though and of course he'd had to sell at a loss; a rather nice Charles II tazza and some monstrous jewellery of which, unfortunately, Mary had been quite fond. But, My God, it would be worth it, just to see the expression on James' face.

'Shall we get on then?' said James impassively.

'If you like,' replied William James setting down his glass. He wasn't in any particular hurry. In fact there was a certain satis-faction in spinning the moment out. He eyed James covertly. My God, he looked grim. You could have skinned a fish on the line of his mouth. Smiling, William James reached inside his coat. 'I think this is what you want, isn't it, James?'

James examined the draft without expression and laid it to one side. Then he pushed a sheaf of papers across the desk. 'If you'll just sign here, William James, beneath my own signature, and initial each page as well.'

When he had done so James blotted the signatures carefully and checked through them again to make sure they were in order. Then he looked up. 'There's just one more thing.' He waited till William James was seated again. 'Whilst I was in London I paid a visit to your bank, also to a firm of money-lenders in Whitechapel.'

The smile clung resolutely to William James' mouth, became fixed, a grimace, as the quiet voice went on. 'I bought your paper from the bank and from the gentlemen in Whitechapel I retrieved the mortgage on Lynhope. In other words, William James, I have bought up your debts. I am your major creditor now, and as such I have the right to immediately call in your loan, to foreclose on Lynhope if necessary.'

William James could not speak. Every function of his body seemed paralyzed with shock. But he knew what was coming and though his mind fought and kicked and struggled against it no sound escaped his lips.

The quiet deadly voice went on. 'I have a document already prepared transferring seven and a half per cent of your share of the company to myself. In payment I will return to you the mortgage on Lynhope.' He held out his pen. 'I think, you know, that's a fair exchange.'

Briefly William James met his cousin's cold eyes, then mutely, without protest, once more he signed his name. He knew now the reason for his lifelong dislike of this man. It was quite simply that he was afraid of him.

December 1st 1883 — Gateshead

The sinking of the new pit had begun at the end of October. There were to be two shafts; the 'Mary' for the downcast and drawing coals, the 'James' for upcast and pumping, each to be served by new winding engines designed and made at the Joicey foundries, as were the shaftings, screens and picking bands. The cages were to be of steel, in two decks, weighing, with chains, some three tons apiece and capable of raising at a single winding some forty hundredweight each. Both shafts were to be sunk to the Brockwell seam, a total depth of nearly nine hundred feet. It was a slow, arduous process; twenty feet of soil and gravel to be dug out by hand, then teams of sinkers lowered in iron kibbles to peck and burrow through tons of clay and shale, and every inch needing to be shored with lengths of wooden tubbing against the ever present danger of collapse. It was the end of November before they'd reached the rock-head and blasting of the solid strata could begin.

The days had grown shorter. There were a few half-hearted flurries of snow. James had felt his spirits sink. It was a bad time for him; the cold, the greyness, the short dark days, all seemed to drag at his heart like lead. He thought often of Marguerite. They corresponded regularly; casual, friendly, unemotional letters — though perhaps if he had cared to read between the lines ... The last he'd had, a fortnight ago now, had mentioned that since her father's health had so much improved, they would be coming north to spend Christmas with friends at Hexham. The thought had filled him with pleasurable expectation. It was due to Marguerite that he was so much easier with life, easier than he had been since Elizabeth's death. He felt he was gradually working himself free of the past, enough to take pride and delight in his sons. He saw them each day now since Eleanor had returned to Whinney house. Hugh had been two on the 21st of November; a dark mischievous child, full of energy and laughter, James Arthur, nearly four, remained solemn and shy.

'They need a mother, James,' Eleanor constantly complained. 'I'm getting too old now to cope with young children. It's time you thought of marrying again.'

And he did think of it — but only that. It seemed a long step from the thought to the deed, to turning his back on Elizabeth forever.

The anniversary of her death came and he went to Jesmond to lay flowers on her grave. He didn't linger. Once there had been some comfort in being so close, but to think of her now, a handful of bones in cold, dark earth ...

He went home reluctantly. It seemed cowardly to stay away. He hesitated though, before going in to see George. Since Elizabeth's death he had become a virtual recluse. Occasionally,

James would bully him into taking a carriage ride but otherwise, he never went out. He didn't welcome visitors either, and spurned every kindness as a gesture of pity. Even with James he was difficult. He never quite knew how he would find him. Some days he attempted a pose of cheerfulness, but more often he was sunk in gloomy introspection. He did no carving now. The effigy of Elizabeth had been the last thing he'd done. Now and then he painted; nightmare canvasses of violent swirling colours that resembled nothing unless it was his inner self. He slept a great deal, heavy drug induced periods of oblivion. He woke to bitter angry thoughts, continuing his private vendetta with a God that he said he didn't believe in. He often asked what sort of God took the life of a young and beautiful woman and spared a hopeless cripple.

As James had expected, just the sight of that thin, bitter face sent his spirits plunging. He looked old and ill, and his skin had the grey chlorotic pallor of a bedridden invalid.

He sat down on the edge of the bed. 'How are you feeling, old fellow?' he enquired gently.

George gave his grimace of a smile. 'Oh, I'm all right. Well, you know ... It's always a bad day, isn't it?'

'Yes ...'

For a moment they did not speak, then George said. 'How are the boys? I never see them. You don't bring them to see me enough.'

'Yes, I know. I'm sorry. It's difficult with Eleanor. I don't always get to see them enough myself. But Hugh was delighted with the wooden soldiers you gave him for his birthday. He's played with nothing else ever since. He seems to have definite warlike tendencies.'

George smiled. 'Yes. He's a fierce little chap, isn't he?'

They fell silent again. James searched for something to say. Often he had wanted to confide in George about Marguerite. This seemed an opportunity. 'Eleanor's very good to them but of course it's not the same.' He hesitated. 'Eleanor says I should marry again ...'

'Marry again?' James was surprised at the vehemence of his brother's voice.

'Yes. Why not? The boys need a mother.'

'They have a mother. Elizabeth is their mother.'

166

James winced. 'For God's sake, George. Elizabeth is dead ...'

'Not to me, she isn't,' cried George fiercely.

'The boys and I can't live on memories, George. We can't live a dream.'

'You're lucky to have memories.' George flung at him bitterly. 'Some of us have nothing. Nothing to look back on, nothing to look forward to.' He fell back on his pillows. 'Oh God, I'm sorry, James,' he muttered through clenched teeth. 'It's just ...'

'It's all right. I understand.' James patted his hand. 'Get some rest now. You look worn out.'

He was glad to get away, glad to escape from that virulent grief. It was morbid, unhealthy, to cling so desperately and determinedly to the past. He went downstairs and into the drawing room. There was a letter waiting for him and he felt a rush of pleasure to see Marguerite's bold decorative hand on the envelope:

My dear James,

I had hoped to be writing to let you know a definite date for our coming north. However, it seems that my plans must remain uncertain. Father has not rallied as well as I had hoped. His doctors advise me that such a journey, especially at this time of the year, is really out of the question.

I need not say how disappointed I am, how much I had looked forward to seeing you as well as escaping from town. London is always dull at this time of the year. All our friends are abroad or gone to the country. Last Sunday Charlie Pickard and his sisters called. (Do you remember Charlie? Fair hair. Squinty eyes. You met, I think, on your last visit) We had an evening of bridge but even they are now gone down to Somerset so I am left to play canasta with Father's nurse. The weather too is abysmal; rain, and of course the usual fog, so that it's quite useless to even think of venturing out. Not that the opportunity presents itself often. Father is becoming increasingly pettish and demanding and wants me with him always. Time as you can imagine lies heavily on my hands. I am reading a great deal; for the hundredth time it seems, Flaubert's Madame Bovary and from this you can judge my mood. It is at times like this that I feel the lack of home and family. My father's poor health makes me increasingly aware that sooner or later I shall be truly alone.

I am grateful for your letters and am following the progress of your new venture with interest although please explain 'cage' and 'headgear'. (A hat?). How I envy you, James, having a purpose in life. Boredom must be the greatest enemy of intellect and it must be a great comfort to know that even if all else has fallen away, you still have your work.

I don't suppose now it will be possible for you to get away until the New Year. Do you have any business that is likely to bring you to town around then? Please don't think I'm pressing you. I understand how busy your days must be. Please continue to write. At the moment your letters are my only source of relief.

Affectionately yours,
Marguerite

He laid the letter aside, stricken with such a piercing disappointment that he swore aloud. He had not realized how much he had been looking forward to her company, how much he missed her quiet charm.

Vickers appeared noiselessly and placed his usual brandy and soda at his elbow. James looked up and smiled his thanks.

'Shall I make up the fire, sir?'

'No. Thank you. I'll see to it myself.'

'Will that be all then, sir?'

'Yes. Thank you. Goodnight, Vickers.'

'Goodnight, Mr Joicey, sir.'

He poured himself a small brandy and swirled it absently around in the glass. He heard the maid's footsteps retreating up the stairs. A door opened; closed; and then silence, so heavy and oppressive as to be actually felt. He lifted his eyes and looked across the room to where the carving of his dead wife stood in shadow. His brother's words came suddenly into his head. 'Elizabeth will never be dead to me.' Would she ever be to him? He stared at the pale image of her face. The light played gently over the smooth honeyed wood giving the features a fleeting mobility. And he knew that if he listened hard enough he would hear her voice; he would heard the whisper of her skirts over polished floors; her laughter, soft and childish ...

He downed the brandy in a single gulp then rose abruptly to his feet. He took out his watch. Ten minutes to ten. Too late to walk up to Whinney House and say goodnight to his boys, too late for anything except sleep — and upstairs, that wide empty bed with hot bricks to warm him instead of soft flesh ... He began to move round the room with quick, purposeful steps as if he were bound on some important mission. One by one he turned the gas jets down till only the oil lamp upon the desk remained. Then he wound the clock, also part of the ritual, taking out his watch to check that it hadn't gained. A minute fast. He adjusted the hands accordingly, snapping the glass shut. The two fat naked cherubs who supported the dial smirked up at him virtuously and he turned away, irritated by their plump smug faces. He glanced about the room in quiet desperation. Darkness and fog hung at the windows, the fire sagged beneath a weight of ash. Behind him the clock gathered itself to strike — once, twice, the sharp, high pitched chimes reverberating from the glacial surfaces of the room. Suddenly, violently, he turned and with a thrust of his hand swept the clock to the floor. He walked away from it, leaving it whirring and sighing upon the hearth. He paused by the carving, reaching out to touch the half parted smiling lips. 'Elizabeth,' he whispered. 'For pity's sake — leave me alone.'

January 18th, 1884
— London

Black suited her, minimizing the generous curves of her body and throwing her glowing pallor into startling relief. She stood by the window, staring down to the busy London street, calm and implacable as ever. The only sign of any distress was the constant movement of her clasped hands. 'I suppose I should have expected it. Father's health had been failing for so long. But it's always a shock, isn't it? Death always seems to take us by surprise.'

'What will you do?' James asked her quietly.

She didn't turn her head. 'Do? What is there to do? Life goes on.' She attempted a smile. 'What do women in my circumstances usually do? Engage a companion? Take up good works?'

James stared thoughtfully at the floor. For the first time since he'd known her she seemed vulnerable. He was moved by her quiet dignity and calm. He looked up at her. 'An alternative,' he suggested, 'would be to marry me.'

She didn't react quite as he had expected. Her expression did not change. She did not even turn to look at him. 'Yes — well, of course, I can see the advantages from your point of view — a hostess at your table, a mother for your sons ...'

He broke in irritably. 'That isn't why I asked you ...'

'Why did you then?' She turned to look at him now. 'You're not in love with me in the least.'

'No. It wouldn't be honest of me to say that I was. But I'm fond of you and I think you're a little fond of me.' He came and stood beside her. 'And we're two people alone who don't particularly want to be alone. We have a great deal in common. We enjoy the same things, we want the same things. Sometimes mutual liking and mutual interests are a sounder basis for marriage than love.'

She smiled drily. 'You make it sound like a business merger.'

James ran an exasperated hand through his hair. 'Yes, I do, don't I?' he admitted ruefully. 'I'm afraid I've had more experience of those. I've only ever proposed once before.'

She turned to look at him then, at his stern patrician face with its hint of cruelty, the ruthless and inflexible line of his mouth. She could feel his power, his enormous strength. She felt there wasn't anything he couldn't have if he put his mind to it. And he thought he could have her. She could tell by the confident way he had asked. Just for an instant she was tempted to turn him down, at least to keep him dangling for another few days. But she wasn't sure enough of him for that. She cared for him too much herself. Then she saw the quick impatient frown draw his brows together. She'd kept him waiting too long already.

'Forgive me,' he said stiffly. 'Apparently, my offer has offended you.'

She gave her low amused laugh. 'No, not in the least.' She

held out her hands. 'Of course, I'll marry you.' She added mockingly. 'But I'm sure you knew that before you asked me.'

June 10th, 1884
— Orchard House, Low Fell

Marguerite glanced curiously round the large airy room. She knew instinctively that this had been Elizabeth's room, that everything in it had been chosen by her. The simplicity of the furnishings, the cheerful decor, all spoke to her of a youthful, unsophisticated taste. And there were other things, things that only a woman would notice; the overt femininity of the bed linen and hangings, the sweet flowery fragrance lingering in cupboards and drawers. She felt the other woman's presence acutely and had done ever since she entered the house. She didn't like the house, Elizabeth's house. An aura of her seemed to cling to the walls; every room evoked something of her personality. And every caller seemed to delight in mentioning her name. 'Well of course, we're delighted that James has married again. It was such a tragedy. She was so young and quite the loveliest creature ...' Even the servants: 'But the mistress always had it so, madam,' 'But madam, the mistress always dined at six.' And if she'd needed any more tangible reminder of Elizabeth Joicey, there was always that exquisite sculpted head with its eternal expression of gentleness and purity.

She looked down at her hands, clasped loosely at her waist. The wedding band, a little too large, hung slackly from her finger and recalled the last four months of her life. They had been married within the week by special licence, a brief almost furtive ceremony as officially she was still in mourning. They had travelled north the very next day. Within hours, it seemed, she had exchanged the elegance of London for this stark dirty town; all her friends had been replaced by strangers. The ugliness had appalled her, still appalled her. She had not expected the collieries to be so close at hand. She hadn't expected pits on her doorstep. And his family — their hostile amazement at her sudden appearance. It had come as something of a shock to realize that James had never mentioned her before, as if she were some dark and guilty secret. The worst moment, though, had been meeting his children. The younger boy Hugh had received her with happy indifference, but the elder son ... pushing her violently away as she had stooped to kiss him, then running from the room in tears. She'd felt quite like weeping herself. Nothing had been quite as she'd imagined. It had never occurred to her that she wouldn't be well received, that she'd be seen as some sort of replacement.

She sat down before the mirror and stared at her face. She knew she wasn't beautiful in the accepted sense, but she wasn't plain either. She was a passionate woman, an ambitious woman and she had married James to satisfy these needs. She was also a jealous woman, a possessive woman. She didn't like the thought of sharing James, albeit with a memory. Nevertheless, she'd known that she'd been taking a chance in marrying James. He had openly admitted that he didn't love her. It hadn't seemed to matter so much in London. He'd cared for her enough to marry her. She'd believed he would learn to love her, in time. But that was before she'd realized how much he'd loved Elizabeth, how deeply he still mourned and grieved for her. Her chin came up, her eyes glinted defiantly. She wasn't going to underestimate herself, though. The assets she had brought to her marriage, apart from moderate wealth, were equal to youth and beauty. She had charm and personality, an ability to manipulate events and people, to open all the doors between here and Westminster. She knew the right people, and even if she didn't, she was able to get to know them without appearing sycophantic and pushy. And yet here, in this house, among these people, her sophistication jarred, her easy manner seemed to patronize. They didn't like her, she knew, though normally that wouldn't have mattered if she'd been sure of James.

For the first time in her life she felt a lack of confidence. Suddenly she wasn't sure of herself any more. People looked at her critically here, without liking or admiration. She felt they were talking about her, comparing her unfavourably to Elizabeth. His family were, that was certain. She had met them all now; William James, Rosandra, the bucolic Jacob and his unspeakable wife, the vitriolic Eleanor. And George, the author of the infamous sculpture . . . She bit her lip. She hadn't handled her first real meeting with George very well. For one thing she'd rather expected a feeble invalid needing to be cosseted and reassured. It had been with a sense of shock that she'd met those fierce intimidating eyes. From the very first his whole demeanour had expressed dislike. He couldn't have said more clearly that she wasn't welcome here, that he regarded her as an intruder. Then after a few moments of having her pleasantries rebuffed, she'd faced him with his own tactics and asked him outright, 'You don't like me do you, George?'

He had answered her with equal bluntness. 'No, I'm sorry, I don't.'

It had been difficult to maintain her composure but still she had smiled. 'May I enquire why not?'

'Do I have to have a reason?'

'Yes. I think you do.'

'All right then. I don't like you because you don't like us. I think you regard us as rather stupid and provincial. You're patronizing and condescending, as if everything outside your own sophistication is laughable.'

She managed to look amused rather than offended. 'Do I take that as an example of blunt northern speech?'

'You asked me and I told you,' he said.

'Well, seeing as we are speaking plainly, you will not be offended if I say that I find you rude and impertinent, narrow and bigoted. You say you don't like me when you know nothing about me . . .'

'I know you don't belong here. You don't fit in.'

'You mean I'm not like James' first wife, Elizabeth.'

'No, you're not.' George said dully. 'You couldn't be less like her.'

Marguerite was silent. Instinct told her not to pursue it any further. It was better if she didn't actually know. Yet she had to know. She had to give some substance to the shadowy figure of James' first wife. She wanted to know about Elizabeth. She said at last, making her voice casual. 'James must have loved her very much?'

'Yes. He did. We all did. She was a very lovable person.'

Inwardly she flinched but still she persisted. 'Tell me about her, then?'

'Why do you want to know?'

'Oh . . .' Her voice was light. 'Perhaps I ought to know what I'm up against.'

George smiled, and fleetingly there was a curious rapport between them. Just by talking about her, she was helping to keep Elizabeth alive, and that was what George wanted. 'Elizabeth,' he said softly, 'was a very special person. Not just because she was beautiful and good, though those things rarely go together. It was her effect on other people that made her special. Her goodness was infectious. She brought out the best in people.' He smiled. 'I was never so kind as when I was with her, and yet I knew quite well that I wasn't kind at all.' He looked at her suddenly with open hostility. 'I don't know why my brother married you but it wasn't because he loved you. He'll never love anyone but Elizabeth, you know. None of us will,' he had added quietly.

And what had she answered to that? She couldn't even remember, so deep had been her distress. Afterwards of course she was able to reason it out. James had sprung her on them like a rabbit out of a hat and they were going to vent their resentment and disapproval on her. It didn't make things easier though. She wasn't used to being disliked. She wasn't used to having to prove herself. But then so many things were different now, even her name. She wasn't Marguerite Drever any more. She was Mrs James Joicey, the second Mrs James Joicey . . . That was really what disturbed her more than she cared to admit. She wasn't used to being second either.

She went downstairs and into the morning room where usually she dealt with her post. Vickers awaited her with the menus for the day and Marguerite scanned them quickly with a practised eye.

'Yes. Tell Cook that will do very well for luncheon.' She frowned. 'Though I see we're to have Cabinet pudding tonight. Surely we had that on Tuesday?'

Vickers looked sullen. 'Well, the mistress . . .'

Marguerite interrupted her. 'I am the mistress now, Vickers.'

'Yes, madam. I'm sorry madam, but it's always been Cabinet pudding on Tuesdays and Thursdays. It's Mr James' favourite.'

'Yes, I dare say. But it's not likely to remain so if it continues to be served with such regularity. Tell Cook we'll have syllabub, if you don't mind.'

'Very well, madam.' Vickers withdrew, stiff with affront. Marguerite sighed and began to open her letters. She smiled with satisfaction as she saw their contents; one from the Lady Pease asking them to dine on the 12th; another inviting them to Emily Straker's wedding. At least the people that mattered had accepted her without question. And this was just the beginning. She had the future all planned. For one thing she didn't intend to spend her life in this grubby backwater. Gradually, she meant to ease James out of industry so that he could concentrate solely on politics. She foresaw a glittering career, a swift and spectacular rise. Anything at all was possible in politics. The first thing, though, was to engineer a move from Orchard House, to rid herself of the shadow of Elizabeth.

She rose to her feet. On the desk by the window was the famous sculpture and she crossed the room to examine it more closely. How cruel, she thought, to have to compete with a memory, to be forever compared with such perfection. This was how James would always see her; ageless, perfect ... She took the effigy between her hands. It was a strange feeling. It wasn't like looking at a portrait where there was colour and expression. This was unreal, elusive, ghostly ... She set the head down but continued to regard it uneasily. She must try and remember that Elizabeth was dead and that she, Marguerite, was very much alive.

August and September, 1884 — Northumberland

'Of course, the whole house needs completely refurbishing.' Marguerite swept a critical eye round the vast and impressive drawing room at Dissington Hall. She glanced at the agent's prospectus — 'an imposing and commodious mansion some seven miles north-west of Newcastle. The grounds are extensive and well matured, extending to some twenty acres of woodland and gardens.'

'I'm not sure that we would want the furniture though the agent's are asking a very reasonable price — and there are one or two good pieces: that rosewood credenza and a rather pretty set of chairs in the morning room.'

James leant with his back against the open door, watching her as she moved about the room: shaking draperies, prodding sofas, dusting with gloved fingers the seat of a chair. She was obviously pregnant though she still managed to look elegant. It unnerved him a little, thinking of Marguerite bearing a child. He'd lost one wife that way. He didn't relish the thought of losing another.

He took out his watch. 'Will you be much longer, my dear?' he enquired mildly. 'Only I promised Jordan I'd drop in some plans ...'

She smiled at him from the far side of the room. 'Well, what do you think, James?'

He smiled. 'Does it really matter what I think? You've obviously set your heart on it.'

'Of course it matters what you think. It does seem ideal though,' she added persuasively. 'We won't find anything else at such a good price.'

'Mmmm, well, I suppose you're right, though I'd have preferred to be a bit nearer the collieries.' He came to stand beside her and slipped his hand through her arm. 'Am I allowed a day to think it over? Perhaps we'll bring George over tomorrow and see what he thinks.'

'George?' She turned to him in dismay. 'Surely George won't be coming with us?'

'Yes, of course he's coming with us.' He couldn't believe what she'd said. 'Where else do you expect him to go?'

'Well, it wouldn't hurt someone else to have a turn.'

His eyes grew cold. He released her arm. 'George isn't a parcel, you know, to be passed from pillar to post. He's my brother. He's my responsibility. He always will be.'

Marguerite lowered her eyes. 'Yes, of course. I'm sorry.' She didn't know what else she could say.

Then he opened the door for her and they went out into the hall. 'You'll think about it then, James?' She smiled at him in an effort to make amends.

'Yes, I'll think about it,' he answered shortly.

He helped her up into the open carriage, waiting till she had arranged her skirts before he climbed in beside her and took up the reins. They drove in silence down the long straight drive flanked by tall firs. Marguerite opened her parasol, tilting it to protect her face from the hot afternoon sun. 'Will you be long at Beamish, James? You haven't forgotten that we are dining with the Peases tonight?'

'No. I haven't forgotten.' It was said with such a note of obvious boredom that she glanced at him quickly, irritated by his lack of interest in this important invitation it had taken her weeks to procure. 'I really wish you'd show a little more enthusiasm, James,' she complained lightly. 'Joseph Pease is an important man socially and politically. He could do you a great deal of good.'

He smiled — was it a smile, that expression of mingled indifference and amusement? Already he was disillusioned with the idea of politics. He hadn't realized it would be such a lengthy business, an endless round of dinner parties and functions, having to be pleasant to people he normally couldn't stand. He said drily, 'You make him sound like a dose of medicine, my dear, Joseph Pease — to be taken three times a day with meals.'

Marguerite didn't answer. She hadn't yet learned to handle his moods, which could charge, in minutes, from high good humour to brooding silence. She found it unnerving how one moment he could be tender and affectionate, the very next, distant and aloof. But that was part of his attraction, his unpredictability; never being sure, never knowing exactly how she stood. She glanced at his face and saw the slight frown that drew his brows together, the angry set of his mouth. That had been a mistake, to let slip her detestation of his brother, George. But the thought of George accompanying them to Dissington ... Her eyes hardened: George with his derisive, knowing smile, his morbid devotion to Elizabeth. Her expression grew sullen as she thought of Elizabeth. She thought of her a great deal now in a jealous, unhealthy way.

Still in silence they swung out onto the Military Road. The fells rose sharply here, massive natural escarpments crowned by the broken line of the old Roman wall that had once marched from Newcastle to Carlisle. She had always thought the Wall a very practical thing, as if the civilized world ended here, as if the wilderness of forest and moorland that swept northwards to the ultimate bleakness of Cheviot was too desolate to ever be of any account. Even in high summer there was a harshness about the landscape; a vastness, an overwhelming emptiness. But at least it was better than the dirt and stink of the town, at least there were no memories here, they would be free to start a new life. Her mouth set in a hard determined line. A new life — without George, without Elizabeth ... Then she smiled happily to herself. It would be all right, once their child was born, once they were away from Orchard House, once they were away from Elizabeth.

He was a few minutes early for his meeting with Jordan and employed the time watching from the safety of the viewer's office as the charges were set for blasting. It was a relatively quick and simple process these days; holes were drilled a yard's depth into the strata then plugged with cartridges of nitro and gun cotton which were fired on the surface by means of an electric spark. It was a perfect, controlled explosion: a brief muffled roar, the faintest trembling of the earth, a cloud of yellow dust belched from the shaft. Within minutes the sinkers were back in the shaft loading the hot and smoking rock into huge iron skips. He turned away, a pleased expression softening his stern features. They were making excellent progress and had already won through some hundred feet of sandstone and shale to the first of the coal measures. Water was the enemy now, tiny feeders from underground streams, threading the porous rock. These could fill up the shaft in half a night and lose them hours in pumping the next morning. Nevertheless, things were going well and he was confident of reaching Main Coal by Christmas. The surface work was also well advanced; housings for boilers, engines and pumps; screening sheds, weighs and offices. He'd decided to abandon the old upcast shaft with its outmoded furnace ventilation. The James pit with its modern fan and pumping system would serve both the Mary and the Air.

He spent an hour with Jordan going over the plans. There were problems with the old Air pit which had continued to draw coals throughout. The vibration of the blasting was working the lining loose and this was the third day running they'd needed to set the men on elsewhere due to the need for repairs. James agreed a list of essential works to be carried out and he was on the point of leaving when the fore-overman shoved his head round the door. 'Bloody linings blown again. There's water pissin' in ...'

At the shaft mouth Davies the engineer had just emerged from the cage. His hair was plastered wetly to his scalp, his clothes sagged beneath a weight of water. 'It's bad,' he said, shaking himself like a dog. 'It looks as if the sinkers have tapped an underground stream by the amount of water that's coming in. Possibly the blasting has caused a fissure in the rocks and diverted its flow. By the force of the water, I would guess it's been building up for weeks and the pressure has finally forced the lining out. I've been down as far as I dare. The pressure of the water coming into the shaft is terrific.'

'How many men do we have down?' James enquired.

The overman got out his book. 'Four in Main Coal on timbering and repairs. Twenty-four in Three Quarter, seventeen in Brass Thill.'

Davies peeled off his wet coat and flung it down. 'The men in the upper seams are safe enough. It's only Main Coal that's in danger of flooding.'

'How long before we can get it under control?'

Davies shrugged. 'That depends how much water there is behind the shaft wall, how long it will take for the pressure to subside. If we set extra pumps on, we might be able to keep pace. We're only geared to handle two hundred gallons a minute. I reckon there's three times that amount coming in. Fortunately, the men are working well inbye at the top of the slant. If they stay put they'll not even get their feet wet.'

'What about the Swelly?' Bill Severs, the under-viewer spoke for the first time. 'If the water roofs in the Swelly the air supply will be cut off. The men won't drown, they'll suffocate.'

Davies looked grave. The Swelly was a trough, a gradual depression that cut right across the main travelling roads. If it flooded it would form an impassable barrier of water, preventing the men from getting outbye.

'Can't we get the men out through the upcast?' asked James.

'Not without stopping the pumping we can't, which would rather defeat the object. Besides, I doubt if the men could get there in time. That's part of the problem. They don't know they're in trouble and they won't know for at least another hour until they try to come up at the end of their shift. By that time all the intakes will have flooded. They'll be cut off from both shafts by the Swelly.'

'Can't we get down and warn them?' demanded Severs.

'We don't dare risk the cage,' objected Davies. 'The force of the water coming into the shaft is terrific. It would knock it clean off its guides and that would put the men in the upper seams at risk. We could disconnect it. Severs and I could go down in a skip.'

'I think we should get the other men up first.' Jordan said. 'There's nothing to say that more of the lining won't give way?'

'I don't agree,' argued Davies. 'It might take nearly an hour to locate all the men and bring them to bank. The whole of Main Coal could have flooded by then. If we don't get them out now they'll have to sit it out until we can stop up and pump out, which might take days.'

'I agree,' said Severs. 'The risk to the men in the upper seams is very slight. It's a matter of life and death to the men in Main Coal.'

'But it's still a risk,' countered Jordan. 'And I'd prefer to take it on the lives of four men than forty.'

The three men turned to James expecting a decision. It wasn't an easy one to make. His first instinct was to side with Jordan and get the bulk of the men to the surface. Four against forty — yet it was the four who were in the most immediate danger. His decision had to be based upon that.

He watched from the winding house as with the aid of hawsers the iron cage was swung out from the shaft and the massive chains loosed from the cable. Jordan and Davies climbed into the kibble, signalling the banksman as soon as the steel ropes were attached. Slowly the great drums began to turn and the two men disappeared into the darkness. They weren't gone long. After only ten minutes the kibble returned. Jordan climbed out, his clothes streaming water. 'We're too late. It's worse than I thought. The pump is completely overcome. There's already a good head of water in the shaft.'

They returned to Jordan's office. 'What now?' demanded James.

'We wait, Mr James. We wait and pray.' Jordan stripped off his waterlogged jacket. 'There's nothing we can do until the rest of the men have come to bank. Then we can get on with rigging up the extra pumps, use kibbles as bailers if necessary.'

'How long, Mr Jordan?' said James heavily. 'How long to get the men out?'

'I can't tell you that with any degree of certainty. I reckon on twenty-four hours at least to dewater the seam.'

'Will the men be able to last out till then?'

'I can't tell you that either. The Air's a bad pit for stythe. It will depend on how badly and how quickly the air becomes foul and the normal health and strength of the men. In favourable circumstances they could last for days.'

The overman broke in. 'Matt Henderson won't.' He tapped his chest significantly. 'He's breathin' through his skin as it is.'

James winced at the mention of Matt Henderson's name. Just to hear it conjured up old feelings of guilt. He'd made no attempt at reconciliation, even when Matt had thrown up his job as deputy and gone back to killing himself with the hewing. Long after the event his conscience had nagged at him and though he'd never known what else he could have done, he'd always felt that he should have done something.

He looked at Jordan. 'How long then for a man with acute pneumoconiosis? Twelve hours?'

'Perhaps. If he's lucky.'

'Then that,' said James, 'is exactly how long you have.'

He changed into oilskins and went out into the yard, waiting impatiently for the men in the upper seams to be brought up. Then he went with Jordan to the pumping shaft and helped to supervise the rigging up of the extra hoses. They were now pulling out three hundred gallons a minute. Then back to the main shaft where they were using kibbles as bailers. He watched as the huge iron buckets were lowered and raised, spewing black water into the yard. The water had a curious iridescent sheen. He was reminded suddenly of Marguerite. She had a gown like that, some sort of silk stuff that changed colour as she moved ... Then guiltily, he remembered that they were supposed to be dining out tonight. He looked at his watch. Nine o'clock. It was too late to get word to her now.

Eleven o'clock and still the high northern light held back the darkness, though in the heapstead it had long grown dark and chilly. He worked with the men now, taking his turn on the chains used to swing out the kibble. There was a strange satisfaction in his growing physical exhaustion, in the aching discomfort of his body. It seemed to him the repayment of a long overdue debt. He was determined to get Matt Henderson out alive.

One o'clock and they'd de-watered the shaft sufficiently for the cage to go down. Jordan, Severs and James took the lower deck; in the upper were men with spare tackle and equipment. The descent was unnerving; a swift sudden plunge into watery darkness, dropping down through a spume of white drenching spray. The bottom landing was still awash, two feet of black water lapping their knees. They stood listening for a moment. Few sounds disturbed the deep silence of the pit; the frenzied panting of the exhausted pumps — and water, dripping, splashing, trickling, falling with a road onto the roof of the cage. Jordan lifted his lamp and flung light across the landing. Empty tubs floated past like wrecked listing ships; a flotilla of drowned vermin flushed from the waste. They waded through into the main haulage. The water was less here but thick but coal dust and fallen earth. It made the going hard. Then abruptly the road entered. They had come to the Swelly, a greasy black lake that blocked the road for a distance of thirty yards.

Jordan called out, his voice reverberating round the dripping walls. In answer, a dull glimmer of light broke the far darkness.

'Thank God,' breathed Severs. 'At least they're still alive.'

'Can you swim?' shouted Jordan. 'Can you get across?'

Out of the darkness came the scornful reply; 'We'd nivver be standin' here if we could, mon.'

'If we could get a rope over,' suggested the overman. 'Set up a line by which they could make their way across.'

A dozen times they tried to get a rope across. It was an impossible task, like trying to thread a needle in the dark. There was only a bare two feet of headroom above the surface of the water and each time the rope struck up against the roof and fell short. Severs and the overman both waded in, despite the fact that neither could swim. After only ten feet they were out of their depth and in a desperate attempt to get the rope over the overman lost his footing and was half drowned before they got him out.

'Christ, man. We'll be here all night.' Impatiently James snatched the rope from Jordan and began to strip off his oilskin and boots. He was a strong swimmer and reckoned he could cross the Swelly with ease. But the water was cold and heavy, slimed by a filthy oil scum that rose up into his nose and mouth. The narrow space restricted his normally powerful stroke and it was an effort to keep his head above the surface and at the same time keep it clear of the hard whinstone roof. Less than half-way across and he felt himself tiring. The stagnant water seemed to drag him down. The trailing rope twined itself around his legs. Twice he went under, black stinking water filling his mouth. He kicked out with his legs. The water lifted him sharply and flung him up hard against the scabby roof. Gasping, dazed, he turned on his back. He clawed at the roof wth his hands and kicked out his legs, propelling himself toward the shallows. Once more in his depth, he stood shivering and retching. Two of the stranded men, Grogan and Withers, waded in and helped him out. A third man loosed the rope from his belt began rigging up the line.

'Where's Henderson?' James gasped.

Grogan jerked his head over his shoulder. 'He's bad, Mr James. Mortal bad. His heading was full of black damp and water. I don't reckon we got to him in time.'

The former deputy was only partly conscious. His eyes were closed, his mouth open, the whole of his meagre body racked by the struggle for breath. And yet he probably looked healthier than he had ever done in his life. His entire face was suffused by a faint rosy glow, even his hands were softly pink in colour. James' heart sank. He knew the symptoms of stythe well enough.

He went over and spoke to Grogan, instructing him as to what they would need; oxygen, a doctor, some means of getting the sick man across. He watched the three men over the Swelly, acknowledged Jordan's shouted message that they would be back within the half hour. Then he went back to where Henderson lay, dropping down on his knees beside him.

Carefully he eased him into an upright position, bending up his knees so that his legs were out of the wet. Then he squeezed in beside him, supporting the thin body with his arms. He shook him gently. 'How, then, Matt?'

Henderson's eyes fluttered open and for a moment they dwelt upon James without recognition. Then he smiled painfully. 'How, again, Mr James?'

His speech was slurred. It was clearly an effort to talk and yet really that was all that needed to be said. 'Save your breath, Matt,' James said. 'We'll soon have you outbye.'

Henderson nodded vaguely. He didn't really believe that. Instinctively he knew that he'd never come up out of the pit alive. He wasn't afraid. It seemed fitting somehow, like the continuance of some old family tradition. And at least he would die dignified like, not splattered around the walls like his father had been. Yes, he would die dignified, all of a piece. There'd be enough of him to bury. He closed his eyes. He felt sleepy and light headed, as if he'd taken a drop too much. That was the stythe. A queer thing, stythe. Sometimes it would kill a man in seconds. Sometimes he'd linger on for hours. Not a bad way to die though, just slipping away, quiet like. No blood or pain or fear. And he'd die with a friend by him, for the arms that held him were the arms of a friend, the voice that comforted him was caring. He didn't question why the Master was here. He had long ago lost the power to reason and order his thoughts. But he was here and he knew he was here because of him. His thoughts drifted at random. Little glimpses of his life flashed before his eyes. Such a drab, pitiful, insignificant life. And yet perhaps not so insignificant. The Master was here. Mr James was here, the strong voice willing him to survive. For a moment he almost believed he could do it. He was suddenly filled with an urgent desire to live. If he could just hold on to that voice. If he could just concentrate his mind on the words. What was he saying? Do you mind the time, Matt . . .? Then the voice grew blurred, became a soft humming in his ears. Then softer still, like the last whisper of air being squeezed from his lungs, a little sigh slowly diminishing into silence.

He stabled the horse and carriage himself and quietly entered the house. It was four o'clock and even the servants had not yet begun to stir, so that he started when he saw her standing there at the top of the first flight of stairs. 'I'm sorry,' he said abruptly. 'I did not mean to disturb you.'

'You didn't,' she said, coming down the stairs toward him. 'Like you, I have not been to bed.'

He saw then that she still wore her evening clothes, her hair still spangled with pearls. He looked away, irritation inspired by guilt rising up in him. 'I'm sorry,' he said again but his voice was rough and without remorse. 'There was some trouble at Beamish ...'

'So I see,' she said, eyeing his damp and dishevelled appearance. Then she turned and walked toward the morning room, obviously expecting him to follow.

He hovered reluctantly inside the doorway. 'I'm sorry,' he said for the third time. 'I really couldn't get away ...'

'But you could have surely done me the common courtesy of sending an explanation ...'

'There wasn't time,' he began. She cut him off.

'In twelve hours you couldn't find time to scribble a few words?' She regarded him coldly. I'd much rather you were honest, James. Why not say that you couldn't be bothered, that you didn't consider our engagement important.'

'All right, then,' he snapped. 'Since you press me. I couldn't be bothered. I couldn't have cared less about dining with Pease.'

'Or about keeping me waiting and wondering?'

'No. Nor about that either.'

Her expression didn't change, in fact there was almost amusement in her glance. 'I see,' she said. 'Well, at least that's honest.'

James ran a distracted hand through his hair. He didn't want to argue, not whilst he was in this bitter frame of mind. 'Look, Marguerite, I'm tired — as you must be yourself. Can't we talk about this later?'

'Is there anything more to say?' Though her voice was quite calm he knew she was furious. 'Unless of course, you have some explanation to offer that justifies offending an important man and placing me in the embarrassing position of having to make excuses for you which I don't expect for one minute were believed.'

'Well, I have an explanation,' he answered savagely. 'But I don't know whether you would think it justifies anything. I was trying to save a man's life — just an ordinary man though, no one of the consequence of Joseph Pease.'

'I see. And there was nobody else who could have performed this heroic deed. It had to be you?'

Her sarcasm inflamed him all the more. 'No, it didn't have to be me but I wanted it to be me.'

She gave a thin smile. 'It seems to me, you know, James, that you need to get your priorities right. There's absolutely no point in my trying to further your interests ...'

'Don't you mean your interests,' he shouted. 'It's you who are so keen to get me to Westminster. Perhaps you think that coalmining is not really a gentleman's occupation unless you can do it by proxy, like Lambton.'

'That isn't true. You know it isn't true. You're as keen to get into politics as I am, although perhaps not for the same reasons. And besides, what I'm talking about has nothing to do with politics. It hasn't even anything to do with Joseph Pease. It has to do with your lack of consideration, your lack of thought for my feelings. I wonder,' she said furiously, her voice rising, 'Did you treat your former wife with such indifference?'

He lost his temper then. 'No, I didn't,' he shouted. 'I would never have had to. Elizabeth would never have whined over something so trivial. Elizabeth would have understood.'

She did not move. Neither did her expression change. Then without looking at him, she moved past him and went out of the room.

It was just a quarrel, she told herself, their first quarrel. There would probably be hundreds more. And when that evening he apologized, she accepted graciously. At least on the surface that was how it seemed. But she felt that things would never be the same again. She wouldn't ever be able to forget it. Quietly she brooded on it and her jealousy of the past grew. She was more determined than ever that James should leave Orchard House. She was convinced that Elizabeth was the barrier between them. And it was George who was the catalyst there, with his morbid devotion, his unassuageable grief. Somehow, she had to get rid of George.

George stared bleakly from the window of his room, the rectangle of polished and beaded glass through which he viewed the outside world. Occasionally, there was movement: a carriage passing, briefly glimpsed through the thinning trees: tradesmen's carts making deliveries. He closed his eyes, listening to the muted sounds of the house; servants' footsteps, brisk and purposeful. Any moment now, his own servant, Rogers, would bring in his breakfast. He'd make an attempt at eating, the very least that his body needed to maintain its strength. He had no appetite, for food, for pleasure, for anything at all. He continued to live purely because there was no immediate alternative, except death by his own hand, and he had too deep a reverence for life, however painful and useless, to think of attempting that. Yes, life went on. He went through the motions, moving doggedly from day to day, but without enthusiasm or purpose. He smiled thinly. No, that wasn't quite true now.

Since Marguerite's arrival he had felt the stirrings of some obscure sense of purpose. He thought about her almost as much as he did Elizabeth. Hatred was too strong a word to describe his feelings: antagonism, resentment, hostility, dislike, a sense ... yes, almost a sense of betrayal. It had never occurred to him that James would marry again, especially so soon after Elizabeth's death. He'd never forgive him for that, for bringing this cold, clever woman into their lives. He resented that the most, her strong personality, her intelligence. He could have accepted someone quieter, unassuming, undemanding, so that their lives would have continued virtually unchanged. Everything was different now. Marguerite had brought with her all the cool impersonality of her breeding and class, a rigid etiquette and formality they'd never known. And she was quietly forceful, demanding and possessive. He could see that she meant to use James to pursue her own concept of success, and that, he was sure, meant status and position. These were the things that were precious to her. She wasn't wasting any time either. Already, she had persuaded James to move to Dissington Hall — all the best people lived in the Tyne Valley.

His heart sank at the prospect of leaving Orchard House, of leaving his memories, Elizabeth, behind. At first, he'd made up his mind that he wouldn't go. He could just as easily go to his sister, Margaret, or there was nothing to stop him setting up a small house of his own. He could manage quite well just with Rogers. Yes, he'd thought about that for a while. Then he'd thought about being without James, without his two little nephews, being alone with his pain, his loneliness. Both Marguerite and Dissington were preferable to that. And, thinking about it, he supposed he hadn't given her much of a chance. He'd been against her even before they'd met. For James' sake, he should make more of an effort.

He opened his eyes. Rogers padded towards him, bearing a tray aloft. George glanced without enthusiasm at the contents of the dish. 'Rogers,' he said quickly, before he changed his mind. 'Would you ask Mrs Joicey if she could spare me a few moments after breakfast? I'd like a word with her, if I may.'

She knocked and entered, without doing him the courtesy of waiting for a reply. That set him on edge to start with.

'Rogers tells me that you wish to see me.'

'Yes . . .'

Marguerite seated herself. 'Well, I am here.'

She gave the impression of bestowing an enormous favour, as if she were granting him a special audience. The propitiatory words stuck in his throat. 'It's about Dissington Hall,' he managed to say.

'Yes,' she responded quickly. 'I wanted to speak to about that myself.' She looked at him thoughtfully with her cool green eyes. 'I was wondering, you know, George, if you're going to be happy at Dissington? Will it really suit you to be out of the town?'

George flushed at the implication. 'Meaning, I suppose, that it won't suit you?'

Marguerite smiled. 'Well, I wouldn't be honest if I said that I relished the thought of caring for an invalid and two young children as well.'

'Elizabeth never complained,' he said provokingly.

Her expression hardened. 'Yes, well, I am not Elizabeth, as you are always so fond of pointing out. As you say, I am nothing like her.'

She rose to her feet. She knew that diminished him. 'As I

188

know you set such store by speaking plainly, George, of saying, however cruel, what is on your mind, I thought I would afford myself the same facility, and tell you, as plainly, what is on mine.' She turned to look at him. 'Firstly, let me say that I have no intention of allowing you to continue to contaminate my life with your morbid passion for Elizabeth. My concern is wholly for the living, and quite frankly, I'm not sure in which category you place yourself. Your preoccupation with Elizabeth is unhealthy, sick ...'

George laughed suddenly. 'My preoccupation!' he exclaimed, sneering. 'Don't you mean yours? Do you know how many times you have mentioned her name?' He looked away from her. 'Anyway,' he lied, 'It's all right, you know. There's no need for all this. I've never had the slightest intention of going to live at Dissington Hall. That's what I asked you here to tell you.'

She didn't believe him. It was said with such effort, with barely concealed pain. She glanced with sudden compassion at his pale, thin face. It must be a terrible thing to be so sensitive to beauty and yet to live always with ugliness and deformity. For an instant she regretted being so harsh. She could so easily have liked him if he had allowed her to. Bitterness and bad temper she could have borne, understood. Hadn't she lived with an invalid father for years? That was part of the reason she had grown to resent him so much. Because he had deprived her of the opportunity to be generous, kind ...

'Well,' she said awkwardly. 'I'm sure you'll be happier ...'

George looked at her suddenly, malice and hatred gleaming in his eyes. 'It won't work, you know. You won't escape Elizabeth just by leaving this house. You think by going to Dissington, by getting rid of me, you're going to get rid of Elizabeth. But what about the children, Elizabeth's children? How are you going to get rid of them?'

'I won't have to. They're just children. They don't even remember her ...' She broke off, appalled at how she'd revealed herself. She'd as good as admitted that what he'd said was true.

George smiled cruelly, as wordlessly she turned from him and went out of the room. Then he turned and stared from the window again, and thought bleakly of the future — alone.

They left Orchard House at the end of the summer. James had no regrets, though he was saddened by George's decision to live on his own. It would be the first time in their lives that they'd been apart. But in a way, he could understand it. It had been hard for George to accept his marriage, harder still for Marguerite to understand why. It was for the best, he told himself, another painful memory behind him. No, he had no real regrets, though it was inevitable that he would leave some part of himself there, not just the years that belonged to Elizabeth, but the last of his youth, the years of struggle and glorious uncertainty. He was thirty-eight years old now, approaching middle age. His future seemed entirely predictable and assured.

And Marguerite, on the surface at least, seemed busy and content. She occupied herself a great deal with the house and establishing relationships with their impressive neighbours. The house itself she quite transformed, and though he couldn't help but admire its air of quiet grandeur — the furnishings sumptuous yet discreet, extravagant but simple — he was never to feel comfortable in the large chilly rooms. It wasn't his home in the sense Orchard House had been. It was too vast and imposing with its massive tomblike rooms linked by chilly passages and a broad winding staircase that coiled through the house like a malevolent serpent. He saw it more as a vehicle whereby they displayed their wealth, where they informed the world of their good taste and respectability, and where he was always to feel more like a temporary and honoured guest than master of the house.

They had separate rooms and he hadn't objected. With Marguerite being so far advanced in her pregnancy it seemed only natural that they should sleep apart. He never thought much about the child. He could never imagine it as belonging to him in the way that Hugh and James Arthur did. But when he did think about it, he hoped for a daughter. He had always longed for a little girl.

But on the whole he felt he couldn't complain. Marguerite managed everything perfectly. Regulating his household so that it ran along the lines of a first class hotel. He was never irritated by late meals or inefficient servants. They entertained a great deal; not friends, but men who had influence in the political world, men, to use her own words, who could do him some good. It showed how little she really understood him. She couldn't grasp the fact that he didn't want patronage, that success had no value unless he achieved it himself. But he admired her persistence, her refusal to be diverted by anything he said. She was, he knew, just waiting for the right opportunity. It came at the end of September with the passing of the Franchise Bill that gave working men the right to vote. The Durham Thirteen was enlarged by another three seats. One of them was right on his doorstep, the newly formed constituency of Chester-le-Street.

October 3rd, 1884
— Gateshead

William Arnold, secretary of the Newcastle Liberal Association, regarded James without enthusiasm. He knew the type. He interviewed at least one every week; successful industrialists who'd made a packet and now looked to politics to provide them with status. 'You've had some experience in politics then, Mr Joicey?' he enquired politely. 'Public office? Committees? Something like that?'

'No, I'm afraid not,' James answered apologetically. 'I never had the time before.'

'I see.' The thin dry smile became tinged with disdain. 'But you have the time now?' The inflexion of his voice was mildly sarcastic. 'And you wish to stand in the Chester-le-Street division at the general election to be held next year?'

'Yes.'

'And for the Liberal Party?'

'Of course.' James frowned, mildly irritated. 'You seem doubtful, Mr Arnold.'

'Yes, I am,' Arnold informed him bluntly. 'Quite frankly, Mr Joicey, as a coalminer, and forgive me, an obvious capitalist —' he smiled deprecatingly — 'It does occur to me that you might be better suited to the Tories.'

'But I do not happen to be a Tory, Mr Arnold.' James' voice wiped the smile from the older man's face. 'I am a Liberal and always have been. And why, may I ask, is being both coalowner and politician suddenly incompatible? My late uncle, Colonel John Joicey, was elected to the Durham division by, if I remember rightly, a considerable majority.'

'Yes, well, of course, things have changed a great deal since the Colonel's day. As I'm sure you are aware, the passing of the Franchise Bill has wrought many changes.' He looked faintly aggrieved. 'Although the Bill was my own party's measure, I myself did not support it. In the past, only responsible house-holders in the boroughs could vote, but now every village clod has the right. I do not say this in a purely derogatory manner, but it is a fact of life that men of this type — working men — by virtue of their education or lack of it, will not able to grasp politics in the broadest sense. Their interests will be narrow, local rather than national, emotional rather than practical. In the Chester-le-Street division particularly, there are now nearly twelve thousand working men eligible to vote, seventy per cent of whom are pitmen.' He eyed James cynically. 'Do you think they'll vote for you, Mr Joicey? The man who to a great extent employs them?'

'Yes, I do,' James answered evenly. 'At least I can assure you they won't vote for a Tory.'

'No, well, of course, one always hopes that, and, really, I wish it was so simple. As I say, things have changed. Did you, for example, know that the Durham Miners' Federation are financing candidates of their own? Strong Radicals of course, but that's really what's needed in working class seats.' He stretched his mouth in a tired and mirthless smile. 'How would you rate your chances then, Mr Joicey? Having to fight it out with union stalwarts like, say, Thomas Cann and John Wilson?'

'Would the situation ever arise?' James enquired drily. 'I was not aware that it was party policy to run two of its own candidates in harness.'

'Quite right, it's not — which brings me to my next point. Perhaps I should have mentioned it before, but we already have a candidate in mind for the particular division in which you are interested. A Mr Lloyd Jones — I dare say you know of him. An outsider, granted, but he's done some good work for the unions, I hear. Very much the people's candidate . . .'

That should have been the end of it as far as James was concerned, but some slight hesitation in Arnold's manner inclined hm to press it: 'Jones has been accepted as the party's official candidate then?'

'Well, no. Not yet. It's early days ...'

'But it is not usual for prospective candidates to appear before a selection committee?' James persisted. 'Whatever your opinion of my chances of election, surely I should be given the chance to put my views?' He gave Arnold a long and searching look. 'I get the impression that Mr Jones is perhaps a favoured candidate!'

Arnold spent a few moments vigorously polishing his spectacles. 'Perhaps I shouldn't be telling you this, Mr Joicey,' he said at last, 'except that I think it only fair that you be put fully in the picture. Mr Jones, in fact, is the nominee of Mr Joseph Cowen, the proprietor of the *Newcastle Chronicle* ...' He paused then said, 'to put it bluntly ...'

'To put it bluntly, you're afraid of offending Cowen!'

Arnold smiled thinly. 'I would not have put it as strongly as that — but yes, in a way, that is true. It would be quite disastrous for the party to lose the *Chronicle*'s support. A partisan newspaper is quite essential for propaganda, especially at election time. I might add that Mr Cowen is a man who is easily offended. And really,' he added, as if to convince himself, 'Mr Jones does seem a very good candidate.'

'I think I would be a better one.'

'I'm afraid I can't agree. Nothing you have said overcomes my original objection — that you are a coalowner, a capitalist, an employer of labour. The inevitable question would be bound to be asked: how can the interests of the working man be served by the man who employs him? In my opinion it would be pure folly to even think of running a coalowner in a purely mining community. Complete anathema to the working classes, I would have thought. Grinding the faces of the poor and all that. Employers, I'm afraid, however decent, are never wholly beloved.' He took off his spectacles and polished them vigorously. 'Though of course, if you were prepared to think of standing in another division ... The Honourable Frederick Lambton, the Earl of Durham's younger brother, has adopted a similar course. As you probably know, he's the sitting member for Mid-Durham. But there's so little chance of him being re-elected that he has very wisely chosen to stand at Berwick; a safe seat as far as we are concerned. Now if an arrangement like that would appeal to you ...'

'No, it wouldn't, Mr Arnold,' James said aggressively. 'It's the men among whom I work and live whose interests I want to protect. What would be the point of standing elsewhere? I don't want to be a member of parliament just for the sake of it.'

Arnold regarded him thoughtfully, even regretfully. 'Then I'm afraid I can't help you, Mr Joicey.'

Marguerite maoeuvred her heavily pregnant body out of the chair and went to stand by the window so that she would see the carriage approach. The gardens looked drab; stretches of wet brown earth set with pruned dwarfish shrubs; bedraggled leafless trees. A frown drew her finely arched brows together. She had expected him back long before now. It wasn't like him to keep her waiting.

She turned back into the room, glancing anxiously at the clock. Surely if the news had been good, he couldn't have waited to tell her. Her heart sunk at the prospect of disappointment. She hadn't ever been happy about his method of approach, going in cold without even a sponsor. When she thought of the countless introductions she could have arranged.

She sat down again, diverting herself by an inspection of the room. Its formal elegance soothed her, so at variance with the cluttered comfort of Orchard House. And to know that Elizabeth hadn't been here, hadn't looked from this window, sat by this hearth. Her lustrous eyes darkened. Why, then, did she still feel her presence so strongly? Why, then, did she continue to overshadow her life? She glanced toward the little walnut desk where the carving of Elizabeth had used to stand. She didn't know what had become of it, except that it hadn't come with them to Dissington. She'd been thankful at first, but thinking about it, its disappearance disturbed her. Now, she imagined it secreted away in his room, worshipped, adored, venerated like some saint. She bit her lip. George had been right. It hadn't been any solution to leave Orchard House, Elizabeth couldn't be contained by bricks and mortar. What was it James had said? 'When you have loved someone very much they are always with you ...' Her mouth trembled, remembering the conversation that she hadn't been meant to overhear. James Arthur suddenly turning to his father and saying, 'Father. Where is Mama? Won't she ever be coming back?'

She could have wept at the look on James' face, the pain in his voice as he had answered. 'No, Jamie. She won't be coming back, although in a way she hasn't ever left us. When you have loved someone very much, in a way, they are always with you. You can't see them or touch them, but still, they are there.'

James Arthur had nodded gravely. 'It's not the same thing, though, is it, Papa?'

James had kissed him. 'No. It's not the same thing — but it's all that we have.'

All that he had! As if she were nothing. As if she didn't exist ... She breathed deeply to calm herself. It wasn't good for the child for her to get upset. Again, she reminded herself that she was a calm and reasonable woman. She must exorcize this thing with calm and reasonable thoughts. Then she smiled wryly. That was the difficulty. She wasn't calm and reasonable any more. She exhibited all the weakness and instability of a woman deeply in love, all the insecurity of knowing that it wasn't mutual. Her marriage was sensible, affectionate, unemotional — at least on James' side it was. They never spoke of love, even in their most intimate moments. And to be fair, he had never promised her any more than that. It wasn't he who had reneged upon the bargain. She would have to be patient. These things took time. It would be different once their child was born. Her face lit up as she thought of the child: a child of her own, untainted by the past, someone who'd never heard of Elizabeth. Surely the child would bind them? Surely a man couldn't help but love the mother of his son?

Then she heard the sound of wheels in the drive, a slamming door, quick irritable footsteps coming down the hallway.

She knew as soon as she saw his face that things hadn't gone well. She swallowed down her crushing disappointment and forced herself to smile. 'You're late, my dear. I had expected you long before now.'

'Yes, I know. I'm sorry. I went for a walk.'

195

She resumed her seat by the hearth. 'Well,' she said, still resolutely smiling. 'How did it go?'

'It didn't. They turned me down flat.'

Marguerite's eyes widened. 'Who turned you down?'

'Mr William Arnold, Secretary of the Liberal Association.' He added with faint sarcasm. 'Someone, apparently, you forgot to ask to dine.'

She flinched at his sarcasm. Was he blaming her? 'Did he give you a reason?' she asked him quietly.

'Oh yes. Half a dozen: that I am inexperienced, unknown, a coalowner, a capitalist. He made it quite clear that I had more chance of being elected to the Senate of Rome than as member for Chester-le-Street.'

He crossed the room and poured himself a drink. 'You were quite right, though, my dear, about friends in high places — except that, in this instance, we were beaten to it. Apart from my apparent unsuitability as a candidate, Arnold said in so many words that Joe Cowen, owner of the *Chronicle* had the thing all sewn up. They're going to nominate his man, a carpet-bagging Welshman by the name of Lloyd Jones.'

He flung himself down in his usual chair. 'You know, it never actually occurred to me that they would turn me down.'

Marguerite repressed a smile. No, it wouldn't, she thought. Failure was something he rarely contemplated.

'And the most damnable thing is, knowing I've been passed over for an old fool like Jones. The man's practically senile — seventy if he's a day!'

'That's usually considered an asset in a politician,' Marguerite observed. 'It will be you who is considered too young.'

He wasn't listening. 'Even Arnold had the grace to look embarrassed about it. He knows perfectly well that he's not the best man for the job. If it wasn't for Cowen ...'

'This Cowen then — he's a powerful man?'

'In certain circles,' James admitted grudgingly. 'He was once a Liberal member himself till he resigned over a policy decision. He's supposed to have retired now but he still enjoys pulling political strings.'

'So his only advantage as far as the Party is concerned is ownership of the *Chronicle*?'

'Well, yes. Without the *Chronicle*, the Liberals have no voice in the north-east. The *Journal* is pro Tory; and the other, smaller papers don't have the circulation.'

Marguerite was silent for a while. Then she looked up and said with gentle provocation. 'So you're giving up then?'

'At the moment, I can't see that I've got any choice. All the time Cowen is dangling his newspaper as bait, I can't see that the Party have any alternative but to accept his nominee.'

'Couldn't you give them an alternative?'

He looked at her, frowning. 'In what way?' he said.

'Match whatever Cowen is putting up. An involvement in a newspaper, perhaps. A great many politicians either own, or have interests in, newspapers.'

He laughed out loud. 'Are you serious?'

'Yes, I'm serious.' She gave him a challenging look. 'Why? Don't you think you could do it?'

'I'm not sure that I would even want to,' James answered thoughtfully. 'I don't know the first thing about it.'

'You don't have to. You could buy something ready made. Something small and provincial; preferably financially ailing, and ideally, a one man affair that could be bought up fairly quickly. It would be worth looking into, don't you think so, James?'

He made no answer except to stare at her in prolonged and thoughtful silence. Then he smiled. 'Well,' he said. 'Why not?'

November 2nd, 1884 — Gateshead

It was typical of him that what had once only interested him vaguely should become an obsession once it was out of his reach. It was an old weakness, to confuse the unattainable with the utterly desirable. His passion now was to out-do Cowen, to thwart Lloyd Jones in his bid for the nomination. Like all industrialists, he indulged in a form of espionage. There were always clerks and runners willing to keep him informed. The 'Change was always a source of gossip. He now extended his army of spies to press clubs and newspaper offices and within just a few weeks he had found what he was looking for. He approached Arnold again at the beginning of November. As before, Arnold's attitude was not encouraging. 'I must say I admire your persistence, Mr Joicey, but really I must tell you that nothing has changed. I won't go so far as to say it's in the bag. Nevertheless ...'

'That doesn't sound very democratic to me,' James observed mildly. 'Surely the electorate has the right to choose.'

'Well, of course — that's how it should be ... But I think you pointed out yourself the folly of running two candidates in harness. We can't afford to split the vote and perhaps let a Tory in. It's not cut and dried that we shall win this election. The party must come first. As it is, we're divided over this Home Rule business. Parnell and the Irish Nationalists have put us in an impossible position by promising the Irish vote to the party that gives him what he wants. In the Chester-le-Street division, that wouldn't normally affect us. Even if Parnell were to instruct his Irishmen to vote for the Tories, we'd still get in. But if the Liberal vote were to be split ... You see what I'm getting at? It's imperative that only one candidate stands, the candidate chosen by the Association ...'

'Yes, I quite see all that,' said James evenly. 'Let me ask you though. If you were not under obligation to our fat friend, Cowen — would Lloyd Jones still be your choice of candidate?'

Arnold looked uncomfortable. 'That isn't really for me to say. I will say, though, that you wouldn't be my choice either. As I said before ...'

'Yes, I know. I'm a capitalist and a hard-grinding employer.' James smiled derisively. 'But then so are Gladstone and Chamberlain, come to that.'

'But they're not standing at Chester-le-Street.' Arnold spread his hands in a helpless gesture. 'Look, Mr Joicey. I don't like this way of doing things any more than you do. But we need the *Chronicle* ...'

'Why particularly the *Chronicle*? Wouldn't some other newspaper do just as well? The *Newcastle Daily Leader*, for example?'

Arnold frowned. 'I can't say that I've heard of it.'

James smiled. 'No. You wouldn't have. It doesn't exist yet. But you may have heard of the *Daily Leader*? Issued from Shields; small, provincial, circulation figures not up to much.'

The arbitrary blue gaze swept over Arnold's face. 'I intend to buy the *Leader*, Mr Arnold. Transfer it, lock, stock and barrel to new and larger premises in Newcastle. I plan to have the first issue on the streets by the middle of next year, in time for the run up to the election. Think of it, Mr Arnold. Newcastle's first truly Radical paper. Eight sides to bring it in line with the *Chronicle*, but at half the price.' He rose from his seat and collected up his hat and gloves. The *Daily Leader* will be entirely at the party's disposal, should they wish it. You might mention this to the Committee, Mr Arnold, before they make their final decision.' He smiled. 'Let them decide which of us they would rather offend — Joe Cowen or myself.'

February 19th, 1885
— Dissington Hall

James Arthur stared solemnly at the cooing baby. 'Is he my brother? Like Hugh?'

'Yes, Arthur,' Marguerite smiled at him from the far side of the crib. 'Sydney is your brother.'

'Sid-nee.' He pronounced the name carefully, to be sure of getting it right — unlike Hugh, who after one brief disinterested look had settled for 'Sidley', and wooden sword in hand had resumed his assault on the nursery bannisters. But James Arthur continued to stare with grave fascination. This was their first real introduction, for since his birth three months before, Sydney had been the object of constant and obsessive care. Marguerite lived in dread of germs and infection. Every cough and sneeze filled her with terror — and those dreadful screaming fits, for no apparent reason. No one could have told her that the cause was her own slavish affection, her constant fondling, the tightness and closeness with which she held him. To Marguerite he was a delicate and sensitive child, a source of constant anxiety; feeding too well or not enough, whining and fretful and difficult. For that reason his half-brothers had been kept at arm's length and even now she was uneasy at James Arthur's nearness, the way he breathed so directly into Sydney's face.

'Sid-nee,' James Arthur said again. Then looking at Marguerite with those large quiet eyes, he added, 'Are you his Mama?'

'Yes.' Marguerite tucked the quilt closer to the slight and sweating body. 'And yours too, of course, Arthur,' she added, seeing the unhappy look that crossed his face.

The boy looked even more distressed. For one thing he didn't like being called just Arthur, as Marguerite insisted on doing. For another, he knew quite well that this woman wasn't his Mama and he resented her pretending that she was. In reality he remembered his mother hardly at all; a vague impression of warmth, the recollection of soft laughter. But mostly his memories were gleaned from other people. He had built up an idyllic picture of her just from things he'd heard. His face grew sullen. He stared at Marguerite with childish dislike. He didn't understand why this woman was here, what she or this ugly creature had to do with him. He looked again at the baby. Eyes of an indeterminate colour looked back. The small mouth, already with a look of petulance about it, opened to reveal white ridged gums. James Arthur turned away, his expression sullen. He didn't think he was going to like Sydney very much.

Marguerite didn't even notice him leave the room. Her attention was entirely focused upon the child. It was an effort not to touch him, not to smooth the damp clustering curls from the pale forehead, not to kiss that tiny perfect mouth. The baby stirred, as if disturbed by the passionate intensity of her thoughts and she moved away in case she should wake him. She smiled happily to herself. She had felt so much better about things since Sydney had been born. Her confidence and optimism seemed to have returned. She hardly ever thought of Elizabeth now and looking back she could see how petty and ridiculous her jealousy had been. That was the trouble when love came so late in the day. She had lost her sense of proportion for a while. She had allowed the sensible pattern of her life to be disturbed by nothing more substantial than her imagination.

She went downstairs. She was expecting William James within half an hour. He called regularly now, every Friday afternoon he stopped off on his way up to Lynhope. She had come to rather dread his visits. She always felt he only came to probe and make mischief and more often than not he succeeded. She always felt irritable and out of sorts when he left. Inevitably that evening she would quarrel with James about something entirely trivial.

He was punctual as always and she went out into the hall, lifting her cheek briefly for his greeting. 'You're looking well, my dear.' He stood back, regarding her with his warm, possessive stare. 'Bonny is the word, I think.' His eyes dropped to her breasts, heavy with milk. 'Motherhood obviously suits you.'

She led him into the drawing room where the tea things were set out. She boiled water herself on a spirit stove. 'Green or black?'

He smiled apologetically. 'Would you mind if I had something a little stronger?'

'No, of course not. Will you help yourself? There's whisky, and I think soda, on the side table there.'

'Actually,' he talked as he busied himself with decanter and glasses, 'one of the reasons I called, apart from the pleasure of seeing you,' he turned toward her and smiled, 'is that we're having a small house party at Lynhope at the end of next week before moving to town for the season. There are one or two people I thought James might be interested to meet.' He reeled off a list of impressive names. 'I thought he might be able to pick up the odd vote, so to speak.' He sat himself down on the sofa beside her. 'I presume politics are still the order of the day? Was it Pliny who said that politicians were not born, they were excreted?'

'It was Horace actually,' she replied, smiling.

He nodded and regarded her thoughtfully over the rim of his glass. 'I hear a rumour that James has bought out the *Daily Leader*. Is it true?'

'Yes. Quite true. It isn't a secret. Obviously, ownership of a newspaper will help his political career.'

'Of course!' There was a hint of a sneer in William James' voice. 'Manipulation of the masses through the printed word ... Banner headlines proclaiming James Joicey to be a jolly good fellow ... His idea or yours? Yours, I would imagine. Far too subtle for James.' He sipped at his whisky, glancing enviously round the exquisitely furnished room; the rosewood bureau he particularly admired, and the carved Louis Quinze chairs upholstered in oyster silk. He thought bitterly of Lynhope, disfigured by his wife's appalling taste; imitation French furniture corroded with gilt, the floors smothered in dingy carpets. And Mary herself, fat and middle aged ... He looked at Marguerite, her glorious pallor, the faint but noticeable shadows beneath her eyes. It gave her an unaccustomed air of frailty. He rather liked that in a woman and it occurred to him that if both had been younger he might have tried to seduce her. Not physically perhaps — his enjoyment of women was mostly in the pursuit — but to flirt a little, turn her head. As it was, he might settle for a little discreet meddling. It would be amusing to see what he could stir up. He assumed a solicitous air. 'Forgive me for asking, my dear, but is everything all right? One can't help but notice that you've been looking a little strained of late. Is everything all right between you and James?'

She coloured faintly. 'Yes, of course. Why do you ask?'

'Oh ...' He was casual. 'I just wondered that's all. I know what a swine James can be. After all, it can't be easy being the second Mrs Joicey when your husband is still enamoured of the first.'

She kept her face expressionless though his words were like a knife sliding between her ribs. Then William James patted her hand. 'I'm sorry, my dear. That was a rather tactless remark.'

She forced a smile. 'No, please. Don't apologize. It's quite all right. I don't have any illusions about how James feels about Elizabeth.'

'Well, if it's any consolation to your, she wasn't the right wife for him. She didn't approve of his ambition. I think she would have stood in his way. Perhaps in time he would have found that tiresome.'

'Well, we'll never know will we.' She rose to her feet. 'Perhaps we could talk about something else.'

'Yes, I'm sorry. I should't have brought the subject up. It's just that I can't help being concerned for you, my dear. You see, I know what James is like.'

She turned to face him. 'What is he like then?'

'He's very ambitious.'

'So am I.'

'There's ambition and ambition. Most of us set some limit upon it. There comes a point at which we're satisfied. That doesn't happen with James. There are no limits. There must be more and more. It's an endless road — and a hard one, I would have thought, for a woman.'

She smiled. 'For some women, perhaps.'

'But not, for you? You think you're a match for him?' He shook his head in a pitying gesture. 'Tell me that in five years time and I might believe you. You just don't have any conception of what he's really like.'

'You were going to tell me,' Marguerite reminded him.

'Yes, I was, wasn't I.' Then he gave a short laugh. 'And now that you ask me I'm not really sure that I know. Perhaps that's what's so unnerving about him. I don't know what he's like and I should do after all these years.' His expression grew sour. 'I know that he uses people, though. He's used me often enough. I think we're all fair game to James. We're all expendable if it means getting what he wants. He sees life as a gigantic balance sheet and people in terms of profit and loss. My father was like that. He absorbed people, gobbled them up. That's how it is with James. In the end you lose your sense of identity. You stop seeing yourself as an individual and become merely an appendage to James; James' wife, James' partner.' He looked at her. 'Do you understand what I mean.'

'Yes, I think so.' At least she understood how it might be like that for him. Instinctively she sensed that he was weak. 'Why do you stay then,' she asked him curiously. 'You must have had opportunities to get away?'

William James smiled. 'I suppose the honest answer is greed. Being with James is like being on a winning streak at the tables. You just can't bring yourself to walk away. It's always been like that. Even when the Colonel and Edward were alive, we all ended up doing things James' way. He has that effect on people. He's somehow able to persuade you that you'll be missing something if you don't tag along, that there's something momentous just round the corner. And so of course we all trot along without the faintest idea of where we are going.'

She smiled. 'As if he were the Pied Piper and we the rats?'

He laughed softly. 'Yes! Exactly like that. That's a good analogy.' He looked at her mockingly. 'Except when you remember what happened to the rats!'

She didn't allow him to spoil the day, knowing full well that his meddling had been deliberate. And that evening she dressed particularly to please James; the pale soft colours she knew he preferred, the diminished gleam of amethyst and pearls rather than the hard icy fire of diamonds. And though she wasn't aware of it, she had a brilliance of her own. Her eyes shone at the prospect of the challenging months ahead; her perfect skin glowed with triumph and excitement. This was how she had always imagined it; the two of them together, working and planning toward the same end.

She raised her glass ... 'To the Right Honourable Member for Chester-le-Street ...'

James shook his head. 'Don't let's tempt providence. It's hardly a foregone conclusion.'

'It's as good as done,' Marguerite predicted confidently. 'The Liberal Association have adopted you as their official candidate. That's half the battle won.'

'Yes.' He smiled but the smile was tinged with unease. He'd had a victory of sorts. After four months of wrangling, the bulk of the Liberal caucus, led by Arnold, had eventually come down on James' side. But what should have been the end of the matter had proved to be only the beginning. Lloyd Jones, despite enormous pressure from the party and even being offered another safe Liberal seat, had refused to concede. Even at the risk of splitting the vote, he had announced his intention of fighting the seat openly, standing as an Independent.

'Still,' he added cautiously, 'it won't be easy.'

Marguerite smiled. 'Would you want it if it was?'

She rose from the table and nodded her assent for it to be cleared. It had been a perfect evening; a quiet supper alone and a bottle of Lafitte '65 which had made her feel faintly light headed, used though she was to strong wine. Perhaps more intoxicating was the warmth in James' eyes, his unmistakable look of admiration and approval.

She poured two cups of thin bitter coffee. 'You think Cowen is behind Jones's refusal to back down?'

'I'm sure of it,' James answered. 'Jones wouldn't have had the courage to stand against the caucus himself and the fact that Cowen is paying his expenses speaks for itself.' His eyes narrowed thoughtfully. 'No. It's definitely Cowen we're up against. Apart from being a threat to his political protegé, I'll soon be a rival to the Chronicle.'

'Will the unions back him?'

'No, I don't think so. At least not openly. Naturally, Jones is plugging his union connections for all they're worth but I don't think they're good enough to impress the Federation. They've got their own man standing at Houghton and they won't want to risk queering his pitch.'

They sat together by the fire. James fell into a thoughtful and relaxed silence. Now and then he glanced across at his wife. She looked radiant tonight. He had forgotten that sometimes she could. He couldn't help being proud of her in his own grudging way. She was exactly the right wife for him; ambitious, intelligent, sophisticated and charming. He knew that people envied him. They were alike in so many things; the urge for power and dominance was strong in them both, although sometimes he felt, that in Marguerite, the need to dominate extended to him: not just his actions, but his feelings and thoughts. He had the feeling that she wanted to exclude from his life anything she didn't like or over which she had no control. It was only a little thing, just one of a dozen little things which seemed to have sprung up between them. Though she hadn't actually said so, he knew that she wasn't happy here. She didn't like the north, she didn't like the pits, and once or twice she'd hinted that if he made a success of politics, it would be an opportunity for him to sell out. He didn't seem to be able to make her understand that coal was his life. Politics would always be secondary. But on the whole he was satisfied. He was growing fonder of her all the time, although he still held back from absolute commitment. He'd always promised himself that he wouldn't risk that again, all his life and happiness hanging by the thread of a single life. Sydney's birth in November had brought it all back; November again — freezing fog and rain hardening into snow. It had seemed like the repetition of some awful nightmare; the snow outside, white, malevolent — and upstairs, the stifled cries from behind closed doors. He had thought then — if Marguerite should die, if he should have to go through the whole business again ... He leant back and closed his eyes. Remembering still made him feel depressed.

Marguerite stared at his closed set face and slowly her elation began to fade. She knew these moments of quiet brooding when suddenly, all expression would die in his face and it would become cold and still; frozen, like a piece of exquisite sculpture. She knew then he was thinking of Elizabeth.

She stirred restlessly. She wanted to talk, to keep at bay the train of insidious thought that William James had begun, to maintain the illusion that everything between them was as it should be. Was it an illusion? Why had she thought that? She knew he cared for her in his way. He was considerate, kind ... But that wasn't the same thing as love. It wasn't anything like the intense feeling she had for him, the feeling he'd had for Elizabeth. Her eyes went to the desk, its naked surface seemed to shout the absence of the carving. She gritted her teeth. She wanted to ask where it had gone, yet was reluctant to speak of Elizabeth. James never did. Somehow, that made it worse. As if the memories were so painful, so precious that he must keep them all to himself. Suddenly she said, as if by mentioning the name she could banish the ghost. 'James? The carving of Elizabeth? Where is it?'

He looked at her strangely. 'Why do you ask?'

She shrugged. 'I wondered. It was such a lovely piece. It seems a shame to keep it hidden.' Her voice was light, casual, relegating Elizabeth to the status of an ornament.

'It isn't hidden.' She couldn't mistake the irritation that crept into his voice. 'My brother George has it. I did not think you would care for it here.'

It was the wrong thing to say, implying a jealousy she thought concealed. She gave a brittle laugh. 'Why should you think I wouldn't care for it here?' She tried to keep her own voice from rising. 'It really doesn't matter. There's no point in pretending that Elizabeth didn't exist. I'm perfectly aware that you still think of her.'

'Naturally I still think of her.' He answered her honestly as she had known he would. 'She was my wife.'

She gave him her quick cynical smile though inwardly she was sick and trembling with rage: at herself for allowing her irrational jealousy to spoil the evening; at him for not lying and telling what she wanted to hear. 'I'm glad that you used the past tense,' she said acidly. 'Sometimes I get the impression that she still is your wife, that half of you is still married to her.'

James looked up at her briefly. The passionate intensity of her eyes unnerved him. He was almost embarrassed by their desperate appeal. 'Marguerite,' he said, gently, reasonably. 'There will always be a part of me that will belong to Elizabeth, as there will, to James Arthur and Hugh. But the rest is yours, if you want it.'

Marguerite lowered her eyes. It was an effort to control her resentment and anger. After Elizabeth, after Elizabeth's sons ... then there might be a morsel left over for her. Her mouth hardened, grew bitter and resolute. She wanted more than another woman's leavings.

March 30th, 1885
— County Durham

The hall was long and narrow and incredibly dirty, another in the succession of dingy halls and cheerless institutes in which she had sat since the beginning of James's campaign. Sometimes there was not even the comfort of roof and walls, only a wagon in a field to serve as a platform. It wasn't how she'd imagined it at all and she thought briefly and bitterly of the extravagant venues she'd planned. James had laughed at her. 'It isn't going to be that sort of campaign, my dear. If you want me to win you're going to have to get your hands dirty.' And her clothes and her hair, even her skin, all filmed with a greyness that seemed part of the air. The hall at West Pelton was worse than most. It smelt of sweat and beer and stale tobacco. The few, small windows opaque with dust, the bare floor awash with mud and the constant hawkings of the two hundred men who sat crowded together in sullen and uneasy silence, waiting for James to speak.

Marguerite glanced anxiously at the other occupants of the platform; John Lucas, James' political agent; two councillors and an alderman here to speak on James' behalf. She saw her own unease reflected in their fixed and anxious smiles. They too sensed the belligerent mood of the crowd. She watched the mass of grimy faces as James began to speak; sullen with prejudice and cold mistrust. They were against him before he'd uttered a word.

And yet slowly, unbelievably, the brutal countenances thawed. James began hesitantly, almost shyly. Like them, he said, this was his first real experience of politics. He hoped they would bear with him if his words came from the heart, rather than from any prepared speech as was usual. He spoke, not loudly, but in a penetrating voice. He spoke to them as equals, of things they knew and understood, of poverty and hardship, of death and disease.

'I am informed by some that I am not qualified to represent you, that as a coalowner I cannot possibly know of these things. But I do know. I was born in a pit house not so many miles from here. I was raised among you. I have lived and worked among you all of my life. My father was a pitman once, and his father before him. Five generations of Joiceys have worked the Northumberland and Durham pits. I am the first never to have actually worked below ground.' His brilliant eyes swept over them, resting briefly on each upturned face. 'I cannot think what better qualifications I could have.'

A low murmur ran round the hall. The men leant forward, listening intently, weighing up his every word.

'I am also told that I am unfit to represent you because I am an employer and that our interests could never possibly coincide.' He smiled. 'I will not try and deceive you, as so many politicians do, by pretending that I only have the workers' interests at heart. I very much have my own interests at heart, but my interests must be yours as yours must be mine. Neither of us can function without the other. How can my company be served by a badly paid and discontented workforce? How can yours be served by employers making low profits or none at all? By a sick and depressed industry? We both of us suffer when trade is bad. If I am elected I shall make it my business to fight against the things that oppress us both: sickness and injury, death and disease, which could be halved if we had enough and better qualified inspectors. Where are all the mine inspectors parliament promised us? And how qualified for the job are the few that we have? And why are they always brought in from outside the industry? Who better to safeguard pitmen than pitmen themselves?'

His voice gained power, resounding from the grey plastered walls of the hall. The men looked at him, then looked at each other, struggling with years of inherited mistrust.

'I am also accused of being a capitalist. But what does that mean? It means I am my own man, and which of you here does not want to be that? The man who founded James Joicey and Company spent his first twenty years in the pits. He was his own man, a pitman and proud of it all of his life. And what I offer to you, what the Liberals offer to you, is the opportunity, the right, for you all to be your own men. My beliefs are simple, easily understood. I believe in work, not slavery. I believe in honesty not deceit. I believe it is the right of every man to make what he can of himself, to live decently, to be independent of charity and hand outs. The Tories would withhold this right from you. Poor you are and poor you shall remain has always been their philosophy. They are the real capitalists, living on privilege and inherited wealth. I inherited nothing from my father. What I have, I made for myself. But these Tories, these aristocrats, they take all and give nothing. It is not employers who are the parasites but the landowners who bleed the industry with royalty rents and wayleaves. Did you know that it costs as much for a ton of coal to cross just seven miles of Church Commissioners' land as it does for the actual hewing? And then the same again in royalties? And what of the London coal dues that impose a crippling tax on coal shipped to London forcing owners to seek less profitable markets abroad?' The muttering swelled to loud shouts of approval and it was some moments before he could proceed.

'You will all know that I am not the only candidate to seek your suffrage. Mr Lloyd Jones, although not the official Liberal candidate, has also chosen to contest this seat. That is his right; but it is also your right to be represented by the man who will serve your interests best. And if I thought this man could serve you better than myself, then gladly I would step down. But I'm afraid I do not know enough about him to form such a definite opinion. Who is he? Where is he from? What really do we know about him except that he is a friend of Mr Cowen? But you do know me and whether your opinion of me is good or bad, you at least know what to expect. Mr Cowen and Mr Jones believe that the labels "capitalist" and "employer" are enough to ensure my defeat. I do not believe it. I know that Durham pitmen aren't so easily fooled. If Lloyd Jones is not a capitalist, he is the nominee of a capitalist. I have no nominee. I have no patron except yourselves, no other cause except the well-being of our trade. If I am elected I shall be answerable to none but the men who gave me their vote.' He paused, his intent passionate gaze sweeping over them. 'A great many of you are employed by me. You must know then from my dealings with you and what kind of man I am. On what you know of me, on what you can expect, I ask you for your vote.'

He sat down and there was silence. Then abruptly a wild cheering filled the hall. The crowd rose and surged forward, shouting his name, calling him down into the body of the hall. Marguerite sat alone whilst James and his entourage went amongst the crowd. She saw his face, flushed with pride. She thought; in a moment he'll look over and share this moment with me, he'll acknowledge that we did this together. But he didn't look at her at all and after a while she got up, brushing her skirts and followed him out into the chilly evening.

July and August, 1885 — Dissington Hall, Northumberland

Marguerite smoothed the skirts of the grey glacé gown and surveyed her reflection with satisfaction. The new gown suited her, the skirts spilling out from her savagely corseted waist, then looped and swathed to fall in a cascade of lace and pool the floor with a diminutive train. She smiled faintly. No one would have guessed that she was three months pregnant and she meant to keep it concealed as long as she could. She hadn't welcomed the news, coming at such an inconvenient time. It was bound to hamper her during the campaign. It was an obsession now; to get James elected, away from this place. That, she was conceived, was the answer. They'd have to live in London for at least part of the year, all the time that Parliament was in session. She'd already made up her mind where they should live; Belgravia or Mayfair, Knightsbridge at a pinch. And once there, James would see. He'd soon learn that political success didn't depend on pleasing the electorate but on pleasing the men in power. That was the way you became one of them. He would appreciate her then, all she had done, all she was still willing to do, if only he had let her.

She went downstairs and into the dining room, running a practised eye over her table; glasses for hock and claret in sparkling crystal, silver cutlery ranked either side of Davenport plates. The flowers were yet to come — blue iris and yellow roses in their election colours. She was determined that everything should be quite perfect.

She moved around the table, setting a knife straight, refolding a snowy napkin whose lines did not quite please. Her guests had been chosen with equally elaborate care. The place cards read like a page from Debrett's: Colonel Sir Charles Collingwood and Lady Collingwood, The Right Honourable Edward and Mrs Liddell, Mr and Mrs Blackett-Ord ... She fiddled unnecessarily with an arrangement of knives. Normally these occasions filled her with pleasure: good food and wine, the company of elegant and witty men, the envy and admiration of their wives. But today she felt depressed and out of sorts. It happened a lot lately; a feeling of self doubt, the plunging of her spirits for no reason. She was doing too much, cramming too much into the day. But she liked to keep busy, keep herself occupied, keep herself from thinking. It was very necessary that she maintain the pretence of being a happy and contented wife. Successful politicians didn't have neurotic wives — unhappy wives — and indeed most of the time she was able to persuade herself that she was happy. After all, she had her her son, and wasn't she on the brink of seeing her hopes and ambitions fulfilled? Except that a child couldn't take the place of a husband, ambition wasn't a substitute for love. James didn't love her and she wasn't even sure now that he was still fond of her. She thought she amused him sometimes. They had a cynical sense of humour in common. But that seemed to be all lately. Ambition for his future was their only other common ground, the only subject on which they could freely speak without fear of quarrelling. They quarrelled a great deal now, privately, behind closed doors. To other people they appeared as an affectionate and devoted couple though the effort of always maintaining this cosy façade, of always being as it were on public display, had bred in James a sullen streak, and in her a brittle despair. There were other delusions, more wounding still, the idea that he needed her, that she would, in some way be instrumental in his success. She had discovered a long time ago that James couldn't be bullied, he couldn't even be led. Nothing was done unless he really wanted it. That was the most painful truth of all and one which she could not yet fully acknowledge; that she needed James more than life and he didn't need her at all.

Upstairs, James stared broodingly from his bedroom window, flung open to the hot summer night. He hated these affairs, these grand formal dinners, pouring good claret down the throats of men he didn't know, didn't even want to know. It had been a bad day all round; first the news that he'd been outbid on a contract. Then Cowen, bursting into his committee rooms unannounced ...

'My dear Mr Joicey!' He had advanced upon James, plump hand outstretched, his large teeth exposed in a beaming smile. 'Forgive me descending upon you unannounced. I couldn't resist the opportunity of spying out the enemy camp.'

It was all very hearty, all very British, reeking of fair play. James, who had done nothing but regard his visitor with mild amusement, now rose to his feet. 'I wasn't aware that we were at war, Mr Cowen.'

'You don't think so, eh?' The jocular manner became a little strained. 'That just goes to show how little you know about politics, Mr Joicey.' Cowen glanced at John Lucas who hovered uncertainly. 'I wonder if I might have the favour of a word. In private,' he added meaningly.

James resumed his chair behind the desk. 'You may speak quite freely before my colleague, Mr Cowen,' He added wih a deprecating smile, 'In fact, I'd prefer to have a witness.'

Cowen's prominent eyes narrowed and he abandoned all pretence of amiability. 'You're very sure of yourself, aren't you?'

'I think I have reason to be. Opinion seems very much in my favour.'

'And cocky too! That's not a good thing in a politician, Mr

Joicey.' He eyed James coldly. 'You might remember that I have forgotten more about politics — and newspapers — than you're ever likely to know. And as I understand you're something of a beginner at both. Wouldn't it be wiser to tread a little warily at first?'

'I might be new to politics, Mr Cowen,' James answered him easily. 'But I'm an old hand at threats and intimidation and bribery. For a coalowner, you know, it's standard practice.'

'Yes, I've heard that,' said Cowen. 'Sharp practice. Undercutting ... If that's how you intend to run your campaign then you'll find yourself out on a limb. Gentlemen don't do business like that.'

James stared at him insolently. 'And how would you know, Mr Cowen?'

Cowen's heavy face became suffused with fury but he kept his temper well. 'Don't you think that a rather provocative remark?'

'No more provocative than the defamatory articles you have been running in your newspaper lately. Let me see; what was today's tit-bit? That my wife patronizes London stores in preference to local traders ...' His mouth curled in disdain. 'Is that the best you can do?'

Cowen smiled. He wasn't easily provoked. 'I must say your attitude inspires me to dig deeper.'

'Dig as much as you like, Mr Cowen. You won't find anything.'

Cowen picked up his hat and settled it firmly on his head. 'Oh, a good newspaper man always finds something, Mr Joicey. Being new to the game that's something perhaps you haven't yet learned.'

James frowned. The recollection of Cowen's words filled him with distinct unease. He didn't feel now that he'd handled the situation at all well.

'James!'

He turned his head. Marguerite stood in the doorway. 'Are you ready to come down? The first of our guests will be arriving shortly.'

For a moment his eyes lingered on her face. She looked quite lovely. he still couldn't help but admire her poise, her cool air of sophistication. His eyes clouded, knowing that this

213

sparkle, this surface allure, was purely for their guests, put on like her jewels and her gown. When they were gone, the brilliance would fade. Only a dim, tarnished lustre would remain. Then he looked away and picked up his gloves. 'Yes, of course,' he said flatly. 'I'm quite ready.'

Marguerite gave an elaborate sigh of relief. The last of the guests had finally departed. 'Well,' she said brightly. 'It all went off very well, don't you think so, James?'

'A triumph, my dear,' James murmured drily. 'Indeed, a positive triumph.'

Her smile faded as she heard the undertones of sarcasm in his voice. 'It was for your benefit, James,' she reminded him sharply. 'It's expected for us to entertain.'

Yes, I suppose so.' He watched her restless, agitated pacing. She never seemed to be still these days. He put that down to her condition, as he did her violent swings of mood, these strained, potentially explosive scenes. A feeling of compassion suddenly swept over him. She looked so pale, so stretched. He said quietly, 'What are you going to do if I don't get in, Marguerite, if I don't get elected.'

Her face grew paler. 'But you will. You must.'

'Is it so important to you then?'

'Isn't it important to you?'

'Yes, but not so much. I'll still have the company left. Politics for me has always been secondary to that anyway. I've only ever seen it as a means of making changes in the trade.'

She smiled bitterly. 'And you're wondering what I'll have left?'

'Yes I suppose I am. I've never really known what you want out of life — what you want from me.'

'That's because you've never bothered to ask me, James.'

'I'm asking you now. What is it you want?'

She was silent, staring down at her small clenched hands. 'Can't you tell me,' he said. 'We've always been able to be honest with each other before.'

She laughed unpleasantly. 'Oh yes, you've always been honest with me, James — brutally so.' Then she turned on him viciously. 'All right then, James, I'll tell you what I want. I want what every other woman wants. I want a husband, a family. I want to be loved, admired. What I don't want is to be

214

forever compared to a woman younger and more beautiful then myself. I don't want to be treated as a some sort of second rate replacement.' Her eyes glittered with tears and rage. 'You weren't honest about that, James. Elizabeth isn't dead. She's alive. She's here. In this house. In you. You keep her alive ...'

James' head jerked up. His face was deathly white. 'No,' he said savagely. 'It's you who keep her alive. It's you who are obsessed with Elizabeth.' He glared at her. 'Can't you see how pitiful that is, how degrading, to be jealous of a dead woman?'

'But you can't forget her, can you?' Marguerite screamed at him.

'No, I can't forget her.' He was shouting himself now. 'You've never given me the chance.'

The next morning it was as if nothing had happened. He enquired politely if she had slept well and she replied that she had. They breakfasted in near silence, which she broke only to remind him that they would be dining early as he was addressing a meeting at Whickham that night. He answered without looking up that he had not forgotten. Then he folded his newspaper and rose from the table. She walked with him as far as the hall and offered her cheek as usual for his brief dry kiss. 'Goodbye, my dear. I shall be at the Quayside if you should need me.'

She stood leaning against the door for a few moments after he had gone. '*If you should need me.*' The words echoed mockingly around the chill marble hall. Oh, dear God. If she needed him! Then she straightened, walking briskly and determinedly across the hall. She had much to do; luncheon with the Ladies Temperance Guild, meetings with printers and canvassers and Lucas, their agent ... She smiled resolutely. The main thing was to keep busy. And indeed the weeks flew by. She was forever occupied, caught up in the mounting fever of the coming election. The polls showed James to be marginally in the lead. Cowen and Lloyd Jones were putting up a determined opposition and in places like Blaydon were even creeping ahead. She redoubled her efforts, working late into the night at the committee rooms in spite of morning sickness and cramps. Nothing mattered now but that James should win.

It mattered to him, but not for the same reasons. Being elected had become almost secondary now. Even Lloyd Jones was just a pawn in the game. It was beating Cowen that really mattered and so far he had matched all of Cowen's moves — double size issues, supplements, cut rates for advertisers. In just six weeks he had halved the *Chronicle*'s sales. Over the poisonous and vindictive articles spewed from the *Chronicle*'s columns he had been slower to react. Cowen accused him of intimidation and tyranny. He countered with scornful and dignified replies. In that respect, though, he was biding his time. There were still two months until the election. He counted on Cowen's running out of steam long before the event. The public had short memories. What they read today they would have forgotten by tomorrow. He was saving this particular sensation till the week before the election, late enough for the voters to go to the poll with it fresh in their minds, too late for Cowen to retaliate. In the meantime he quietly gathered together his ammunition. He knew it had to be good. Cowen was popular with the man in the street. They liked his extrovert and stagey manner, his long and extravagant speeches. They would need to be outraged. They would need to be shocked. He was going to make sure that they were.

November 30th, 1885
— Dissington Hall

November again, the last of the month — four years lacking a day since Elizabeth had died. It was also the day of the election and he saw it as an omen; November, the month of the Scorpion, the month of loss and bitter defeat.

He stood at his bedroom window, staring out into the spectral dawn. It was a day of soft and curious melancholy. Mist hung opaquely over the bleached, dormant fields and in the distance, the chimneys and pitheads that ringed the city seemed like the wreckage of ships lost in some white milky sea. He shivered, turning up the collar of his quilted robe. The room was cold, the fire long dead. Only pale ashes blew in the cavernous grate. He hadn't slept well, hadn't slept at all, so terrified was he of failure. And to fail openly, publicly, before thousands of eyes ... To have to witness Cowen's triumph, to have to smile and shake that fool Jones by the hand ... He gnawed at his lip. He wasn't usually pessimistic. He hadn't even any real cause to think of failure. Predictions for the outcome were all in his favour. Neither Cowen nor Lloyd Jones had had time to recover from his scathing and bitter attack launched just three days before polling. The revelation of Cowen's past political dealings; stories of bribery and vote rigging. His protegé Jones had not escaped though the charges against him were less severe. Enough though to discredit him in the working man's eyes; the disclosure that once, nearly thirty years ago, he had campaigned for a Tory against the Liberal hero Cobden. Every paper in the north had taken it up. Banner headlines proclaimed Cowen and Jones traitors and hypocrites ... The hard lines around James' mouth relaxed. Oh yes, he had every reason to feel confident. Why then didn't he?

He moved away from the window and the ache in him intensified as he looked round the chill and shadowy room. He thought of Elizabeth. He often did these days, more, it seemed, than he had ever done. He found that strange. He had expected the memory to fade with time. It hadn't though. He could recall her face, her joyous smile as clearly as if she had just walked from the room. Perhaps Marguerite was right. Perhaps, unconsciously he did keep her alive. He'd never really come to terms with losing her. Marrying again hadn't been the answer, at least not a woman like Marguerite. They were too much alike. She mirrored all that was worst in him. Her pride, her possessiveness, her demanding nature, these were all reflections of things he saw in himself. And yet sometimes he still believed that he could care for her. Sometimes when he looked at her, he was overwhelmed with a curious tenderness. He never thought of it as love. He had only ever loved once; foolishly, slavishly, or so it seemed in retrospect. That intensity of feeling had died with Elizabeth. But he still believed himself capable of love, a different kind of love, a quieter and easier happiness. Perhaps when the election was over ... He bit his lip. He couldn't even begin to think about the future. It was hard enough to project his thoughts beyond today. Only tomorrow seemed certain. Tomorrow was Sunday, the anniversary of Elizabeth's death. Tomorrow, then, he would take his boys to Jesmond and lay the customary flowers on their mother's grave.

He went through into his dressing-room and drew his morning bath himself, tepid verging on cold as he liked it. He had no valet, though Marguerite protested that all gentlemen did. He didn't like the idea of being watched and fussed over. A man had to have some time to himself.

He dressed carefully; a morning coat of severe but elegant cut, a waistcoat of dove grey silk. Then he went downstairs and ate a solitary breakfast. During her pregnancies Marguerite had hers sent up to her room. He glanced through the early editions; Cowen's *Chronicle*, his own *Leader*, strongly partisan as was to be expected. The neutrals like the *Echo* predicted a close run thing.

He looked up as Marguerite entered the room, elegant in blue velvet and astrakhan. She looked pale, he thought, even a little sickly and he tried to put warmth into his smile. They went into the hallway where the servants had gathered to see them off. Marguerite left him to greet John Lucas his agent. James bent to kiss his three small sons: Sydney, sleeping peacefully in his nurse's arms; Hugh, noisy and exuberant as ever; and James Arthur, staring up at him with those large anxious eyes. 'Good luck, Papa. I hope you win.'

Marguerite was already settled in the corner of the carriage, a fur rug over her knees. Depite the raw weather, she had insisted they use an open carriage and already her limbs were numb with cold. She swallowed hard as they moved away, refusing to acknowledge the spasms of nausea that rose in her throat, the violent protestation of her pregnant body within the vicelike constriction of her stays. Nothing, but nothing must be allowed to spoil the day. She glanced at the sky, opaque with pale cloud. Rain was the only eventuality she couldn't provide for. Bad weather always meant a poor turnout, though she had done what she could to minimize the threat by arranging to have a fleet of conveyances on hand for voters who had any distance to travel. Feverishly, she went over the final details in her mind. She had planned the morning's itinerary with almost military precision. First port of call, Newcastle and the committee rooms to give last minute directions to their helpers. Then the round of the polling stations — she had allowed ten minutes for each — and finally back to Gateshead for eleven o'clock for the count and the declaration. She shivered with anticipation. He would win. She knew he would win. Even now the feeling of triumph was upon her. And this would be just the beginning. A position on the front bench was her next objective.

The sound of cheering broke into her thoughts. A small crowd had gathered by the south lodge gates and all along the road there were people. She looked at James. What was he thinking? She could tell nothing at all from his face. Then suddenly he turned and looked at her and his hand slid out to cover hers. 'It's all right,' he said. 'It's going to be all right. We're going to win, my dear.'

She nodded and stared straight ahead. She felt like crying. ' We're going to win, my dear.' Suddenly, miraculously, they were together again.

They were an hour late starting the count and by one o'clock, with still no result declared, the strain was beginning to show. Yet throughout all the agony of delay she managed to keep smiling. She maintained her air of quiet confidence whilst steeling herself for the faint possibility of defeat. And it did seem a possibility, with Lloyd Jones's colours to be seen throughout the hall. It was going to be a close run thing, not the runaway victory she had hoped for. She dabbed her face with a handkerchief soaked in cologne. The large hall was hot and noisy and crowded, a sea of faces and moving lips. Outside a band played tunelessly, shrill against the bass of the gathering crowd. The atmosphere was tense, even mildly aggressive. Already there had been one or two verbal skirmishes and twice fighting had broken out in the street below. She looked for James. He stood, tense and preoccupied, making desultory conversation with Lucas. She closed her eyes and prayed silently that he would not have to walk away in defeat. She would never get him so far again. She licked her dry lips. The returning officer was mounting the platform. The three candidates rose and stood at his back; Ashworth, the Tory, already with a resigned smile fixed on his face. Lloyd Jones stared thoughtfully at his feet. Only James looked straight ahead, eyeing the crowd, as if he were defying them to reject him.

'I, Richard Curtis, Under Sheriff for the borough of Newcastle-upon-Tyne and Returning Officer for the Parliamentary Decision of Chester-le-Street, hereby declare the votes polled in the above election to be as follows: Mr Charles Ashworth — Conservative. Two thousand and eighteen ...

She didn't dare look at James but fixed her eyes instead on the face of the clock at the far end of the hall.

'Mr Lloyd Jones — Independent. Three thousand, six hundred and six.' Her eyes widened in dismay. So many! Already some of the crowd were setting up a cheer.

'Mr James Joicey — Liberal.' Her heart began to beat in thick unsteady strokes. 'Four thousand —' He raised his voice against the mounting roar. 'Four thousand, four hundred and nine. And I therefore declare the said James Joicey to be the duly elected member ...'

Nobody heard him. The hall erupted into a frenzied cheering. The band struck up, tinny and raucous, hats and caps whirled through the air. Laughing, crying, Marguerite went to him and flung her arms around him. 'You've won,' she cried. 'You've really won.'

James looked at her, smiling, and she thought her heart would burst with happiness. 'We've won, Marguerite,' he murmured. 'I could never have done it without you.'

August 21st, 1886
— Dissington Hall

Marguerite stared round the walls of the drawing room, looking strangely naked without its pictures. It didn't seem that long since she'd been putting them up. She smiled. It has been an eventful year to say the least, a marvellous, wonderful year. In January they had moved to London, taking up residence in exclusive Belgravia at 58, Cadogan Square, and it was there, in April that Drever, her second son, had been born. Also in April, James had begun negotiations for Longhirst Hall, a prestigious estate twenty miles north of the Tyne, comprising some four thousand acres, two entire villages, a colliery and thirteen farms. They now had all the outward trappings of worldly success. Politically though, things hadn't gone so well, the Liberals were no sooner in office than they were out of it. James had made an impressive début with a fiery maiden speech on employer's liability. But it was the Irish question that dominated these days. Chamberlain's resignation and defection to the Tories, followed by the Government's defeat on the Home Rule Bill, had forced Gladstone to dissolve and call a second election within six months of the first. James held his seat, doubling his majority but overall, the Tories swept the board. When Parliament resumed it was on the Opposition benches that James had taken his seat.

On the social side though, things couldn't have been better. Marguerite was in her element here. She was on her home ground and no longer felt diminished by the spectre of James' first wife. It hadn't taken her long to establish herself again and her guest lists were always sprinkled with distinguished persons and she numbered many wealthy and titled families among her friends. James was less in awe, and viewed all the new faces with the same detached and impassive air. It was a source of mild but not serious irritation to Marguerite. Often she wished that he could be a little more humble, that he could pay court to the men that mattered. But all in all, she couldn't complain. She was happier than she'd been since they'd married.

At the end of August, Parliament had risen for the summer recess and they were to return to Dissington for the last time. Marguerite had come on a few days ahead and her high spirits were only slightly diminished by the knowledge that she was pregnant yet again. She had spent the days before James' arrival supervising the packing up of the things they did not need and arranging for their removal to Longhirst. She expected James tonight though and accordingly had his rooms prepared. Despite the summer heat she ordered a fire, for the rooms quickly became damp when they were not used. She looked in after luncheon to see that all was in order. The quiet austerity of the room was soothing. It was a man's room, all dark mahogany and pale gleaming silver; faded Turkey rugs thrown down upon a polished floor. There were two further rooms leading off the main bedroom; a dressing room and a small sitting room he used as a study into which she had never yet been.

She wandered through into the dressing room. Silver-backed brushes were laid out with military precision. His clothes, dis-embodied, ranked behind mirrored doors. She touched them lovingly; rough tweed jackets that carried the faint scent of moorland, formal suits of cashmere and barathea. She held the sleeve of the grey Cheviot overcoat against her check. It smelt of cigars and wild heather and coal tar soap.

Then, without meaning to pry but more in a mood of pleasurable exploration, she went through into his private sitting room. There were books everywhere. On the floor, on the chairs, weighty leather tomes piled upon the desk — and preserved lovingly in a small glass case, the dozen or so stained shabby volumes that had once belonged to his father. There were other discoveries; paintings and old photographs she had long thought discarded; a set of insipid watercolours by his sister Dolly, a violent self portrait of his brother George ... Then the light drained from her face. Of course, she should have known. Smiling at her from the shadows, the pale lovely face of Elizabeth.

She sat down abruptly, knocking a pile of books onto the floor. At first she felt sick, only that, a vile bitterness rising up into her mouth. Then anger, slow, insidious, feeling its way cautiously through her mind. And not just the anger of the moment, but the anger of months, years ... He had lied. He had lied. He had said that he had given it to George. And all the time she'd been here. Hidden, gloated over, worshipped like some perfect saint. She had never been so angry, so overcome with rage. She felt humiliated, betrayed and she began to tremble, her hands shaking as if with palsy. Staggering a little, she got to her feet. She snatched the effigy from the pedestal and for a moment stood with it held in her hands. Then she crossed to the fire and flung it with all her strength into the heart of the flames. She watched it burn. Yellow hair, yellow flame, blistering and blackening, the smiling lips parting to emit a hissing scream. She knelt by the hearth, snatching up a poker to thrust the head deeper into the coals. Heat seared her hands and face — and so intent was she on her murderous task that she neither heard the outer door open, nor his quiet foot-steps crossing the room.

She looked up eventually, aware, with the draining away of her rage, of his presence. He stood in the doorway watching her. He did not speak. He just looked at her and in that look she saw the death of hope and the end of dreams. Then, still

222

without speaking, he turned and walked away. She sat quite still, staring after him, her stricken gaze following him beyond the limits of the room; along the passage, down the stairs and out of the door that only minutes ago he had entered. A dreadful coldness assailed her, a black despair as frightening as death. She sat for a long time, unmoving, till the light was gone, till Elizabeth was only charred and crumbling ash — and the tears ran slowly and silently down her face.

February 21st, 1891
— Longhirst Hall, Northumberland

It was uncommonly cold, even for February, and despite numerous fireplaces stacked high with coal, the rooms at Longhirst Hall remained perpetually chill. Marguerite lifted the lid of a silver warming dish and spooned a little kedgeree onto her plate. She was fond of kedgeree, of all spicy food. They reminded her of her father and their days in India. Yet she ate sparingly and after only a few mouthfuls laid her fork down. Then she said, pitching her voice down the length of the table to where her husband sat. 'I thought I might go up to town a few days early. The day after tomorrow perhaps.'

James glanced up from his newspaper. 'Yes. Why don't you, my dear? London always seems to suit you better.'

Marguerite scraped a film of butter onto a small triangle of toast. 'When may I expect you, then?'

'I'll try to get down before the end of the week. I'm reluctant to leave while this dispute at the Londonderry collieries drags on.'

'Try not to get too involved,' Marguerite said, frowning. 'The Rochester girl's wedding is this coming Saturday. We are duty bound to attend.'

'Yes, of course.'

He immersed himself in his newspaper again and she inwardly winced at the indifference in his manner. Since that shameful episode five years ago, their life together had dwindled down to these cold impersonal exchanges; her impassive questions, his brief, sometimes monosyllabic replies. They still quarrelled occasionally; sporadic little outbreaks of malicious bickering; hot wounding words followed by long cold silences, in the end, more wounding still. And yet strangely, their antagonism bound them just as surely as love. They lived for each other's pain, continuing to inflict their subtle cruelties upon each other, to exact payment for the disappointment of their lives. It was emotion of a sort, and for Marguerite, it was better than nothing. She glanced at him covertly. Physically at least, he did not seem to change. His hair was greyer perhaps and thinning at the temples. But the strong aesthetic face was virtually unlined and what lines there were, were of cynicism and amusement. She often wondered what it was that amused him, what pleasure he could still find in their sterile and empty life. She often wondered why she continued to love him. For her at least, there were compensations, of course. She had her children; her sons Sydney and Drever, her four year old daughter, Marguerite. And she had position and status, wealth and prestige and sometimes she was able to convince herself that these things were enough. Only in one thing did she continue to pursue him although even in this he frustrated and baulked her. He could have achieved so much. He had men like Gladstone and Rosebery eating out of his hand. They appreciated his blunt approach, his real concern, his insistence on remaining a lowly back bencher. My God! When she thought of the opportunities he had failed to grasp, opportunities that she had worked and schemed to create . . .

She looked at him directly, schooling her features to an expression of unconcern. 'Will you be at home for luncheon?'

'No.' His voice assumed a faint irritation. 'I thought I'd already mentioned I was lunching with Richard Lamb.'

'Well, perhaps you did.' She rose from the table. 'I'll see you before dinner, then? You haven't forgotten we have guests?'

'No. I hadn't forgotten. I don't expect to be late.'

She went out into the hall and mounted the three flights of stairs to the nursery. She stood for a few moments outside the schoolroom door. There was a little glass panel through which she could watch them unobserved. She smiled to see Sydney, his fair head bent close to the page, his tongue curling over his lip in fierce concentration. He was a clever and precocious child, advanced well beyond his seven years. Drever, her second son, was a little less so, a stolid, rather unimaginative child but with a shy and engaging personality. Then reluctantly, a little resentfully, her eyes dwelt upon James' elder sons; Hugh at ten, already darkly handsome, savaging the end of his pencil with strong white teeth. And Arthur. She moved her position so that she could see his face, and as if he sensed her presence, he lifted his head and stared at her. She looked away before their eyes should meet. Even after all these years he could still make her feel like an outsider.

She entered the room. The governess, Miss Peak, rose to greet her; a thin fussy woman who schooled the boys in Art and English as well as having charge of their little sister. The boys also had a tutor, Mr Griffiths, who came in daily the three miles from Morpeth.

'Good morning, Miss Peak,' she said in the brisk, condescending voice she used to the servants. 'I see your pupils are working hard this morning.'

'Oh yes, indeed. They are always most industrious. We have already completed today a charcoal study of a lapwing. Master Arthur, especially, has made the most delightful sketch ...'

Marguerite barely glanced at the proffered drawing, looking instantly for Sydney's effort. She repressed a smile, for the lapwing bore a strong resemblance to Miss Peak. With humorous malice he had quite cruelly caricatured her long sharp nose and small beady eyes. Even the bird's ruffled feathers were reminiscent of the woman's drab but fussy gown. She frowned a little as she came upon Drever's attempt; solid, unimaginative, the paper scored right through in a dozen places where he had pressed so heavily with his pencil. Hugh had made no effort at all. The drawing was no more than a token gesture, boredom and restlessness showed in every scribbled line. She glanced across to where he sat, taking advantage of this welcome diversion to fire ink pellets at the back of Sydney's neck. And Arthur was smiling, that quiet secret smile that so enraged her. Her own mouth drew down into a sullen line. It was time they thought about schools for those boys.

She spoke about it to James that night. There was always a half hour to spare between dressing and dinner and it was usually at this time she approached him on matters concerning the children or the house. She glanced at him first to gauge his mood. He stood by the long windows staring out over the lawns and she was instantly warned by the rigid stillness of his face, the hard cynical set of his mouth. She decided she would not come too quickly to the point and made an attempt at pleasantries. 'How was your luncheon with Dick Lamb today?'

'Oh!' He shrugged. 'Much as usual, you know.' His voice was flat and dispirited and heavy with lassitude. He had been thinking, without relish, of the weeks ahead: the return to London, which he had grown to dislike; the resumption of Parliament, the endless meetings and committees and late night sittings — but never anything actually done, never anything achieved. And this coming session, he thought, would be the final disillusionment. Six years of wrangling and bitter debate to get the amendment to the Employers' Liability Bill through the Commons and now it seemed almost certain that the Lords would throw it out. Bitterness deepened the lines around his mouth. The real power remained firmly in the hands of just a very few men; men like Durham and Londonderry, smug little lordlings, secure in their wealth and years of privilege, blind, arrogant, stupid men, who couldn't see that they plotted their own destruction.

He moved away from the window, suddenly cold. His eyes moved broodingly round the vast palatial room with its elaborate gilded ceiling and silk hung walls. In spite of the deep chairs, the cushioned sofas, the room offered him no invitation to rest. It was a room to be admired, to show off to one's guests. He never thought of it a room to be lived in. And sometimes he couldn't help but feel the hypocrisy of it all: this house, this grandeur, this extravagant way of life — and every day a step nearer to the men he pretended to despise.

Marguerite waited till she thought she was comfortably settled. She noticed now that he never sat beside her. He seemed to pick always the most distant chair so that she needed to raise her voice. 'You know, James,' she said suddenly, as if the thought had just occurred, 'Isn't it time we thought about schools for Arthur and Hugh? They're getting much to old to be taught at home. There are dozens of good preparatory schools in the county. And then Harrow perhaps. Lord Byron went to Harrow, you know, and the Churchills send their boy Winston there ...' She looked up at James. 'Are you listening?'

'Yes of course. I was just thinking that perhaps they are still a little young ...'

'Not at all,' Marguerite rejoined briskly. 'Arthur will be eleven in just two months, and Hugh is ten in November. Didn't you go away to school yourself at ten?'

'I'm not sure that it would quite suit Arthur.'

'Nonsense. It would do him good. He needs bringing out of himself. You can't coddle him for ever, you know.'

He looked at her coldly. 'I do not coddle him. But one cannot help but be aware that he's a shy and sensitive boy.'

She smiled above her mounting annoyance. 'That is just the side of himself that he shows to you. In reality he can be quite spirited, quite rebellious in fact. And devious enough to take full advantage of your very obvious favouritism.'

He fixed her suddenly with his chilly eyes. 'I don't think it is I who can be accused of favouritism, Marguerite. After all, they are all *my* sons.'

They were only a small party for dinner that night; William James and Mary, John Straker and his wife, the Hodgson-Cadogans from the neighbouring estate. Marguerite sparkled with emeralds and malicious wit ... 'and so after sitting through this long and dreary play, Mr Wilde was asked his opinion of Meredith's work. He replied, "Chaos, illumined by flashes of lightning".'

Amused and genteel laughter rippled through the company. As always, in public, she was the focus of all eyes.

Then Mrs Hodgson-Cadogan said avidly, turning to William James. 'Now tell me all about the Prince of Wales. I hear, you know, that he is quite a rake; women, gambling, all the vices. One can't help feeling sorry for Alexandra, his wife, even though she is a foreigner.'

William James obliged her with a suitably debauched and knowing smile. He moved in very exalted circles now; the Prince of Wales was a frequent guest at Sunningdale Park, and on familiar enough terms to talk about him as 'Bertie'. In consequence, he exuded a delicious air of scandal, a faint aura of depraved sophistication. It was well known, even here in the north, that he rubbed shoulders with women like the 'Jersey Lily' and the infamous Daisy Warwick.

Marguerite pretended amusement and interest as William James regaled them with the gossip of the Court, the intimate details of 'Bertie's' latest affair. She glanced curiously at James. Of course, it had occurred to her that he might have a mistress. He wasn't the sort of man who would enjoy celibacy and that side of their marriage was completely dead. And yet, instinctively, she knew that he hadn't, if only for the reason that he wouldn't have been able to resist telling her so, and enjoyed every minute of the telling. It was strange, though, how she could accept the thought of physical infidelity with such equanimity, and yet the thought of Elizabeth still sent her into paroxysms of jealous rage. In a way, she could almost envy Alexandra. At least her rivals were mortal, women of flesh and blood. They would age, lose their beauty, their charm would grow stale. She didn't have to compete with a ghost.

With an effort she gave her attention to her guests. Emily Straker was asking what she thought about the latest fashions. She murmured some vague conventional reply. Suddenly she wasn't in the mood for conversation. Now and then she glanced covertly at James. She had so few opportunities to see him animated and relaxed. It came home to her then, what a sham, what a pretence, their marriage was. The sense of failure was overwhelming, having to acknowledge that she'd brought most of it on herself. It was ironic, really, that in her desperation to have all, she'd ended up with nothing. There must be a moral here somewhere, some awful cliché ... *Half a loaf was better than no bread at all.* But it hadn't been for her. She hadn't been able to settle for just half, and so she starved, emotionally and physically. And yet the hunger was still with her. Her appetite for him had never diminished. The banquet was still spread before her starving eyes. She closed them briefly, shutting out the hot and brilliantly lit room. Perhaps if he'd been a naturally cold man, incapable, in himself, of love ... But she knew that he wasn't. She knew how affectionate and tender he was with the children. She knew how he had loved Elizabeth. That was the most wounding thing, the most unforgivable thing — to know that he was capable of love, but not of loving her.

She opened her eyes, making an effort to concentrate on her guests. They were talking politics, about Charles Parnell, the

228

Irish leader, now the centre of a scandalous divorce.

'Of course, Parnell's finished in politics,' John Straker announced. 'His party appears to be going to drop him like a hot brick. The Catholics, naturally, have already disowned him ...' He looked at James. 'I'm surprised to see that you're backing him, old man. I saw your paper carried a rather strong editorial.'

'Oh yes, Mr Joicey,' added his wife. 'I thought your headline most poetic: "There is an entire nation in slavery, and they will keep it there because they have a quarrel with a single man".'

'My editor's words actually. I really can't take the credit.'

'But surely, Mr Joicey you must endorse his sentiments?'

'Yes,' said James. 'I do to a certain degree. I think Parnell's being rather badly treated. A man's morals do not necessarily effect his ability as a politician. Does it matter what he has done privately, when publicly he has devoted his entire life to the Irish people? For them to turn their backs on him now seems to me the worst kind of hypocrisy.'

William James gave a hoot of derisive laughter. 'And their pronouncement, I might say, comes from an expert on the subject.' With mild belligerence he looked at James. He was just moderately drunk, though he'd consumed a bottle and a half of Veuve Cliquot even before he'd sat down to dinner. 'I was thinking, old boy, seeing as we are talking of hypocrisy. All this ...' He swept his hand around the long sumptuously furnished room ... 'It doesn't exactly fit your image as champion of the oppressed. Isn't it going to be a bit of an embarrassment next year, when you come up again for re-election?' He grinned maliciously. 'Going to stretch the credulity of the electorate a bit, isn't it? Make all your sanctimonious claptrap about equality and social justice seem just a little bit feeble?' He turned to his fellow guests, oblivious of their uncomfortable silence. 'The trouble with James is that he can't decide whether he's a hound or a hare. He's a bit of a fraud in that respect. He's a "have" who spends his time explaining to the "have-nots" that if they're good chaps and work hard to make him an even bigger "have", then one day they might be "haves" themselves ...'

'Unless, of course,' James interrupted him smilingly, 'They are fortunate enough to manage to hitch a free ride and let somebody else do all the work.'

For a moment they stared at each other in open hostility, then William James laughed. 'Touché, *mon cousin.* I asked for that.' He turned to the silent and shocked little audience. 'My apologies. You must think us incredibly rude to bicker so openly. But I'm afraid that when James and I sit down together, it's rather a set course, coming indigestibly between the pudding and savoury.' There was a murmur of relieved and embarrassed laughter. Then John Straker said, taking a practical line, 'There seems to be rather a deadlock over this Silksworth business, James. Neither Londonderry nor the union seems willing to budge.'

James looked thoughtful. 'Yes. I must admit it seems be getting a bit out of hand. I understand Londonderry's given the order for evictions.'

'I don't really see what else he can do. We can't have men being bullied and intimidated into joining the Union ...'

'No. I agree with that. Nevertheless. I think evicting the men is a little drastic — especially as we'll soon need to ask for a reduction in wages. It can only antagonize, provoke ...'

Straker looked irritated. 'I'm sorry, James. I don't agree. Quite frankly, I think there's been too much of the soft approach.' He reached for the decanter and poured himself another generous glass of port. 'In my opinion, Londonderry's got exactly the right idea. If the beggars won't work — turn 'em out. A night or two in the cold will teach them a lesson.'

It was not quite dark; the short February day still clung to the horizon with grey, leaden fingers. The crowd stood in silence — two, three hundred men, women and children, massed at the end of the narrow colliery street. Impassively they watched the wreck of their homes; furniture and bed linen piled roughly in the street; a child's cot flung from an upstairs window; an old man carried out forcibly, still in his chair. Yet they made no move. They uttered no cry of protest. It was their silence that was so menacing; total, immense, overwhelming even the quiet snivelling of the bairns, the rough laughter of Londonderry's hired thugs — candymen, they were called; men with a natural taste for violence; bully boys and criminals, ex-army men cashiered from their regiments, prize fighters grown too old for the ring. It was the second week of the strike, the second day of the evictions. One hundred and forty families had been turned out so far. Most had gone quietly, gathering up what few possessions they could, seeking shelter in churches and schools. Others, not so lucky, burrowed for warmth into slag heaps at night or slept huddled together in doorways. For the men anyway, it wasn't too much of a hardship. When a man lay on his back in dirt and darkness for ten hours a day he was immune to bodily discomfort. Physical pain, hunger, these were all things of the body and could be suffered. But humiliation, loss of pride and dignity, these touched the spirit and could not be borne. Few of them were actually clear as to why they were on strike: some thought more money, others, more knowledgable knew it to be some wrangle between the union and the masters, something about deputies not joining the union. They didn't need to know. There wasn't any question of taking sides. If the union said they were out then they were out. It didn't really matter why.

It was fully dark now. Gas lamps filled the street with a sickly yellow light. Sounds sharpened in the darkness; the wind moaning softly through the ropes and struts of the headgear; the eternal throb of the pumps. And still they stood, silent, watchful, as the bailiffs, finished for the day, laid the chains across their doors.

At the far end of the street, the police sergeant whose task it was to oversee these affairs, shifted his feet uneasily. He didn't like this. He didn't like it at all. He should have ordered them to disperse long ago, except that it had seemed foolish to provoke them unnecessarily. He hadn't wanted a rowdy mob on his hands. Yet this was worse, this deadly murderous quiet. He beckoned to one of his men. Time to call it a day. No point, was there, in asking for trouble. He wasn't paid for heroics, only to keep the peace, to see that the evictions took place without incident. It was a filthy job at the best of times. It was the lasses and the bairns he felt sorry for.

He blew his whistle to signal their departure. The bailiffs, about twenty of them, had moved on ahead. The sergeant and his men brought up the rear, orderly ranks, four abreast. Then suddenly, at his back he heard a sigh of movement, the cracking of boots and clogs over splintered glass. The mob were advancing, slowly, unhurriedly. He saw their faces as they passed under a lamp, gleaming with hatred and murder.

Sweat pricked at his skin despite the cold. 'Keep going, lads,' he muttered. 'There's no cause to panic.' Yet it was hard to resist the urge not to break into a run, not to keep glancing over his shoulder ... He weighed up the odds. They were outnumbered two to one at least. But the mob wasn't armed. They carried no weapons except their clenched fists. He fingered the lead-weighted baton that hung at his waist, and the 'candymen' he knew, carried brass knuckles ... Then he gave a little scream of pain as a stone struck him full in the back. Another, sharp, flintlike, sliced at his cheek.

He spun round to face the mob. They had halted and seemed to be crouching, waiting to spring. He saw their eyes, glaring back at him with murderous intent.

Londonderry's agent thrust him forward. 'Pull yourself together, man. They're only scum. For God's sake give the order to charge.'

February 24th 1891
— Exchange Buildings, Newcastle

'I tell you, Mr Joicey. In thirty years as a union man, I've never heard the like.' John Wilson, Member of Parliament for Mid-Durham and the newly appointed secretary of the Durham Miners' Federation, regarded James with earnest gravity. He was obviously ill at ease, perched on the very edge of the deep leather chair, his brown Derby cradled between his hands. 'Such dreadful inhumanity,' he went on aggrievedly. 'The police turned upon the men entirely without provocation...'

James regarded his visitor with mild incredulity. 'You don't think being pelted with stones provocation?'

'No more so than being brutally turned out of house and home.' It was said without the least aggression. John Wilson was by nature a placid man, his placidity born of long endurance, from years of being hounded and persecuted for his ideals and beliefs. Every blow had hardened him, made him strong, so that now he could deal pleasantly and amicably with the men who had been his oppressors.

'You don't think, Mr Wilson,' said James, equally amiable, 'that the Federation should bear at least some part of the blame? As I understand it, the entire dispute revolved around your Executive's insistence that certain deputies at Silksworth belong to the union, whether they wished it or not. Naturally, Lord Londonderry as owner, objected to the men being coerced ...'

'Persuaded, Mr Joicey. They were not coerced.'

'Well, whatever the finer points of the method you used, you instructed the men to come out on what was essentially a trivial matter.'

'Unity is not trivial, Mr Joicey. Unity is strength.'

'Yes. I quite agree — and yet you object when coalowners themselves resort to it.'

'I object to any sort of violence, any show of force ...'

'Unless of course, the violence is meted out by your members.'

Wilson smiled but he would not be drawn. 'The dispute is settled now, Mr Joicey. I can see no profit in dragging it up. That isn't why I came here.'

James' eyes dwelt briefly on the bland, amiable face. On the surface he seemed harmless enough, and it was true, he had a reputation for being a moderate, always ready to negotiate, to compromise. And yet beneath the calm and peaceable smile, James sensed a deep and hidden resentment, a latent and suppressed desire for real power. He said at last. 'Why did you come then, Mr Wilson?'

The older man took his time in answering, choosing his words in accordance with what he knew of this man. It was said that he was a fair man, but he didn't rely on that. He was a master — and he knew all about masters. But he was also a Member of Parliament with a reputation to think about. He knew all about reputations too, and the lengths to which men would go to preserve them. 'I am here, Mr Joicey, because I am anxious to know your feelings on the Durham Coalowners' Association's latest demand for a ten per cent reduction in the men's wages. I cannot believe that you will sanction this, knowing your supposedly Radical views — and also bearing in mind the fact that next year you will be seeking the votes of these

233

very same men.'

'Mr Wilson,' James spoke patiently and slowly. He'd experienced this conversation many times before though not on such a personal level. To James, haggling over pay was like haggling over anything else. The owners put in for a hefty reduction, the unions countered with demands for a massive rise and usually they settled somewhere in between. 'Only last year the men were awarded an increase of five per cent, on the understanding that the price of coal was likely to rise. Unfortunately it did not. In fact it's dropped by five per cent. A reduction of ten per cent would therefore only restore the status quo.'

'That isn't any justification to men who can barely feed their families as it is.'

'Yet they can always afford to pay the union dues.' He was being harsh, he knew, yet it seemed important to draw this man out.

Wilson smiled his passive smile. 'If I cannot appeal to your better nature, Mr Joicey, perhaps I can appeal to your common sense. The men will not accept ten per cent. In fact they have already been balloted regarding acceptance and out of a membership of some fifty-four thousand, three quarters have voted overwhelmingly to strike.' He looked at James. 'You know the mood of the men. Silksworth will have told you that. If the owners insist on pressing for ten per cent then every pit in Durham will be stopped — including yours.'

'Are you threatening me, Mr Wilson?' James enquired amiably.

'No. I'm asking you to be reasonable, to use your influence with your Association to get the amount reduced.'

'I don't know why you think I have any influence. I am merely a member of my Association as the deputies at Silksworth are now members of yours, out of necessity rather than preference. Unity, you know, is not solely a union prerogative — and the same rules apply. What you are asking me to do is ... "blackleg", I think is the term. It's a question of loyalty, you know.'

For a moment they stared at each other in mute antagonism. Then Wilson said. 'You don't think you have a loyalty to the men who sent you to Parliament? You don't feel that you should try to protect their livelihood?'

'Yes, I would feel that, if the owners were demanding more than their due, if they were breaking the terms of any agreement.'

Wilson was silent, seemingly lost in contemplation of the dome of his hat. He wondered how much he could tell this man without giving ground. Desperately he wanted to avert this strike. Strikes cost money — union money. The funds that it had taken years to amass could be dissipated in as many weeks. It took a thousand pounds just to give every man fourpence. He didn't despise wealth as so many of his kind did. Money he knew was the key, the source of all power. It was money that made the masters impregnable. He said, carefully, 'The Federation — the Executive — we don't want this strike.'

'Then why do you not prevent it? You only have to agree to the reduction.'

Wilson raised his large hands in a helpless gesture. 'I wish it was as simple as that. Unfortunately, the men, the membership, will not grant the Executive the power to settle.' For a moment anger darkened his eyes. It had been a bitter blow; to be rejected, suspected, to be reduced to the status of messenger boy, by the very men to whom he had devoted his life. He knew the culprits, a handful of hotheads and troublemakers, men burning with hatred and reforming zeal. He had heard them speak, never of peace and conciliation, but of revenge and violence, anarchy and strikes. He despised that kind of man; for their lack of vision, their lack of real purpose, their lack of deep and utter commitment. Their passions were violent, but they had no real depth. They thought to conquer injustice with kicks and blows. They couldn't see beyond the moment, all had to be here and now. They couldn't see ahead to the greater glory — a massive army of workers, welded together in strength and unity, a single brotherhood bound by peace and justice and equality. This was the dream that had sustained him all his life, that transcended all hardship and suffering. He didn't approve of strikes. They were a last resort, when all else had failed, when every possible avenue had been explored. He knew from bitter experience the futility of strikes. After the first glorious heady euphoria of rebellion came the gradual dwindling of resources and eventually of hope; the harsh reality of empty pockets, the even harsher reality that they could not win. And then the final despair; crawling back, beaten and humiliated ...

He glanced up suddenly, aware of James Joicey's eyes upon him, hard, uncompromising, merciless eyes — and yet ... He tried again. 'If the men do come out, they'll stay out until the bitter end. It won't then be a dispute just about pay. It'll be about pride and dignity and honour. These men are on the bottom. There's no lower to go. They know these are bad times but they want some gesture, some sign from the employers that their plight is recognized and understood. They can not, they will not accept ten per cent.'

James was silent for a moment then slowly he said, 'What will they accept then, Mr Wilson?'

'Five per cent. Seven at a push.'

James nodded. 'Very well then, Mr. Wilson. I'll see what I can do.'

April 12th, 1892
— Cadogan Square, London

James listened, half listened, to his wife's low and still sensual voice. She was speaking to Sydney, for she would never have addressed him in such a tender voice. Her voice when she spoke to him was quite different; dry, emotionless, as his own was when he needed to make a reply. Between them they had perfected the art of arid conversation, of speaking and saying nothing. It was almost like a dialect of their own, a way of speaking peculiar to themselves with all the phrases and sentences devoid of inflexion, all ambiguous and emotive words edited out. He often thought of their marriage as a rather long and boring game of chess where all the moves were defensive, both players reluctant to sacrifice even a pawn. Or a stalemate. That perhaps was a better analogy; all the moves made with equal loss and just the two of them left upon the board.

He picked up the evening edition of *The Times*. The eight-week long strike still dominated the headlines. His mouth tightened. Eight weeks of wrangling, of demand and counter demand, of acrid and furious confrontation. He'd kept his word to Wilson. During the year-long negotiations that had preceded the strike he had, harrassed, nagged, pleaded with both Federation and owners to come to a settlement. Nothing had worked. In March, at the end of their tether, the men had handed in their notices. And still there was no agreement. After two months both sides were still deadlocked, the owners hanging out grimly for the full ten per cent, the union as solidly entrenched to resist. It had seemed that they must just sit the thing out; crumbling faces and flooded seams versus hunger and want. His own collieries had suffered. They were kept going with less than twenty per cent of the usual workforce: Irish mostly, imported labour, just enough men to keep the workings from irrepairable damage. Even so they'd lost two entire faces at Beamish, and at Tanfield Bute the water was rising dangerously in Seventh Pillar Flats. But he'd been hopeful of a settlement during the past week. Attitudes had softened, at least on the part of the men. They'd asked for talks, a sure sign of weakening which the owners had ruthlessly exploited by upping the demand for a reduction to thirteen and a half per cent. He thought again of the wire he'd received that morning from his agent, Ramsay. 'Situation getting desperate. I beg you to make time to come north without delay.'

He glanced up, smiling. Sydney was bidding him goodnight. And Marguerite was speaking, her musical voice dropped to its usual passionless key. He thought about E Flat. 'I'm sorry,' he said 'I didn't catch what you were saying.'

'I was saying that we'd been invited to the Asquiths for the weekend.'

'I'm afraid I shan't be able to go. I have to go north.'

He saw her frown, the nearest she ever came to expressing annoyance. 'Is it necessary?' she enquired. 'Surely you've done and said all that you can. With or without you, the strike will go on. What on earth do you think you can do?'

'Probably nothing. But I have to try.'

'James. Please.' It was the first time for years he'd heard concern in her voice. 'Don't let yourself get caught up in this thing. Let them fight it out alone. With an election less than three months away it would be madness to get involved.'

Well, of course, she would be concerned at the thought of him blotting his political copy book. He threw her a scornful look. 'For God's sake! How can I not be involved, with nine collieries idle?'

'There is no need for you to draw attention to yourself. This isn't the time for heroics. You've already caused enough of a stir with those damning articles you ran in the *Leader*. Can't you see that it's pointless to antagonize, on any front? Whatever you do, you won't come out of it well. Your fellow coalowners will see your interference as some sort of a betrayal. And at the end of the day, it won't matter to the union whether you behaved well or not. You'll still be just another employer.'

'Yes,' agreed James. 'I know all that. Nevertheless, I must go.'

Ramsay met him at the station and had a closed carriage waiting, though the Coal Trade Offices in Westgate Street were only a stone's throw away. 'I thought it a sensible precaution to take,' Ramsay explained as he ushered James inside. 'Strikers are on the rampage all over the town. Londonderry is talking of calling in the Military.' Ramsay's heavy ponderous face looked grim. 'There's a heavy turn out today; men from pits all over the county. They're trying to prevent the masters attending the meeting. Londonderry has been turned back and Joseph Pease had his carriage pelted with mud.' He looked at James. 'I'm not sure, you know, sir, that you'd be wise to attempt it.'

'Mr Ramsay,' said James heavily. 'I have not come three hundred and fifty miles only to turn tail again.' He banged his cane on the roof of the carriage. 'Drive on.'

On Ramsay's advice they took the more circuitous route, via Clayton Street and Pink Lane, past the elegant frontage of the Assembly Rooms. There were men on every corner; grey faces beneath shabby, greasy caps, hands thrust deep into trouser pockets, collars turned up against the wind. They stood huddled together as if for protection. He thought — like sick cattle awaiting the slaughterer.

They turned into Westgate Street. James caught his breath as he saw the seething, struggling crowd massed outside the Coal Trade Offices. They drew up outside, and at the sight of the carriage the crowd let out a maddened shout. They surged forward; famished, rabid faces pressing against the glass. The horses reared, screaming in panic. Two men went down and stayed down, bludgeoned by the iron shod hooves.

'Christ!' Ramsay swore as the carriage began to rock under the pounding weight of the crowd. He tried to open the door but the pressure of the surging bodies held it shut. 'My God,' he said. 'They're going to turn us over.'

Then James brought the head of his stick down on the window. The shower of flying glass sent the front ranks reeling back. James flung open the door and at the sight of his face the crowd quietened and fell back a little to give him room.

Without haste, James descended from the carriage, incongruous among the poorly clad men in his immaculate broadcloth and silk top hat. He surveyed them expressionlessly though the hair rose on the back of his neck. He saw their faces; unknown, unrecognizable faces with their open expression of savage hatred. For the first time in his life he felt threatened and intimidated. He had seen hatred before, but not this blind unreasoning hatred that would never judge him on his merits or take account of anything but who and what he was, an employer, a coalowner, and therefore the enemy to be defeated.

He addressed them coldly. 'What are you doing here? What do you want?'

A voice came from the back of the crowd. 'We want to eat, maister, nowt more than that.'

'Then get back to work,' shouted Ramsay impulsively.

The crowd roared and swayed dangerously toward them. There was a twisting sensation beneath James' ribs which he refused to acknowledge as fear. Then a man thrust his way through the crowd. He was young, with famished cheeks and fanatical eyes. 'Oh aye. We all know that's what ye bastards are wantin'. And ye'd hev us grateful that ye're only takin' the thirteen per cent. Di ye think we can feed wa'selves on that? At least if we starve now it'll be our own choice. We'll not have it forced upon us.' He thrust his face close. 'Di ye knaa me, maister? Well, ye bloody well should di. Aa've warked for ye for fifteen year and nowt but an empty belly to show for it.'

James regarded him calmly. 'And do you think this riot, this demonstration is going to put food in your mouths? Do you not want a settlement? How are you helping yourselves by preventing the owners from meeting?'

'It's the bloody masters who divvn't want to settle.' Another voice came from out of the crowd. 'That's what ye buggers are here for, ti see how much more ye can take off us.'

'That isn't why I am here,' shouted James. 'I am here to plead reason, to prevent if I can, the further destruction of both your living and mine. If any of us are to survive in the long term there must be a settlement — but a fair settlement. Ten per cent is a fair settlement and that is what I have come here to say. But I can say nothing unless you let me pass. I can do nothing out here in the street.' He watched their faces, saw their changing expressions of optimism and mistrust. Then slowly, grudgingly they fell back and let him through. Grim faced, he walked between them and up the steps into the Coal Trade Offices.

He was late and the meeting had already begun. He saw that there were less than thirty actual coalowners present. Many had been intimidated by the crowds outside and had sent agents and managers to vote by proxy. Durham was there though, also the Priestman brothers and Lindsay Wood.

He sat down at the back of the room. Durham had already begun his speech. 'There has been much said regarding the decision to increase the amount of the reduction by a further three and a half per cent. Why, I am constantly asked, have we done so. Surely, gentlemen, I don't need to explain. We all know the terrible losses this strike has entailed on the owners. Are we not entitled to some restitution?'

James listened intently, making the odd note. Now and then he raised his head and his eyes would stray to Jack Lambton's face. In ten years his aversion for this man had not diminished. He still offended his pride, his sense of achievement, he still aroused in him that old bitter fury.

'Gentlemen, we are within a hair's breadth of victory. The men's resources are gone. The union's funds are exhausted. All we have to do is wait.'

The earl sat down to loud applause.

At the same instant, James rose to his feet. The sight of him brought immediate silence. 'May I enquire of his lordship, on

240

whose authority the demand was raised to thirteen and a half per cent? I myself was certainly not consulted and I know of others who were not.'

It was Lindsay Wood as President who answered him. 'It was the Committee's decision. There was not time to consult every individual member.'

'Then may I suggest that the Committee makes time, Mr President. Even the union allows their members the privilege of a vote.'

There was silence, an exchange of glances, then Durham's pale eyes swivelled toward him. 'Do I take it, Mr Joicey,' he enquired stonily, 'that you are against this further demand?'

'Yes, you may take it that I am, my lord. If we persist in demanding more than we know the men can or will concede, then we have only ourselves to blame for the continuance of the strike and any resultant losses. Both the men and the union are agreed to settle on the ten per cent which was our original demand. That should be enough of a victory, if it is victory you want.'

Durham regarded him down the length of his prominent nose. 'It isn't so much a question of winning, Mr Joicey, as of not being seen to lose. We have made our stand on thirteen and a half per cent. I can see no reason why we should think of backing down, in fact I can think of a dozen why we should not. The union is climbing down. Once they would not have countenanced seven per cent, now they are ready to concede ten. To make voluntary concessions now can only be seen as weakness.'

'To compromise is not necessarily to concede, my lord.'

'You think not? Then our interpretation of the word obviously differs. To me it means surrender which I shall never do. I will not be dictated to by ignorant riff-raff.'

Jame's eyes hardened but he did not reply. He turned instead to his fellow members. 'Gentlemen, I ask you to think carefully before you give your consent to what is already being hailed as a cruel and unjust demand. You are being led to believe that the men will capitulate. I can tell you that they will not.'

He was interrupted by Durham's thin nasal voice. 'One wonders if Mr Joicey has some private arrangement with the men, that he knows so well what they will or will not do.'

James waited till the ripple of laughter had died away. 'My lord, gentlemen, I am a busy man, as I assumed all of you were also. I did not realize that I was coming here to listen to the views of a single man and to witness so gross an exhibition of bigotry and prejudice as would put any decent man to shame. As I see it, gentlemen, if the view of Lord Durham is always to prevail then we are heading for industrial chaos.' He moved into the room so that he could be heard. 'I heard his lordship say confidently that we have weathered strikes before. He may weather them, but there are dozens of colliery owners who will not; the small men, the owners of single pits with minimal resources for whom a long strike can mean financial disaster. Of course, his lordship may see that as also in his interests. When small men go under it means less competition, more men thrown onto an already glutted labour market who will work for a pittance rather than not work at all. These are the attitudes with which our grandfathers would have been familiar. Every man for himself. The survival of the fittest. But perhaps his lordship has not yet realized that the days when employers believed they had a divine right to brutalize and exploit their workers, are well and truly over. Those days are gone, as are the days when anything black could be sold for coal. There was a time when Great Britain raised two thirds of the world's coal instead of the third that we are producing now. There was a time when the Durham Miners' Federation consisted of a handful of fanatics meeting in a derelict shed instead of the fifty-five thousand membership they have now.' He paused and his eyes rested for a moment on Durham's furious face. 'And there was also a time when the grandson of a pitman and the grandson of Radical Jack would never have even stood in the same room together.' He regarded his audience with open amusement. 'As you can see, gentlemen, times have changed.'

He left to thunderous and good humoured applause, leaving Ramsay behind to cast his vote. He went downstairs and into the smoking room to await the result. Despite the good humour with which his speech had been received he wasn't at all confident of victory. He didn't underestimate Durham's influence. He was known for a powerful man and vindictive man.

He looked up as Dick Lamb came into the room.

'I'm afraid it went against you, old man, though only by two votes.'

James swore softly. 'A defeat is a defeat, Dick,' he remarked acidly, 'Whether by two votes or two hundred.'

'Yes, I know. I thought for a minute you'd swung things, you know. But then Durham gave them the thumbs down.' He beckoned to the steward and ordered two brandies. 'Not that I blame him. You were a little bit rough on him, you know.'

'I meant to be. It's Durham who's keeping this damn strike going and entirely from motives of personal greed.'

'Actually, that's not quite true. You must have heard that Lambton's are in a bit of a hole financially?'

'I hear a great many things,' said James evasively, 'but I don't necessarily always believe them to be true.'

'Well, you can believe this, James. I have it from a very reliable source that the Lambton Collieries are on the verge of bankruptcy.'

James raised his eyebrows in an expression of disbelief. And it was unbelievable, that this once flourishing concern could have become a liability, that the massive profits that were the main source of the Lambton's wealth could suddenly have dried up.

'Oh come on, James. It's a common enough occurrence. One generation makes it, the next breaks it. The Lambtons have always believed that the company could run itself. They've always seen themselves as no more than figureheads. But decisions still have to be taken, choices made.' Lamb shrugged. 'Obviously they've been the wrong decisions, the wrong choices. For one thing their investment over the last ten years have been practically nil. They've never put any of the profit back. And of course they've only ever worked the thick and easy seams. Now that they're faced with deeper winnings they haven't got the modern equipment needed for thin seams or the capital with which to buy it. Add that to a ten year depression in the trade ... In fact, I have it from an impeccable source that these past three years they've made a thundering loss.'

'And may I enquire who this impeccable source is?'

Lamb grinned. 'Ted Martin; Lambton's head viewer. His

243

wife is my wife's cousin.' He emptied his glass. 'Actually, I can't help feeling a twinge of sympathy for Durham. It'll be a bitter blow to him if he's forced to sell. The collieries have been in his family for generations.' He emptied his glass. 'Another brandy, James?'

'No. Thank you, Dick, but I have to go. I'm due back in the House for a vote tonight.'

Humming faintly under his breath he made his way out into the hall. Then he paused. Coming toward him was the Earl of Durham. They stared at each other in silence for a moment, then Lambton said, 'I think you ought to know, Mr Joicey, that your remarks today will not be forgotten. As I'm sure you are aware, I am not without influence, in both political and business circles, and as the largest colliery owner in the whole of the north east . . .'

James interrupted him. 'At the moment, my lord,' he said quietly. 'But that may not always be so.'

September 9th, 1891
— London

Settled comfortably with a brandy in a private room at the Reform Club, James eyed his host speculatively: Sir Edward Grey, Liberal member for Berwick and parliamentary under-secretary. He couldn't help wondering why he was here. He and Sir Edward were colleagues, associates, but he had never thought of them as friends. In his book, invitations to dine with members of the cabinet meant that somebody was looking for a favour.

They made desultory conversation, about unemployment in the coal trade, the recently ended strike. That had dragged on till the end of June, till pressure from the government forced the owners to capitulate and settle for ten per cent. It was a hollow victory for the men. Collieries were closed, hundreds of men laid off in the face of collapsed and flooded workings. Castle Eden and Hutton Henry were completely abandoned. In all a total of thirteen pits that would never work again.

They turned to politics. James had won the July election by

the skin of his teeth. Thankfully, his only opponent was a Tory, and though much was made of the three month strike, the majority obviously favoured a Liberal devil they knew, than a Tory one they did not. More important, it had been a complete Liberal victory. Gladstone was Prime Minister for the fourth time.

'And the last, I think,' Sir Edward said regretfully. 'The Grand Old Man isn't so grand any more. He's getting on you know. Eighty-three this year. I don't think he'd have taken on another term at all if it hadn't been for this wretched Irish bill.'

James nodded in silent agreement. The issue of Home Rule overshadowed everything these days. It hung round the neck of the Liberals like an albatross. It had split the party, turned friends into enemies, enemies into friends. Twice it had lost them an election and it had soured the last years of Gladstone's brilliant career, keeping him hanging on long past his time. He was determined this time that he would see it through. In February the bill had passed its second reading in the Commons and hopes were high for a smooth passage the third time out.

Then Sir Edward returned to the subject of the recent election, saying that he wished they'd had a stronger majority. He looked at James. 'I understand you had something of a rough ride this time out. Didn't I hear that the Earl of Durham and some of your fellow coalowners mounted some sort of campaign to discredit you?'

'They tried to.' James dismissed Lambton's vicious attempt to destroy him politically with a thin and bitter smile. He'd survived, but only just. Perhaps he wouldn't next time. And there would be a next time. Jack Lambton didn't give up easily. He added with wry humour. 'As a matter of fact, I think it all rather worked in my favour. The electorate took the view that any enemy of Lord Durham's must be a friend of theirs.'

Grey smiled. 'Nevertheless, Lord Durham is a powerful enemy to make. I've always believed that a man should choose his enemies with the same care that he chooses his friends — and as sparingly. I don't have to tell you how important it is to achieve some stability in your industry. The coal trade is the hub of our industrial wheel, a prime target for agitators. The last thing the Prime Minister will want is a feud between employers.'

245

James answered him bluntly. 'I'm afraid you'll never have stability in the coal industry or any other whilst men like Durham and Londonderry are in control. Bad masters are the real agitators; skimping on safety, treating their workers like slaves. They run their collieries inefficiently, with obsolete and out of date equipment. They house their men in squalid, insanitary hovels and pay them the minimum wage for the maximum hours. Then they whine that they can make no investment because they are making no profits, and yet if they are making no profits why do they remain in the trade?'

Sir Edward nodded, eyeing his guest thoughtfully. He couldn't say he knew him well though he'd dined out in his company on many occasions. But then James Joicey wasn't the sort of man you ever got to know well. On the surface, he seemed a tame politician. He was loyal, predictable, obedient to party doctrine; a Home Ruler, a Free Trader; anti-Imperialist, and all that. It was easy to underestimate him though, to miss that air of quiet ruthlessness, the remorselessness beneath his easy manner.

Then he said, aware that he had been silent for some time, 'The reason I wanted to speak with you privately — one of the reasons — the Prime Minister is concerned by this rumour of further strikes. He's heard that the unions are pressing for a national stoppage. How much is truth, James? And how much is put out as propaganda by the union?'

'That depends on whom and what you mean by union. At the moment they're all mostly separate and individual organizations, all with different rules and regulations. A year or so ago, the Midlands and Yorkshire amalgamated to form the Miners' Federation of Great Britain. It's the M.F.G.B. who are attempting to pursuade the smaller county organizations to strike. I'm not convinced they will succeed. Unemployment is high. Men think twice about giving in their notices now. All I can say with any certainty is that neither Northumberland nor Durham will answer the call.'

'You are sure? You know this for a fact?'

James nodded. 'Durham has already been approached by the M.F.G.B. and have refused to come out. The county has just weathered the most crippling three month strike. The resources of both men and union are nil, and the men are

246

canny enough to know that if every other pit in the country is on strike then every Durham pit will need to be in full production. And shortage of coal elsewhere will push up the price per ton. Their pay could double overnight.' James smiled. 'When it comes to making a profit, I've never found there's much difference between the men and the masters. Few men labour for the love of it.'

Sir Edward looked at him askance. 'Isn't that a rather cynical point of view?'

'I'm afraid I am a cynic as far as money is concerned. I've never been able to underestimate it, to think of it as some vulgar and debased commodity. Man is by nature a competitive and predatory animal. He is born greedy and ambitious and no amount of refinement can ever breed these things out. It is just a question of degree; how little a man wants as opposed to how much. That's where men like Durham make their mistake. They never think of the working man as wanting to be any more than he is. They believe it's enough for him merely to exist.'

'That sounds almost like a Socialist belief to me.'

'No,' argued James. 'The Socialists' concept is purely idealistic — that all men are born equal and must remain equal. I am not an idealist. I believe all men are born equal but that there is no necessity for them to remain so. Isn't that what the Liberal party is all about? That no matter what a man's birth, no door is closed against him?'

'Well, yes — at least, that's the way it's supposed to work in theory. I'm not sure that it always does in practice. Some men are inclined to shy away from advancement because they see it as some sort of betrayal.' James smiled. 'I presume that remark is directed at me?'

Sir Edward inclined his head. 'Well, one wonders. Politically speaking, you could have done more for yourself than you have. I must assume that you haven't out of choice.'

'Yes, I suppose that's true.' James shrugged. 'I've always found that the higher one climbs in politics, the harder it becomes to look down. Primarily, I am a coalowner. Politics only interest me insofar as it concerns the trade. Frankly, I can get a clearer view from grass roots level. I've always preferred to keep my feet on the ground.'

Grey inclined his head. 'I'm afraid that makes what I am about to say almost inappropriate.' He smiled. 'The main reason I asked you here tonight was to tell you that the Prime Minister has put your name before the Queen, recommending that you be created a baronet.'

He watched James closely, but none of the expected gratification showed upon his face. The slight widening of his eyes betrayed his surprise but otherwise he looked merely amused. Then James said slowly, 'You don't think that might prove to be something of an embarrassment in my present constituency?'

'I don't see why it should. In fact I would think it a magnificent advertisement for the principles of Liberalism.'

'Nevertheless, I can't help feeling it would be a little dishonest. I've spent a great deal of my life speaking out against rank and privilege ...'

'Against the abuse of rank and privilege. It's not the same thing, you know.'

James nodded. He was silent for a moment and then enquired with mild sarcasm. 'Without seeming ungrateful, Sir Edward — may I ask the reason why I have been chosen for such an honour?'

Grey's pale eyes flickered. 'The Prime Minister obviously feels that some recognition is due for the services you've rendered both to the coal industry and the party.'

'That could apply to dozens of men. Why particularly me?'

Grey looked mildly irritated. 'My dear fellow. Are you always so suspicious?'

'Always.' James smiled. 'There's no such thing as a free gift.'

'It isn't free in that sense. It's a reward, if you like. It's a means of expressing the party's gratitude for all you have done for the Liberal cause. We're all aware that you're running the *Leader* at a loss, that you've kept it going purely in the interests of the party ...'

'As I'm sure you must be also aware that I'm seriously considering closing it down.'

Sir Edward looked grave. 'It would be a severe loss to the Liberal cause if you did, James.'

'But not so great a loss that any would think of putting their hands in their pockets.'

'There are other rewards besides money, James.'

'So it would appear. Though you might tell the Prime Minister that it wasn't necessary. He had only to say the word and I would have kept the *Leader* going as long as he'd wished ...'

'He already knows that, James. That's the reason he wants you to have this honour. It wasn't ever meant as a bribe.'

'Wasn't it, Sir Edward?' James looked sceptical. 'I wonder.'

He was impatient to tell her, to see the look of surprise and elation light up her face. It was a revelation, as if he had touched some hidden spring, immediately and vibrantly she came to life. 'Oh, James. I'm so glad. This is wonderful news.'

He eyed her mockingly. Already she was making plans, issuing invitations to balls and soirees — 'Sir James and Lady Joicey request the pleasure of your company ... 'I haven't accepted yet,' he reminded her.

'But you're going to?' She still smiled but a note of anxiety had crept into her voice.

'I'm not sure,' he said slowly and saw the brightness drain from her face.

'But you must.' He could see she was really worried now. 'It's a great honour, a marvellous tribute. It's recognition for everything you've done, everything you've worked for.'

'Everything you've worked for, you mean. You're the one who's always so enamoured of status.'

Her face became still, settled back into its stiff, haughty lines. 'I can't believe you're serious,' she said coldly.

He rose and went to stand by the window. With his back to her he said, 'Yes, I'm quite serious. It isn't quite as simple as all that.' He turned to face her. 'Can't you see how the whole thing would smack of hypocrisy? For years I've given out to the constituency that I don't approve of titles. I'm the loudest voice when it comes to speaking out against the power of the Lords.'

'Is that what concerns you? The opinion of a few ignorant and illiterate men?'

James stared at her coldly. 'I might remind you that those ignorant, illiterate men help to put the clothes on your back.'

'Oh, you don't have to remind me where your money comes from, James — where you come from. We're none of us ever allowed to forget.'

'I don't particularly want to forget. It's not something I'm ashamed of.'

'No, you're not ashamed of it but you're afraid to leave it behind. You're afraid to go forward, to take a step up.'

He laughed, that harsh brittle laugh that told her he was furious. 'You're talking nonsense, my dear,' he said to her amiably. 'You know perfectly well what I believe ...'

'I know what you think you believe, what you think you ought to believe.' She looked at him scornfully. 'I know you, James. You want to be persuaded, to be able to say that you accepted because of me. Don't think I don't know how you use me as a scapegoat; Longhirst, this house, the servants, the carriages. You pretend to yourself that they are all for me. But nothing is for me. Nothing is ever for me.' She glared at him with cold fury. 'You're a selfish man, James. I've always known that. Selfish and cruel and thoughtless. But I never thought you were a fool. I never thought you'd turn your back on something you want, purely in order to spite me.'

He laughed softly. 'I think you overestimate your influence in my life, Marguerite. Quite frankly, your wishes don't enter into this at all.'

'Then why bother telling me?' she shouted furiously. 'Why bother mentioning it at all, unless you take some perverse pleasure in seeing my disappointment.'

'My dear Marguerite, it's years since anything you felt or did gave me any pleasure,' he said cruelly. 'I'm just surprised, that's all, that something so superficial as a title could be important to you. But then I suppose that's all you've ever wanted really. I suppose that's why you married me, for rank, status, all the things you couldn't achieve by yourself?'

'Yes, James,' she said bitterly. 'That's exactly why I married you. If you remember, that was all you ever offered me.'

With an effort, he kept the sneering smile on his face. Memory suddenly overwhelmed him. In his mind he saw again the confident smiling woman he had once coveted and admired. How could something that had promised so much in the beginning, have come to such a disastrous bitter end? What had happened in the intervening years to turn her into this acrimonious, sharp-tongued shrew, and him into a cold, vindictive bully? For a moment he found it difficult to speak.

Then at last he said, 'Well, I suppose in the circumstances. I'll have to accept. I wouldn't want to think you'd been short changed, my dear.' He added mockingly. 'My lady.'

June, 1895 — Longhirst Hall, Northumberland

White-gloved deferential hands poured iced lemonade into tall frosted glasses. 'Will there be anything further, my lady?'

'No, thank you, Jessop. That will be all.'

Jessop bowed and retreated silently into the house. From the sunlit terrace at Longhirst, Marguerite watched James attempt to teach their sons the rudiments of cricket.

'No! No! Drever. Keep the bat straight. Yes, good, Sydney, but try and get some lift into the ball.'

Hugh and Arthur were fielding; Hugh dancing with impatience on the edge of the pitch as Arthur fumbled yet another catch. An expression of sympathy crossed her pale face. Poor Arthur. If there was a ball to be dropped, an obstacle to stumble over then Arthur would be the one to do it. That would have irritated her once; that clumsiness, that painful awkwardness that accompanied everything Arthur did. Why it no longer did she wasn't sure. There were a great many things of which she was no longer sure. Things were different. She was different, though she didn't understand herself well enough to know in exactly what respect. But she was more tolerant of Arthur, of James, especially she was more tolerant toward herself. She supposed what had happened was that she had given up, not loving James, but hoping that he would ever love her in return. It had come almost as a relief, the complete abandonment of hope, to be no longer struggling against something that had always been beyond her control. When she thought of James now, it was with sadness and regret rather than her old rancour and bitterness. She expected nothing from him now and at least that way she was never disappointed. Having taught herself contentment and called it happiness, she lived quietly now and tried to find fulfilment in her children. And sometimes she thought that quiet content-

251

ment was preferable to violent emotion. Perhaps happiness only came after all other emotions had been exhausted.

She rarely left Longhirst, only for weddings — last year the marriage of Rosandra's daughter Alice; and funerals — two months ago, James' brother George had died. A faint smile turned her mouth. Yes, that had added to her sense of peace, though not for the reasons she once would have imagined. She was glad now that she had seen him again before he died. She so very nearly hadn't gone. She'd been startled and suspicious upon receiving his letter asking her to call. They hadn't met for years, though she knew James visited him often. She had hesitated a long time before making up her mind, almost too long. The instant she had seen him she knew that he was dying.

George had understood her expression. 'Yes,' he said. 'I thought it only fair to give you an opportunity to gloat.'

Marguerite hadn't answered him, but had felt only an overwhelming pity. She had never seen death so clearly: the shrivelled diminished limbs, the sickly pallor of his face, the skin stretched and taut over the fine bones.

George had smiled his bitter, caustic smile. 'Sympathy, Marguerite? That's not like you. I would have expected triumph, mild satisfaction at least.' His voice faltered. 'You see? Even now I can't resist the urge to provoke a quarrel.'

'Is that why you asked me here? To quarrel?'

'No. Quite the reverse, in fact. I am embarked on the dreary business of what legal men call, "putting one's affairs in order". You know, last will and testament, paying my debts; that sort of thing.'

Marguerite regarded him steadily. 'And what do you think you owe me?'

'An apology. An explanation at the very least, of my appalling behaviour toward you.' He was silent for a moment. Even to speak tired him. Then he said. 'This is difficult for me to say, even after all this time. I've always had a horror of revealing myself. But I can't die without telling you, without attempting to put things right. Elizabeth would have wanted it.'

Marguerite stiffened. Her lips compressed. She felt a brief flaring of the old bitter rage. Elizabeth, Elizabeth, always Elizabeth. Somehow it always came back to that in the end. All her pain seemed to stem from her own stubborn refusal to come to terms with her memory, to allow her a place in James' life.

'Marguerite,' George sensed her withdrawal. 'Please don't, my dear. There is no need. That's why I asked you to come.' His head fell back. 'I lied to you, you see — or at least, I didn't tell you all of the truth. I didn't just love Elizabeth. I was in love with her, in exactly the same way that James was. I always deluded myself that if I'd been a normal man ...' He broke off for an instant, as if to catch his breath. 'But I wasn't a normal man, so she married James. That seemed to me the next best thing. But when a man doesn't have the use of his body, his mind, his imagination takes over. I imagined myself married to Elizabeth. I was her husband in all but the physical sense. It was just a dream, and yet when she died, I wasn't able to give the dream up. She continued to exist, as really she'd only ever existed for me, entirely in my imagination. And for the first time in our lives, James and I were on equal terms. Neither of us could have Elizabeth.' He turned to look at her. 'And then you came, so confident, so assured, so willing to be happy. I couldn't bear that. I couldn't bear to see Elizabeth replaced. I couldn't bear James to be happy without her. It wasn't you, Marguerite. It was James I was so angry with. It was James I couldn't forgive. But I was too cowardly to own up to that so I took it out on you. I tried to make you believe that you were a substitute, that the past was stronger than the future ... I didn't tell you that nothing would have made Elizabeth happier than for James to marry again. She would have wanted you to be welcomed with open arms. And James knew that, you see. He felt no guilt about caring for someone else because that's what she would have wanted. She'd have been ashamed to know what I had done.' He turned and looked at her and saw her expression of pain. 'Can you forgive me for taking so long to tell you, my dear? I'm afraid I'm taking full advantage of my condition — the dying man's last request.'

She sat quite still. Silence grew like a wall between them and she thought suddenly of how many moments like this there had been in her life, how many silences that had remained unbroken. Then she answered him calmly. 'Yes, I can forgive you, George. It doesn't really matter much now.' She managed a weak smile. 'And you're not entirely to blame. I brought a great deal of it upon myself. Another woman would have shrugged it off — perhaps I would have, if I had believed that James had cared for me.'

'But he did care for you. I wouldn't have needed to do anything at all if he had not.' Suddenly he reached out and took her hand. 'Perhaps it's not too late. You still love him, don't you?'

Tears pricked her eyes. 'Oh yes, I still love him. Nothing will ever change that. But we've hurt each other so much. I think we've destroyed in each other what was decent and kind. There's no trust, no affection, no liking between us now.'

George said nothing. There was nothing really to say. For a while they sat in silence. Then Marguerite got to her feet. 'Thank you for telling me, George. It's been a comfort of a sort.'

He held out his hand. 'Well, goodbye, then, Marguerite. I don't suppose we shall see each other again — at least, not in this life.'

Compassion softened her haughty features. 'I'm so sorry, George . . .'

He patted her hand. 'Don't be, my dear. All that you see is the final disintegration of a body from which the spirit departed a long time ago.' He smiled. 'Death for me has a kind and compassionate face.'

He died two days later. She hadn't pretended to grieve. There seemed no need. He would be with Elizabeth now.

Her own life continued without much change. She saw little of James. Of necessity he still needed to spend a great deal of time in London and she did not often accompany him now, preferring to remain at Longhirst. Even when he came north during the recess they weren't together a great deal. He was always busy, at the office, at the collieries, closeted with his agent Nesbit over the running of the estate. She was busy herself. She had her charities and committees — a wealthy titled patron was always in demand — as well as managing the army of servants needed to run Longhirst and Cadogan Square. And on the rare occasions they were together they were never alone. There were always guests or the servants or the children between them. She preferred it that way. She could never be wholly at ease in his presence.

She glanced up at the sound of approaching laughter. James was coming toward her, his sleeves rolled up, his bare arm flung casually round Drever's neck. Their daughter Marguerite whose name over the years had been diminished to Margot, scrambled up and ran to meet him. 'Look Papa, I have drawn a rose. Mama says it's very good. Do you think it's very good?'

James lifted her up and kissed her and then whirled her round so that she screamed with excitement and delight.

Marguerite lowered her eyes to her work. It still hurt to see him so loving and tender. With the boys he was sterner but with their daughter he was openly adoring.

'Mama. Did you see? Did you see?' Sydney's voice, cocky and self important, already with the undertones of a sneer. He leant against her, assured of her favouritism. 'Didn't I play well, Mama? I got Drever out three times in a row.'

Drever thrust out his full lower lip. 'I still got more runs than you when you were batting.'

'Only because Arthur kept missing the ball,' Sydney retorted. 'You know Arthur's hopeless at everything.'

Arthur said nothing. He was used to being ragged; at home, at school, especially at school. He hadn't done well in his first year at Harrow. It hadn't brought him out of himself as Marguerite had imagined. In fact, he was quieter and more introverted than ever. She eyed his pale face with a mixture of exasperation and compassion. It was strange how suddenly she should feel his isolation so keenly, that self imposed loneliness that was also in her. It occurred to her sometimes that they were both outsiders here, each in their own way.

She resumed her stitching again as the children went into the house, hungry for their tea. She said quickly before James could follow, 'Jessop tells me that you won't be dining at home tonight.'

'No. Something's come up. I'm dining with a colleague at the Northern. I hope it doesn't put you out.'

'No, of course not.' She answered in her usual impersonal manner. She could have added that she was used to dining alone — to sleeping alone, to being alone. But she said nothing and continued placidly with her stitching.

The smoking room of the Northern Counties Club was discreetly lit; shaded brass lamps burned night and day, for the heavily draped windows allowed in the minimum of light. The furniture consisted mostly of chairs, high backed leather chair placed a measured distance apart, near enough to permi conversation if members required it, far enough apart fo solitude if they did not. There was a fire too — there wa always a fire, even in high summer — heat was a necessary ingredient of the room's atmosphere; a mingling of leather and cigar smoke, port and linament.

James occupied his usual corner. He eyed his guest specula tively; a tall stooped man with thin dry lips and a marked deferential manner.

'Another brandy, Mr Marchant?' suggested James, 'I think you will agree this is an exceptional vintage?

Edward Marchant, a well placed official at the Lambton Collieries — though not so well placed as he felt was his due — allowed his glass to be refilled. 'It has been an exceptiona evening, if I may say so, Sir James. It's not often I have the opportunity to exchange views with someone so well versed in the trade.'

'Nor I, Mr Marchant,' James said expansively. 'I must admit I envy Lord Durham your services.' He paused and then added, 'If you should ever be seeking a change of employment, you need look no further than my company.'

Marchant looked gratified. Now they were coming to it, the point of the evening. That there was some point, he was perfectly aware. Men like James Joicey didn't wine and dine obscure men like him unless there was something they wanted. And what it was that he wanted he was also perfectly aware. They had observed the niceties, working round to it gradually. All evening they had hedged and fenced around the subject, sounding each other out before committing themselves openly. By now Marchant was sure that James Joicey was in the market to buy information and as equally sure that he, himself, was ready to sell.

He answered James easily, recognizing his cue. 'That day may come sooner than you think, Sir James. I dare say you already know that the Lambton Collieries are in difficulty.'

'I know that their order books are practically empty, Mr Marchant; that they're producing poor quality coal that nobody wants to buy and that eight out of thirteen pits are idle.'

Marchant inclined his head in a respectful gesture. 'You are well informed, Sir James.'

James took his time lighting a cigar. He regarded Marchant thoughtfully through a fragrant blue haze. He had chosen this man carefully — well placed enough to have access to what he wanted, but not so well placed that he couldn't be bribed. It helped, too, when they had a grudge. Marchant had been passed over for promotion a half dozen times and it was inevitable that when companies went to the wall, heads would roll. Marchant knew that his would be one of them. He said, smiling. 'I would be better informed, Mr Marchant, if you understand what I mean.'

'In what way, Sir James?'

James leant toward him. 'Tell me about the Lambton Collieries, Mr Marchant.'

He listened thoughtfully, interrupting now and again to put a question. The picture that emerged was much as he had expected, confirmation of what Dick Lamb had surmised. The Lambtons hadn't kept up with the times, relying on sweated labour instead of mechanization. Their equipment was archaic; one winding engine had been in service for eighty years. At some pits pumping and ventilation was almost primitive. He heard too, tales of graft and bribery, viewers and overmen being paid to turn a blind eye; massive purchases of job lots and bankrupt stock; accidents due to cheap timber and faulty props.

'So, Mr Marchant,' he said, summing up. 'From what you tell me, it seems that Lambtons are virtually hanging on the edge. It could, at the moment, go either way. But the loss of one of their staple contracts, say, could push them over the edge? I was thinking particularly of the contract to supply the London and North Eastern Railway which comes up for renewal next month. Lambtons have always seemed to be able to hang on to that, irrespective of what bids other firms put in. I've always found that rather curious.'

Marchant smiled drily. 'That is easily explained, Sir James. Lord Ravensworth, the chairman of L.N.E.R., is one of Lord Lambton's closest friends. The arrangement, I presume, is mutually beneficial, though I don't know in what particular way.'

James looked thoughtful. 'Could you get proof of that? That Lambtons got the contract despite putting in a higher bid?'

'Well, I could find out the amount of their last bid. You could then compare it with some of the other firms who lost out.'

James nodded. 'I would be grateful if you could obtain that information for me, Mr Marchant.' For a moment he was silent. Then he said, 'Assuming then, that something of that kind happened, that Lambtons lost the L.N.E.R. contract and were forced into a position where they had to sell . . .' He paused. 'If that were to happen, Mr Marchant, then I dare say that within the company, you would be one of the first men to know. I should like to be the second.'

Marchant nodded. 'I see no difficulty in that.'

James smiled. 'Assuming that to be so, it's general practice to invite sealed bids. You, Mr Marchant, or one of your clerks would be responsible for opening those bids . . .'

'I understand, Sir James,' Marchant said quickly. He had been way ahead of Sir James there. Then he added, 'With respect, Sir James, run down or not, the Lambton Collieries are a vast undertaking. You would be talking about a very considerable sum.'

'How considerable?'

'Somewhere in the region of a million pounds, I would think. Three quarters of a million at least.'

'And what exactly would I be getting for my money, Mr Marchant?'

'Well, leaving the actual pits aside for the moment: gas works, brick works, a hundred miles of railway and rolling stock, a fleet of thirty-odd steamers . . .'

'I'm thinking about coal, Mr Marchant,' James interrupted him. 'I would need to know Lambton's reserves, exact figures rather than rough estimates. Also land surveys and geological reports, details of rents and leases, profit and loss accounts for the past ten years . . .' James refilled Marchant's empty glass. 'Would it be possible for me to obtain such information, Mr Marchant?'

Marchant moistened his lips. He hadn't intended to go quite that far. Verbal information was one thing but written reports were quite another. He said, prevaricating. 'Forgive me, Sir James. But I cannot see how to know these things will give you any advantage. If and when the collieries come up for sale, such information will be common property, given out as a matter of course to prospective buyers.'

James smiled. 'It's a matter of timing, Mr Marchant, of always being that one step ahead. Besides, information given out to prospective purchasers is always dressed up; a nought left off here, added on there. I want the real figures, Mr Marchant, to know the worst.' He refilled the other man's empty glass. 'As I said, Mr Marchant, timing is all. In six months perhaps this information will be worthless to me. At the moment, it commands a high premium.'

Marchant hesitated only briefly. Perhaps more than the promise of money he was swayed by this man's overwhelming personality. He wouldn't care to cross him and that's what he had to think of if he backed down now. Furtively he nodded. 'Very well, Sir James. I'll see what I can do.'

James escorted his guest out to the waiting hackney and stood for a moment in the slowly darkening street. It was an impossible idea, a fantastic idea and yet he couldn't quite abandon it, the thought, the dream, that one day he would own the Lambton Collieries.

'Sir James.' Arthur Ravensworth advanced toward him extending a smooth white hand. 'This is indeed a pleasure.'

James smiled, wondering how much longer the old fraud would continue to think so. 'It's very good of you to see me at such short notice, my lord.'

'Well, I must admit I was curious. Your letter made it all sound very mysterious.' He resumed his seat behind the imposing desk. 'Now tell me. What exactly can I do for you?'

'Actually, my lord, it's rather what I can do for you, or more to the point your company.'

'Oh,' said Ravensworth. 'In what way, Sir James?'

'It's regarding the contract for steam coal which comes up for tender at the end of the month.'

'Oh?' Ravensworth said again. 'And how do you think I can help you with that? Naturally, your firm is invited to tender along with the others.'

259

'Yes, of course. And in the past, we have done so on several occasions, but we have never seemed to be able to dislodge Lambtons, no matter how competitive our bid.'

Ravensworth's affable smile faded. 'Obviously, then, it wasn't competitive enough, Sir James. I must say we've always found Lambtons very reasonable.'

'You're saying that Lambtons have always put in the lowest bid?'

Ravensworth looked uneasy. 'Within reason, yes. But price isn't everything. One has to take quality into account.'

'And yet there are frequent complaints from your managers about the high ash content of Lambton's coal. Are you telling me that that's good business practice as well?'

Ravensworth flushed. 'I'm not telling you anything, Sir James. Quite frankly, it's a matter between myself and my fellow directors.'

'And your shareholders,' countered James. 'You're not a private company, my lord. You are answerable to your shareholders as well.'

'Now look here, Joicey. What exactly are you getting at?'

'I'm merely pointing out, my lord, that your shareholders, of which incidentally, I happen to be one, are entitled to value for money and that means the best product at the lowest price. I happen to know they haven't been getting that. Perhaps it's time they knew that as well.'

Ravensworth inclined his head slowly, acknowledging the threat. 'What is it you actually want?' he demanded coldly. 'Perhaps the same favourable terms as you accuse me of offering Lambtons?'

'Not at all, my lord. I have never needed to rely on patronage and favouritism to make my business a success. All I am asking is for your assurance that when you put out the tenders this coming month, that the contract goes to the lowest bidder.'

Ravensworth frowned. 'Very well then, you have my assurance.' He eyed James mockingly. 'You seem very sure that it's going to be you.'

'I can guarantee it, my lord,' James assured him. 'Even if I have to give the damn coal away.'

After that, there wasn't much he could do except await the outcome, although he was fairly sure that neither Lambtons nor any one else could better his rock-bottom price. They couldn't, and at the end of the month he received official confirmation that the L.N.E.R. contract had been awarded to him. Then more waiting, to see if his strategy had been successful. Had he been able to push Lambtons over the edge? It was an unnerving time, when he veered between euphoric confidence and nervous misgivings. It was like a kind of madness. He couldn't ever remember being so emotionally involved, to the extent of jeopardizing all that he had. By the end of September he had still heard nothing and reluctantly returned to London for the resumption of Parliament. Marguerite did not accompany him. She seldom did now and though at first he had welcomed this, after a while his own company had begun to pall. His life assumed a dreary pattern; the mornings spent dealing with company business, then lunch at his London club, arriving at the Commons by two. Invariably the House sat late. He was rarely home before ten. He was used to having Marguerite there. It irritated and vaguely depressed him that she was not. He put this down to the inconvenience of having to see to everything himself and his general disillusionment with politics.

It had been a bad year for his party, out of office again after another forced election. Gladstone's resignation over the defeat of his Home Rule Bill had sounded the death knell for the Liberals. His successor, Lord Rosebery, a flighty young aristocrat whose only interest in the Irish was in the blood lines of their horses had divided the party even further. After eighteen months of having every measure killed off by a hostile Lords, including the Employers' Liability Bill over which James had laboured so hard, Rosebery had also resigned. There had followed another election, another defeat. James had kept his own seat. His re-election now seemed just a matter of course, but the Liberals were out, impotent under a fifty seat Tory majority. It had been the final disillusionment. He was seriously thinking of not standing again.

Then at the end of October, he heard from Marchant; the information he had asked for, thirty foolscap pages covered in his neat clerkly hand; together with an accompanying note, the news he had been waiting for — the Lambton Collieries were to be put up for sale in the New Year at an asking price of a million pounds.

'A million pounds! My God, James, you can't be serious?' William James stared at him in mounting incredulity. 'But you are, aren't you? Yes, of course you are. You're always serious about money.' He went and stood with his back to the fire. He wore evening dress and had called in at the office between dinner and the theatre in answer to James' request.

'Yes, I'm perfectly serious.' James' voice was assured. It was important that William James believed him to be so. Just the suspicion of a doubt on his part and he knew the argument would go against him. He went on confidently, 'If you'll look at the figures I've drafted, you'll see ...'

'I have looked at them and all I can see is a white elephant.'

'Then you obviously haven't looked properly,' retorted James. 'The coal is there. Reserves for at least another sixty or seventy years. It's just a question of working it economically.'

'But can it be worked economically? The Lambtons obviously don't think so, or they wouldn't be selling.'

'Perhaps in the short term it can't,' said James carefully. 'But in the long term ...'

'Meaning that it would be years before we saw any return?'

'That applies surely to any investment.'

'But not on this scale, James,' William James protested. 'A million pounds, perhaps a quarter as much again to reorganize and re-equip. For God's sake, where do you think we're going to find that sort of money?'

'We'd have to borrow of course — something probably in the region of three hundred thousand.'

William James stared at him. 'Now let me get this quite clear in my mind,' he said slowly. 'You're proposing that we mortgage ourselves and the company up to the hilt in order to buy a near bankrupt company, invest thousands of pounds in the hope that we can put it on its feet — and all at a time of the greatest depression in trade?'

'Depressions don't last for ever.'

'You've been saying that for the last five years but coal is still fetching less than five shillings a ton. It isn't the time to

262

speculate, in my opinion. Most coalowners are trying to consolidate rather than to expand.'

'That's exactly why it is the right time to speculate. If trade was booming we wouldn't even be in the running for Lambtons, it wouldn't even be on the market.' James came out from behind his desk. 'A million is just the asking price. It'll go, I'm certain, for a great deal less. There won't be too many bids for an undertaking of that size. It's the chance of a lifetime. It won't ever come again. Just think, William James, just take time to think. We wouldn't just be the largest coalowners in the north, we'd be the largest coalowners in England.'

He couldn't keep the passion and longing from his voice and William James' eyes narrowed thoughtfully. 'You really want this, don't you? I wonder why? Because it's Lambtons? You've always had a bit of a thing about Lambtons, Haven't you?' He smiled, seeing from James' expression that he'd struck the nail on the head. Suddenly he knew that he had the upper hand. 'This isn't just a business deal, it is? It's far more personal than that. That worries me even more, James. I've never known you let personal issues get in the way of business. It inclines me more than ever to say no.'

'Is that what you're saying, then.'

'Yes, I'm afraid that it is.' It gave him more pleasure than he would have believed to turn him down. It wasn't just a business deal for him either. A great many old scores were being settled here. He thought of all the years he'd been dominated by this man, all the times he'd been talked down and over-ruled. James — Sir James ... His eyes hardened ... His mouth drew down. That perhaps was the greatest source of his envy and resentment. When he thought of all the money he'd poured out, all the years spent cultivating his aristocratic and titled friends, his slavish devotion to his dear 'Bertie'.

Then James said quietly, 'I'll do it without you if I have to, you know.'

William James smiled unpleasantly. 'I don't see how you can, old chap. You might be the major shareholder but you would need seventy-five per cent before you could carry it through without my consent.' He smiled at James happily. 'I'm afraid you'll have to admit it. You're just not going to be able to bring this one off.'

James sat for a long time in the quiet room. Only by keeping very still could he contain his anger and disappointment. He had been afraid of this. He'd been aware from the beginning that this wasn't something he'd be able to force through. It had all depended on the way he'd put it across. And he'd over-played his hand. He'd let William James see how desperately it mattered — and why it mattered. He gnawed at his lip. He'd asked himself the question a hundred times. Did he want Lambtons just to settle an old score? Had his hatred of Jack Lambton clouded his judgement. Even now he wasn't sure. Instinct told him that this was the chance of a lifetime, one that would never come again. And yet it was an enormous gamble, everything staked on a single throw of the dice.

He went to stand by the fire and poked at the dead coals broodingly with the toe of his boot. He would have liked to talk about it except that he couldn't think of anyone who would want to listen. It was a strange feeling, to feel so suddenly alone and without a friend. He missed George. George would have listened, offered honest advice. And Marguerite? Yes, once upon a time he could have gone to her. Though he'd never have admitted it, he missed her support. When it had been withdrawn he wasn't quite sure. He was only sure that it was gone, that she was no longer interested in anything he did. He didn't blame her. They'd neither of them had much joy out of the last twelve years. Twelve years. So long — and still strangers.

He moved away from the fire and stared broodingly at old James' portrait. The eyes mocked him, sneered at him for a fool.

'You wouldn't have been beaten, would you, old man?' His eyes hardened. 'And neither, damn it, will I.'

She was asleep, heavily so — lately she'd been in the habit of taking a little laudanum with her evening milk — so that when she saw him standing by the bed, she thought it part of some vivid dream.

'Marguerite.' His voice, harsh and resonant in the absolute silence of the room quickly dispelled the illusion. He looked away. 'Forgive me for disturbing you — but there's something quite urgent I need to say.'

She sat up. 'I — yes, of course. Just give me a moment.' She reached for her robe, thrusting her arms into the sleeves before she slipped from the bed. She stood for a moment smoothing her hair, watching him as he attempted to stir the fire to life. He looked tired, she thought and the broad shoulders of his coat were dark with rain. 'You're wet,' she said. 'Did you walk from the station?'

'Yes,' he answered. 'It's not so far as I thought. Probably just over the mile.'

'Would you like some tea?' she offered. 'I keep a small spirit stove here in case I wake in the night.'

He smiled faintly. 'Yes. Thank you,' he said. 'Some tea would be very welcome.'

She was glad of something to do, to cover up the trembling of her hands. She had expected this, not quite so abruptly or dramatically, but yes, she had expected it. James was selfish enough to want to confess. If he was nothing else he was always honest. And of course she'd remain calm, dignified, unconcerned. He wouldn't have the added satisfaction of knowing that it mattered. She set the kettle to boil and laid out two cups and then went and sat in the chair facing him. She kept her eyes lowered. She couldn't bear to see as well as hear. Then she asked him outright. 'What is it, James? What is it that you wanted to say?'

James glanced down at his hands. There wasn't anything to do but come straight to the point. 'I wouldn't normally bother you with business but I'm afraid in this instance I don't have any choice.'

She looked up at him then. What was he saying? Something about the Lambton Collieries? Silent laughter welled up in her throat. Not another woman then but a coal mine, another damn hole in the ground.

'I won't bore you with all the technicalities. The long and the short of it is that William James refuses to back me and I'd like to have a shot at going it alone.' He glanced at her uncertainly. 'It would mean borrowing a very great deal of money, mortgaging Longhirst, Cadogan Square, in fact, we'd need to put up practically everything we have.'

She looked at him gravely. 'Is it then such a very great risk?'

He answered her, equally gravely, 'I can't pretend to you that it's not.'

Marguerite was silent. The kettle pulsed out a thin ribbon o steam and she rose, making the tea with deft, unhurried move ments. She handed him his cup and sat down again. 'Thi means a very great deal to you, doesn't it? The acquisition o these collieries?'

'Yes, it does. A very great deal.'

She didn't ask him why. She didn't ask him anything at all It was enough that he needed her, perhaps only this once, bu he needed her. Then she said, 'Well, if it would help at all have some money of my own, probably some fifty thousand pounds now, with interest. And there are the shares that my father left me in de Beers.'

James looked at her strangely. He didn't understand women. Especially this woman he didn't understand. 'Thank you ...' For a moment he found it difficult to speak. Then he said, 'You're very calm about it — considering that by this time next year you might be destitute.'

'Am I?' She smiled. 'That's because I don't believe it will ever come to it. I don't believe that you will fail.'

For a long time they looked at each other then Marguerite rose and brought paper and pens from her writing desk. 'Now, to get down to practicalities. How much exactly do we need to raise?'

James smiled. Suddenly he remembered why he had married her.

January 14th, 1896 — London

Marguerite leant to the carriage window as it turned the corner into Lennox Gardens. The rain of the last two days had turned to a light snow, frail, nebulous flakes that melted the instant they touched the glass. She looked out on the sweep of tall grey houses. She felt some apprehension now, uncertainty as to whether this was a wise move. William James might not even be at home. She had sent no word of her intended visit. She was here purely on impulse and quite unknown to James.

She leant back against the soft padded seat. She was plainly dressed; a dark woollen costume, a high beaver hat. She wore the minimum of jewels; the rest were deep in the vaults at

Lloyd's, together with the Titian and the Rembrandt etchings, held as security on a fifty thousand pound loan.

The carriage halted outside William James' house. She glanced at the watch pinned inside her jacket. She had just over an hour. James wouldn't be back much before six. He had a meeting in the city, the third this week — a German banker this time, ready, no doubt to lend any amount, but at a crippling rate of interest. It was the same everywhere. The City wasn't in the mood for speculation. Though one or two merchant banks had made interested noises, they were holding out as long as they could, hopeful that market conditions would improve before they committed themselves absolutely. But time was something they didn't have. The bidding for Lambtons closed at the end of the month and as yet, they'd only raised two thirds of the money. She'd decided two days ago that William James was the only answer. If he could only be persuaded to back the venture then they could put the company up as security. It hadn't helped, the whole world knowing that William James was against it. It didn't inspire confidence, as one banker had pointed out, the knowledge that a man's closest business associate wanted nothing to do with it. But there was no possibility of persuading James to approach him again. As he'd said himself, he'd rather have gone to the Jews. She'd hesitated to go herself. For one thing James wouldn't have approved and now that things were so much better between them, she'd been anxious not to provoke a quarrel. And for another, she hadn't really been convinced that it would do any good. She knew William James and knew that his motives for standing in James' way weren't altogether personal. But they hadn't been so desperate then. Anything at this stage was worth a try.

He opened the door to her himself. 'I saw the carriage,' he said as he showed her upstairs. 'It's very distinctive with that abysmal crest of black diamonds and miner's picks all over the door.'

'Sherry?' he enquired. 'It's not too early for you, is it?'

Marguerite shook her head and glanced appreciatively round the room. There were some fine examples of the new French decorative furniture, some lovely Satsuma, a piece of exquisite Cloisonne. The only jarring note was a large heavy oil above the mantle. A Landseer, she presumed. That man never seemed to paint anything but dogs and stags. 'You need a Renoir there,' she said lightly. 'Or perhaps a Cezanne.'

'Yes, I know,' he replied, smiling. 'I'm afraid Mary, my wife, is rather traditional.' His eyes appraised her as he handed her a glass. It was a long time since he had seen her and he saw that she was changed; softer, more relaxed, almost beautiful in a rather distant way.

'It's rather early in the year for you to be in town,' he remarked. 'Parliament doesn't resume for another three weeks yet.'

'No, it doesn't,' she agreed. 'But we had to take the boys back to Harrow for the beginning of term so we thought we'd come on a week or two early. Also James has some pressing business in the City.'

'Oh?' Something in her manner aroused his curiosity. 'What little scheme is he hatching up now?'

Marguerite replied vaguely. She was deliberately evasive. It was important that William James made all the running. 'Did you enjoy the play?' she asked, changing the subject. 'We saw you at the theatre last night. Unfortunately we left it rather late to get tickets so we had to sit in the stalls.'

'My dear, you should have joined me. One can always make room in a box.'

'I might have,' she said, 'but I don't think that James would have thought it a good idea.'

He pulled a face. 'I suppose I'm still in high disfavour over this Lambtons business?'

'Well, you did make things rather difficult for him,' she answered with mild reproach.

He shrugged. 'Well, I dare say he'll come round. He always does. As a matter of fact I had expected to see him long before now. James doesn't usually give up so easily.'

Marguerite smiled enigmatically. 'What makes you think that he has given up?'

He looked at her in sudden consternation. 'Well, naturally, I assumed . . .'

Marguerite interrupted him. 'You needn't worry. It's nothing that involves you.'

He grew even more concerned. 'Is he still going ahead then?

I don't see how he can without my consent.'

'He doesn't need your consent. He's going to put up the money himself.'

William James raised his eyebrows. 'Well, you do surprise me, my dear,' he said airily. 'I wouldn't have thought your resources ran to that.'

'We have an independent backer.' She lied blatantly. 'A friend who has offered to put up the rest of the money.'

William James paled visibly. It had never occurred to him that James would go ahead without him, let alone that he would involve a third party. 'Well, I wish him luck.' He laughed nervously. 'I still think he's getting in over his head. It's too much of a gamble for me.'

She smiled at him provocatively. 'I thought you were a gambler, William James.'

He laughed uneasily. 'Yes, I am, at reasonable odds. In my book this must rank as an impossible outsider.'

'Outsiders sometimes come in. You should know that James never gambles unless he's convinced he can win.'

William James was silent, irritated by the supreme confidence of her manner. He rose to his feet and went to warm his hands by the fire. He would have liked another drink but thought that it might betray anxiety on his part. And he was anxious. He was having second thoughts now about breaking away from James. Christ, he thought, he must be sure of himself. He must have mortgaged his very soul to be able to go it alone. What if he pulled it off? Marguerite certainly seemed to think that he could. And he'd be out of it, completely in the cold. He glanced covertly at her calm and composed face. That perhaps disturbed him the most, her complete conviction, her total assurance that James would win. And he remembered now that he usually did; he remembered other occasions where he hadn't taken advantage of James' Midas touch; those South African shares that had rocketed unexpectedly; his prediction, ridiculous at the time, that Mercantile Iron would go to the wall. He gnawed at his lip. Perhaps it wasn't so impossible after all. Perhaps, in retrospect, he had been a bit hasty. He wouldn't have put it past James to have engineered the whole thing. This might just have been a clever way of easing him out. He said, casually, 'This backer — this friend. Has James made any firm commitment as yet?'

'Not that I am aware of. The money is there if he wants it, but he's still having discussions with various banks. Naturally, he'd rather manage without a third party.'

'Well, that's exactly my point.' He grasped eagerly at that. 'I'm not altogether keen on the idea of having to bring in someone from outside. I was wondering if I oughtn't to take a second look at the proposition myself.'

She looked doubtful. 'Isn't it a bit late for that?'

He rose wonderfully to the bait. 'I don't see why. You say that nothing has been finalized. We've always been a family concern, I'm sure that at the bottom of him James would rather keep it that way.' He smiled at her with what he thought was fatal persuasion. 'I'm sure that you could arrange something, my dear. Women are always so good at these things.'

She looked up at him, smiling. She saw an old man, nearly sixty, though like all the Joiceys he retained the impression of youth. But still as vain and shallow and egotistical as ever. It had not even occurred to him to wonder why she was here.

July 26th, 1896 — Newcastle

'This agreement, made and entered into on the twenty-third day of July, eighteen hundred and ninety-six, between John George Lambton, Earl of Durham on the one part and Sir James Joicey, baronet ...'

The two men faced each other, separated by the length of a long mahogany table and a battery of agents, solicitors and clerks. They did not speak, and except for a cursory nod — the briefest acknowledgement of each other's presence — had not done so since they entered the room.

'And whereas the said John George Lambton, Earl of Durham has sold and disposed of the whole of his share and interest in the collieries and coalmines and seams of coal, ironstone and fireclay known as the Lambton Group of Collieries ...'

Lambton listened with an air of quiet bewilderment — and anger, confusion, fury and dismay — but mostly bewilderment. That it had come to this. That the Lambton Collieries should need to be sold — and at half their real worth. And to this man, this nobody, this upstart. He repressed the urge to look at him. He would not give him the satisfaction of seeing his defeat. And it was defeat; the end of six months of haggling and furious bargaining that had whittled almost a quarter from their original price. It was a buyer's market, his advisers had told him; a scoundrel's market more like, an opportunist's market where cut throat tactics were the order of the day. It wasn't any consolation that, privately, the trade thought James Joicey had made a bad bargain. The general consensus was that the collieries were too far gone to be profitably redeemed. And he knew himself how much needed to be spent — unbelievable, staggering sums. For a moment he dwelt pleasurably on the thought of Joicey going under. Predictions were all for it happening. But the predictions had been made by men like himself, men of the old school, who were equally aghast at this man's sudden rise. These were the new times; new money, new men, a new world where tradition and heritage counted for nothing and money, however come by, was all of its creed.

His thin elegant shoulders twitched in a spasm of helpless rage. He was incredulous still. The very air around him seemed tinged with disbelief, seemed to tremble from the shock of his fall. He glanced at his brothers, his fellow directors and saw his own astonishment reflected in their faces. Of course they all blamed him. Censure and recrimination was in their every glance. Even Freddie, his twin brother, always before on his side, eyed him with mild reproach. None of them had actually said so outright but they thought he'd bungled it, handled things badly. They thought, he knew, that he should have done more. Yet what more could he have done? The catastrophe was upon them before he had known it. Bad times, bad management, all come together . . .

His bitter thoughts intensified. He would not be their scapegoat. There were others equally to blame; the unions for one with their insatiable demands, more money, better conditions, as if they were the master and not he. And closer to home; the agents and managers whose duty it had been to advise him and who now smilingly bartered away his inheritance. Balefully he eyed them. Yes, it was clear to him now. He'd listened to the wrong advice, trusted the wrong men. He wondered now how

271

many had betrayed him, how many had lined their pockets at his expense? He cast about in his mind for others to blame and thought with quiet loathing of his barren and unstable wife. Even she must come in for some share of the blame. If he'd had a son it might have been different. A man worked the harder when there was a son to hand things on to. As it was, everything would go to Freddie and his boys. Oh yes, there were so many, equally culpable. Even the dead; his own father, that prolific old goat, leaving him saddled with nine brothers and five sisters, all to be housed and endowed as befitted the Lambton name. And even further back ... He raised his eyes to Lawrence's massive portrait that dominated the far wall. There, perhaps, was the real culprit. His grandfather, the first earl — 'Radical Jack' with his free-thinking and liberal views that had allowed men like James Joicey to get their foot in the door. He eyed the smiling face with bitterness. Would he be smiling now, he wondered, if he knew that the grandson of Radical Jack had been bested by the grandson of a common pitman?

Then Stobart, his agent, touched his sleeve. 'My lord, if you would just sign here and here ...'

The earl raised his eyes, struggling to maintain his bored and indifferent front. He would not let them all see how this pained him. And then as he glanced about the room he saw that it didn't matter any more. He was no longer the focus of other mens' eyes, they were already paying service to their new master. He looked at him then, met full the brilliant and icy gaze. For a few moments they stared at each other and then James slowly smiled. Oh, yes, thought Lambton bitterly. I remember that smile. He heard a voice, a long way off, as it seemed, from a great distance. *'One day, my lord, I shall exact payment for that remark, and with a very great deal of interest.'*

James sat slumped in the corner of the first-class compartment. He felt tired, depressed and the constant movement of the train made him feel slightly sick. He supposed anti-climax had been inevitable. At the bottom of him he'd never really believed that he would pull it off. All through the negotiations he'd had the feeling that Lambton would cry off, that he'd be outbid by a rival coalowner. But Lambton hadn't cried off, he hadn't been outbid. Everything had gone very much according to plan. For better or for worse, the Lambton Collieries belonged to him. It was only now that the doubts came creeping in. For the first time in his life he was financially vulnerable. He squirmed in his seat. He must stop thinking about it, just thinking about failure often brought it about. There was much to be done. Firstly, with William James to inspect every inch of their new domain, to cut out all the dead wood. He already had a list; names of managers and officials who hadn't earned their keep in years, those who took bribes, who gave concessions to particular freight companies, others who were just generally incompetent. But that was tomorrow. There was still today and this agony of uncertainty to be overcome.

He walked from the station. After sitting all day he was glad of the chance to stretch his legs. It was a fine evening, the sun still visible over the distant hills. He lifted his face and the soft radiance warmed his pallid skin. I had forgotten, he thought; forgotten what it was like to walk in the sun, forgotten that all the world was not drab and gritty. He breathed deeply; green leaves, warm earth, the sweet scent of hay — and yes, even here, the faint odour of coal, blown from the Ashington complex three miles away. But just to be out in the air was exhilarating, after weeks of being cooped up in one office or another, months of poring over ledgers and files.

He walked through the village, down the single street of neat houses. The street was deserted except for a couple of basking dogs. He noticed as he passed that the door of the school needed a new coat of paint and that the broken window of old Hodge's cottage was still boarded up. He would have a word with Nesbit in the morning. These last few months he'd been forced to neglect the estate. At the thought, his shoulders slumped imperceptibly. He remembered again the crushing burden of his responsibilities; all this, the company, politics as well — and the greatest burden of them all, his new acquisition, the Lambton Collieries.

He turned in by the west lodge. Again the feeling of tiredness overwhelmed him. His legs grew heavy, his footsteps dragged. He felt that all he wanted to do was sleep, not just for hours, but for weeks — months.

He came in sight of the house and stood for a moment,

contemplating its elegant and impressive façade. He'd never really liked it. That extravagant pillared portico reminded him of a church. He'd always felt dwarfed by the vast dimensions of the rooms. Tonight particularly he felt a reluctance to enter. The polished windows, like mirrors, reflected back the light. It could have been empty and in a way it was. It was walls and a roof, nothing more. It was where he slept and ate on the occasions he did not do so elsewhere. It was Marguerite's house; chosen by her, furnished and decorated by her. Was that why he didn't like it? Because twelve years of anger and disappointment had prejudiced him against all that she touched? He was vaguely ashamed of that. It seemed to emphasize the terrible waste of their marriage. It made him feel guilty, aware that in some way he was also to blame. It was hard to admit now that he had misjudged her.

She was waiting for him, and the sight of her sitting there, calm and smiling, suddenly gladdened and reassured him.

She had champagne ready, plunged in ice. 'I thought,' she said, 'that we should celebrate.'

He drank, the icy liquid scalding his throat. 'How did it go?' she asked him, eagerly.

'Oh,' he shrugged, 'all according to plan. It's all signed, sealed and delivered.'

Marguerite glanced at him, hearing the lassitude of his voice. She had expected triumph, jubilation. Instead he moved like a man weighted with chains. 'Is anything wrong?' she asked him with concern.

'No.' His voice had that distant, irritable note. He sat down heavily. 'I'm just tired that's all.'

She did not press him, seeing the approach of one of his black and unfathomable moods. She'd never learned the art of turning him from these depressions. Like sudden storms they had to be weathered, endured. She relapsed into silence and when she looked at him again he was slumped in his chair with his eyes closed. Her lips tightened. So that was how it was. The truce was over. He'd got what he wanted and now she was no longer of use. She felt herself trembling with anger and disappointment. When she thought of all she'd done, willingly, gladly; all the days and nights spent listening, encouraging, putting him and his needs first.

274

She stuffed her sewing down the side of the chair. 'I'm going to bed,' she announced in a harsh angry voice.

James opened his eyes. He looked vaguely surprised. 'Very well,' he said in an expressionless voice. 'Goodnight then, my dear.'

She sat in her room, staring at nothing. For an hour she sat in the darkness, struggling against the resentment and anger that were at the heart of her deep unhappiness. She'd been a fool to hope, to lay herself open to the prospect of more anguish and despair. She wasn't angry now, merely hopeless and depressed. She felt only the pain of his continued rejection.

She moved her head as she heard James come upstairs, heard his footsteps approach her door. A few seconds passed before he knocked.

She hesitated for an instant before going to open it. He looked embarrassed, a little shamefaced. 'You're not asleep then?' he said unnecessarily.

'No. I'm not asleep.' She turned back into the room leaving the door open so that he could enter or not as he pleased.

He closed it quietly behind him. 'I didn't feel much like sleeping myself. I thought perhaps we could talk.'

She rounded on him. 'What about?' she demanded coldly. 'About your collieries, your stocks and shares, how much you owe at the bank?'

He went white. 'And what is that supposed to mean?'

'It means exactly what it appears to mean. Business is all you ever want to talk about. You only need people to listen, to approve. But that's how you see everybody, in terms of profit or loss, of how useful they can be to you.' Her eyes glittered with suppressed anger and tears. 'Well, I've served my purpose. I'm no longer of use. You've got what you want. You've got Lambtons. Now leave me in peace. I'm tired of being disappointed.'

'And I suppose you think you're the only one that's disappointed,' he snapped. 'You haven't so many endearing qualities yourself.'

'No, but at least I'm human enough to own up to having faults. I don't try to hide them, pretend they don't exist. You're not human, James. You're a machine, a cash register, your only love is for power, your only passion for making money ...'

'Well, perhaps that's a good thing,' he shouted furiously, 'seeing as you have a similar passion for spending it.'

'Oh, I think you've had more than your money's worth out of me, James.' She laughed wildly, her voice rising. 'You know, I used to blame Elizabeth. I used to think you were like you were because she died. I used to think you were human enough to feel something like loss and grief. But it was only the loss you felt, wasn't it? You only grieved because you thought you'd been short-changed. Dead after two years! That wasn't much of an investment, was it? That wasn't value for money...'

Then she screamed as he struck her hard across the face, 'You bitch,' he said softly. 'You cruel, unlovable bitch.'

He turned and walked out of the room, slamming the door. Marguerite stood with her hand pressed against her cheek. The she sank down, still dressed, upon her bed. The tears came then; hot, bitter tears of pain and anguish, all the pent-up misery of her life.

PART III
1908–1936

And oft a chilling damp and unctuous mist,
Loosed from the crumbling caverns issued forth
Stopping the springs of life.

Jago

December 22nd, 1908
— Ford Castle, Northumberland

Evenings, before dusk, it was James' habit to climb the worn stairs to the battlemented roof of King James' Tower. This was the larger and more solid of the two medieval towers that Ford Castle still possessed. The rest was a hodge-podge of Elizabethan grandeur and violent gingerbread Gothic, with late additions of solid Victorian restraint. This tower though, King James' Tower, was his own particular retreat. His first action on acquiring the Ford and Etal estates had been to commandeer it for his own private use. No one ever came here except by invitation and these were issued sparingly. Every evening he came here; rain or shine. From here, on a good day, he could see clear into Scotland, and southwards, at his back, the meadows and lush pastureland of the Millfield Plain. To the East was the sea, glimpsed across miles of heather clad moorland. The view to the west was lost behind the dark sprawl of the Cheviots; long, low featureless hills that faintly reminded him of gigantic slag heaps. There were no pits here though, at least not of any consequence. Just one or two drifts worked to supply the estates; discreet, small capacity pits hidden away behind walls of trees; toys for an old man to play with.

He took a last turn about the roof before descending the short flight of stairs to the lower chamber. This was his favourite room; bleak and baronial. He liked its grimness and austerity, the thought that kings had walked here before him — one king at least. The inscription above the chimney piece bore witness to that: 'King James ye Forth of Scotland did lie here. A.D. 1513'. And did lie a day later, hacked to death on Flodden Field and all of Scotland's chivalry with him. James pursed his lips. Bad generalship that, to have allowed the English to sneak round to the high ground. Now, if it had been him ... He shook his head, smiling faintly. He'd played that particular game too often, amusing himself with the tactics of the battle that had been fought within sight of these walls. He'd often thought that he might have made a passable general. It pleased him that his son Hugh was making strides in that direction, a major already in the 14th Hussars, although on the debit side, it meant that he didn't see as much of Hugh as he would have liked. For the past two years his regiment had been stationed in India.

He seated himself at his desk, leafing idly through the catalogue that had arrived from Christie's that morning. There was a Cezanne coming up for which he'd half a mind to bid. Art was his main diversion now, the enlargement of his collection of modern paintings. A few hung incongruously around the ancient sandstone walls and he eyed them with a pleasure that had nothing to do with their worth: a solemn Sisley, a nubile Renoir, two pastels by Degas and a rather fine Manet. And his particular favourite, a harsh Vlaminck seascape, all dark slashing strokes and ridges of steel grey. Yes. He smiled to himself. He would have the Cezanne. He'd go up to town and attend the auction himself. It would probably do him good to get away.

He lit a cigar. He still smoked those thin, evil smelling cheroots. He sighed, an exasperated sound from deep in his throat. The long and the short of it was that he was bored. There were no challenges left, and it occurred to him that even if there were, he was too old for challenges now. He was sixty-three this April and yet strangely, he didn't feel old. If age was apathy and creaking bones then he wasn't old. And he'd always kept himself fit; cricket and tennis in his younger days, shooting and golf now he was getting on. But he could still walk to the top of Flodden Hill without losing his breath, which was more than you could say of some younger men. And his mind was just as sharp, though it was true he was becoming more pedantic in his habits. He'd noticed certain phrases creeping into his conversation — 'When I was a boy ... In my younger days ...' Old men were always saying that, always looking back, like old soldiers recounting past battles. For him, too, all the good days were in the past, all the excitement, all the uncertainty.

Often he recalled those first years after he'd sunk everything in Lambtons. They'd all thought him a madman, throwing good money straight after bad. New methods, new equipment including the first mechanical coal cutter in the entire north east. Oh yes, they'd all laughed at him, spewing up tons of coal that nobody had wanted to buy when every other coalowner was cutting production. He's often wondered himself if they hadn't been right. The trade had continued its downward plunge. Export markets had closed one after the other as the Americans slammed high tariffs on imports. For him the crisis had come at the end of 1899, when it became obvious that the once profitable Joicey group could no longer support its poor relation. Interest rates were spiralling, the banks growing uneasy at the lack of return. For the first time in his life he had been faced with the prospect of failure. He might have gone under — he would have gone under — if it hadn't been for the South African war.

Perhaps, looking back, it hadn't been totally unexpected. That particular pot had been on the boil for the last twenty years, ever since gold had been discovered in the Transvaal. The Boers, naturally, had wanted rid of the foreigners exploiting their wealth whereas the British couldn't believe that there was any more glorious existence for a nation than to live under the protection of the British flag. Even then it need never have come to it if the government hadn't bungled their handling of Kruger. They hadn't taken the Boer leader seriously and had been confident of being able to bluff it out. In August Kruger had called their bluff. By September they were at war. And there he was, with millions of tons stockpiled, able to guarantee immediate delivery, constant supply. The contracts had come flooding in, from steelworks, railways, shipping lines and munitions factories. He'd landed the contract to supply Armstrong's ordinance works and had held it ever since.

Of course, morally or politically, he hadn't approved of the war. It had offended his sense of fair play, the might of Empire against a handful of Boer farmers. It wasn't as if it were a worthy cause; the protection of gold diggers and diamond magnates headed by that arch-villain Rhodes. Nevertheless, he had never doubted but that the British would win. Hugh had written confidently. His regiment had been one of the first to mobilize, being, as it were, on the doorstep. So that it had been with shock and disbelief that he had heard the news of the British defeat at Lombards Kop. Defeat had followed defeat; Mafeking and Kimberley both under siege, the battles of Magerfontein and Stormburg lost. Casualties had been heavy. Hundreds dead and dying every day, and always the thought that one day his son Hugh might be one of them.

The new year had dawned, 1900, the first of the twentieth century. Not an auspicious start, he remembered, with blizzards raging throughout the north and Drever and Margot down with scarlet fever. Outside of Longhirst, the war had still dominated but at least now they were on the offensive. Victories began to outweigh the defeats. March saw the capture of Blomfontein. By May both Ladysmith and Mafeking had been relieved. In June the British had entered Pretoria and Kruger himself was on the run. It had all seemed over bar the shouting.

Another year, 1901, the first that Lambtons had been officially out of the red. Coal was still selling magnificently at thirty shillings a ton and with five million tons raised in the previous year, they'd made a clear quarter of a million pounds profit. It had seemed cause for celebration, and then one cold January morning, a black clad messenger had ridden out from Osborne House. Victoria, Queen and Empress, was dead and half the world was instantly plunged into mourning.

He'd attended the state funeral, walking between crowds a hundred deep, behind kings and princes, dukes and earls, alongside foreign statesmen and ambassadors from countless dominions and colonies. It was as if no one had ever died before, as if reigning over them for sixty-four years had rendered her immortal. And for James, who could never remember a time when she hadn't been there, it had seemed an end to something. Not the war though. That had dragged on into the Spring of 1902. Not until the end of May was peace declared and he had received the news with relief rather than triumph. Hugh had come home in June, something of a hero, the proud possessor of the King's Medal for gallantry. But none of them felt it had been a war they could be proud of. They'd won — but at a cost of some twenty thousand lives and two hundred and twenty million pounds.

James had devoted more of his time to politics then, lobbying against the Tory imposed tax of a shilling a ton on exported coal. For the Liberals at least it had been a sterile nine years, the Tories in power for every one of them. Though James had retained his own seat throughout, it wasn't until 1906 that the Liberals again formed a government. Ironically, he was not to be part of it. In January of that year, for services rendered to the coal industry, he had been created a peer. He was Baron Joicey now.

He ground out his cigar with an impatient gesture. So where did he go from here? What else was there still to be done? The company didn't need him. Arthur and Sydney were perfectly capable of handling everyday affairs and they had an excellent right hand man in Austen Kirkup. Soon he would be just a figurehead, a signature on the contracts that other men drew up. And yet on paper at least, he was a busy man: Chairman of the Lambton Collieries, the Tanfield Steamship Company and the Albion line; the Great Northern Coal Company of Australia. His directorships were numerous and he was president of a dozen different associations. And there was still his political life, although becoming a baron had meant giving up his constituency. He wasn't so happy in the Lords and besides, his interest in politics in general had waned. They were all new issues now; votes for women, socialism, placating an aggressive and overbearing Germany. New faces too; that devious little Welshman, David Lloyd George; the ex-miner Keir Hardie and his avid socialism, the garrulous Mr Winston Churchill. All the old faces had gone: Gladstone, Salisbury, Rosebery and Parnell, and closer to home, his own brother Jacob had died at the end of 1899 and Eleanor, just last year. Out of the old faces, he and William James seemed to be the only ones left. Not that they saw much of each other now. Even that old rivalry had deteriorated into a passive contest to see which one of them would die first.

A brooding look settled on his face. He didn't often contemplate the future. At sixty-three there was no telling how much of it was left. But when he did think about it, his heart sank. When he thought about retiring, about giving up his place at the head of the firm ... He knew he should think about it. It was inevitable that one day he would have to move over and make room for Arthur. He frowned, thinking about his eldest son. Sometimes Arthur worried him and he often wished that he had a little more confidence, that he wasn't so painfully shy. He'd had high hopes when he had married though he'd been mildly surprised in his choice of a wife. James could never make up his mind about Gina. On the surface it seemed to be just what Arthur needed, a good strong hand behind him. And in all other respects, Georgina Burdon had been eminently suitable as a wife; good landed family of respectable wealth besides being slavishly devoted to Arthur and the two daughters and a son she had speedily produced in the four years of their marriage. Ambitious too. Already he had the feeling that she was trying to ease him out. That was the trouble with the young, they were so contemptuous of age, as if being past sixty meant senility and decay, as if forty odd years experience counted for nothing.

He went down the stairs and out into the courtyard. He stood for a moment staring up at the darkening sky before entering the main house. Marguerite came out of the Little drawing room and called to him.

'James. Aren't you changed yet? Arthur and Gina will be here any minute. I sent the carriage to the station ten minutes ago.'

James regarded his wife with his usual impassive stare, this woman he had so casually and thoughtlessly married. It still irked him to admit to failure, but if he was honest, that was what their marriage was. Years of vicious bickering that had deteriorated into this bland, impersonal exchange of words. Sometimes he thought he preferred the bickering. At least then he'd known he was alive. 'All right, my dear,' he said mildly. 'There's plenty of time. I'm getting too old to be rushed.'

Marguerite smiled thinly. Old wasn't a word that sat easily on James. To her eyes at least he hadn't changed so much. Still lean as a whippet and hungry as a hawk and what lines there were on the dark autocratic face seemed to be the result of some deep inner amusement. Of course, a little weathering was considered flattering in a man. Women weren't so fortunate, she thought acidly. A woman was considered old the minute she was past childbearing, as soon as the first grey hair appeared. She wondered if James noticed how much she'd aged, how thin and sharp her features had become. Probably he hadn't. He'd been too preoccupied building empires and fulfilling his own dreams. And it was a long time since she'd thought of herself, at least, as an individual, as separate from James. She was James' wife, the mother of James' children. She no longer felt that she had a personality of her own. She could remember that someone had warned her about that happening. But it had happened. He had gobbled her up, swallowed her down. He had absorbed her into himself so thoroughly that now she only saw herself as a dim reflection of him. She no longer fought him, struggled against his will. Well, that was what he had wanted. And James always got what he wanted in the end.

Of course, they still quarrelled, usually about the children, though with Arthur a year off thirty and Margot, the youngest just turned twenty-one, they no longer warranted that description. But yes, they still quarrelled, about her favouritism toward Sydney, her eldest son, about his toward Arthur and Hugh. There was the nub of it all. Sydney was *her* eldest son but not his father's, a fact which Sydney resented bitterly and in consequence bore Arthur a monumental grudge. Naturally, she defended Sydney. She knew what it was like to be always in second place. Except that with Sydney it was third place. In the family hierarchy, Arthur and Hugh took precedence. Since coming down from Cambridge, Sydney's life had been a series of compromises. He'd gone into the firm but of course Arthur was being groomed for the top job there and consequently Sydney bullied and humiliated him unmercifully. Oh very subtly, of course. Sydney was nothing if not subtle. She frowned critically. Although she loved Sydney passionately, she'd never been able to like him. There was a cruel streak in Sydney, a sadistic side to his nature that took pleasure in people's pain. She felt a little responsible for that. Sydney thought he was special. She'd always made him feel he was special. It was she who had created that monstrous ego ...

She looked up. James was speaking. 'It's a pity,' he said regretfully, 'that Hugh couldn't get leave. It would have been nice to have the family together for Christmas.'

'Yes, it would,' she agreed but with less enthusiasm. She always dreaded the family being together; herself and James being strenuously pleasant for the children's sake; and Sydney and Arthur, Sydney cruelly whittling away at Arthur's prestige

— and Arthur? Well, of course you never knew with Arthur. Who could tell what went on behind that quiet façade?

'And so I said to this fellow — who by this time was more than three parts drunk ...'

Sydney was telling one of his famous stories. He seemed to have a fund of them, witty little anecdotes all centred around himself, with the joke always at someone else's expense. They were all amused, James and Marguerite smiling indulgently, Margot and Drever laughing outright. Even Gina, Arthur's serious young wife, managed to look diverted. Only Arthur refused to be amused. He kept his eyes determinedly upon his food as his half-brother drew to the hilarious climax. His half-brother. Arthur reminded himself firmly of that. It made him feel less guilty for not liking Sydney, for never having liked Sydney, almost from the day he was born. And over the years Sydney had more than justified that irrational and childish dislike. Sydney was a bully, not in the physical sense, but with his sneers and sarcasm and malicious wit of which Arthur was often the victim. And of course, Sydney was clever, brilliant in fact, sailing through Harrow and Cambridge, emerging with a first class Masters degree whilst he'd had to struggle for a B.A. And brilliant at everything. Sydney had coxed the Christ Church eight, he'd excelled at rugby and cricket. Arthur impaled a brussel spout upon his fork as if it were Sydney's head, flushing as another slid wetly onto his knee. No one had noticed. Sydney's rich languorous voice still held them rapt. Arthur stared at him; sleeked back hair glistening with brilliantine, pale hedonistic features. He had his mother's eyes, mocking and supercilious and Arthur had once thought that his feelings for Sydney stemmed from his old resentment of her. But no. He'd thought about it a great many times. He loathed Sydney just because he was Sydney.

He pushed his plate away, refusing dessert. Thinking about Sydney always ruined his appetite. He wished for the hundredth time that Hugh was here. He'd been bitterly disappointed when his brother had written from Bangalore to say that he couldn't get leave till Easter. Hugh was his real family, his brother in every sense of the word. He didn't feel so anxious about things when Hugh was around. When they were together it was as if he took on something of his brother's aura. He was more confident, more resolute. People listened when he had something to say. And Sydney wasn't so full of himself when Hugh was at home. Even Sydney couldn't outshine Hugh.

He smiled inside himself, looking forward to Easter. Perhaps he could persuade Hugh to spend a few days at Longhirst before coming on to Ford. It would be like old times, himself and Hugh out riding together — 'Come on, Jamie, I'll race you to the paddock ...' Arthur's smile became wistful. Only Hugh ever called him Jamie now. He was plain Arthur to everyone else. He still resented it. It made him feel only half a person, and worse, he had lost the half that enabled him to identify with his father. He raised his eyes and fixed his father with a look of fanatical devotion. He lived in perpetual terror of proving a disappointment, of not, in the end, being up to the job. He knew that so far he hadn't come up to expectations. He wasn't as forceful and assertive as his father would have liked. He found it difficult to deal with certain kinds of men for he was by nature a thoughtful and compassionate man, full of kindness and solicitude for others. Ever since boyhood he'd had a deep and secret fear of people and left to himself, he would have taken refuge from the world in his dreams.

He still day-dreamed a great deal, a boyish habit that he'd never been able to give up. The dreams only varied in time and place, all featuring himself as a bold heroic figure. The endings were always the same though, his father embracing him after the accomplishment of some incredible and dangerous feat, tears of pride and joy in his eyes. The reality of his life was a little different; years of self doubt, of a deep inner loneliness, of trying to live up to his father's image. He swallowed nervously. He hadn't yet told him about the Murchiston contract. He'd made a mistake, he knew, in letting Murchiston talk him into that penalty clause as well as the cost of shipment and despatch. But he'd been so keen to get the contract, to show his father, to show Sydney that he could do it. He'd been too keen, he realized that now. Murchiston had sensed that ...

'Arthur, old chap. The port's with you.'

Arthur blinked. He had not even been aware that the table had been cleared, that the ladies had left the room. 'I'm sorry,' he smiled apologetically, poured himself a small glass and

287

passed the decanter on.

Then Sydney said, fitting one of his pretentious cigarettes into an equally pretentious holder, 'I read Sir Edward Grey's speech on the train coming down. A bit tame I thought. All this business about standing by our old allies. When have the French ever been our allies? More often than not they've been the enemy.' He pursed his lips and blew out a cloud of smoke. 'In my opinion, if Britain needs to ally with anyone it should be Germany. I wouldn't trust a Frog as far as the corner.'

'Well, that's what Asquith wants,' said James. 'What all the Liberals want. But I have to agree that the Kaiser is attaching rather a lot of strings, one of them being that any treaty with Germany must exclude our support of the French. I don't know that we could do that in the interests of peace. The Kaiser is obviously trying to manoeuvre France into a position of isolation. If she is left defenceless, Germany is bound to provoke a war.'

Sydney shrugged. 'Don't you think that inevitable, sir? War in Europe, I mean? The Kaiser is obviously spoiling for a fight. With France or Russia, even perhaps with us. I don't think he really cares which.' He gave his light sneering laugh. 'There's one thing about war. It's good for trade.' He looked at Arthur. 'Don't you think so, old chap? Perhaps you had better step up production.'

Arthur returned his look coldly. 'Actually, I don't think we should get involved at all. Europe isn't really any of our business. If we start meddling in Germany's affairs we're bound to get dragged in.'

Sydney looked scornful. 'Don't you think that's rather a pacifist point of view?'

'I am a pacifist,' retorted Arthur.

Sydney's eyes glittered with smiling malice. 'How much of a pacifist, Arthur? Would you refuse to raise coal to supply a war, to supply an ordinance works, for instance, knowing that you were helping to make weaponry and guns?'

Arthur flushed. 'No, of course, I wouldn't. What I meant was the actual fighting, the killing . . .'

'Oh I see! So you'd be perfectly happy to make money out of a war but not to actually get out and fight.' His lip curled. 'That doesn't make you a pacifist, Arthur. It makes you a damned coward.'

The hot tide of mortification flooded Arthur's face. He was aware of every eye upon him and desperately he tried to think of something clever to say. But before he could say anything their father intervened.

'That's enough, Sydney.' James said sharply. I insist that you apologize to your brother at once.'

Sydney did so grudgingly but the damage had been done, Arthur had heard the irritation in his father's voice. He had seen the disappointment in his eyes.

'Honestly, Arthur. Sometimes I wish you'd show a bit more spirit.' Gina brushed out her dark hair with quick angry strokes. 'I don't understand how you can let people talk to you like that — and Sydney of all people.'

Arthur sat on the edge of the bed, buttoning his pyjamas carefully. He wished he hadn't told her now. Gina was always so fiercely loyal. He might have known she'd make a fuss.

'And what should I have said,' he enquired mildly. 'Sydney was quite right. I am a coward.'

'Oh Arthur,' Gina looked at him with exasperation. 'You 'Why must you always think so little of yourself? Can't you see that Sydney provokes you deliberately? Can't you see that he's jealous?'

'Jealous?' Arthur laughed. 'Of what?'

'Of you, of your position in the family as the eldest son, of the fact that one day you'll have everything he wants.'

Arthur frowned. He did not care for these emotional scenes. 'You speak as if I am to get everything, Gina. Sydney, like Drever and Hugh, will get his share.'

Oh Arthur,' Gina looked at him with exasperation. 'You really don't understand people, do you? Sydney isn't interested in sharing anything. It isn't just money he wants. He wants all the things that would have been his by right if your father hadn't been married before. He wants the title. He wants to be at the head of the firm. Don't you see, my dear. Sydney is after your job.'

Arthur looked unhappy. 'And he might get it,' he observed bitterly, 'when Father finds out I bungled the Murchiston contract. You see, Gina? I can't even do my job properly.'

'That's only because you're never allowed to do it. Your father's to blame for that. You don't realize it, Arthur, but he undermines your confidence. He always knows a better way, a cheaper way . . .' Her small pretty face hardened imperceptibly. 'It's time he retired. It's time he stood back and gave you a chance.'

Arthur said nothing but she saw the withdrawn look creep into his face. 'Arthur, my dear.' She went and sat beside him and slipped her bare arm around his shoulders. It destroyed her to see him so miserable and unsure and she often thought it strange that she should feel so much more protective toward this full grown man than she did toward any of their three children. But Arthur needed to be protected. His gentleness, his kindness made him easy prey, and people, even people who loved him took advantage of him. 'Arthur, my dearest.' Gently she stroked his thick fair hair. 'If only you'd believe a little more in yourself. If only you'd stop trying to be like your father and thinking you're a failure because you're not. Your father is unique. No one will ever be quite like him. But his time is past. The gifts he brought to the company aren't needed any more. It needs different handling now. It needs calm, sensible and competent management and these are your gifts, my dear, and every bit as valuable.'

Arthur looked at her and smiled. It always amazed him that he'd had the courage to ask her to marry him, even more amazing, the fact that she had accepted. Gina was so strong, so forceful, so unlike himself. He sighed. 'I'd like to think you were right. Truly I would.'

'I am right, Arthur. You'll soon see that I am. But you have to learn to be more decisive, to stop worrying about other people's feelings. You have to learn to trust your own judgement. It doesn't matter if sometimes you're wrong. Everyone makes mistakes, even your father. The only difference is that he isn't afraid of making them, he's not afraid to take chances.' She looked at him gravely. 'You must speak to him, my dear. You must explain to him how difficult it is for you to be always waiting, as it were, in the wings. You must persuade him that it's time to let go, that you need a free hand if you're to get anywhere.' She patted his hand and smiled. 'Will you do that, Arthur? Will you do that for me?'

Arthur nodded and Gina leant toward him and kissed him.

'Now come to bed, my darling. Forget about Sydney. Forget about Murchiston. It'll all look quite different in the morning.'

But it didn't look any different. The sense of his own inadequacy grew throughout the morning. He brooded upon Sydney's accusation and it occurred to him that in a way he was right. There was something craven deep inside him, something that shrank away from the reality of life, something shifting and fluid that had him trembling as he stood outside his father's door.

James greeted him smilingly. He seemed in high good humour and Arthur accepted the whisky and soda he offered him though he didn't really care for the taste. James said something about the weather. Arthur agreed, took a sip of his whisky and plunged straight in.

'I thought I ought to have a word with you, sir, about the Murchiston contract.' He swallowed tremulously. 'I'm not sure that I've struck the best possible deal. I — I'm not sure you'll approve ...'

'Oh?' said James easily, seating himself and crossing his legs. 'What seems to be the problem?'

He was smiling but Arthur was never sure about his father's smile. It did not always signify pleasure. He took another sip of whisky. 'I'm afraid I've allowed Murchiston to write in a penalty clause. I know that normally you're not keen on these things but Murchiston was insistent. And as I wouldn't budge on the price, he seemed to need some sort of concession, you know and I thought ...'

James was still smiling though it was with an effort. Silently he ground his teeth. He'd have seen that old dog Murchiston in hell before he'd have saddled himself with a penalty clause. He knew Murchiston's clauses, tight as an actress' corset and with about as much room for manoeuvre. He said quickly, before his irritation showed on his face. 'You thought quite right, Arthur. Murchiston wouldn't have signed unless he felt he'd scored a point. Admittedly, a penalty makes it a tight piece of business but the main thing is you stood firm on the price.' His gaze softened. 'You worry too much you know, Arthur.'

Arthur coloured. He felt almost sick with relief. All that anguish for nothing ... 'Yes, I suppose I do,' he admitted ruefully.

'You see, Arthur,' James smiled at him encouragingly. 'You need to be able to feel your way with a man. You have to know what he wants and how badly he wants it. Talk to his clerks and his office boys. Find out what you're up against; how well he is doing, what orders he has in hand, how much is actually in the till.'

Arthur winced. 'Yes, I know. I'm afraid I'm not very good at that sort of thing. It all seems so underhand.'

'It is. And you don't have to do it. That's what we employ agents and managers for. It's they who should be keeping you informed.'

'Oh they do, sir,' said Arthur loyally. 'Really, I have a first class team, It's just that ...'

'It's just that you think it a mite dishonourable to pry into a man's affairs?'

'Yes, I do, sir. We shouldn't have to do business that way, at least not anymore.'

James groaned inwardly. Arthur was a gentleman in every sense of the word. He didn't understand that men like Murchiston were not. It worried James a little, that inner core of sensitivity that bordered on timidness. Arthur felt things, worried about things, suffered from feelings of conscience. He shrugged lightly. Perhaps Arthur was right. Times had changed. Intuition wasn't so important. They dealt with faceless companies now rather than individuals. 'You're probably right, Arthur. Old habits die hard, you know. It wasn't so easy in my day ...' He winced. That phrase again. In my day — as if it were over, finished. As if he were finished ...

'Of course. I know that, Father.' Arthur regarded him with that look of earnest intensity which always made him feel slightly uncomfortable. 'No one knows better than I how much you have achieved. I shan't ever achieve anything like so much. Probably, if I'm honest, nothing at all ...'

James rose abruptly to his feet. It irritated him to hear Arthur talk like that. 'Things were different then, Arthur,' he said lightly. 'There were more fools about then.'

Arthur smiled, that shy hesitant smile that always tore at his heart and reminded him so poignantly of his mother. He only ever thought about Elizabeth when he looked at Arthur. Perhaps that was why he was so protective toward him, so tolerant of his bland personality.

He refilled their glasses and for a while they talked of other things; Hugh, Arthur's children, how well Drever was doing running the farms and estates. Arthur sat smiling, warmed by the whisky and his father's glance. Then Arthur said, breaking in upon the companionable silence. 'How do you see the future, father? Of the company, I mean?'

James stared thoughtfully into his glass. 'Gradual expansion, I suppose, within our means.'

Arthur looked startled. 'Expansion!' he exclaimed. 'Don't you think the company has grown enough. We're the largest already in the north.'

'Our size is our strength, Arthur. That was always my concept; a large group of collieries all serving each other and all served by a single administration.'

'Yes, I understand that. But surely there comes a saturation point, a point beyond which we cease to become efficient and merely become unwieldy?'

'Yes, there is. But we haven't reached it yet. To my mind the ceiling would be annual production of something like six million tons, two million up on our present output.'

Arthur frowned. 'But could we find markets?'

'One can always find markets for cheap, good quality coal. It's the one thing industry can't do without.' James looked at him thoughtfully. 'How do you see the future then?'

'Certainly not in such grandiose terms.' Arthur shrugged. 'I suppose I saw us jogging along much as we are now.'

'You don't agree then? That we ought to expand?'

'I don't disagree. I just never thought of it. Naturally, I shall be happy to abide by your decision. You are still Chairman after all,'

James averted his eyes from his son's open face. 'Only as long as you want me to be, Arthur. As soon as you feel you want to go it alone . . .' He broke off. He hadn't meant to say that, at least not yet. He didn't know why he had except that some instinct had told him that Arthur wouldn't make his own decisions as long as he was around. Arthur would always be content to follow where he led. And that wasn't good for Arthur. It wasn't good for the firm. Inevitably, one day, he wouldn't be there. Even though he dreaded the answer he asked him again. 'If you ever want me to step down, Arthur, you only have to say.'

Arthur stared at his feet. Here was his chance, his opportunity to keep his promise to Gina. Except that it suddenly dawned upon him that the thought of life without his father beside him, the thought of bearing the crushing responsibility alone, filled him with misery and terror. That's what Gina didn't understand, not so much that he was afraid to stand alone but that at the heart of him he didn't want to. He smiled. 'I don't think, you know, Father, that I'll ever be ready to go it alone. I don't even believe I really want to. It wouldn't be the same without you. You made the company. You are the company.'

The taut grey lines of James' face relaxed. 'Thank you, Arthur.' Suddenly his voice was soft with tenderness. 'You don't know how much I wanted you to say that.'

Arthur smiled contentedly. Oh, but he did know. He'd always known what his father wanted. Pure happiness welled up inside him at the thought, that just this once, he'd been able to give him what he wanted.

February 16th, 1909
— Stanley, County Durham

At the beginning of a particularly bleak and dismal February, Arthur began his yearly inspection of the company's twenty-eight pits. His father had always insisted on this, that they keep in touch with the workforce, that they didn't become faceless and distant profiteers. Arthur didn't look forward to these occasions. The actual pits depressed him with their grimness and meaness. He hated the air of Victorian oppression that still seemed to persist despite all their up-to-date methods. And he was also aware that he didn't have his father's rapport with the men. They were inclined to regard him with a mixture of scorn and suspicion, quietly contemptuous of his soft white hands and Harrow voice. It didn't seem to count that he was good at his job, that theoretically at least, he knew the business.

Tuesday, February 16th, 1909. In his neat careful hand

Arthur inscribed the date at the top of his memorandum. He glanced at the clock on the wall of the colliery office. Half past three. If he could get away within the next fifteen minutes he might catch the four o'clock from Stanley. He sighed inwardly. So far it had been a long day, spent for the most part listening to the grievances of both management and men; first at Beamish Mary and for the last hour and a half, here at the Jackie pit in Stanley.

'You see, Mr Arthur,' Bill Severs, manager of the Beamish and Stanley Collieries recalled his eyes to the page, 'with respect, it's little use complaining that production figures aren't up to scratch when we're working with out-of-date equipment. Of course, I realize that the Jackie is a short-life colliery and investment must be kept to a minimum. But it's impossible for the men to produce the coal when they're working in such a depth of water as we've had in Shaft Winning.'

'Yes, of course, Mr Severs. I quite understand.' Arthur accordingly wrote in his memo; Item. Problem with water in Shaft Winning Flat in Maudlin seam. Costing for increased capacity pump. He replaced the top of his fountain pen. 'Is there anything else, Mr Severs? Only I'd like, if possible . . .'

He broke off. A noise like a distant firing of cannon, a single muffled shot. He stared at Severs, straining to identify its cause and direction. For a few moments he heard nothing, yet all the time he was aware of a gradual gathering of sound, a tangible vibration of the air. Severs opened his mouth to speak and it remained a tremulous gaping void as the burgeoning sound erupted in a sudden cateclysmic roar. The walls of the office shook. Windows shattered. The earth actually moved beneath their feet. Then silence, as if the building had shuddered and sighed and settled again on its foundations.

'Oh my God,' whispered Severs. 'There's been an explosion.'

For a moment Arthur could not move. He stared at the shattered window, watching the glass slowly fragment. Then Severs leapt to his feet and dashed out of the door. Arthur followed. He felt sick and his legs would barely carry him.

Out in the pit yard the same air of shocked immobility prevailed. Men stood about, arrested in all sorts of queer positions, staring at the cloud of yellow grey smoke that hung like a pall over Stanley.

Then Wilson, the overman lunged across the yard. 'It's the Burns,' he cried. 'The West Stanley's fired. I saw it. Oh God, I saw the flames.'

In the North Brockwell, at a hundred and sixty fathoms, the lowest seam in the Burns, Pat McKenna, known as Irish, lay on his back in the two-foot heading. He was working broken, kirving out pillars in six yard lifts; Irish undercutting the mass of the coal, Geordie Carr coming behind, ramming chocks and filling. Both men worked at a furious pace. You had to be fast on pillars, to get the coal out and the props in while the stone groaned and sighed above your head, anticipating the moment the timbers were withdrawn and the roof allowed to collapse.

Irish twisted sideways under the jud. He was naked except for pit boots and drawers and the sweat rolled off him, streaming down the runnels in the dirt-cake of his back. He grunted and swore alternately with each savage swing of the pick. It had been a sod of a day, the coal hard and stony and a bugger to get. It was a sod of a place too; hot and dusty and where the seam had been watered to damp the dust down, the wet ran down from the roof and walls and pooled the thill with a black oozing slime. He felt uneasy, more so than usual. He didn't like working pillars in any case even though he was paid twopence extra on the score. He didn't like being so near the gob either. All day she had groaned like a bitch in labour. It got on his nerves, hearing the slither of rats between the pack walls, the dull rumble of shifting rubble. Several times he'd had the urge to get away outbye. He would have done, even at the risk of looking daft, but with a wife and two bairns, he couldn't afford to lose the pay. He thought briefly of his young and pretty wife and the silly little hat in Moscrop's window that she'd been saving for weeks to buy. He smiled and fought down the nagging unease. It was near the end of his shift anyway. Just this last lift then, and still time enough to prepare a fresh jud so he'd have an easy start in the morn. He spat on his hands. This next ton for his Mary then, and he rammed the wedges hard into the top coal, nodding with satisfaction as three tubs came down.

He helped Geordie fill the coal into tubs. There was a lot of small, a lot of dust and they needed to take frequent sips from their bottles. Then Irish wiped his face and chest with his singlet and slipped it on. 'Reckon that'll do us the day, eh Geordie?'

Geordie coughed up a stream of gritty black phlegm. 'Aye,' was all he said. Geordie never said much at the end of a shift. The dust always took his chest bad.

They put on their top clothes and collected up the pokes. Irish squatted down on the edge of the gob and waited, vaguely impatient with the older man's slowness. Again the feeling of unease swept over him. He glanced over his shoulder, peering through the forest of creaking props to the impenetrable darkness of the waste. And quiet now, those few seconds of intense quiet that preceded a fall. It came, a dull rumble as another section of the roof gave way, a rush of rank and gassy air into his face. The hair on the back of Irish's neck lifted as firedamp drew up the flame of his lamp.

'Gas,' he cried hoarsely. 'Prick down, man. Prick down.'

Geordie didn't hurry himself. He was used to falls, he was used to gas and merely turned his wick down as a precaution. 'It's nowt, mon,' he said scornfully. 'There's allus gas in the waste. Ye should knaa that by now, Irish, lad.'

All Irish knew at this minute was that he wanted to get outbye. He ducked out of the heading and ran down the slant into main haulage. His nerve had quite gone now. He imagined the gas pursuing him, insidious, invisible, diffused by the air into an explosive mixture. He reached the landing and a little of his panic subsided. It was light on the landing and there was room to stand. All seemed as usual. The boys still working, switching the full tubs from their Galloways onto the mechanical haulage.

Jefferson, the deputy, advanced toward him. 'Ye're a mite soon aren't ye, Irish? Aa hevvn't called lowse yet.'

He needed to shout above the noise of the engine and Irish shouted back. 'There's gas coming out of the waste in number four pillar.'

'Oh aye?' said the deputy. 'So ye've come runnin' outbye like a lassie.' He gave a scornful laugh. He knew Irish's sort, jumpy, hysterical as all Papists were. Bad sort in his opinion to have down a pit. He said with a sneer. 'Ye're nivver feared of a breath of gas ...' He broke off as the light on the landing dimmed. The two big free standing lamps that illuminated the curve now burned with a distinct blue flame. The deputy called out for them to turn down their wicks. He began to advance ponderously across the landing. But before he was even half way across, the glass housings had filled with flame. Then the glass shattered. Red flame spurted up then seemed to die away in a brief muffled explosion, smothered by rising clouds of coal dust.

Irish staggered back and cannoned into a set of empty tubs. For a moment all was blind, choking darkness. And then at the end of an instant that seemed as long as a year, a burst of pain and terror and blinding white light. The blast took Irish full in the face, flung him like a cloutie ball across the landing. All around him there was screaming, a vivid orange light. He saw a man. He thought it was a man. He had no face, just corroded skin and red weeping flesh and a ragged hole where his mouth had been. And out of this hole came a dreadful, desolate animal sound ... Then the flames engulfed Irish, surging up into his shocked and stunned eyes; a scorching wind seared and shrivelled his skin. Blinded and gasping he fell. Beneath him there were bodies, scraps of torn flesh, his cheek was pillowed against the ripped flank of a Galloway. At first he felt nothing, not even pain. He was conscious only of the fact that he was naked. The blast had ripped away even his drawers. It worried him, that. It didn't seem right. It wasn't decent and feebly he tried to cover himself with his burnt and mutilated hands. He thought of his Mary, his darling Mary. She wouldn't be getting her silly little hat ... It was his last conscious thought before he died.

In the Busty seam, six fathoms higher, only one man was left alive. Matt Elliot, the Busty onsetter cautiously opened his eyes. Darkness, silence, a weight of foul air crushing his lungs. For a moment he was only aware of the darkness; hot, heavy darkness, stinking darkness, full of the stench of sulphur and burning ... He rolled away from the wall where the force of the blast had flung him. He felt a rawness on his back, then waves of searing pain as the air met his blistered skin. He lay very still. A little whimpering noise came out of his mouth. He felt as if the whole of his body were on fire. He tried to think, to concentrate his muddled and painful thoughts. It was difficult to remember what had actually happened. The last thing he remembered clearly had been looking at his watch. 3.45. Fifteen minutes to loose. He'd sent a boy along to the Bugle Flats to tell the lads to get their head tubs up. Jack Forster, the pumpman, had stopped by for a word. He'd carried on working; pulled six empties out of the cage, fed six full ones in. Then he'd heard a bit of a bang; the empty tubs in the sidings had rattled together; the electric lamps at the shaft pillar had gone out. Or had the two things happened together? He couldn't really remember. He retained only vague impressions of what had happened after that; a dull roaring noise, as if a set of tubs was coming full tilt toward him. Then smoke, clouds of gritty, choking smoke ... He'd run then. He'd still been running when the force of the blast overtook him ...

Gritting his teeth against the pain of his burnt skin, he sat up and tried to focus his streaming eyes. He hadn't got very far, a few yards into the engine plane. Dimly he could see the shape of his cabin, the dense looming bulk of the shaft pillar. If he could just get to the phone, get word to the surface. He crawled forward, picking his way through the wreckage of smashed tubs. He saw with relief that the hanging lamp in his cabin still burned, a dim button of light, gleaming through the dust. His spirits rose. He lifted the lamp down tenderly, rubbing the soot from the glass with the rag of his sleeve. Holding it aloft he went toward the shaft. He saw the telephone, what had been the telephone, the wires all melted, fused together with the heat. He saw the body of Jack Forster, a naked, hairless, shrivelled corpse. Suddenly there was a sickness in him, a violent shivering that rattled his teeth. The whole of the shaft was blocked. Wreckage spilled out onto the landing, an avalanche of bricks and twisted steel. He licked dry cracked lips. He must get a grip of himself. He mustn't panic. He would just have to find another way out. He went back and sat among the charred wreckage of his cabin. He forced himself to think. Coal from all levels except the Brockwell were drawn via the Busty, that from the Townley seam above dropped down the staple, that from the Tilley came down the drift. He'd never make the drift. Even if he could have got round to the other side of the shaft, the drift was nearly a mile inbye. That left the

Townley staple then, a seventy foot shaft linking the upper seam with the Busty. Anything, he supposed, was worth a try.

He began to make his way along the spur of the engine plane. Now and then his foot touched something soft. There were bodies, parts of bodies, hands and feet. He looked at their faces to make sure they were dead; Joseph Ager, John Mackay, little Ned Manistre, just thirteen, wizened and wrinkled up like an old man. At the foot of the staple he found the body of old Jack Simm. His head lay ten feet away under a tub. It watched him with wide, terrified eyes.

He went into the staple, clambering over the debris of a splintered tub. The rope was still there, a lifeline of plaited steel rising up into darkness. He tested it with his weight and found that it held. It was still attached to the creep engine in the Townley. He felt his courage ebbing. He'd never make it; a seventy foot climb up a thin slippery rope. The alternative was to stay put, wait for help to come. That might take hours, even days, with only Jack Simm and the rats for company.

He gripped the rope. It was cold and oily and where constant friction had roughened the surface, thin splits of wire pricked at his hands. He hauled himself up. The first few feet were not so bad. The lamp hanging at his waist sent dull streaks of light round the staple walls. He could see where the falling tubs had torn the lining away. He could see water seeping through the shattered brickwork. Another ten feet and his strength began to ebb. His arms had to bear the whole of his weight as his boots could find no purchase on the rope. Half way up and his hands began to bleed. He wept with despair and pain. Somehow he forced himself to keep going, knowing that not to do so now meant instant death. He thought of the forty foot drop beneath him, of his body impaled on jagged timbers. He eased himself up a few feet more. Blood from his lacerated hands trickled down over his wrists. The muscles of his arms were locked in pain. He couldn't go on. He'd never make it. He had no idea now how far he had progressed. Was he halfway? Nearly there? He could see nothing but darkness above him. Oh Christ, he thought. He was going to die. Oh, Jesus Christ, he was going to die. The thought drove him up a little way more but he knew there was no hope. He clung to the rope, slippery with his own blood. He began to pray, not a real

300

prayer but the words of a hymn, his cracked, sobbing voice echoed around the shaft. Then suddenly he felt a movement of air against his face, the downdraught from the seam above. He looked up and saw the dim shape of the engine beam. Oh God. Oh wonderful God. He'd made it. He was there. Crying and laughing he caught hold of the beam and dragged himself over the lip of the shaft. The he took a deep breath and the gas filled his lungs. He slumped down on the landing, unconscious.

In the Tilley seam, midway between the Townley and the Busty, Mark Henderson, deputy in charge of the Second South Flats was making his way inbye. He had reached the putter's landing when the explosion occurred. The shock waves actually lifted the iron flat-sheets beneath his feet. He spun round, alarmed, and peered down the ropeway from which he had just emerged. He could see nothing, hear nothing except the steady drip of water from the roof. He went back out into the ropeway and stood listening. Suddenly there was a roaring in his ears. Wind filled the ropeway, scorching and hot. He flattened himself against the wall, heard a thump as the air reversed, then wind again, a fierce gust laden with smoke and grit rushing back the way it had come. The props shuddered. There was a grinding roar as a section of the landing collapsed. Then silence.

He stood for a moment, blinded by the smoking dust of the fall. Then faintly he heard voices, the sound of men running hard and stooped in the dark, the squelch of pit boots tramping through clarts. Shadows detached themselves from the murk surrounding him. A bloom of light filled the ropeway as men crawled out of side roads, retching with the dust.

A boy's voice called out, shrill with terror. 'Oh God. What's happened? What's up?'

Back came the scornful answer. 'The bloddy pit's fired, ye daft beggar. That's what's up.'

The deputy held up his lamp as a marker and shouted out. The big hewer, Tommy Ross crawled toward him.

'How, then, deputy?'

'How, again, Tommy?' The two men greeted each other as if nothing had happened.

'Fourteen of us here,' Ross came abreast and dropped back

301

on his haunches. 'Couple of the young un's a mite shook up but otherwise we're all of a piece.'

Henderson's heart sank. Only fourteen out of forty-two. There must be others still at the face. He looked at Ross. 'Stay here,' he said rapidly, 'Keep the lads together until I get back. I'm going inbye to fetch the others.'

He ran down the ropeway and up the slant. At the top of the incline four men stood, anxiously debating what they should do. He sent them up to the landing and pushed on toward the face. The water was bad, worse than usual, streaming in cataracts from the sagging roof. Two men staggered out of a heading supporting a third. He shouted at them to get away outbye and ran on, stumbling, falling, crawling on his belly now as the roof bore down and narrowed the seam to a bare two foot. He found another three boys huddled down behind a set of tubs and a little further on he found Robert Brown, his fellow deputy, but Robert Brown was dead.

He went back to the landing. More men had arrived on their way outbye. He counted them up. There were thirty-six of them together now. He eyed the circle of subdued faces, tallow white beneath their dirt: John Stark, Tommy Ross, William Batty and Geordie Young; Ned Pace, famous as a survivor of Wingate; Fred Manistre — 'Manny' — talking in his slow calm voice to the truculent Andrew Dean. Then Tom Wheatley, union stalwart and religious fanatic; Harry Whitehead, renowned as a pillar of the Chapel but whose language when kirving out an awkward jud was known to have stripped paint from a door. The boys stood a little way apart, separated by youth and inexperience; Billy Gardner and Issy Ager, both seventeen; little Ned O'Brien, three years younger. The other men he did not know so well: the hewers Lawson and Riley, a driver named Craig.

Then Riley said anxiously, 'How bad is it, deputy. Can we get outbye?'

'I don't know,' said Henderson. 'I don't know anything yet.'

'Well, we cannot just sit, for Christ's sake.'

Henderson remained silent. He wasn't sure what they could do. Their options were limited. The Tilley was virtually a blind alley, almost like an upper level of the Busty seam with only thirty odd feet between them. The only entrance and exit was by the sloping stone drift that connected them with the Busty below. Getting out depended on what conditions were like in the Busty. It would have borne the brunt of the explosion, perhaps it had even originated there. There were bound to have been falls. Almost certainly there would be gas ...

'What about the airways?' suggested Harry Whitehead. 'Couldn't we travel the airways, win out that way?'

'Ye can forget about the airways,' said Manny quietly. 'We've already tried them. Both the intake and the return are full of gas.'

Gas! The word fell into the silence like a stone into a pond, sending out little ripples of panic. They all knew what it meant. After-damp, a lethal mixture of carbon dioxide and monoxide that could suffocate a man in seconds.

'Well, I reckon we should try, like,' said Geordie Lawson, a young hewer. 'The gas might not be so bad on the outbye side. If we travel the workings we might be able to break into the main intake nearer the shaft.' He looked at the deputy. 'Well, it's worth a try. Anythin's better than stoppin' here.'

The deputy maintained his air of quiet calm. Lawson he knew, was tempted to make a run for it, to take his chance on reaching the shaft. Aye, and he'd have been tempted himself at that age. He was a middle-aged man now and thirty odd years underground had knocked some sense into him. And he was a religious man. His belief sustained him, kept him calm. Lawson's only belief was in himself, in his youth and strength, his desperate desire to live. But if he'd thought about it, if there was gas in the airways then it would be coming up the drift, which meant that the travelling roads outbye would be thick with it. But they couldn't stay here either. The landing was too exposed. All the secondary roads inbye converged here. In a matter of hours it would be filled with the gas.

'Reet then, lads,' he said cheerfully. 'Let's give it a try.'

For an hour they scurried through the workings like rats, but every exit was blocked off by a fall or gas. They found seven more men, all dead, suffocated — and a boy who was nearly so, a young pony driver called Jimmy Gardner. He was unconscious, half buried beneath a fall of stone. It was hard to know whether he was alive or dead.

'Is he breathing?' said Henderson, staring down at the still white face.

'Just about,' said Ned Pace. 'Though I don't know for how long. He's badly hurt and I reckon his legs is crushed.'

They began moving the stones tenderly by hand. A boot emerged, an ankle, a knee — a bloody mass of pulped flesh and crushed bone. The deputy swallowed, his gorge rising at the reek of blood. Ned Pace said, 'If the Lord is kind, he'll let him die.'

They improvised a rough stretcher, thrusting splits of timber through the sleeves of their coats. Then they turned and retraced their steps inbye, more slowly now, hampered as they were by the injured boy. They kept to the workings, staying as near the main haulage as they dared, all thirty-six of them squeezing into a low gallery between the intake and the return where there seemed to be a reserve of good air. They squatted down and eyed each other dismally. They had to face facts. They were trapped. There was nothing to do but sit it out and wait for the gas to lift.

'That might take days, mon,' said Riley dismally. 'I had a brother at Seaham. It took three days te get him out.'

'Whey, man, there's no comparison,' one of the younger men scoffed. 'Seaham's three thousand odd feet. We're only a quarter of that here.'

Riley looked unimpressed. 'Aye. It's all reet for you young uns. Y've naa responsibilities. Aa've a wife and eleven bairns at home to think on.'

'All the more reason for ye to bide below then,' said Manny drily. 'I'd ov thought ye'd be glad ov the quiet.'

They all laughed, even Riley managed a wry smile.

They settled down to wait and the first couple of hours were not so bad. They took turns in jowling, beating out a distress signal against the coal. The steady repetitive sound helped to keep their spirits up. They were afraid but they didn't show it and talked a great deal to cover their fear. Ned Pace recounted his experience at Wingate. They all listened eagerly, especially the younger men. Ned's presence comforted them. Ned was living proof that they could survive.

Henderson let them talk, though every word used up a little more air. Strangely, he was more afraid than any of them. He understood their predicament better than they did and his knowledge made him fearful. It was hard not to imagine the worst. He looked covertly at his watch. Seven o'clock. They'd been entombed for three hours already. He reckoned that both shafts must be blocked, either by wreckage or gas, otherwise help would have reached them by now. It was just a question of endurance, of waiting for rescue or for the gas to disperse. Both, he knew, might take days. He wondered exactly how long they could survive. They had light and air, at least for the moment. They had four lamps between them. If they were lucky they might last out for another ten hours. The ventilation was off, all the stoppings blown out. There was no air coming in and what air there was left in the workings would eventually be polluted by after-damp. They had no food, though that wasn't important. They had water, gallons of it, streaming down from the walls and the roof. He realized now that it was the wet that had saved them from the worst of the explosion, diverting the flames away from the Tilley. He tried to look on the bright side. They had a chance. They had a good chance. He looked up and saw the men watching him. He smiled. 'They'll come,' he said confidently. 'Give them time, lads. They'll come.'

Ten o'clock. Silence. At Henderson's suggestion they had stopped jowling for a bit. The noise had been getting on their nerves. Now every man sat quietly, shoulder to shoulder, knee to knee, each wrapped in his own private thoughts. Harry Whitehead thought of his stomach. He'd had nothing since his breakfast of crowdy and dripping and a slab of cold bacon for his bait. His mouth tasted like a midden. He could have murdered a pint and he promised himself that as soon as he was out he'd be straight to the pub and drink himself sick. Aye, that'd be the first thing he'd do, the minute he got out ... He shivered. If he got out. If any of them got out.

Tommy Ross was thinking anxiously of his prize whippet bitch, due to whelp that very night. He couldn't rely on his lass to see to her. She'd be up at the pit-head, waiting for news. And his girl wasn't strong, delicate as a rose. His eyes grew moist at the thought of his darling girl in pain and without him by her to hold her head. He closed his eyes. Perhaps he'd be in time. He prayed hard that he would be in time.

Fred Manistre wondered what things were like in the Busty where his two young sons worked as drivers; Ned, thirteen; John a year older. Fine boys, fine strong boys and with their wits about them an' all. They'd have found a way out, sure as like. Ned now, he was the quick one. Always got an answer, his Ned had ... His mouth trembled. Tears welled up in his faded eyes. Oh, God, he prayed silently. Keep my bairns safe. Don't let them feel any pain.

Henderson, the deputy, was also thinking about death. He thought of his father who'd died down Beamish Air. A long time ago. Twenty odd years but still he didn't forget. Like father like son? For the first time it occurred to him that he might not get out. They had been entombed for seven hours now. They were cramped and cold though their clothes were stuck to their bodies with sweat. It was getting harder to breathe. The atmosphere was hot and heavy with moisture.

Then Geordie Lawson said suddenly; 'Bugger this. I'm not stoppin' here. I'm gannin' to try and get outbye.'

The deputy regarded him mildly. 'Now sit theesel' down, Geordie, mon. If there's a way out, then there's a way in. If there was one, they'd be here by now to fetch us out.'

'Mevvies they are here,' said the old hewer Riley. 'Mevvies they're looking for us and cannot find us. How'll they find us if we're hiding away in here?'

'They'll find us,' said Henderson firmly.

'Aye, so ye keep saying, deputy,' shouted Lawson. 'I'm not si sure that we should be listening te ye. We'll nivver get out unless we shift wa'selves.' He glared at Henderson defiantly. 'Well, I'm gannin' anyways.'

'Well, if ye're gannin', Geordie lad, ye'll gan in the dark. We've no lamps to spare, ye mind that.' Henderson spoke harshly, aware that it needed only one man to break away and he would have lost control of the others. 'Now, bide, lad. It'll not be for long.'

Lawson sat down and dropped his face in his hands. He had begun to sweat profusely and his heart beat up so fast he could hardly breathe. He could feel the walls of the narrow gallery closing in; crushing his body, squeezing the air from his burning lungs. He had to get out. He knew he could make it.

He wasn't affeared of a bit o' gas. He looked up suddenly. 'I want a piss,' he announced.

'Well, have it then,' said Harry Whitehead. 'But get away outside. We've wet enough here as it is.'

Lawson pushed himself to his feet and reached down for a lamp. Manny said quietly, 'Ye divvn't need te see te piss, Geordie, mon.'

Lawson sat down. It seemed for a moment that he had given up, then with a queer sideways movement he cleared John Stark's legs and was out into the ropeway. Without a word, old Riley got up and followed him. None of the men spoke. They sat in silence, listening to the footsteps moving away from them. Then Tommy Ross spat. 'Daft buggers,' he said. 'They'll not get far in the dark.'

An hour ago they'd have all agreed with him but now there was doubt on some of the faces. The thought of darkness, even the thought of the after-damp, seemed to diminish beside the prospect of remaining here. They were consumed now with the idea of getting outbye. A few of the men exchanged glances, seeing who would be the first to speak.

Then Batty said, 'I reckon that's reet. I reckon we ought to see what's gannin' on out there. We might all be sittin' here for nowt.' He looked round the circle of grim dirty faces. 'Happen the gas's lifted by now. Leastways, enough for us to get down the drift into the Busty.'

'And what if it hasn't?' asked Henderson quietly.

'Well, if it hasn't, we can always turn back.' He sprang to his feet. 'Come on lads, who's going to try it with me?'

Four of the men joined him immediately and after a few moments another three. Henderson shrugged. There was no point in arguing. He couldn't keep them against their will. He let them have a lamp. At least then they'd have half a chance.

At midnight, the boy Jimmy Gardner died. He'd been semiconscious for about an hour, though only toward the end did he become really alert and seem to feel any pain. Ned Pace sat him up so that his head and shoulders were pillowed on his chest. Davidson talked to him, telling him stories, trying to make him laugh, anything to keep him from crying out. Then Harry Whitehead, who had assumed the role of spiritual leader, suggested that they say a few prayers. They prayed for a while, even old Harry Gill who hadn't seen the inside of a chapel for years, even Harry put his hands together. Then they sang a hymn. Lead Kindly Light seemed appropriate. They encouraged the boy to join in. 'Come on, Jimmy lad, let's hear you.' It was a grand sound; the men's deep bass overlaid by the boy's pure clear voice.

Some of the men had stopped singing so that they could listen. The boy's voice rose, ragged with exhaustion and pain but piercingly sweet. Harry Whitehead said feelingly, 'If the Good Lord doesn't hear that, He'll never hear owt.'

Then all of sudden the voice died away in a sighing of air. There was a silence which all of them seemed reluctant to break. After a while Ned Pace blew his nose. 'He's gone,' he told them quietly.

'Bloody good job,' said Tommy Ross. 'Poor little beggar.'

Harry Whitehead added in a pious voice. 'At least he died with the Lord's name in his mouth.'

They didn't speak for a while. There didn't seem to be anything to say. Henderson, watching their faces, saw that the atmosphere was subtly changed. Death was an actual presence among them now.

They sat a while longer. There were twenty-six of them now with just two lamps between them. The flames grew dimmer as the wicks burned down. They could not see each other so clearly now. And the air was getting slack. There was a heaviness in the men's chests. One or two complained of feeling sick and drowsy.

The minutes slipped by, lengthened into an hour. Then Issy Ager let out an awful groan. 'Oh Christ,' Issy said. 'We're not going to make it. Oh Christ! We're going to die.' He began to shout. 'Help! Oh help. For God's sake, get us out.'

'Shut yer gob up, Issy, mon,' said Manny savagely. 'If I'm gannin' to die, I'll die quiet, if ye divvn't mind.'

Issy relapsed into silence and dropped his head in his hands. One of the boys started to cry.

Manny looked at the deputy. 'It doesn't seem like any of the lads could have made it. A rescue party would have been in to us by now.'

'They'll come.' The deputy persisted in his optimism. 'They'll be into the Townley first, looking for survivors there.'

'Aye,' Manny nodded. 'Wastin' their time with dead men

while we're quietly dying down here.' He looked at the deputy urgently. 'We've got to do something, man. We've got to let them know that we're here. We cannot last out much longer.'

Then somebody thought of the telephone, the telephone to the compressor house at the end of the drift.

A flicker of optimism showed on their faces. 'It'll nivver be working, mon,' said Tommy Ross scornfully.

'It might be. It might be possible to get to the end of the drift and telephone the surface even if we couldn't make it all the way to the shaft.'

'Well, I'm not riskin' it,' said Harry Whitehead. 'There's ten men tried it already and lyin' out there dead, like as not. At least here we've a chance that they'll get to us in time.'

'Aye. And as good a chance that they'll not. We cannot just sit it out and . . .'

'I'll go,' said Henderson suddenly. 'One man might be able to make it on his own.'

There was silence for a moment then Manny said, 'Ye'll not leave us wonderin', will ye, deputy? Ye'll come back and tell us?' He added quietly. 'If ye can.'

Holding his lamp at arm's length so that he could observe any change in the shape and colour of the flame, the deputy made his way outbye. At the junction with the main haulage he paused. The gas seemed to have lifted. The air was damp and stagnant but breathable. He stepped out into the road, moving slowly and cautiously to conserve his breath. The silence was absolute, broken only by his own footfalls slithering over heaps of rubble, the sudden rattle of stones disturbed by his weight. His confidence grew as he reached the shattered air crossing. He knew then that he wasn't so very far from the drift. So far so good, he thought. Perhaps Riley and the others had made it after all.

They had made it, as far as the mouth of the drift. He found Riley and Geordie Booth there and a little further in he came across Batty and the rest. All of them were dead.

He lowered the lamp to their faces. Batty looked back at him with wide staring eyes. Poor Willie, he thought. Batty by name and Batty by nature . . . Then suddenly the flame of his lamp grew dim, he felt a soft stealthy breath against his face. He retreated instantly, breaking into a stumbling run. Twice he fell, skinning his hands. The second time his lamp went out and he was plunged into an awful blackness. He lay quite still, shocked by the sudden darkness. He could see nothing. All was a solid uniform black. He lifted his head. He seemed to have lost his sense of direction. He wasn't sure now which way he had come. He crawled about, this way and that, his hand fluttering helplessly in front of him till it encountered the line of the wall. Now, left or right? He wasn't sure. He had completely lost his bearings. He listened acutely — nothing but his own breath and the steady drip of water from the roof; long and sharp as it fell the full distance to the thill; softer, with less vibration as it hit the props. And different again, softer still, the impact muffled and absorbed as it struck the sodden bodies at the mouth of the drift. He crawled toward the sound, touched a cold dead face. Then he was in the drift, inching his way tentatively along the wall. He halted. His eyes were becoming accustomed to the gloom. He found he could differentiate between shadow and solid objects. Just ahead of him he could make out the bodies of the dead men. He moistened his lips. What if the stythe were still there? He could be walking straight into it.

He edged forward a few feet more, keeping low to the floor. If there was gas, likely, it would be up a height. The something soft and furry brushed his hand. He saw the dark shape of a rat streak ahead of him. He felt better then, seeing the rat. It meant that he wasn't alone. It meant that if the rat could survive then so could he.

He followed the rat, allowing it to get some way ahead of him. Sometimes it doubled back and they almost collided. Sometimes it tacked across to the other wall. Often he lost sight of it altogether and had to follow the sound of its scrabbling feet. Then both he and the rat were forced to halt. The way ahead of them was blocked by a fall from the roof, and not rubble either, but solid slabs of whinstone that it would have taken a regiment to move.

Henderson sat down and his eyes filled up with tears of despair. No wonder that rescue hadn't reached them yet if they were having to cut through falls of this size. We're all dead men, he thought. Me and the lads back in the heading . . .

But the rat hadn't given up. Its dark shape swarmed up the

mountain of debris, weaving its way from side to side. It disappeared into a crevice and emerged again. Henderson heard the scratching of its paws as it scrabbled for purchase. Then he could hear nothing. The rat had disappeared.

He got to his feet and scrambled up the slope of the fall to the point where the creature had vanished. Yes, there was a gap, very very small, where the fallen stone hadn't quite filled up the void of the roof. He could feel a definite draught coming through. Hope rose in him again. He reckoned if he could clear away a foot from the top of the fall he would be able to follow the rat through. With his bare hands he began to scrape away at the loose rubble, easing the small stones from between the larger ones so that they toppled down under their own weight. Soon he had widened the gap sufficiently to be able to squeeze his body over the fall. Once on the other side it was only a matter of yards to the end of the drift. He remembered the telephone was on the left hand wall at the junction with the Bugle way. He found it easily, even in the dark. He said a short prayer and lifted the receiver. Then he spun the handle twice and waited.

A voice came, distorted over the distance; 'Hello, hello. Is anybody there?'

The deputy answered in his quiet and calm voice. 'Aye,' he said. 'There's twenty-six of us left. Can you get us out?'

Twenty-six men — twenty-six out of perhaps two hundred and nobody was even sure about that, for no proper record had been kept of the men who were down. Heslop the under-viewer had put it at a hundred and fifty, Jones Todd, the lamp man, thought it was more.

'Another cup of cocoa, Mr Arthur, sir?'

'Yes. Thank you.' Absently Arthur accepted a fourth cup. It was cold in the colliery office despite the fact that it was full of men. John Henry Burn and his brother Frank, owners of the West Stanley, were here surrounded by engineers and mine inspectors, viewers and under-viewers; owners and officials from every one of the neighbouring pits, most of which were Arthur's. Outside there were more men; medical men and newspaper men, shaftsmen and sinkers, overmen and deputies; men from Armstrong's ordinance works, grotesque in rubber

311

breathing masks. Since six o'clock they'd been working to clear the shafts. They worked in relays, teams of eight men for half an hour at a time. In nine hours they'd shifted twenty tons of debris and only minutes ago had they reached the Townley. At this very minute Mr Burn was organizing a party to go down; selected persons, fellow coal owners, gentlemen of the press, as if it were some sort of bloody outing. Arthur didn't go. He didn't need to go. His imagination had already conjured up horrific visions of the scene below ground. Of course, if it had been one of his dreams he'd have been in the thick of things, the hero of the hour. But it wasn't a dream. This was real, and so he sat quietly and uselessly in his corner. He didn't even know why he was still here. There was nothing he could do. And yet it seemed important that he maintain this vigil. It would have been obscene to go home to his warm comfortable house whilst there were men dead and dying here. He hoped they had died quickly, especially the children. That preyed on his mind, the thought of the children. Some of the boys were only thirteen. He couldn't help but feel guilty. It wasn't his pit, not this time. But next time it might be. How did a man live with all those dead men at his door?

He went outside to take the air, blinking in the glare of the arc lights. He was surprised at how quiet it was; so many people crowded together and yet he could hear the whirring of the pulley wheels quite clearly and the banksman's periodic cry of 'Bend on.'

There were more people gathered outside the gates. Women mostly, row upon row of grey anxious faces waiting with quiet patience to be told they were without husband or sons. His heart went out to them. He would have liked to have offered some word of comfort but he sensed that his presence among them would not have been welcome. However much he felt for them he was still one of the masters, an exploiter of their misery and grief.

He felt ashamed and turned away, walking back toward the shaft. A hush of expectation had fallen over the crowd. They were bringing the first of the survivors up, the three men who'd been found alive in the Townley. Slowly the cage rose up over the lip of the shaft and settled noiselessly on its makeshift keeps. Two men emerged, pale with shock. And a third man,

312

Matthew Elliot, the Busty onsetter, carried tenderly on a stretcher. Arthur saw his burnt and blistered flesh, his torn and lacerated hands. He saw his face, contorted in such an expression of unutterable horror that it imprinted itself indelibly on Arthur's mind. He looked away and a cold despair settled on his heart that was to remain with him for the rest of his life.

June 14th, 1909
— Longhirst, Northumberland

Hugh came home in the summer. The prodigal returned, Marguerite thought wryly, though in Hugh's case it wasn't a fatted calf but rather a succession of dances and suppers and tennis parties. Of course, in a way it was only natural that the family should put themselves out. They didn't see so very much of him. He only had home leave twice in a year. That wasn't the only reason though. Even Marguerite had to admit there was something special about Hugh. He brought excitement and a kind of glamour into their lives. Everyone was so much more agreeable when Hugh was around, even Sydney wasn't quite so surly.

Arthur, more than any of them, was looking forward to his brother's return. For weeks he'd been thinking about it. Thinking about Hugh took his mind off himself. It stopped him brooding about the Stanley disaster.

He'd gone back to Stanley the following day, drawn by some awful morbid fascination. He wasn't the only one. Stanley was famous, besieged by sightseers and newspaper men, surveyors and engineers. There had even been a telegram from their Majesties. People said useless things like, 'Terrible, terrible — such a tragedy.'

There were no more survivors — just the thirty-six men who'd been rescued the night before. Arthur watched as the dead were brought to the surface. One hundred and sixty-six bodies; parts of bodies, lumps of charred and blackened flesh in canvas sacks that bore no resemblance to men at all. They used the joiner's shop as a mortuary and hospital as there was no proper establishment nearby. He thought that terrible, for the living to have to lay among the dead. And so many dead, row upon row of shrouded corpses, score upon score of grim silent women come to look for husbands and sons. The scene affected Arthur profoundly. He was shocked by the stark indecency of death. Of course he did what he could and made a large donation to the Widows' Relief Fund and another toward the foundation of a local hospital. It didn't seem enough, it didn't seem anything at all set against the terrible carnage. It continued to prey on his mind. He couldn't stop thinking about it and for nights afterwards he would wake suddenly in a sweat of terror. He could never remember these dreams except that there was darkness and death and a noise like the end of the world. And always, yes, always, he was there. Oh yes, Arthur was looking forward to his brother coming home. He would feel himself again, as soon as he saw Hugh.

On the first day of Hugh's leave they went riding together, over Middle Moor and Broom Hill, as they had done when they were boys. Arthur sighed pleasurably as they dismounted and flung themselves down in the grass. He knew this view so well; the gleam of the river caught between steep wooded banks, the line of hills tumbling across the western sky. He could just see Longhirst, roofs and chimneys shadowed by trees. Behind him were the collieries, the slag heaps of Ashington. He looked across at his brother, sprawled on his back. He couldn't help thinking how dissimilar they were. Hugh was as dark as he was fair though both had the same intensely blue eyes. They were like two sides of a coin, both struck from the same mould but quite different. Hugh was so vibrant, so wonderfully alive. His face, deeply bronzed from the fierce Indian sun, had strength and definition and purpose.

Then Arthur said, 'When do you go back?'

Hugh propped himself up on his elbow and grinned. 'You always ask me that. The first day home you always ask when I have to go back.'

'Well, I want to know how long we've got.'

'Three months this time, although this will be my last long leave for a while. We're being posted to some hell hole east of Nepal.'

Arthur looked disappointed. 'Do you ever think about giving it up, the army I mean?'

'No. Not really. I've never wanted to do anything else. In fact what else could I do, come to that?'

'You could come into the firm.'

'No, I couldn't,' argued Hugh. 'And besides, I would hate it, being shut up in an office all day. I wouldn't be able to stand it for more than a minute.'

'What if you marry?'

'I shan't, at least not while I'm still in love with the army, I shan't. It's no life for a woman, especially if you get a colonial posting. Women die of boredom or die with the heat. Either way, it's not much of a life.'

Arthur nodded and fell silent for a while. Then he said, because it was still very much on his mind. 'Did you hear about the disaster at Stanley?'

'Yes. The Guvnor was telling me.' Hugh always referred to their father as the Guvnor. 'Pretty awful by all accounts.'

'Yes. Yes, it was.' Arthur looked depressed. 'One can't help feeling, you know, just a bit guilty.'

'Why should you feel guilty? It wasn't our pit.'

'No, I know that — but we're all in the same business. We're all employers . . .'

'Oh come on, Jamie. You make it sound like a dirty word, as if all employers were exploiters and oppressors.'

Arthur smiled. 'Well, I do feel a bit like that sometimes. Somebody once said that all employers were of necessity oppressive because they exploited a man's need to live.'

'Employers need to live too, you know.'

'Yes, but perhaps not quite so extravagantly. Perhaps the gap between us shouldn't be so great.' He looked at his brother earnestly. 'Oh, Hugh, you weren't there. You didn't see. It was shameful. There wasn't even anywhere to put the injured men. They had to lay among the dead till they were well enough to go home. And there were rats, Hugh, dozens of rats just running over the corpses. They had to employ boys day and night to keep them off . . .' He shook his head. 'Anyone with any conscience would have felt responsible.'

Hugh looked at his brother with tenderness and concern. 'You mustn't take everything so much to heart, Jamie. It happens. It's part of pit life. The men know the risk they're taking. The risk of death and mutilation is part of their job as

315

in a way it's part of mine. There's no reason for you to feel guilty. If I had my head blown off in some war or other, you wouldn't feel that I'd been exploited.'

'That's different, Hugh. Wars aren't for profit.'

'Oh Jamie. Sometimes you really are naive. All wars are about profit; the pursuit of wealth, the defence of wealth. What on earth do you think the Boer War was all about?'

Arthur looked doubtful. 'Well, perhaps you're right. It's just that I can't help thinking . . .'

Hugh leant across and ruffled his hair. 'That's your trouble, Jamie. You think too much.' He leapt to his feet. 'Come on, I'll race you back.'

Arthur smiled. Yes, that was his trouble. He thought too much. He cared too much. It didn't make for the easy life.

September 24th, 1910
— Cathedral Buildings, Newcastle

Arthur stared dreamily from the window of his office. Not that there was anything to see, just more offices, rows of windows with gilded letters gleaming through the dirt; J. Croxley & Son, Coalfitters; R. Brown, Marine Engineers — just more and more of the same. He'd preferred their old offices in Exchange Buildings. At least from there he'd been able to see the river; he hadn't felt quite so shut in. He moved his head slightly. The warm September sun beat down through the glass and roasted the left side of his face. He thought that he ought to move his chair. Being fair, too much sun didn't agree with him and he'd often wondered how Hugh survived the fierce Indian heat. His shoulders sagged a little, thinking about Hugh. He'd only been gone a week and yet he missed him like hell. They'd had such a time. It had been just like the old days, the two of them going about together, all the places that Gina wouldn't have approved of; White's, Boodles, the Bodega Refreshment Rooms where he'd won fifteen pounds at roulette. He never gambled unless he was with Hugh. Hugh was lucky and it seemed to rub off. He'd even backed the winner of the Gold Cup at Ascot.

He looked back into the room. His father was going over the half yearly figures, always a strenuous time for Arthur who lived in dread of some error on his part coming to light. Not that there was ever any foundation for thinking this. Arthur was always meticulous over the returns and never once had he made a mistake. All the same he worried, about the business, about himself, about everything.

In a chair by the door, Sydney lounged. That really irritated Arthur, Sydney's habit of tilting his chair back on its hind legs. Why couldn't he sit square like other people did. Why did he always have to sprawl and lean as if standing on his own feet were too much effort? And those clothes! Balefully Arthur eyed the light-coloured lounge suit and two-tone shoes so at odds with his own dark morning coat and pin stripes. Arthur always dressed as their father dressed, as all other men of business dressed, all other men except Sydney.

Then James said, frowning. 'I see the Hetton wayleaves have gone up again. That's the second time this year.'

'Yes, I'm afraid so.' Arthur roused himself. 'I have written a strong letter to Sir Lindsay Wood but as yet I have had no reply.'

'I think we'll have to do better than a strong letter, old chap.' Sydney straightened himself from his lounging position. 'Those wayleaves are just the tip of the iceberg. Hetton have been making difficulties over concessions for years.'

'I've done everything that could be done,' said Arthur defensively. 'It's a difficult situation and one where we can never hope to have the upper hand. In the circumstances I've always felt it best to act with tact and diplomacy.'

Arthur flushed with gratification as their father backed him up. 'Arthur's quite right, Sydney. I'm afraid that's the only way. Hetton have got us over the proverbial barrel in as much that, economically speaking, coal from our Sherburn Collieries needs to cross Hetton land. It isn't a new problem and of course, in the old days it wasn't a problem at all, when Lord Durham owned Lambtons and had Lindsay Wood and every coalowner for miles around in his pocket. Hetton were only too glad too oblige, then. I'm afraid we have never been accorded the same privilege.'

'And never likely to be either,' Sydney said drily. 'Honestly, sir, I think it's time we made some sort of stand.' He rose casually to his feet and went to stand before the framed linen map that covered the far wall. The red coloured areas marked the extent of their own collieries; the original Joicey Group, diminutive beside the mass of the Lambton group and farther south, the smaller and less profitable Sherburn pits, isolated from its Lambton parent by the pale coloured area of Hetton Coal. Isolated, cut off, necessitating the payment of extortionate wayleaves to Hetton, the alternative being to ship by the long and tortuous river route which was both expensive and inconvenient.

Then he said, turning toward his father. 'I've often thought, you know, sir, that in the long term we'd be better off disposing of the Sherburn pits all together. Quite frankly, their geographical situation makes them a liability rather than an asset ...'

Arthur interrupted. 'I think you'll find, Sydney, that Father's policy is to expand rather than contract.'

Sydney looked at him with derisive amusement. 'Thank you, Arthur, but if you'll just allow me to finish. Actually, I wasn't thinking of contracting. Consolidating was more the word I had in mind.' He looked at James. 'I think we ought to make a bid for Hetton.'

There was silence. Even James looked mildly surprised. 'But Hetton isn't for sale,' Arthur protested. 'And neither is it likely to be. There's absolutely no reason for the Woods to sell.'

Sydney smiled — their father's smile. 'Well, perhaps it's time we gave them one, Arthur. Sometimes these things have to be helped along.'

James spoke then, his voice low and thoughtful. 'What exactly do you have in mind, Sydney?'

'Well, it's only an idea. It might not come off. I dare say you'll find dozens of snags.' He paused and lit a cigarette. 'As you already probably know, the Hetton Coal Company originally had three directors; Nicholas Wood, old Burrell and Philipson. On their death the shares passed to their sons. Then Burrell's son pulled out when the company floated and sold his shares back to Lindsay Wood and Roland Philipson. At the same time they divided the issue into two distinct types of shares — voting and non-voting on a proportion of thirty to

318

seventy. The voting shares they retained themselves, the ordinary shares were quoted as usual on the market. This was obviously their way of keeping control of the company strictly to themselves. The other shareholders got a piece of the company but no rights, no power to go with it.' He glanced at his father. 'Do you see what I'm getting at? Control of Hetton rests on acquiring just sixteen per cent of the voting stock not seventy five per cent as is usual. And yes, I know, in the ordinary way we wouldn't have a hope in hell. But — and this is the point — Roland Philipson was killed in a motor accident two weeks ago. His sixteen per cent voting stock is now held by his widow, who I'm fairly confident could be persuaded to sell. Even if we could acquire just ten per cent, it would give us enormous clout with Hetton's board.' Sydney looked at his father. 'It's worth a try, don't you think, sir? After all, we've nothing to lose and everything to gain.'

James nodded thoughtfully. 'Yes, indeed, Sydney, it's worth a try.'

Arthur opened his mouth to protest. Really! He didn't approve. It was tantamount to sharp practice ... But neither his father or Sydney were looking at him. He fell silent as he saw the smile that passed between them.

December 15th, 1910
— Sunningdale Park, Berkshire

James descended from the train at Sunningdale and walked briskly along the platform. He moved with a lightness and agility unusual in a man of nearly sixty-five and on this clear and crisp December morning he didn't feel his age. Since this Hetton business had come up he had felt almost young again, like an old hound who'd suddenly picked up the fading scent of his youth. He'd forgotten what it was like — the tension, the excitement, imposing his will upon life rather than letting life impose its will upon him. Except that it was more of a game to him now, more an exercise of his wits and power. There wasn't the same urgency, the need to win at all costs. It wasn't a

319

question of survival as Lambtons had been. He merely wanted Hetton because it was there. And things were moving along very nicely. Approaches had been made to Philipson's widow and Sydney was confident of having the matter settled within the week. In the meantime they were quietly buying up such ordinary shares as they could. It was important not to alert the market too soon. Once his interest was known, Hetton stock would rise, and so they needed to work through a complicated network of brokers and middle men who could be trusted to act with discretion. There was only one man James felt it necessary to confide in fully, though even that was really a formality. William James hadn't taken an active part in company business for years. His health had not been so good of late and this visit to Sunningdale was a mixture of duty and courtesy. It was a long time since they had met. Even so, within minutes, antagonism had sprung up between them.

'So. It's Hetton now, is it?' William James said with heavy sarcasm. His voice was faintly slurred, the aftermath of a mild stroke that had left him with a drooping eyelid and dragged the left side of his mouth into a permanent leer. It gave him a slightly drunken appearance which more often than not was justified.

He cast James a brief inhospitable look. If he had known he was coming he'd have bothered to spruce himself up a bit. Being with James always made him very aware of himself and he was conscious now of his unshaven and somewhat seedy appearance, the glass of whisky at his elbow though it was barely eleven o'clock. As if in a mirror he saw himself, how age had diminished his once elegant stature and endowed his shoulders with a permanent stoop. He saw his scalp showing pinkly through his thinning hair, the bones of his face sharp and prominent. His skin too had a yellow liverish tinge and there was about him that curious apathy that came to a man when he'd nearly reached the end of his life and had nothing better to do with the remainder of his days than reflect on his disappointments. He flushed as he felt James' sympathetic glance. Usually he drew attention to his delicacy and poor health but from this man he wanted to conceal it. In vain he searched his cousin's face for similar signs of decay, examining his eyes for the sickly yellow tinge of illness, listening for a querulous note in his voice. Then he said, trying to inject strength and vitality into his own voice, 'Well, I dare say you know what you're doing, James. You seem confident, as always, of pulling it off.'

James answered with his habitual caution. 'Well, I am providing we can obtain Philipson's shares. In that case I don't see that Lindsay Wood has too many options. He can give in gracefully and sell outright. If he fights it, then he's in for an open wrangle for control which will send Hetton shares plummetting. Assuming that we hold an equal amount of voting stock, then it's stalemate. We can block any decision Hetton's board tries to make. We can bring the company to a virtual standstill.'

William James smiled drily. 'It doesn't sound to me as if Lindsay Wood has any options at all. He either sells or you will ruin him.' He gave James a searching look. 'What, I wonder, has he ever done to you?'

'Why should you think there's anything personal in it? It's purely a business proposition. Hetton have been a thorn in our flesh ever since we bought Lambtons out. By taking them into the group we get over the nuisance of wayleaves and outstroke rents apart from increasing our royalties by some eight thousand acres. Also Hetton has the advantage of a private railway direct to the staithes at Sunderland. That alone cuts our haulage costs by some fifteen per cent.'

'Well, let us hope that Lindsay Wood sees it in the same glowing light.'

James shrugged. 'It's a risk we all run — that one day somebody stronger and more powerful will come along and gobble us up. He'll be paid a fair price, more than a fair price . . .'

'And of course, money compensates for everything, doesn't it, James?'

James gave him an amused look. 'You used to think so, if I remember.'

William James' voice was suddenly wistful. 'Yes, yes, I suppose I did.' He knew better now. Money wasn't everything. In fact, money by itself was nothing at all. And, looking back, he saw now that it wasn't really money he'd wanted. The money had just been a means to an end. He glanced around him and felt a sudden pang of nostalgia. He saw the room filled with candlelight, gleaming white shoulders, the glitter of jewels and the sound of laughter. Yes, he often looked back — those heady summer days when the Prince of Wales had virtually been his permanent guest. Dear Bertie. Dear, false and fickle Bertie, the roistering, hard-drinking companion of years suddenly transformed into the majestic King Edward VII. A sad smile touched his mouth. Amazing really, how Bertie had dropped him as soon as he'd become King. Well, he supposed he could understand that. Princes had a licence that kings did not. They needed to keep up appearances at least. But he'd expected some sort of pay off, some recognition, some reward. He'd been confident of a knighthood at least. Of course, he knew now why he'd been passed over. Bastardy, it seemed, was an indelible stain. It meant that you weren't, and never could be, quite a gentleman. That, for him, had been the last and bitterest blow, the realization that he'd been used, that to Bertie and his crowd he'd been just a convenience, like the proprietor of a first class club or hotel ... 'So convenient for the course at Epsom' ... And now Bertie was dead. He'd whored and drunk himself into an early grave and it looked like he was following in his footsteps. That had depressed him. It had made him feel vulnerable. There was only a year or two between them.

They had a new king now, George V, a solemn, po-faced and dutiful young man who seemed determined to make amends for his father's excesses. That he supposed was one of the ironies of life, that men like himself and Bertie should produce such dull and dreary sons. He thought bitterly of his own son, Jimmy, to whom he had not spoken for the last two years. His mother did of course, behind his back, indulging him as she had done all his life, leading him down the path that had ended last year in the bankruptcy court. He still burned with the shame of it. All those thousands of pounds, hundreds of thousands of pounds, and not spent on riotous living which he could have understood, but on butterflies and moths, dead insects in glass cases impaled on steel pins ... Of course, he'd had to bail him out, though he'd grudged every penny. Shameful to have to admit it, but his son was a fool. That worried him a great deal, the thought of leaving his son at the mercy of a man like James. He knew he was dying. Part of his sickness was the loss of the ability to deceive himself. Occasionally, when sober, he saw himself with frightening clarity. And when he saw himself, inevitably he saw James. He'd never been able to stop making comparisons. Of course, he'd never measured up. James could still make him feel an abysmal failure. His father, old James, he'd been like that. Just a look, a glance, holding a wealth of contempt. And as he'd hated his father he now hated James. In his mind, the two men had become inseparable.

He pushed himself unsteadily to his feet and poured himself another whisky. He didn't bother to ask James. James never indulged in spirits before dinner. He found himself smiling, though he had no idea why. Between the chair and the sideboard he seemed to have lost the thread of his thoughts. He frowned. Now, about what had he been thinking? Oh yes. About Jimmy, about James, what would happen once he was dead. He took a stiff pull at his drink. The whisky helped to concentrate his thoughts. He could see it all so clearly. The minute he was out of the way, James would be on to Jimmy to sell him his shares. And of course, Jimmy would sell. He was bound to be strapped for cash, and probably he'd let them go for less than they were worth. There was a way round that. He'd been thinking about it for some time, though he'd always hesitated to hand to James on a plate the very thing they had fought and bickered over all their lives. It was the only battle that James had never won and the thought of surrendering now ... But at least it would be surrender upon his own terms, honourable surrender to protect his son. If it was inevitable that James should have his share of the company, he could at least make damned sure that he paid for it.

He finished his whisky. He felt more like his old self. He'd show James that he still had a trick or two up his sleeve. He said casually, 'Getting away from this Hetton business for the moment, I suppose you heard about Jimmy's bit of trouble last year?'

'Well, I heard something,' James admitted tactfully.

'Yes. Well, it was all very unfortunate. I've been meaning to have a word with you about Jimmy for some time. I've kept putting it off. You know how it is. It's regarding my shares in the company. The truth of it is, I don't want Jimmy to have them. For one thing he's interested in nothing but his damned insects. He'd be an embarrassment to the company in all respects. Obviously you would think about buying him out and I dare say that Jimmy would be inclined to sell. But to be frank, he isn't to be trusted with any amount of money. He'd run through it in no time at all.' He lit another cigarette. 'I'd feel easier in my mind if the thing were settled now. That way I could tie the money up and restrict Jimmy to an annuity. Perhaps next time I'm in town we could meet and discuss it?'

James threw him a questioning look. 'I'm not sure what it is you want to discuss.'

William James smiled slyly. 'I'm offering to sell you my shares in the company, James.' His inner amusement increased at James' prolonged silence. No, you hadn't banked on that, had you, you old scoundrel? You were going to wait till Jimmy was in Queer Street and then buy him out for next to nothing. He said, mockingly, as the silence went on. 'What's the matter, James? Can't you afford it?'

'Yes, I suppose I can. I'm just rather surprised, that's all.'

'Are you, James? I wonder why. It's what you've always wanted, isn't it? It's what you've angled for all these years?'

James murmured something non-committal, sensing that William James was working up to a quarrel. He rose to his feet, suddenly anxious to leave. 'By all means let's talk about it,' he said mildly. 'Let me know when next you expect to be in town. We'll lunch at the Bodega ...'

William James didn't appear to be listening. He went on in his queer drunkard's voice. 'One has to be practical. Neither of us are getting any younger, you know, James. Three score years and ten, isn't it? Do you realize that by that reckoning you've only eight years left?' He smiled maliciously. 'You're going to mind that, aren't you, James? You're going to mind like hell leaving all this behind.' He began to laugh, feebly and malevolently. 'Don't you think that's funny, James? All that struggling and striving, all that effort to get on, only to end up as bones and dust. That's going to be a bit of a poser, isn't it, James? To be faced in the end with something that can't be bribed or bought off or taken over.'

James stared at the sickly wizened face, wrinkling and smiling before him. A coldness crept over him. In spite of all reason, in spite of his health and strength and money and power, he had the strangest sensation that he wasn't looking at William James at all, but at himself in years to come.

Three score years and ten. The thought depressed him and nagged at him all the way back to Cadogan Square. He'd never really thought about death. He'd never cared to admit that there was an end. Seeing William James had shocked him. It made him uneasy. He felt suddenly vulnerable when he remembered that there was only ten years between them. To think that in the end it all came down to that; old age, sickness, senility and death. It was a sobering thought. Death was the one challenge that couldn't be met, the one obstacle that couldn't be overcome.

His mood was still sober when at last he got home.

'You're late, James,' Marguerite said in her cool impersonal voice. 'Sydney couldn't wait. He'd have missed his train. He said he'd telephone in the morning.'

She brought him his sherry. 'And how was William James?'

'Not too good,' said James. 'Not too good at all. In fact, I think he's about on his last legs. Do you know, he offered to sell me his share of the company.'

'What about Jimmy, his son?'

'I think it's because of Jimmy that he's doing it this way. If Jimmy inherited the shares it would only be a matter of time before we'd want to buy him out and Jimmy being Jimmy, would sell. By selling out to me before his death, he can prevent Jimmy getting his hands on a lump sum. Also, I think it's a precaution against me getting his shares on the cheap.'

Marguerite smiled drily. She had never believed William James to be so perceptive.

They sat in silence for a while. Then Marguerite said, 'I thought we'd leave for Ford quite early tomorrow. At least then we'll have one quiet day. Margot isn't coming up till Sunday night. She's bringing a few friends; Vere Bertie and the Roddam girls and Everard Lamb.'

James frowned. 'She's seeing a lot of young Everard lately, isn't she?'

Marguerite glanced at him. 'Do you object?'

'No. I suppose not. At least he's an improvement on the last one. I don't know why she has to have such peculiar friends.'

'They aren't all peculiar, James,' Marguerite objected. 'I've always thought Vere Bertie to be charming.'

'She's a lame duck,' James said unkindly. 'She's got no guts or personality of her own. Margot seems to delight in collecting people like that. Anyway, it's more her taste in young men I was referring to.'

'You're prejudiced, James. Fathers always are. I think you'd be perfectly happy if Margot never married at all.'

'It's not that at all, but I don't see as there's any rush.'

'She's twenty-four. If she doesn't find someone to suit her soon all the eligible young men will have been snapped up. Once a woman's past thirty she doesn't have so much of a choice. It isn't so easy to find a husband then.'

James eyed her mockingly. 'You managed, my dear.'

'That's what I mean.' She gave him a faint smile. 'You were a last resort.'

He returned her smile. He had forgotten how once she had amused him.

They dined alone, and he couldn't help notice how frugally she ate. He watched her covertly, and noticed the air of exhaustion that accompanied her movements. She had lost weight too, the dress that had once fitted her perfectly drooping at her throat. It was her hands he noticed the most, the rings hanging slack upon suddenly skeletal fingers where once they had sat comfortably on her smooth flesh. He remarked upon it and saw how, quickly, she avoided his eyes.

'I'm a little tired, that's all,' she answered him lightly. 'I'm getting old, I suppose. One's appetite — for everything — diminishes with age.'

He stared at her hands. Those hands really worried him, lying so thin and weak upon the table. 'Perhaps when this Hetton business is over, we'll get away, if you like. Cannes, perhaps, or even Venice again.'

She nodded. 'Yes, that would be nice. Perhaps in the spring.'

He looked at her anxiously. Something was wrong. He had never seen her so worn, so passive before. 'Are you all right, Marguerite?' he asked her sharply.

'Yes, of course — well, just a bit out of sorts, that's all.'

'Why don't you drop in and see David Barty? He'll probably give you something to buck you up.'

Marguerite nodded, avoiding his eyes. 'Yes,' she said. 'Perhaps I will.'

Of course she knew, long before she entered David Barty's elegant consulting rooms. It was February now. It had taken her these weeks to pluck up the courage to discover whether her fears were real or imaginary. It had been an easy thing to put off. She wasn't in any pain, she didn't even feel ill — just tired, very tired, and this vague inner feeling that all wasn't well. But knowing, really knowing, no longer being able to dismiss it as nerves or her time of life ... It wasn't the same, and now as she stood again outside the black painted door flanked with brass plates, she felt sick and dizzy and ill.

The porter was solicitous, and seeing that she had no conveyance to meet her offered to fetch her a cab. Marguerite shook her head. She preferred to walk. She couldn't face going home quite yet.

She walked quickly down Harley Street. The world looked strange; blurred, indistinct, as if her vision were affected. Colours burned her eyes; hot reds and yellows, sickly blues and greens. Her breath didn't seem to be filling her lungs.

She turned into Marylebone Road. Beyond lay the park, Regent's Park; an oasis of quiet, a cool green island moated by traffic. Abruptly she stepped out into the road and a cab driver shouted out as she forced him to swerve. She walked on, repressing the urge to break into a run, through the wrought iron park gates, along the wide carriageways choked with rotting leaves. People passed her; nurses and governesses with small noisy children; shopgirls and clerks taking the air. She saw a girl walking toward her. She was young, not very pretty, her clothes shabby and cheap. But her flat cheeks glowed with robust health, her strong young body pulsed with vigorous life. Marguerite's eyes clouded with quick and bitter tears. It wasn't fair. It wasn't fair. Why must it happen to her?

She sank down on a bench and stared at the trees; dark skeletal shapes like the bones and arteries of a fleshless corpse. A light wind touched her face, pungent with the smell of damp earth and decay. Somewhere, high above her, a bird sang persistently, the same sharp sweet note repeated. She closed her eyes and listened intently, as if by fixing her mind upon the sound she would maintain her grip upon reality. She tried to remember what David Barty had said. But all she could remember were his hands upon her body with their queer sterile smell, the coldness of probing intrusive steel. She breathed deeply and placed her hands upon the place where this thing was. She hoped there wouldn't be too much pain. She could perhaps bear it if there wasn't to be pain. And what would she tell James? Would she tell him at all? He was always repulsed by any kind of illness. She rose from the bench and dusted her skirts and walked slowly back the way she had come. Outside the gates she waved down a hackney and sank back into the dim and shabby interior. No. She'd made up her mind. She wouldn't tell James. Probably, he wouldn't care. Probably, the news would be a relief, that slowly but surely, she was dying.

Lindsay Wood kept him waiting as James had known he would. A full five minutes kicking his heels in the plush oak panelled office. He glanced around him. The walls were hung with past and present Woods; old Nicholas flanked by all four of his sons; Collingwood, John and Nicholas, all of whom were dead — and Lindsay, who was very much alive. James stared at the long haughty features thoughtfully. The portrait had been painted some years ago and showed a middle-aged man with light indolent eyes. Was it wishful thinking on his part to imagine that there was a hint of weakness in the faintly smiling mouth? Perhaps there might have been then, years ago. Lindsay Wood was an old man now, older even than he was. There wouldn't be many tricks he didn't know.

He sat down again and went over his plans for the hundredth time. He was confident that he had left no loophole. All that really stood in his way was this man's personality, whether he would capitulate and take the easy way out or whether he'd make a fight of it on principle. He was relying a great deal on the element of surprise. So far he'd been able to keep the market ignorant of his interest. After today that wouldn't be possible.

Then he rose to his feet. Lindsay Wood advanced toward him, his hand outstretched. 'My lord,' he smiled his quiet restrained smile. 'I'm so sorry to have kept you waiting. I was held up on the telephone. That's the trouble with these things. One never quite knows when they're going to ring.'

'Won't you sit down?' He gestured with an elegant hand to a nearby chair. 'Can I offer you some refreshment? Whisky? Or a glass of sherry perhaps?'

James accepted sherry. He's nervous, he thought jubilantly. Wood hadn't stopped talking since he entered the room. That was always a sign that a man was on edge.

'Now then, my lord. How can I help you?' Sir Lindsay seated himself behind a half acre of mahogany. 'If it is regarding the wayleaves, I think I might have anticipated you there. My board have already made a reply to your firm's letter. Unfortunately, they were unable to make any further concession.' His perpetual smile was suddenly tinged with malice. 'Times are hard, my lord, I'm sure you'll agree. We all have to make profits where we can.'

For the first time James spoke. 'I'm glad you think so, Sir Lindsay. I had rather hoped that you would take a realistic view.'

Wood looked puzzled. 'Of what, my lord? At what am I supposed to be looking?'

'At my company's offer to buy up Hetton Coal.'

Not a muscle of Lindsay Wood's haughty countenance moved. 'You are perhaps suggesting some sort of merger, my lord?'

'No. I'm suggesting that you sell to me the remainder of the Hetton voting stock.' He smiled. 'I am already in possession of the rest, plus twenty per cent of the common stock.'

There was a pause which lengthened into an uneasy silence. Then Sir Lindsay said; 'May I enquire how these shares were obtained?'

'In a perfectly legal manner,' James replied. 'I made an offer which was accepted. I now make the same offer to you. I think you'll find our terms generous. Two per cent on the quoted price and a seat on the board should you want it. As our American friends would say, I'm making you an offer you can't refuse.'

'And if I do refuse?'

'I don't know if that would be wise, Sir Lindsay. Certainly it wouldn't be in the interests of your shareholders. As I said, my company holds an equal share of the voting stock, which gives us equal rights, equal power. You could make no decision without my agreement.'

'And conversely, neither could you without mine.'

'That is so,' said James. 'And in that case no decisions could be made at all. I'm sure you are aware what would happen then; trading would be suspended, Hetton shares would plunge . . .'

Wood interrupted him. 'And has it occurred to you, my lord, that if you render Hetton shares worthless and the company bankrupt, you stand to lose a great deal yourself?'

James smiled. 'But I can afford it, Sir Lindsay. Can you?'

Lindsay Wood was silent. For all his mild and ineffectual appearance he was an astute and clever man. One of his qualities was that he was an excellent judge of character and out of all of his contemporaries, he was one of the few who had never underestimated James Joicey. He supposed he should have anticipated this. It followed though that after Lambtons, Hetton would be the next on the list. He'd become complacent, allowed matters to drift. What a colossal blunder not to have safeguarded Philipson's shares. He stared down at his pale gentleman's hands. He wondered how much was bluff, how much was really meant. How far would this man go to get control of Hetton? He considered the odds if he were to make a fight of it. Could he count on his own board to back him? And even as he weighed up the pros and cons, he looked up and met James Joicey's eyes. He smiled faintly and inclined his head in a gesture of resignation. 'As you say, my lord,' he said with mild irony. 'It's an offer I cannot refuse.'

They celebrated, the whole family together. Even Hugh had managed to come home on leave.

'To the Lambton, Hetton and Joicey Collieries.' Sydney, flushed and smiling, proposed the toast. Arthur responded with a pale set face. Gina too looked grim on Arthur's behalf. Quite clearly, Sydney considered the acquisition of Hetton a personal triumph.

Absently Marguerite sipped at the cool champagne, aware of the undercurrent of discord. Since the discovery of her illness she had seemed more sensitive to atmosphere, indeed all of her senses had become more acute. Everything was suddenly endowed with a febrile brilliance, everything suddenly sharp and clear. She found she noticed things more now, things about people: her daughter's pale and translucent beauty. How thin she was and her skin had a milky bluish tinge like a piece of rare and delicate porcelain. She sighed inwardly. She would have liked to have seen Margot married and settled. She didn't really care for the crowd she ran around with; vaguely Bohemian types, refined, aristocratic young people from wealthy backgrounds who talked earnestly and incessantly about 'art' and 'psychology'. Pseudo-intellectuals, as James called them and great supporters of causes like women's suffrage and social reform. They pretended to despise wealth and old fashioned values and morality, all in well bred, cultured voices.

Her eyes moved on; Drever, her youngest son, gazing shyly and adoringly at Mary Gray, the daughter of their bailiff at Ford. Not perhaps the match that she would have hoped for, though she didn't doubt that Mary would make Drever an admirable wife. And Sydney. His arrogant laughter drew her eyes to his face. She was vaguely ashamed to admit it, but out of all of her children she still loved him the best although she had no illusions about him now. There was a cruel streak in Sydney, an unpleasant side to his nature that delighted in provoking Arthur and gained obvious pleasure from his half-brother's discomfort. And against all this, Arthur's appalling sensitivity, made infinitely worse by Gina's protective love. It worried her, this covert hostility. She wondered what would happen when she was no longer here to keep the peace. Her fingers tightened on the stem of her glass, for the prospect grew more certain every day. And yet in herself she was calm. She had found courage and peace of mind in quiet and constant prayer. To the idea of death, even painful death, she had gradually become resigned. But the pretence of normality was becoming an effort. Keeping it from her family had been more difficult than she had thought. She tired so easily. Even now, though the evening had barely begun, her thin body was drooping with fatigue. Uncomfortably, she was aware of James' glance and she wondered sometimes if he had been deceived by her vague explanations of the outcome of her visit to David Barty. Perhaps only because he wanted to be. He would have shied away from so unpleasant a truth.

At ten o'clock she went upstairs and once inside the safety of her room, the smiling vivacity fell away. She undressed herself, slowly and clumsily. She had no servant to attend her now. Since her illness she guarded her privacy. Trembling with fatigue she drew on the heavy lace nightgown and went toward the bed. She did not hear the door open. She was not aware that anyone was there until she heard his voice.

He stood, just looking at her with pain in his eyes. For all the ruffles of lace at her throat and wrists, she could not disguise her pitiful thinness.

'What is it?' he asked quietly. 'Won't you tell me?'

She didn't answer and he came toward her. 'Tell me,' he demanded roughly. 'I have a right to know.'

She shook her head mutely, It was so hard to say. She dreaded to hear the actual words. Then she said at last in a small tired voice. 'I'm ill, James, very ill. I have cancer of the uterus.'

His face whitened with shock. He sat down beside her on the edge of the bed. 'Cancer of the uterus. What does that mean?'

She gave a tired, painful smile. 'It means, James, that I am dying.'

They stared at each other and it seemed as if all of their life together before this moment, all the bitterness and anger, all the unhappiness and pain, it was as if they had never been. For a long time they looked at each other, pride forgotten, all pretence gone. Then James asked her quietly, 'How long?'

'Six months,' she whispered. 'Perhaps less.'

He turned his face away from her and she saw his shoulders heave as if he struggled for breath. Then she realized he was crying. Tears of real anguish streamed down his face.

'James?' She touched him uncertainly, the first time in years. 'James, it's all right. Please don't, my dear.'

Then suddenly he was in her arms. He clung to her like a child, his face hidden against her breast. 'Marguerite, don't leave me. Don't leave me alone.' He looked up into her face, and in a voice full of tears and pain and remorse, he spoke the words she had waited twenty-five years to hear.

July 5th, 1911 — Cadogan Square, London

Six months she had said, but in the event it was less. By June she was in considerable pain. They returned to London, partly so that she could be near David Barty, and partly because she refused to admit that she wouldn't be well enough to attend the King George's coronation set for the end of June. As it was, he needed to go without her. He felt this deeply, that she should have been denied the glittering occasion. She'd always said it would be her proudest moment, to see him in his baron's robes kneeling in homage to his king.

After that she seemed resigned and tranquil. It was James who was rebellious, pestering David Barty out of his life, demanding second and third opinions. Part of her pain was his inability to come to terms with the inevitable. He could not accept this gradual fading before his eyes. Not until the last week did he finally give up and it took something out of him, to be so completely and utterly defeated.

The pain was sporadic, it came and went. Some days she was almost like her old self. They talked together a great deal, always about the past, aware that for her at least there was no future. She slept quite a bit, sometimes naturally, more often than not with the aid of morphia. But whenever she woke, James was there. Night or day, he was there. He was stubborn about this and despite Barty's advice that at his age he was in danger of killing himself, he always kept himself within a minute's call. He'd never forgotten the suddenness with which Elizabeth had died. He'd always thought it cruel to have been denied a farewell. And yet this seemed crueller, this long farewell, this slow grinding away of her life.

The last day — today — was a good day. In the morning she woke bright and lucid — enough for her to fuss about her appearance and insist that her hair be put up. It looked grotesque, the mass of heavy lustreless hair, top-heavy above her thin wasted face. She wanted to talk. She asked about the children, though all of them came several times a day. She asked about Hetton, how things were going. She seemed pleased when he told her that three days ago the final papers had been signed, though he had told her this twice before. He knew then that it wouldn't be long and at six o'clock sent for David Barty. They were all here now, grouped around the bed, all of the family except Hugh.

She was quiet now, her eyes closed though she wasn't asleep. The room was dim, curtained against the bright summer light. Dim and full of flowers, great cabbage roses that gave out an overpowering smell so that forever afterwards he could not bear their scent.

'James. James.' He leant toward her, her voice was so faint and weak. 'Yes, Marguerite? Yes, my love?' But his name was all she said.

August 4th, 1914 — Ford Castle

'BRITISH ULTIMATUM EXPIRES AT MIDNIGHT. WAR WITH GERMANY IMMINENT.' James read the banner headline with a sinking heart. It was all of the news; the war, the prospect of war, the culmination of weeks of negotiation and bluff, of threat and counter threat, warnings and ultimatums, which had blown up since the shooting, four weeks ago, of the Austrian Arch-Duke by a pimply Serbian youth. The fatal shot had reverberated all around Europe. Austria had declared war on Serbia and Russia's championship of the Balkan state had inevitably drawn them in. Then Germany, in support of Austria, had declared war on Russia, involving France, who had treaty obligations to the Czar. The advance of German troops into France via Belgium had dragged in Britain, for though she was bound by no treaty to go to the defence of France, she was pledged to preserve Belgian neutrality. James sighed. This ultimatum was really a last ditch effort. As far as the Cabinet was concerned, war was a certainty and orders for a general mobilisation had already gone out. The Foreign Secretary, Sir Edward Grey, had made a stirring speech, reported at great length on the front page. James studied it thoughtfully: a great deal about British obligations and British honour, then pointing out, on a more practical note, that Britain could not allow France to be crushed, if only for the reason that an aggressive and power-mad

Germany in control of the Channel ports was a threat to their own security.

He looked across at his son Hugh, who was similarly occupied with the *Telegraph*. 'It looks like we're in, then,' James observed gravely. 'I can't see the Kaiser backing off now.'

'Mmm,' said Hugh. 'Grey seems to be making a final effort to try and head things off but I don't think he'll succeed. We're going to have to make a fight of it, like it or not.'

'How will that affect you?' asked James. 'Will your regiment be brought in?'

'I doubt it,' Hugh answered with an air of regret. 'It would take a good three months to get our chaps mobilised and into Europe. It'll probably be all over by then.'

'You don't see it lasting, then?'

'No. Not now that we're in. I shall probably have to cut my leave short and report in. With any luck I'll get a secondment to a service regiment. I could do with seeing some action.'

James flinched inwardly. Though he would never have admitted to a favourite son, if he had one it was Hugh. Perhaps because he could never feel easy about him. There was always the risk, always the thought ... He said suddenly, 'Aren't you ever afraid, Hugh?'

. Hugh grinned. 'Of course. All the time — not so much of cashing in my chips altogether but of getting crocked up; badly I mean. I'd hate that, being crippled or blinded.' He smiled. 'I try not to think about it. It doesn't do to be a pessimist in a game like mine.'

James nodded and after a while returned to his paper, ploughing through the report of the Finance Bill. Lloyd George was out with the begging bowl again, this time proposing to tax income from foreign investments. He yawned. Politics were inclined to bore him these days. For one thing he had little opinion of the current mealy-mouthed policies, or of the men that formulated them either; the suave and aristocratic Balfour, the meekly ambitious Bonar Law; the Labour men, Ramsay MacDonald and Keir Hardie. Even the men of his own party: Asquith the Prime Minister, often the worse for drink; Lloyd George, that lecherous little Welshman with his blatant efforts to get his foot in the door of Number Ten, an ambition shared by that rising star in the political firmament, the truculent and aggressive Winston Churchill.

He turned the page and briefly scanned the society columns; lists of marriages and engagements, the endless round of balls and suppers to mark the end of the season. 'The King and Queen dined with Queen Alexandra at Marlborough House ... also present; the Empress Marie Feodorovna, Queen Olga of Greece, Prince and Princess Louis of Battenburg ...' and so on and so on for an entire half page. And his own name, prominent among a list of guests who had attended a luncheon at Clarence House in aid of Queen Alexandra's Hospital Fund. That had been an event, one of the few for which he bothered to stir himself and make the effort to go up to town. Since Marguerite's death three years ago he had lived, for the most part, quietly at Ford. He missed her still and continued in his own way to mourn her, not with the agony of grief that he had mourned Elizabeth, but quietly, unobtrusively, within himself. In retrospect it had been a time of mourning, a time of loss. William James had died the following January; Rosandra, Colonel John's widow, a few weeks later. And friends as well as family: Dick Lamb had been one of the fifteen hundred lost when the Titanic had gone down in April. Small fragments of his life slipping away, like flotsam on an ebbing tide.

He moved on to the commercial page. All unease and gloomy speculation there. The Stock Exchange was closed until further notice as the City braced itself for the financial chaos of investors withdrawing their money from Europe. International securities were selling heavily. Bank rate up from four to eight per cent. There was good business on war risks, high rates quoted. He ran his eye quickly down the closing quotes. There'd been a run on steel and armaments. Dorman Long and Consett had closed two points up. Armstrong–Whitworth was a whole five points up on the day. He smiled his dry and cynical smile. War meant money for some and the profiteers would already be rubbing their hands, buying up bankrupt stock and job lots in anticipation of the inevitable shortages. He pursed his lips thoughtfully. Perhaps he should have a word with Arthur about increasing production. If the war went on for any length of time... But that wasn't the forecast. Nobody seemed to see it as being of any duration. A sharp rap

336

on the Kaiser's knuckles was what the Cabinet had in mind.

He sighed inwardly. It wasn't really any of his business now since, although technically he was still chairman of the board, he'd handed the general running of the company over to Sydney and Arthur. And he couldn't complain, with production figures for last year of some five million tons and a profit per ton, free on board, of a comfortable one and threepence. Nothing spectacular, of course, but good steady progress and all very well in ordinary times... Except that if the war went on beyond the predicted three months they wouldn't be ordinary times. Then he smiled ruefully. The truth of it was he was dying to get back in. The life of a country gentleman didn't really suit him, all munificence and good works, opening homes for aged miners, old men like himself, put out to grass like winded ponies. They should have been grateful, after years of hardship and risk, to be able to take their ease. But they weren't. They were bored, like him. Coal was something that was in the blood.

He picked up the paper again. Yorkshire out for a hundred and ten. Kent had beaten Somerset by eleven wickets. Though he no longer played, he kept up with the scores. Golf was his game now, suitably paced for a man of his age, and after August there was shooting and he was reminded that the grouse season opened in just eight days. The birds were good and plentiful this year and he looked forward to some days of excellent sport. And what else? he wondered with a sinking heart. What else did old men look forward to?

He folded his paper and laid it aside. For a few moments he sat staring. Hugh was still reading and the stillness of the room made him feel drowsy. He got up and went to the window, open to the heat of the August day. The countryside was replete, overwhelmingly and opulently green; a radiant mist of sunlight drenched the hills. On the home farms the harvest was well advanced, a golden haze hung over the stubbled fields, the stooks of corn stood ready for threshing. He looked down to the parched lawns where his family enjoyed the afternoon sun; Drever and Mary who were to marry next year, Sydney drinking champagne with his rackety friends, his daughter Margot and little Vere Bertie who seemed to be a permanent guest these days. His three grandchildren romped happily beneath

Arthur and Gina's benevolent eyes, Sylvia and Norah, demure and angelic in frilled organza pinafores, young James, 'Jimmy', in a sailor suit. On the terrace the tables were being set up for tea; snowy lace cloths lifted in a negligible breeze, the sun glinted on polished silver, glowed through the translucence of fine porcelain. It was a scene that Renoir might have wanted to paint; women in pale silk dresses and wide flowered hats, men in white flannels and coloured blazers. Suddenly the idea of war seemed absurd. It seemed impossible that any of this could ever change. And yet even as he thought it he was overcome by a feeling of cold premonition. He knew suddenly that this was the last summer, the last of the golden carefree days. After today nothing would ever be the same again.

November 24th, 1914

Sydney lounged nonchalantly in the doorway of Arthur's office. He looked splendid in his uniform, a Captain in the 10th Battalion Northumberland Fusiliers, complete with swagger stick and Sam Browne. And nothing off the peg for Sydney. The khaki drill was perfectly hand tailored to suit his lean proportions. Even his high boots had been hand made. He selected a cigarette from a slim gold case. Arthur watched him; the slim hands cupped around the flame, the fastidious disposal of the spent match in a silver ashtray. Arthur cleared his throat. 'So you're off on Friday then?'

'Yes, thank God.' Sydney came into the room and perched himself on the corner of Arthur's desk. 'The Battalion sails for France on Saturday night. We expect to be at the front by Sunday.'

And no doubt the war would be won by Monday, thought Arthur cynically, once the army had had the benefit of Sydney's advice. He pressed his lips together in the nervous way he had. The war was all Sydney ever talked about, the war, the regiment, the Bosch; and all so casually, as if he were going off to a rugby match, as if it were all a bit of a lark, like a day trip with a few of the chaps. Arthur didn't think of the war like that. He thought of the bloodshed and violence, of ordinary decent men getting themselves blown to bits. Not that it would be like that for Sydney. Impossible to think of Sydney as less than whole, to imagine that immaculate uniform defiled by blood. Naturally, Sydney would return a hero and Arthur envisaged the rest of his life listening to accounts of Sydney's glorious exploits — how Sydney had tackled a gun emplacement single handed, how he had saved the life of his C.O.

But then he didn't think that Sydney really knew what he was getting himself into. None of them at home really knew what was going on. They only knew what they read in the papers, exaggerated headlines meant to promote morale — 'SPLENDID EFFORT BY B.E.F AT MONS'; 'SEVERE REVERSES FOR GERMANS ON THE MARNE'; 'VALIANT DEFENCE OF YPRES BY ALLIES'. But reading on, reading between the lines, they were just vague accounts of piecemeal offensives and sporadic attacks. Nothing was ever actually accomplished.

Hugh was in the thick of it, seconded to the Life Guards serving in France. He wrote cautiously but Arthur sensed that things weren't going well. Everyone had expected the German advance to run out of steam by September but despite heavy losses they were still pressing on. The British, so far, were heavily outnumbered, at Mons, by something like six to one. Reinforcements were desperately needed and at the end of September, Kitchener had called for volunteers. Of course, Sydney had been one of the first to step forward, which apparently gave him the right to sneer at and disparage all those who had not. Arthur had high priority upon this list of shirkers. As a Major in the Territorials, he had naturally been expected to volunteer for France. That he hadn't had provided Sydney with endless opportunities to humiliate and provoke him. Arthur consoled himself with the thought that, at least for a few months, he'd be free of Sydney's presence, of his constantly questioning and criticizing his decisions. He looked up, a faint smile lighting his pale earnest face. 'How long do you expect to be away?'

Sydney smiled mockingly. 'Probably not for as long as you'd like, old chap. I reckon it'll all be over by the spring.'

'Father doesn't think so,' said Arthur peevishly. 'He thinks it might go on for as long as a year.'

'Oh, I don't think so,' said Sydney airily. 'Not now that

339

we're putting some men on the job. Kitchener anticipates having seventy divisions at the front by the New Year. It won't go on much beyond that.' He looked at Arthur. 'I must say the response has been quite amazing, from our own sort at least. Willie Armstrong, Hugh Liddell, and the Lambtons have volunteered practically to a man.' He ground out his cigarette. 'I wish we could have put forward such a good contingent ourselves. It's a damn shame that they won't take Drever, though of course there's no point in a chap going unless he's perfectly fit. As it is, it looks like the family honour rests with myself and Hugh.'

Arthur flushed. He knew quite well what Sydney was getting at. This subtle campaign had been going on for weeks. 'We couldn't both go,' he said stonily. 'Someone has to keep things going here.'

'And you decided that it would be you.'

'That's not true. Father decided. We discussed it. As you seemed so keen to get into it, it fell to me to run things here.'

Sydney shrugged. 'Well, if you say so, Arthur. I dare say you have your reasons for hanging back.'

Arthur stood up. His face was very white. He'd been enduring this subtle goading for weeks. 'Why don't you come straight out with it, Sydney? Why don't you say exactly what you mean? That you think I'm shirking, that I'm afraid to go.'

'Well, aren't you?'

Arthur swallowed. 'Yes. I'm afraid. I'm not ashamed to admit that. But that isn't my reason for not volunteering for active service. Don't think I don't know what you're trying to do. You're trying to goad me into . . .'

Sydney cut him off with a mocking laugh. 'Actually, Arthur, you've completely got the wrong end of the stick. Pushing you in was the last thing on my mind. Quite frankly, the army doesn't need men like you. You're the nervous type, Arthur, just not suited to command. Of course, you've managed all right in the Territorials, but this is the real thing. The men need officers they can rely on, and let's be honest, Arthur, you've never been able to keep your head in a crisis.' He smiled his tight sneering smile. 'So you needn't feel guilty about staying at home, Arthur. It's probably all for the best.'

Arthur stared at him, wondering why he didn't bother to

defend himself. But then Sydney had a way of putting things, as if his cruel remarks were merely honest statements of fact rather than deliberately calculated insults. He would have pretended amazement that Arthur should take offence over what, after all, was only the truth.

Then Sydney stood up and after a moment held out his hand. 'Well, I'll say cheerio then. I'll be running about a bit the next few days so I probably won't see you again before I leave.'

Arthur shook hands briefly. 'Goodbye then, Sydney.' He added grudgingly, 'And good luck.'

Arthur went out for some lunch but found he had no appetite. He walked instead, along the waterfront jammed with ships, through the labyrinth of stacked crates that cluttered the wharves. He stood for a moment looking through the gloom of drifting smoke. It was like a scene from Dante's Inferno; a sulphurish sky tinged with the dusky glow of reflected flame, a leaden wind, heavy with the fumes of iron and steel works, the dry choking smell of liquid amatol. The noise was tremendous, a cacophony of harsh metallic sound; the dull throb of ship's engines, the whine of the cranes, the pounding of steam hammers from the Swan Hunter yards. A train thundered across the High Level Bridge. The freight wagons bore the Armstrong insignia. Another shipment of arms for the front.

He turned his head and looked up river to where the Paradise Works of Armstrong-Whitworth sprawled along the Scotswood Road. Paradise! What an incongruous name for a place given over to the manufacture of death. But one of their best customers, he mustn't forget that. Armstrong's consumed nearly two million tons a year.

A wave of depression swept over him. There was no getting away from it. They were all part of the monstrous machinery of war. And doing very nicely out of it with coal selling at fifty shillings a ton. Oh yes, everyone was making money; coal-owners, shipowners, bootmakers, clothiers — khaki drill was at a premium. Factories were springing up everywhere, churning out shrapnel and Mills bombs, shells and grenades. There were people everywhere and every man that passed him seemed to be in khaki; every wall was plastered with patrotic slogans; everywhere Kitchener's accusing finger pointed. Suddenly he felt wretched; conspicuous in his sombre city clothes. He felt, ridiculously, that everyone was looking at him, that they were saying to themselves 'warmonger', 'profiteer.' Or perhaps they were just wondering why he wasn't in uniform. Perhaps the accusation he imagined they levelled at him was simply one of coward. He shivered. War. War. War. The word beat like an insistent drum in his head. And he couldn't help thinking about what Sydney had said. 'You needn't feel guilty, Arthur, about staying at home.' He didn't even know why he did. Men in his position, married men with occupations essential to the war, weren't expected to volunteer for active service. Nevertheless, he couldn't help feeling a secret shame. People made you feel like that. If you were under forty-five and not in uniform, they wanted to know the reason why.

He halted at the corner of Grey Street. There was a recruiting office next to the theatre. A military band played outside, appropriately, 'Onward Christian Soldiers.' A sergeant in full dress uniform, all scarlet and brass, strutted the pavement and harangued the young men in the gathering crowd. A queue had already formed; young men, ordinary men — ordinary when they went in but not when they came out. King's men now, heads held high, their expressions at once sheepish and cocky. And then out of nowhere, this ridiculous little man strapped inside sandwich boards, marching boldly down the street. Large crimson letters proclaimed; 'Stop the War. Stop The Slaughter. Government Incompetence Is Killing Our Boys.'

A hostile silence fell over the crowd which quickly gave way to jeers and insults. Someone threw a stone. The man staggered a little as it struck the side of his head but otherwise he did not falter. He marched on, like Daniel into the lion's den. He was close to Arthur now. He could see blood oozing from the wound on his head and his prominent eyes, behind thick spectacles were wide with fear. But he faced the crowd defiantly, shouting above the clamour of the band. His voice was strangely accented. It had a faintly guttural note. Someone shouted out from the jeering crowd, 'He's a bloody German. Belt him, lads.'

Suddenly they had surrounded him. He was like a beast in a ring, being pushed and prodded from one side to another. The women were worst, screaming and spitting, then some of the men began to lash out with their fists. There was the thud of a steel toed boot.

Arthur looked at the sergeant. He was bound to intervene — but the sergeant stood grinning in tacit approval, his arms folded across his beribboned chest.

Something broke in Arthur then. A queer bitter anger rose up in his chest. He ran across the road and confronted the sergeant. 'If you don't stop this at once, I shall report you to your commanding officer for failing to quell a riot.'

The sergeant stopped grinning. Instinctively he responded to the authority in Arthur's voice. 'All right then, lads. That's enough. Break it up.' At the loud, bullying voice the crowd fell back instantly and Arthur pushed his way to the injured man's side. But the crowd were reluctant to disperse and a hand made a grab at him. Arthur wheeled round in fury. 'Take your hands off me, you filthy lout. If you're so keen for a fight why don't you put a uniform on?'

'Why divvn't ye, mister? Happen you're workin' for the Germans as well.'

The sergeant stepped between them. This was a good moment for him. Emotions were running high, the crowd was drunk with patriotic fervour and men who had never even thought of enlisting were now suddenly clamouring to join up. With a benevolent smile he shepherded them toward the recruiting office. 'Come on then, lads. Let's put that fighting spirit to some practical use. We'll soon give you a taste of the real thing.'

Arthur helped the man up, helped him look for his spectacles among the wreckage of his boards. Both were smashed beyond repair.

'Are you all right?' he asked anxiously. 'There's a cut on your head.'

'Yes. Yes. I am all right.' The man smiled. 'At least thanks to you, I am, my friend. Perhaps I may know your name, sir?'

'Joicey. Arthur Joicey.' Arthur held out his hand.

'Rolfe. Frederic Rolfe — at your service.'

'You're quite sure you're not hurt? Perhaps I could fetch you a cab or something?'

'No. Thank you. Really I can manage. It has happened before.' He shrugged. 'It is a shame about the spectacles

343

though. They are expensive to replace.'

'Yes, I'm sorry,' Arthur said, as if it had been his fault. 'I'm afraid the crowd behaved very badly.'

'Oh, I do not mind so much. I do not expect to be popular. While the war is on there are only going to be two kinds of men; cowards and heroes, those who fought and those who did not. To these people I am one of the cowards.'

'I am sure that you're not,' said Arthur politely. 'It must take a great deal of courage to stand out alone for something you believe in.'

Rolfe smiled regretfully. 'It is the wrong sort of courage, Mr Joicey. It is not patriotic, this thing that I do. Everything must be patriotic now. The army, they sell patriotism like corn-flakes.' An expression of enormous sadness crossed his face. 'My son, Albert, he was patriotic. He enlisted just four days after war was declared and was killed two months later at Mons.'

'I'm sorry,' said Arthur. 'That must have been terrible.'

'Yes. Yes, it was. He was only nineteen.'

They walked in silence for a few moments then Arthur said, 'Forgive my asking, Mr Rolfe, but you're not English, are you?'

'No,' Rolfe smiled. 'I have lived here for more than forty years and still I am not English. I am a Belgian,' he added. 'It is my country your army is fighting to protect.'

Arthur glanced at him in surprise. 'And yet you're a pacifist?'

'I am not a pacifist, Mr Joicey. I am not against the war. I am merely against incompetence and waste and the exploit-ation of innocent men by politicians and big generals who never get within miles of the front line.' He looked at Arthur. 'Did you know, Mr Joicey, that half our troops do not have proper uniforms? That they are being trained with broomsticks because we do not have enough rifles? Did you know that the entire British Expeditionary force only have a total of seventy heavy guns? That factories in England are producing only twenty thousand shells a day, compared with a quarter of a million a day in Germany? Our own government is killing almost as many men as the enemy. They send these boys to war but give them nothing to fight with. They have not proper clothing, proper equipment; not enough guns or ammunition and much of what they have is faulty — bombs with dud fuses, grenades with loose pins. I told you of my son Albert. He was killed at Mons — but he was not killed by the Germans. He was killed by a faulty grenade blowing up in his face.'

He halted. They had reached the tram station. 'Perhaps I might trouble you further to put me on the right tram, Mr Joicey. Without my glasses, you understand, I do not see so well.'

'Yes, of course,' said Arthur. 'It's no trouble at all.'

Then Rolfe said, 'May I perhaps know what your business is, Mr Joicey?'

'Coal,' Arthur answered shortly. 'My family own the Lambton and Hetton Collieries.'

'Ah,' said Rolfe. 'Then these perhaps are good times for you?'

Arthur flushed. 'I suppose that's what everyone is bound to think,' he said bitterly, 'that we're just raking in the money and doing nothing to help. But it isn't true. Two of my brothers are fighting in France.'

'But not you, Mr Joicey?'

'No.' Arthur's colour deepened further. Why did everyone make it sound like an accusation? 'Actually, I ...' He had been going to say that he was needed here. But he wasn't. That was just an excuse. There was nothing he could do that his father and Austen Kirkup could not. He began to feel wretched again. If only he could explain. 'You see,' he said unhappily. 'I thought I was going to be able to keep out of it, that it would all be over in a few weeks. I didn't expect that it would all drag on like this. And now they're asking for men, I seem to be faced with this awful choice. It doesn't seem enough any longer just to do nothing.'

'No. You are quite right,' Rolfe agreed. 'It is not enough to do nothing. But what we do must depend on our capabilities and conscience. If I were a young man I would go and fight but as I am not, I content myself with my little protests. My wife, she knits gloves and socks for the troops. Me, I go out into the streets and make a fool of myself. But it is something. I am involved.'

'Yes,' said Arthur gravely. 'I suppose that's the important thing, to be able to say that you did your bit, that you were part of it. Not that I'd be any good at it,' he added wistfully. 'I'm not terribly good at ordering people about. I don't seem to have any authority.'

'That dragoon sergeant seemed to think that you had,' Rolfe observed.

Arthur smiled shyly. Yes, he hadn't made a bad job of that. But then he hadn't been thinking. He'd just acted instinctively. He shrugged. 'That was just a one-off thing. I'm not sure that I could do it again.'

'But you'll never know, will you, until you try?'

Arthur was saved from a reply by the arrival of the Benwell tram.

They shook hands warmly and after watching the tram out of sight Arthur turned and made his way back to the office. But he didn't go in. Instead he walked round to the station and hailed a cab. He instructed the driver to take him to Fenham Barracks.

It took him almost a week to pluck up the courage to tell his father. He waited till Friday when they were to dine together at the Liberal Club. And Arthur, having no subtlety, plunged straight in as soon as they had reached dessert.

'Father ...' It all came out in a garbled rush. 'I've been meaning to tell you ... I — I've volunteered to go to France.'

James raised his eyes slowly from the piece of fruit that lay peeled and dissected on his plate. His expression did not alter. 'May I enquire why, Arthur? I thought we had agreed that your place was here at home.'

'Yes, I know we did,' said Arthur miserably. 'And I would like to think that was true. But it isn't true. I'm not needed here and with all of our friends rushing to the colours, I can't be the only one to stay behind. It's a question of example, don't you see. You once told me that when it's a matter of duty and sacrifice, it's the rich and privileged who must step forward first. How can we expect the ordinary man to accept his responsibilities when it's quite clear that some of us are shirking ours.'

'You have other responsibilities, Arthur. A wife, children. How does Gina feel about all this?'

Arthur swallowed. He didn't particularly care to recall that tearful scene. Of course it was difficult for a woman. They didn't see things in the same way. They hadn't the same conception of duty. 'Oh, Gina's all right,' he said evasively. 'I think she understands.' He looked at his father. 'Do you?'

'No, I don't,' said James furiously. 'I suppose as usual you've allowed yourself to be pressured into doing something entirely unnecessary. You've been listening to a load of emotional clap trap about honour and duty ...' He broke off, seeing his son's stricken face. It wasn't even Arthur he was angry with. It was the war, this filthy war, and the stupid short-sighted men who had plunged them into it. Dear God, he thought, weren't two sons enough to have at risk. And now, Arthur, especially Arthur, his first born son, Elizabeth's son ... He shook his head. 'You're a fool, Arthur,' he said bitterly. 'And you've let other fools convince you that you want to go.'

'I don't want to go, Father,' Arthur said quietly. 'In fact I can't think of anything that I'd less rather do. But I have to go. For myself I have to go. Nothing you can say will change my mind.'

James was silent. Despite his anger he couldn't help a feeling of pride. This to him was a very special kind of courage, the best kind of courage, to face up to something that you didn't want to, to be afraid, yet get on with it all the same.

'Arthur ...' He hesitated. He hadn't always found it easy to express his feelings toward his sons. He'd always been afraid of embarrassing them by being sentimental. 'You're very like your mother, Arthur,' he said at last. 'She was also a thoughtful and compassionate person. She felt for people very deeply, especially people who were less fortunate.' He smiled ruefully. 'She hated the pits, you know. She hated the dirt and the poverty and because she hated it so much she was always trying to do something about it. We — we often quarrelled about things like that. I disapproved you see, of her being involved, but she never really understood why. I disapproved because I loved her and wanted to protect her. I didn't want her threatened or exposed ...' He looked at his son with tender eyes. 'Do you understand what I'm trying to say?'

Arthur blinked. 'Yes, Father, I think so.'

Then James cleared his throat and attempted a cheerful briskness. 'Well then. When do you expect to get your marching orders, my boy?'

Arthur finished blowing his nose. 'Oh, not for some time yet. Probably not till the spring. Some of the men haven't had any training yet.'

'So,' James stretched out his hand in an affectionate gesture. 'You'll be with us for Christmas then. That's good.'

Arthur smiled and thought that his heart would burst with happiness. It was like one of his old boyish dreams; his father's hand resting lovingly on his shoulder, pride and admiration in his eyes. He thought extravagantly, that even if it all turned out badly and he never came back, it would have been worth it just for this one perfect moment.

January 27th, 1915
— Ford Castle

From his vantage point on the roof of the Flagstaff Tower, James watched the hunt come over the hill; the Master and Whippers-in, conspicuous in pink coats and white buckskin breeches; the field in black jackets and low crowned silk hats. There were a few uniforms, a few farmers in tweeds and canvas leggings — a sparse turn-out considering their usual numbers, but then that was the war, shortages of everything; servants, farm workers, shop assistants and clerks. It seemed that every second man had enlisted.

He breathed deeply. It was a glorious day, the fields starkly beautiful, glittering with frost, white winter grass bent by a harrowing wind. It was cold — but not so cold as to kill the scent and they'd found one already up in High Wood, running a vixen three miles to Sleafield before losing her in a bog. Now they were drawing the little wood below Watchlaw, the field waiting a little way apart whilst the hounds flushed out the covert. He lifted his field glasses. They were close enough now for him to pick out individuals by their different mounts; Drever on the big unruly bay, Mary Grey on a steady but spirited chestnut gelding; Margot on an even tempered cob. He sighed faintly. It was strange not to be able to pick out Sydney or Arthur. Arthur had been gone three weeks now, down to

Catterick for preliminary training. And Sydney — Well, of course Sydney had been in France for some time now. He'd heard from him just this morning, not the cocksure Sydney that had gone off to the war and expected to be back for the Boxing Day meet. This letter had been written by a different man; sober, disillusioned, bitter at the way the war was being handled, the deprivations being suffered by both officers and men.

Since Ypres, the war had deteriorated into a kind of stalemate, a strange underground war fought from ditches, a series of blind offensives against a similarly entrenched enemy, both struggling for possession of a strip of useless land. The whole thing was turning into a shambles. Thousands were paying with their lives for the blunders of a few pompous and self-opinionated men. James frowned. He'd always felt the appointment of Sir John French as C-in-C to have been an obvious mistake. Excitable and emotional, French just wasn't up to it and he'd always reckoned Douglas Haig to be far the better man. You couldn't blame the generals for everything though. The government came in for its share as well. Though Balfour and Asquith and agreed a truce for the duration, the petty squabbling and wrangling still went on. And the truth of it was that neither the politicians nor the generals were really running the war. It was a profiteers' war, speculators forcing prices sky high, exploiting shortages of practically everything.

Then suddenly the fox broke cover. The shrill music of the hounds carried on the clear air as the leading bitches burst from the wood. For an instant the riders remained motionless. The Master was holding the field till the fox was free and clear — a hundred yards clear now, streaking across open ground, skirting a wall, leaping a ditch, then turning right handed toward the Common. Through his glasses James could see him clearly; the slavering jaw, the sly golden eye — a wily old dog fox that knew the ground, doubling back to maze his scent, then plunging into a culvert in an effort to check the hounds.

The hounds were running strongly, fast on the scent though the following field was making heavy going of the Bottom Pasture. For a moment he lost sight of them as they dropped down toward the Lowick Road. Then up onto open ground again, floundering across the swollen burn, picking up speed on the firm ground of the Common. James murmured encouragement. Drever was going well, hard on the Master's heels. He saw him put the big bay at the high blackthorn hedge, saw it check in its stride, its head going down. He's going to refuse, James thought wildly. Get its head up, boy. Use your legs . . . He held his breath as his son fought for control of the horse and it seemed for a moment that he was going to make it as the bay launched itself into the air. But he'd bungled the landing, miscalculated the blind ditch on the other side. Horse and rider came down together . . . Then horsemen were pulling up, riders dismounting. He saw Margot running, her hat awry, her habit trailing. Then his vision blurred as the inert body was lifted carefully from the ditch. The head lolled back, swinging as if from a broken hinge . . .

The glasses slipped slowly from James' hand. He clutched at the parapet. 'Drever . . .' The cry echoed round the courtyard like the howl of a wounded dog. Then slowly he turned his back and stared across at the hills. He was still standing there twenty minutes later when they came to tell him that his son, Drever, was dead.

Sunday, April 25th and 26th, 1915 — Wieltje, near Ypres, Flanders

With eyes red-rimmed from lack of sleep, Major the Honourable James Arthur Joicey stared blankly round the walls of the ruined schoolroom at Wieltje that now served as Brigade Headquarters. The room was crowded with men; senior officers of the 149th Infantry Brigade, all talking in loud hearty voices about the progress of war. Speculating on the reasons for this emergency briefing — and all with such gusto, such sickening enthusiasm, as if they couldn't wait to get their heads blown off. Looking at them, listening to them, Arthur wondered if beneath all that hearty bravado, any of them were afraid. They didn't look afraid, although perhaps, like him, they covered it well. That was the secret, that was the drill — to keep up a front no matter what. And he was good at that, good at pretending, hiding his feelings behind that air of quiet reserve. A steady sort of chap, that was how he was described, because his voice was always calm and he exuded an air of quiet reliability. And yet inwardly — inwardly his stomach churned in constant panic, his skin crawled and sweated with terror ... He wallowed down the saliva that persistently filled his mouth. He felt slightly sick. Tinned meat and dry biscuit lay in his stomach like lead and the muscles of his wet and frozen body, squeezed behind a schoolboy-sized desk, suffered increasingly from attacks of cramp. It was his fourth day in France, although he supposed as it was two in the morning, it was really the fifth.

He looked back at the confusion of the last few days: the 21st: disembarked Boulogne 2 am — six hours in a cold and unlit train; the 22nd: raining — marching all day then billets at a place he couldn't pronounce; the 23rd: raining again — marching for six hours — reserve trenches in the rear sector; the 24th: today, yesterday, whenever it was — still raining — reserve trenches again then marching all night ... He moved his head in a gesture of vague irritation. He'd lost track of the days, his senses dulled by shock and noise and lack of sleep. He couldn't remember the last time he'd slept, though he'd lain down somewhere on the road to Ypres. But he hadn't slept. Sleep had been impossible with G.S. carts and artillery limbers continually screaming up to the front; Red Cross wagons coming back laden with cargoes of injured men. And the guns were the worst, the eternal pounding of the massive German howitzers bombarding Ypres, the reply of the inadequate French and British artillery. He hated that the most, the continual and never-ending assault of noise ...

He shivered. It didn't seem possible that just a week ago he'd said goodbye to his father at Folkestone. That had been his last sight of England; his father's grave face among a sea of grave faces, the white line of the cliffs slowly receding, getting smaller and smaller, further and further away. He thought about England a great deal, about Longhirst, looking her best now in the first flush of spring, about Gina, his dearest Gina, expecting their fourth child any day now. Yes, he thought a lot about home, and the thoughts seemed to lay a protective membrane upon his mind. They kept him detached from all this, kept the full horror of it all at a distance. He always felt that if ever it touched him, if ever he had to acknowledge that this was real ...

351

He started nervously at the scrape of benches and chairs. General Riddel, G.O.C. Brigade, was about to begin the briefing.

The General surveyed them gravely, a stout middle-aged man with a fierce upswept moustache. 'I'm not going to beat about the bush, gentlemen. I dare say you already know what a devilish tricky situation we're in. Three days ago the Germans launched a massive offensive against Ypres. Heavy bombardment by Krupp naval guns and powerful seventeen-inch howitzers, followed up by a despicable attack of poison gas. The French and Canadian divisions holding that part of the line suffered the most appalling losses, opening up a breach of four miles through which the enemy advanced until checked by the splendid efforts of the 13th and 14th Canadian battalions lying north of St Julien. Ever since, the entire German effort has been concentrated on the area between the apex of the salient and Kitchener's Wood in an attempt to turn the Canadian flank, thus opening up the way to Ypres. Yesterday, a further enemy gas attack was launched against the 28th division, forcing them back to a position three miles south-east of Ypres on the Fortuin/Grafenstaal road.' He paused impressively and leaned his knuckles on the edge of his desk. 'An hour ago I received an order direct from High Command. We are to launch a counter attack, together with the forces of the 150th and 151st Brigades under the leadership of Brigadier-General Hull. The attack to be made in the general direction of St Julien with the object of driving back the enemy and securing the exposed flank of the 28th division.'

He waved a piece of paper in front of them. 'I have here a message from our Commander-in-Chief, Sir John French. "Every effort must be made at once to hold and restore the line about St Julien, or the situation of 28th division will be severely jeopardized."' He read it as if it were a directive from God, as if this were part of some glorious crusade. Arthur felt a sudden surge of resentment against these men who issued orders from the comfort of French chateaux and never came within thirty miles of the line. Perhaps if they saw all the smashed and broken bodies, all the crippled and mutilated men ... The awful thought occurred to him — in a few hours' time he might be one of them.

The attack was timed for 4.30, which gave them less than two hours to prepare. In a way that was a good thing. There wasn't time to think, to contemplate the madness of putting hungry, exhausted men in the field, to speculate on their chances of success against an artillery superiority of five to one with no telephone communication, no protection against gas. Yes, it was important to keep busy and Arthur spent his time organizing runners to maintain contact between battalion and brigade, ensuring that stretcher bearers and Red Cross cars would be standing by. Then at 3.00 they were called together for a final briefing. Nine men crouched down in a crumbling waterlogged dug-out; Colonel Jackson, their C.O.; Captain and Adjutant, Harry Archer; the N.C.Os; Quartermaster Neville and R.S.M. Casey. The four company commanders Arthur knew quite well: Jack Merrivale and Hugh Liddell hunted the Morpeth pack; Harry Smails had been with him at Cambridge. And Johnny Lambton, the Earl of Durham's nephew — well, everyone knew Johnny Lambton. Arthur averted his eyes from the smooth confident face. Lambton reminded him of Sydney, everything he despised and yet everything he wanted to be. Sydney would have been just like Lambton on the eve of his first battle; eager, confident, in absolute control of himself and the men he would lead. Whereas he couldn't even concentrate on what the Colonel was saying.

'I'm afraid it's not very good but it'll have to do.' Colonel Jackson spread a small dog-eared map on the ammunition box between them and pointed to a spot to the north-east of Ypres. 'This is our objective — an enemy position about five hundred yards inside our front line, just outside a place called Fortuin. It's all open country so we're bound to be in for some heavy shelling. Fortunately it'll still be dark for the major part of the advance though it'll be fairly tricky once we reach our own G.H.Q. line as we'll have to defile through two narrow gaps.' He took out his pipe and made a business of lighting it. 'Stand to at 3.15 ack emma. Order of advance — in lines of platoons, artillery formation. Number 1 and 2 companies in firing line, 3 and 4 in support. Battalion to deploy approximately a thousand yards from enemy position and wait for Battalion H.Q. to come up. Any questions?'

'What about artillery, sir?'

'I think Major Joicey has seen to that.' The Colonel looked at Arthur, who replied in a slow and expressionless voice. 'Not as much as we'd like, I'm afraid. Thirty minutes covering fire by the heavy guns. After that we'll have to rely on half a dozen thirteen pounders. There'll be an artillery observation officer in the front line with us to direct the firing.'

'What about gas, sir?'

'Make do and mend, I'm afraid,' Jackson said cheerfully. 'Wetted handkerchiefs are the only instructions I have. Pee on them if you have to, if you can't find water, though I don't think there'll be much chance of that.'

A ripple of restrained laughter ran round the company, a signal for the Colonel to bring out a flask. 'I think this calls for a toast, gentlemen. Our first action, our first chance to show what the Terriers can do.' He slopped whisky into tin cups and raised his own. 'To the 7th Battalion, gentlemen — and victory.'

Outside it was still raining, blinding heavy rain that rattled like stones on the revetting of the trench. Arthur stood for a moment in the concealing darkness. Tea and whisky welled up in his throat and he thought for a moment he was going to be sick. He breathed deeply; lyddite fumes and blasted earth, chloride of lime from the nearby latrine — rather like smelling salts. He lit a cigarette and inhaled deeply. Mercifully the guns had stopped, at least the heavy bombardment. There was still sporadic shelling and now and then enemy star shells gave brief vivid glimpses of the stricken landscape. To the west Ypres still burned, staining the sky like a lingering sunset, black smoke drifted towards them on an easterly breeze. That was a comfort at least. It lessened the prospect of a gas attack ... Arthur shivered. Bullets and shrapnel he had been prepared for, but this filthy new weapon that burned a man's eyes out and flooded his lungs. It was like drowning, they said, but on dry land.

He pulled up the collar of his greatcoat and slopped his way along the trench. Men peered up at him out of funk holes, others sat shivering under sodden groundsheets. He stopped for a word: 'Everything all right, corporal?'

The man was on his feet instantly. 'Yes, sir. Thank you, sir.'

Arthur couldn't see his face but his voice was young, then as a star shell exploded overhead, he saw just how young. Eighteen at the most. He didn't even look that. His growth of beard was patchy and soft like down. 'Have you had something to eat?' Arthur asked him.

'Yes, sir. Hot soup, sir.'

'And all right was it?'

'Yes, sir. Thank you, sir.'

Arthur nodded and moved on. He wished he could have thought of something inspiring to say — like Henry V before Agincourt — 'O God of battles! Steel my soldiers' hearts.' He supposed it would sound rather silly coming from him. Then he glanced at his watch. Stand-to in fifteen minutes.

Dawn broke slowly over the saturated fields of the Salient; greyness giving way to greyness, revealing a glutinous landscape of churned mud and stunted trees continually erupting under a constant barrage of shells.

Roofed in by a solid arc of noise, Arthur stood on the fire step of the rearward trench and watched the gradual spreading of the light. He couldn't see much; a fog of rain and smoke and flying earth obscured his view. He couldn't even make out the men of his own battalion among the sodden mud spattered troops that made up their ragged and tentative front. Even harder to distinguish were the living from the dead. There seemed to be bodies everywhere, crouched in ditches and shell holes, sprawled under hedges and trees; bedraggled motionless figures pinned down by vicious shell fire and machine gun enfilade.

Arthur glanced at his watch. Two hours into the attack now and they'd made little progress. The first wave had been halted after five hundred yards and any further advance had been killed off by their own artillery, who, unable to range their guns accurately enough, were killing more of their own men than they were Germans. And so they waited, though Arthur wasn't sure exactly what for. He didn't understand this static kind of war where men dug themselves into the ground and fired at each other blindly across a strip of useless land. It was turning out to be an artillery war, a contest between the guns. The men were almost superfluous, a diversion to keep the generals amused, something for the guns to aim at. He felt there was something obscenely impersonal about being blown up by a gun fired from miles away, as if you were nothing, an insect to be crushed. They didn't even know that you were there.

He peered dismally through the smoke and rain. He knew instinctively they didn't have a chance. They hadn't enough men, enough equipment, just four Lewis guns between the whole battalion. In contrast the enemy seemed plentifully supplied; heavy machine guns, trench mortars — most of all, men, an anonymous field grey hoard that never seemed to diminish. As soon as one man fell another rose up to take his place.

He put up his binoculars and tried to get a clearer view, to estimate what men they had in the field. The tattered flank of the Canadians was on their right. Even further right, on the far side of the Grafenstaal road there were supposed to be two battalions of Suffolks. To their left, forward of their position by about two miles, two other brigades of the 50th Division pressed the main assault against St Julien. Their immediate right was unsupported, though. The French, as always, had failed to come up.

'Well, that's the last of the H.E. support.' Colonel Jackson slid back into the waterlogged trench, rain streaming from the peak of his cap. 'They're short of ammo, or so they say. Apparently we've had our ration.' He took the binoculars from Arthur. 'Anything going on?'

'Message from 1 Company, sir,' Arthur replied woodenly. 'Requesting permission to fall back to right of Canadian line. Also a reply from Brigade to your B/12. No reinforcements available. Will review position again at noon.'

'Damn!' The Colonel swore mildly, then both men ducked. A storm of shrapnel burst overhead. A rain of bullets spattered down into the trench. There was a cry for stretcher bearers. One of the battalion runners had been hit. Arthur watched numbly as his body was manoeuvered tenderly along the trench though it was perfectly obvious that he was dead. A sliver of shrapnel was lodged in his neck. Blood sprayed like a fountain from the severed artery.

Arthur looked back toward their thin and beleaguered front line. There was no movement of troops except the regular passage of R.A.M.C. Shells shrieked overhead, rifles cracked, machine guns tore and shredded the air as both sides, locked in an endless immobile struggle, bombarded each other with fire and lead across a strip of useless ground.

Two o'clock in the afternoon and for the first time in six days it wasn't raining. The pale eye of the sun peered through low scudding clouds. Light flooded the landscape and drew a faint steaming warmth from the sodden fields.

Inside Battalion H.Q. dug-out, it remained almost solidly dark. No vestige of daylight penetrated the canvas sheeting that served as a door. Only the stump of a guttering candle relieved the blackness.

'Second Lieutenant F.W. Smail ... Second Lieutenant A.W. Kent ...' The adjutant was reading out a list of officers killed and wounded — seventeen so far out of thirty. 'Also unaccounted for, Captain Liddell and Captain Merrivale, though R.A.M.C. think they've probably got lost, as neither of their bodies have been brought in.'

There was a little silence and then the Colonel started to speak in a bracing voice as if everything was going according to plan. The truth of it was that none of them really knew what was going on. They'd received orders from Brigade after a silence of six hours. They were to hold their present position until half an hour past dusk, when they would be relieved by a battalion of Suffolks. That meant another five hours for the men in their exposed position, five hours lying in water and mud. They'd been forty-eight hours without rest as it was, and fighting for at least fifteen of them. And all for what? Arthur thought — to end up more or less back where they started from. Hours ago they'd abandoned all hope of sustaining the attack and fallen back alongside the Canadians.

'Well, I think in the circumstances, all we can do is to consolidate our position,' the Colonel said. 'Digging in will give the men something to do.' He looked at Arthur. 'I'd like you to take command of 1 Company, Major, seeing as they seemed to have misplaced their O.C. Also I shall need a senior officer in the field to co-ordinate our withdrawal. C.S.M. McAllister will be there to show you the ropes — Oh, and see that the men smarten up as best they can. We don't want the Suffolks to think we're commanding a rabble.'

Arthur went outside and blinked in surprise as the sunlight fell in his eyes. He smiled absently. He had forgotten about things like sunlight, about beauty and warmth. It was comforting to know that they still existed.

1 Company H.Q. was a waterfilled shell hole among a series of waterfilled shell holes in which the men of the four platoons were scattered. In terms of distance it was less than a hundred yards from Battalion H.Q. though it took Arthur a good half hour to get across; running, sliding, rolling from shell hole to shell hole. He crawled the last fifty feet and rolled over the lip of the crater into a foot of mud. A young second lieutenant sat nursing a shattered hand. He looked blankly at Arthur, saw the crown on his lapel and made a painful effort to salute.

Arthur eased himself up into a sitting position. 'Where's your O.C., lieutenant? Who's in charge?'

The second lieutenant blinked. 'I am, I think. We haven't seen Captain Liddell for some time.'

Arthur stared at the boy, for that's all he was, a gangling boy sick with fear that he was visibly trying to conquer. 'Well, I'm in charge now.' Arthur smiled at him. 'What's your name, lieutenant?'

'Herriot, sir.'

'Well then, Mr Herriot, do you think you could find your C.S.M.? Apparently we've got some digging to do.'

By five o'clock they had linked up the shell holes and transformed them into the semblance of a trench complete with a crude firestep and parapet. Arthur had taken a turn at the digging himself. It was a relief to do something physically demanding. It relieved the pressure on his stretched nerves. And yet he was managing far better than he'd thought he would. It helped enormously being out here with the men, knowing that he was responsible, that they stood or fell by his actions. Yes, that steadied him, working with the men, being part of a team. He'd always felt he'd have made a much better captain than he had a major.

At six o'clock it started raining again, a heavy downpour that extinguished the last of the light. It was the signal for the German artillery to open up, aware that any movement of troops in and out of the line would take place under cover of darkness. Star shells soared; the ruined landscape leapt into sudden relief, a hail of mortars battered their trench. There was nothing to do but sit it out, cowering under an avalanche of cold wet earth and wondering what the hell their own guns were doing.

Gradually the sound of gunfire died away, though the silence that followed it was infinitely worse. Arthur glanced anxiously at his watch. Eight o'clock and still no sign of the promised relief.

'Will they be much longer, do you think, sir?' Herriot regarded Arthur worriedly. 'I mean, they will come? They won't just leave us here ...'

'Of course they'll come,' said Arthur calmly. 'They're late, that's all. It's not a train service we're running, you know.'

Herriot returned his smile weakly. 'Couldn't we send someone to see what's going on ...' Herriot broke off and dropped his head in his hands. 'I'm sorry, sir. I don't seem to be able to get a grip of myself.' He looked up at Arthur. 'I didn't think it was going to be like this. I don't mean the fighting — of course I expected that — but the trenches, the mud, this bloody awful mud. I think I mind that more than anything. Always being like this, filthy and stinking. There's no dignity, is there? It's all so squalid and mean.'

'I'm afraid war is rather squalid,' Arthur said.

'Yes, I suppose so.' Herriot smiled weakly. 'They say you get used to it after a while — except I don't think I'll ever get used to it.' He have a shrill laugh. 'Sometimes, you know, I wish I could get a bullet in the head and get it over and done with. At least that way I wouldn't have to keep thinking about it. I wouldn't have to worry about making a hash of the thing, of letting people down.' He looked desperately at Arthur. 'Aren't you ever afraid, sir? I know I shouldn't ask ...'

Arthur smiled. 'All the time, actually. We're all afraid, Mr Herriot. Don't let anyone fool you about that. Nobody wants to die. It's just a question of not thinking about it, of getting on with the job.'

'But I can't help thinking about it. I can't hear a shot without imagining how it would feel entering my body. Every time I see a man with his head blown off I think next time it'll be me. I suppose the long and short of it is, I'm just a rotten coward ...'

Arthur leant forward suddenly and gripped his arm. 'No, you're not. There aren't any cowards in this battalion. We're all heroes to be here at all. But there are different kinds of heroes. The most obvious kind unfortunately are the ones who get all the gongs. They don't think about what they're doing. They don't think about death and even if they are unlucky, it happens only once. People like you — like us — we'll have suffered the same moment again and again in our imagination. We die a thousand deaths instead of just one.'

Herriot stared at him and his body grew still. 'Yes, I see, sir. Thank you, sir for telling me that ...'

Within minutes he was asleep, his cheek pillowed in the mud of the trench wall. Arthur sat staring into the darkness. He wondered where Hugh was — well out of this show he wouldn't mind betting. The cavalry didn't like getting their feet wet. And Sydney? He smiled grimly. So much for it all being over by the spring. He'd remind him of that the next time they met. The last time had been at Drever's funeral ... His eyes grew moist thinking of Drever. And his father. My God, he'd never seen the old boy looking so grim. It must be hell for him now, to have all three of his sons fighting in France. By the law of averages not all of them would come through. His spirits plunged. Which one, then? Which one would be the subject of that impersonal buff form — Army Form B/101 — Dear Sir or Madam, It is my painful duty to inform you ... A paralyzing coldness swept over him suddenly. Of course, it would be him. He'd always associated death with noise and violence ... Then he stiffened as he heard stealthy footsteps squelching through the mud. To his rear, but that didn't mean anything, an enemy raiding party could have circled right round. There were enough gaps in the line for them to slip through. He glanced at the sentries — still staring out toward the German lines — obviously they hadn't heard. He drew his revolver and slipped the safety catch off as a shadowy figure dropped down beside him.

'I say, steady on, old chap!' White teeth gleamed in the darkness. 'Captain Trewitt. 1st Suffolks. Your relief.'

He slept for eight hours, the deep dreamless sleep of utter exhaustion. The guns woke him, like a hellish dawn chorus. Through the cracked and pitted window a weary sunlight fell.

Arthur opened his eyes and stared blankly at the damp stain above his head. It took him a few minutes to get his bearings, to realize exactly where he was — back in billets in Wieltje, in the attic room of the local estaminet that he shared with the adjutant and Major Mackay.

He swung his legs over the edge of the rickety bed and dragged his hands across his face. There was a filthy taste in his mouth and his skin itched beneath a layer of dried mud. He would have given anything for a bath, but hot water was a luxury here, every drop needing to be boiled up in pans.

His batman came in with his shaving water and tea. 'Breakfast in fifteen minutes, sir. Mr Liddell asks if you will join him.'

'Yes, thank you. I'll be down straightaway.' Arthur gulped a mouthful of tea and glanced at himself in the fly blown glass. His light hair was lank and the colour of brass, his neat moustache merged into a dingy yellow stubble. He smiled ruefully and began to lather his face. Thank God Gina couldn't see him now.

The shave bucked him up a bit and he felt almost cheerful as he went downstairs. The back parlour of the estaminet served as an officer's mess and a delicious dry heat pulsed from a pot-bellied stove. The room smelt of simple everyday things, baking bread and frying bacon, tobacco and wine.

'Hallo, Liddell. What happened to you? I heard you were on the missing list.'

'Couldn't tell you, old man,' Liddell replied cheerfully. 'Last thing I remember was a Bosch whizz-bang going off under my nose. Next thing, I was lying up to my neck in mud in a filthy ditch. Spent the night wandering around looking for H.Q.'

'Well, you were well out of it,' said Arthur. 'We had a hell of a time.'

'Yes, so I gather.' Liddell offered him a cigarette. 'Although you didn't do as badly as those poor devils pressing the major attack on St. Julien. It's all supposed to be pretty hush hush but of course everyone's heard. Apparently the whole thing was a complete fiasco. Their attack was timed for an hour before ours, a really big push, fifteen full battalions in all. Well, due to the lateness of some of the units getting up to the line, the powers that be decided to postpone, except that they forget to tell the damned artillery who loosed off their barrage at the appointed time which succeeded in putting the enemy on their guard. And when the attack eventually got going, the men had to advance without artillery support, whilst the Bosch were blazing merrily away, mowing our chaps down like ninepins. Most frightful balls-up by all accounts. Appalling losses on our side; seventy-three officers and nearly three thousand men.'

'My God,' whispered Arthur. 'What on earth do G.H.Q. think they're doing?'

Liddell shrugged. 'And that's just the good news, old man. The bad news is that it's our turn next. We're supporting an attack by the 4th and 6th Fusiliers. C.O.'s briefing at eleven ack emma.'

The Colonel's voice droned on ... creeping barrage ... order of advance ... necessity of avoiding bunching under fire. Arthur listened impassively, doing grisly sums; seventy-three officers and three thousand men — that was the equivalent of three whole battalions ...

'Any questions?'

There was an uneasy silence, then Jack Merrivale said. 'What about artillery, sir. You haven't mentioned ...'

'Er, well, no. I have no clear instructions at present. I'm told that we're desperately short of guns, ammunition too. They can't offer full support anywhere along the line. We may have to take pot luck with the other battalions as to whether we get any or not.'

Another silence, then Arthur said mildly, 'Is that wise, sir? To mount a daylight assault with questionable artillery support. I would have thought ...'

'Those are my orders, Major,' Jackson snapped. 'Whether it's wise or not, that's what we're going to do.' He dismissed the men abruptly but as Arthur went to leave, he called him back. 'Might I have a word, Major?'

Jackson waited till they were alone. 'Sit down, Arthur. Smoke if you want to.' He lit a cigarette himself. 'We've known each other for a few years now, Arthur, long enough I think for me to offer you a word of advice. I don't have to tell you that it's not done to question orders in front of junior officers. It makes for an uncertainty which is bound to be felt by the men. It's imperative that the men believe we know what we're doing.'

'But we don't do we, sir,' said Arthur urgently. 'It's against everything we've ever been taught — infantry advancing over open ground in broad daylight without adequate support. Our losses are going to be enormous.'

Jackson avoided his eyes. 'Well, on the surface perhaps the strategy might not seem sound. But there may be other factors to the situation of which we know nothing. We can't take an individual point of view. We can't fight our own personal war.' He hesitated. 'What I'm trying to say, Arthur, is that whatever our doubts, whatever our private thoughts, they're better kept to ourselves.'

'I'm afraid I can't do that, sir,' Arthur responded stiffly. 'I can't just say nothing when perhaps hundreds of men ...'

'You're taking a purely sentimental view. This is war, Major. There are bound to be casualties. In any major offensive one expects to lose the odd battalion.'

'The odd battalion!' Arthur's voice rose. 'Sir, a battalion is nearly a thousand men.'

The colonel gave him a hard look. 'Take my advice, Major. Don't question it, don't even think about it. Just get on and do the job.'

Don't question it. Don't think about it. Easier said than done with ambulances and burial parties continually rumbling back from the front.

'Post's up, sir.' R.S.M. Casey met him at the top of the dug-out steps. 'Shall I give it out to the men?'

'Yes, Sar'nt Major. Give it out.' There was one for him, addressed in his father's bold decisive hand. It was brief and to the point; hoping he was safe and well, telling that his sister Margot had joined the V.A.D. — and congratulating him on the birth of a daughter, Angela Georgina, three days ago on the 23rd.

April 26th, 1915 — London

'Quite frankly, my lord, I can't say that I find your attitude patriotic. Profit should be the last consideration during a war.'

'It's not profit I'm concerned with, Prime Minister.' James protested in an exasperated voice. 'It's a pack of civil servants attempting to run my collieries. Probably none of them will ever have been near a pit shaft in their life.'

The two men glared at each other. They had argued the subject back and forward at length: the proposed Coal Mines Emergency Act, by which the government planned to take over the coal industry for the duration of the war.

Then Asquith sighed. 'Look James, let's be practical. I know this isn't the perfect solution but that's because there isn't one. The government can't allow the coal industry to hold the country to ransom — and before you say anything, I'm not accusing you. But not all coalowners are as scrupulous. A great many have been stock-piling, manipulating output, causing a deliberate shortage to push the price up. Unless you can undertake to supply the country's entire needs single handed, we've no choice but to control. Coal is a necessity. The entire war effort would collapse without it.'

'Control, yes. I'm not arguing with that. Control of prices, profit, output. But for the state to attempt to run the pits themselves? Have you any idea what long-term damage could be caused? By trying to avoid a national emergency now, you are going to create one for the future.'

Asquith looked grim. 'James, if we don't win this war, then there won't be any future. It won't be the state who'll be running your collieries. It'll be the Germans.'

James was silent. He knew, instinctively, that he was going to lose this one. You couldn't argue efficient business practice against the country's desperate need. He glanced at the Prime Minister. Asquith looked tired. The long aristocratic face was pale with strain. His hands, as he lit a cigar, were trembling.

'Is it going so badly then?' James asked him quietly.

'It's not going well,' Asquith admitted with a nervous laugh. 'Kitchener's screaming for more troops, more guns, more ammunition. The only thing we can supply him with is plenty of men. The other stuff, we just can't turn out quick enough. To be perfectly frank, the whole thing has become a shambles, made infinitely worse by the French, who insist on pressing these narrow attacks against a fortified line. I admit we've had a limited amount of success, but we haven't yet discovered any decisive means of maintaining or exploiting a break-through.'

'What about Churchill's plan to open up another front in the

East?'

'I don't hold out much hope. It'll be just another side-show. It's the Western Front that's the decisive area. That's where the war will be fought and won. But it's stalemate at the moment and unless a way can be found out of the deadlock, I'm afraid it's going to be a question of battling it out to the bitter end, till one or the other of us run out of men.'

'How long?' James asked. 'How long do you think it will go on?'

Asquith's expression was bleak. 'Kitchener reckons another two years — another two years at least.'

Two years! Another two years of wondering and worrying, of waiting for the blow to fall. As James walked back to Cadogan Square through the glorious spring day, he felt old and tired and depressed. Drever's death had hit him hard. He still hadn't recovered from the sense of anger and shock. He supposed it was ironic really. All his prayers and fears had been for the three elder boys. It had never occurred to him that Drever ... And ever since he'd had this feeling, this premonition that for him the grief and misery had just begun. It was the war of course. That made everything uncertain and he lived every day in fearful expectation, pouring over the daily casualty lists, looking for names that he knew. And there had been so many: two of Freddy Lampton's brothers, one of his sons, the two Sanderson boys ... And young Everard Lamb. Margot hadn't said much. If she grieved she'd kept it all to herself. But then what was there to say. Soon the loss of friends and loved ones would be commonplace.

He walked through the park. Everything looked normal. Everything looked the same. It was hard to believe that there was a war on. The daffodils were out, sheets of brassy, brazen colour. The band, in the bandstand, played brassy, brazen tunes. He thought of his sons. He hadn't heard from Hugh for a few weeks now, but then Hugh hadn't ever been one for writing. Sydney wrote regularly: bitter, complaining letters, despairing letters ... But it was Arthur he worried about. He wished now he'd been firmer. If he'd been firmer then perhaps Arthur wouldn't have gone ... He sat down on a bench and stared across the pond. He wondered what Arthur was doing now.

April 26th, 1915 — Flanders

It was like the end of the world, the earth heaving and shuddering beneath his feet, a hurricane of flying steel above his head.
The voices of the guns screamed in his ears; the roar of the
howitzers, the shrill whine of five nines, the infernal chatter of
machine guns — and they all spoke in German. From the
British artillery there was no reply.

Crouched down behind the ridge overlooking St Julien,
Arthur waited with the men for the signal to advance. They
stood in rows, herded together like submissive sheep, heads
bowed, shoulders slumped beneath the weight of sixty-pound
packs, hands clasped loosely on the stocks of their rifles. They
might have been praying and really that was all there was left
to do. Pray that you came out of this all in one piece, that you
survived until tomorrow, even though tomorrow you might
have to go through the whole thing again; Over the top,
advancing at a hundred and sixty-five paces a minute, rifles at
the high port.

There were just three minutes to go — perhaps only three
minutes more of life and sanity. And yet strangely enough, he
wasn't afraid. In fact he didn't feel much of anything at all.
Brain and body and spirit were numb and he viewed the
proceedings quite dispassionately as if he were an observer
rather than an actual participant. With the same detachment
he took part in the customary pre-battle show of heroics, the
exhibitions of bravado meant to inspire the men. He often
thought only the British were capable of such divine lunacy;
officers reading magazines and discussing the latest scores
from Twickenham; Brigadier Riddell in gleaming top boots and
spotless white gloves strolling the front line as if he were umpir-
ing a cricket match instead of a life and death struggle. It was a
game, of course, a grotesque charade where nothing was as it
seemed; young men looking like old men; old men preening
and prancing like reckless boys. They didn't know of course.
For them the horror was still to come. But Arthur knew. He'd
fought this battle a hundred times in his mind. He'd seen all the
dead, the spilt entrails, and ripped bowels. He'd seen himself
. . .

Then whistles shrilled all along the line. The raucous voices of C.S.M.s rose above the guns. First wave moving forward, leaden footed, bayonets stabbing the lowering sky. Second wave; more men scrambling up the muddy incline ... Third wave; Arthur and Battalion H.Q. bringing up the rear, stumbling out over open ground, dodging gunfire, bursts of shells. Enemy machine guns were traversing, mowing the forward platoons down like stalks of corn. Men were falling all around him; screams and sobbing, cries for help. He gritted his teeth and kept going. The shell fire increased. Fountains of wet earth rose up in front of him. Clouds of yellow smoke blew back in his face. Then suddenly the smoke cleared — and Christ, oh Christ, there were bodies everywhere, corpses spread like a carpet underfoot. He saw men with bellies laid open with shrapnel; faceless, headless, without arms, without legs ... The reality burst upon him with sickening violence, forcing open the locked door of his mind. He felt a little mad, possessed of an insane and killing rage. He rushed forward. There were men ahead of him, the remains of 4 Company, a thin ragged line. He plunged blindly through their ranks. There was more smoke ahead, greyish green, a sinister fog rising up before him like a solid wall.

'Gas.'

The terrified cry froze him in his tracks. He had a terrible urge to turn and run, and some of the men ahead of him were already falling back. Men were running in all directions, blinded, gasping, coughing up green froth. And the men around him were beginning to panic, fumbling in their trousers, trying to squeeze urine from paralysed bladders. Others flung themselves face down and tried to bury themselves in the mud.

'Get up. Get up!' He ran round the men, kicking them to their feet. The gas cloud was only yards away now, still moving, diffusing, thinning at the edge. Wet or not, he ordered the men to cover their faces. 'We're going to run through it,' he shouted. 'That way we'll be in it for the shortest possible time. Don't hold your breath but breathe lightly. Now on my order — run'.

He didn't give them time to think but plunged straight in where the gas seemed to be thinnest. The vast amorphous cloud engulfed him. Within seconds his eyes were streaming. There was a sharp burning pain in his lungs. This is it, he thought, I'm going to die. I'm going to be choked to death by this filthy gas. He thought of Gina, of the little daughter he would never see ... Then suddenly they were through, choking and gasping but breathing clean air. He staggered on. There were trenches in front of him and at first he thought it was the enemy until he heard the voices of the men cheering him on. He smiled weakly. He'd made it after all. It was their own front line, manned by a platoon of Seaforth Highlanders.

Under cover of darkness they trudged back to Wieltje, a straggling column of shambling scarecrows with blank empty eyes. Not so many, though as had marched that way fifteen hours before. All three Northumbrian battalions had suffered heavy losses. Brigadier Riddell had been killed and Jack Merrivale and Fred Smail; many others, they didn't know how many yet.

In a field outside the town the men fell in and R.S.M. Casey called the roll.

'Armstrong, Austen, Adamson, Anderson ...' Silence, silence, long minutes of silence broken by the occasional hoarse reply.

'Tomkins, Trotter ... Wallis, Watson ...'

Arthur sunk his head in his hands and the tears trickled slowly through his fingers. Out of the thousand men of the 7th that had left England six days ago they could only muster two hundred.

August 7th, 1915
— Ford Castle, Northumberland

Margot glanced anxiously at her father. He looked tired and drawn and the fine bones of his face had a cadaverous look. 'Will you have some more tea, Father?'

'Mmm. Yes,' Absently James passed her his cup. 'Has the afternoon post been yet?' He glanced at his watch. 'I thought there might have been a letter from one of the boys.'

'If there'd been anything I'm sure Jessop would have brought it in.' Margot handed him his tea. 'And anyway, I'm not even sure there still is an afternoon post. You know how things are with the war.'

James glanced at his daughter, frowning. He couldn't get used to seeing her in her nurse's uniform, though the long striped dress with its neat collar rather suited her. He didn't approve of course. He didn't like the idea of her changing dressings, emptying bed pans or whatever it was that V.A.Ds did. It wasn't healthy. You never knew what you would catch. He'd noticed lately that she'd had this dry persistent cough. And she was too thin as it was, although they said that was fashionable. All sorts of queer things were fashionable now. But at least she was doing something. At least she was useful. She didn't spend her time just thinking, imagining ... He tried to concentrate on his paper. Lloyd George was making the headlines again, openly challenging Asquith's leadership. His money was on the garrulous little Welshman. Asquith wouldn't last the course and Churchill wasn't even in the betting anymore since the disasterous failure of his Dardanelles campaign. Personally, he didn't care much. None of them had come up with any solution for ending the war.

He looked up and caught his daughter's eye. 'Will you be home to dinner tonight?' he asked.

'No, I'm afraid not. I'm on duty till ten.'

'Oh, I see,' He tried not to sound disappointed. 'Well, what about having a run down to Newcastle tomorrow. There's a good review on at the Theatre Royal. And I thought we could look in on Gina and the girls.'

'Well, actually,' Margot looked regretful. 'Actually, I've asked Vere to dine with us tomorrow ...'

'For God's sake,' exclaimed James irritably. 'Hasn't that girl go a home to go to?'

'Really Father, that's unkind. Vere's a jolly good sport. Besides, I thought you rather liked her.'

'Yes, I do. Of course I do.' James smiled apologetically. 'It's just that she's so painfully shy. She's damned hard work some-times you know and I'm not sure that I'm up to making idle conversation.'

Margot came over and slipped an arm round his shoulders. 'Don't be such an old grouch, Father. Vere isn't shy. You just terrify her that's all.' Laughing, she dropped a light kiss on his cheek. 'Well, I'm off then to do my bit for King and Country. We've got a new intake coming in today. Some of them are from Arthur's battalion. Why don't you come over to Etal and have a word?'

'Yes, I might. I'll see.' He wouldn't go, of course. He was cowardly like that, and often, ashamedly, he regretted allowing the army to use Etal as a military hospital. It didn't help, having to see all those broken and mutilated men, to see the horror, the terror in their eyes. And the last thing he wanted was to talk to the men of Arthur's battalion, to have to acknowledge what his son might be going through.

He went for a walk after his tea, down to the little church that lay within the grounds. Marguerite and Drever were buried there.

He sat down carefully on the painted bench and gazed across the sun drenched valley. He saw the vague shape of the hills, drifting like smoke against a cloudless sky. The sun was hot on his face, dazzling in his eyes. He closed them and thought about Marguerite, embarking on one of the silent, wordless conversations he often had with her. 'It's me, my dear,' he would say, as if he needed an introduction. Then he would tell her what had been happening, how the children were getting on. He would tell her his plans, his hopes, his fears, his disappointments, and wished he'd done so whilst she'd been alive.

He walked back to the house through the accumulated heat of the hot August day. The second post had been. His heart began to beat in hard heavy strokes as he saw the small official buff envelope. He picked it up. It seemed to weigh heavily in his hand, an object of terror. Then with trembling fingers he tore it open ... He frowned. It was from Arthur's commanding officer. Arthur was sick. He was coming home.

September 22nd, 1915 — Longhirst

Arthur sat by the window watching the steady drift of beech leaves onto the lawn. For hours he would sit there, his eyes blank and opaque. It was unnerving, that fixed empty stare that suddenly without warning would become fluid and tearful, luminous with pain borne at an intolerable cost.

It was a glorious day, a day of brazen colour and blinding clarity, where every blade of grass stood out sharply and the shadows were heavy and dense. But Arthur saw none of this. He saw a waste of shell holes and barbed wire entanglements. He saw columns of bedraggled marching men. He had been home a month, at least physically he had. His mind still wallowed in the mud and misery of the trenches. The sound of the guns still kept him awake at night. He thought that strange. When he'd been in the trenches he'd thought of nothing but home. Now he was home he thought of nothing but the trenches. He wasn't well though, he realized that. Trench fever, it had said upon the official form, but that was just the army's way of saying that he was no damned good — 'unfit for command' was how the brigadier had put it. He smiled faintly. He supposed it was the equivalent of getting the sack except that the army didn't sack serving officers. If you were no good then they packed you off on three months' leave then hid you behind a desk somewhere where you couldn't do any harm. He supposed he should be thankful to be out of it at last. He should be grateful that he didn't have to go back.

Tears welled up behind his eyes. The sense of shame and failure was overwhelming. He couldn't stop thinking about it. Every day he went over every little detail in his mind. At night he dreamt of it vividly — that last day when suddenly everything had got out of hand, when without warning his nerve had finally snapped. And yet he felt, looking back, that it had been a gradual process, a steady and relentless erosion of his nerves. After St Julien they had remained for a further three months in the Salient; four weeks at Hell Fire Corner, two months in the infamous trenches around Hill 60. Every day had been for him a fresh ordeal, a never ending battle against noise and fear and the awful monotony of existence. Five days in the line, five days in support, five days supposedly of rest, but the men were always on fatigues or digging parties. And always the mud, waist high in some places, a solid slime in which sometimes they had to stand for days. It rotted the flesh as well as the mind. He'd seen men lose their legs up to the knees. It had worn him down, the constant pressure, the awful brutality grinding away at his nerves. He hadn't given in though. He'd

371

stood the racket day after day. He'd learned to live with fear and stress.

Then at the end of July they'd been moved to Armentiers, a relatively quiet part of the line. His spirits had lifted. After Hill 60 it had seemed like heaven; good well revetted trenches, solid earth underfoot, and though there was shelling it wasn't the planned bombardments they'd suffered at Ypres. Perhaps that was why it had happened. He'd lowered his guard. He'd allowed himself to relax. He'd left the door of his mind swinging carelessly open. He remembered that day now, though for a long time he couldn't; a hot, quiet drowsy day. There'd been no movement at all from the enemy trenches. He'd been writing letters of condolence to the bereaved families of the men. They didn't vary much except for the name and number. They'd all died instantly and painlessly no matter how long and lingering their deaths. They'd all died bravely, for King and Country. They'd be sadly missed by both officers and men ... he had laid down his pen and lit a cigarette. Sunlight poured down the steps of the dug-out and he'd imagined himself at home at Longhirst, sprawled in the grass with Gina and the children. It seemed so long since he had seen them. He supposed he could have wangled leave. All the other officers seemed to. Perhaps it was the thought of having to come back, knowing this time what he had to face. He wasn't sure he could manage that yet; he wasn't sure that he'd be able to stand it. He knew now that he didn't dare relax. He couldn't afford to drop his guard for a moment. Even at night whilst he slept, he still needed to be vigilant. He was always afraid he might say something in his sleep, inadvertently give himself away. So he always waited till the others were asleep before he dared to drop off himself.

Abruptly he got to his feet and paced round the walls of the dug-out. It was quite luxurious compared to some that he'd known; chairs and a table, bits of carpet upon the floor; the walls were hung with pictures and maps, a captured German helmet had pride of place. Home from home, with books and magazines, real china cups. There were even flowers outside the door; scarlet poppies and yellow coltsfoot sprung from seeds that had lodged in the warm damp earth. He watered them assiduously with the dregs of wine and tea since water could not be spared. It pleased him to see the brave bright colours. They seemed symbolic of something — that life went on, that no matter how man destroyed himself, life itself could not be extinguished.

He went outside. It was hot and close and a veil of flies hung over the trench. The flies worried him, knowing as he did that they feasted on the unburied corpses of No Man's Land. That worried him too, the thought of men being left out there to rot. Sometimes the stench was appalling. He moved along the wide and spacious trench, all properly sandbagged and revetted — and dry, that was the real joy, to feel solid ground beneath his feet instead of trudging through filthy slime. He stopped for a word with the sentry. All was quiet, monotonously so. The enemy must also be feeling the heat. He took a look through the periscope. There wasn't much to see, just a waste of scarred and ruined earth stretching away to the German wire. He passed on, moving easily among the men who lounged in the sun or played at cards. None that he really knew. All the old faces were gone. These were the raw recruits of Kitchener's New Army.

'Good morning, Mr Arthur, sir.'

He turned his head sharply, a reprimand on his lips. Other ranks didn't address officers by their Christian names. Then it dawned on him. Mr Arthur! It seemed years since anyone had called him that.

He stared at the gawky private, scarlet with embarrassment as he realized his gaffe. 'I'm sorry, sir. It just slipped out.'

Arthur looked at him with interest. 'It's Rawlinson, isn't? From Vending?'

'Yes, sir.' Rawlinson looked gratified that Arthur remembered.

'How long have you been with us?' Arthur asked him.

'Just a week, sir.'

Just a week, thought Arthur. Still with the bloom of England on his cheeks; his eyes still eager and bright. 'Well, good luck, Rawlinson,' he said cheerfully. 'Come and see me if there's anything bothering you.'

He moved on a few yards more then halted as the sentry yelled a warning. There was a low whining noise. All the men instinctively scrambled for cover. Arthur looked back at

373

Rawlinson who stood uncertain of what to do. He took a step toward him, shouting at him to get down ... Then suddenly there was a blinding flash against his eyes. He was caught up in a vortex of ferocious light and sound. Darkness overwhelmed him, an avalanche of earth forcing him into the ground. He could not see. He could not move. Something heavy was pinning him down. He struggled against the weight, a solid object, warm and wet, against his face he felt the roughness of a khaki sleeve. A scream rose up in his constricted throat. Rawlinson. It was Rawlinson, his smashed body spreadeagled across him, his blood trickling down into his eyes ...

Arthur blinked. He couldn't remember much after that. He'd cried a great deal, he remembered that, curling himself into a small tight ball and crying, just crying, for nearly three days. On the fourth day he'd slept. On the fifth he'd been up before the Divisional Commander. A white haired general, all bristling efficiency and common sense, an ex-cavalry man too, naturally prejudiced against the sweaty infantry of the territorial drafts. What had he said? He couldn't remember — something about him being able to serve the army better in another capacity, something about him being sent home to await orders ... He had his orders now. He was to report in two weeks' time to Catterick Camp. He'd been relieved of active service.

He swallowed down the sick feeling that rose in his throat. My God, Sydney would have a field day over this. And how was he going to face Hugh? How was he going to face his father?

Then he saw his father's big Wolseley sweep up the drive and he was seized with a sudden desire to weep. He still cried a great deal, in secret, behind closed doors, into his pillow at night.

'How are you, Arthur?'

His father's voice was tender and compassionate which made him want to cry even more. He tried to smile. 'Much better,' he said without meaning it.

James patted his shoulder and his heart broke within him as he looked at his son. He looked like an old man, his face wizened, his eyes like glass and his habit of drawing his brows quickly together had become a permanent expression.

James sat down beside him. 'You ought to get out more, Arthur. It would do you good to get a bit of fresh air. I thought, if you're up to it, we might take a run out.'

Arthur's face tightened. He screwed his eyes up. He didn't like going out. He couldn't get used to the space and the light and he thought everyone was looking at him, pointing him out.

James didn't press it and after a while Arthur relaxed. 'How are things with the firm?' he said.

'Oh, as well as can be expected with government busybodies poking their noses in and half our workforce in khaki.' He smiled wryly. 'If it eases your conscience, Arthur, we won't be making much money out of this war. Government control for the duration is a certainty now. They're very graciously allowing us one tenth of the excess profits. The rest is going to the Exchequer.'

'Oh,' said Arthur. 'I see.'

He fell silent again and James made a fresh attempt to get him to talk. 'Have you heard from Hugh? He said that he'd written.'

'Yes,' Arthur brightened. 'He's going out to Salonika he thinks.' He stared down at his hands. 'That must be a relief, having at least one son that isn't going to let you down.'

'Don't talk like that, Arthur,' James said irritably. 'You're talking nonsense as you know.' Then he took Arthur's limp hands between his own. 'You haven't let anyone down, Arthur. It's shock, that's all. You'll get over it in time. My God! If I had my way you wouldn't go back ...'

Arthur pulled his hands away. 'Well, that's it, you see. I'm not going back. They don't want me back. I'm no good as an officer. I'm not up to the job so they're putting me out of the way — a nice desk job where I won't have to make any decisions. That's the army's way, do you see? They just sweep you under the carpet and forget about you ...' He covered his face with his hands and his shoulders heaved. 'I wish I was dead,' he whispered. 'I really wish I was dead but I haven't even got the courage for that.'

James closed his eyes in sudden anguish. This bloody war. This bloody awful war.

March 21st, 1916
— Calonne, near Ypres

Lieutenant George Bond, temporary adjutant of the 10th Battalion Northumberland Fusiliers flexed his frozen fingers and took up his pen. It was bitterly cold. Snow drifted beneath the gas curtain that covered the door. His breath issued whitely from between chapped lips. He was relatively new to the adjutant's job and wasn't too sure of the form. He was making a bit of a hash of the weekly report. He blew on his fingers and carried on:

A POSITION. CALONNE SECTOR.
March 18th: Quiet day.
March 19th: Quiet day. Second Lieut. Palmer wounded on patrol. 9 Other ranks wounded by rifle grenades.
March 20th: Quiet Day. Captain and adjutant S.J.D Joicey killed whilst visiting a sap. Three attempts made by Private Green and one attempt by Captain Llewellyn failed to recover his body. At 7 pm enemy bombarded our sap and trenches under cover of which they took in Captain Joicey's body.

James stared at the crumpled photograph; himself and Marguerite; Sydney, Margot and Drever. It wasn't very good, one of those strained studio portraits with Grecian urns in the background. He frowned, trying to remember when it had been taken. About ten years ago, he thought. Sydney couldn't have been more than twenty. He turned it over. There were stains on the back, dark ugly smears of blood — and yes, as he had thought, the studio's name. 'Caxton Photography, 112 The Strand'. He remembered now. It had been Sydney's birthday. He'd been just twenty-one ...

He cleared his throat and looked again at the contents of the large buff envelope. There were only a few other things; Sydney's pass book, some letters; two from himself and one from Margot — and of course, the usual letter from his commanding officer ... 'brave and gallant officer' ... 'great loss to the regiment' ... 'He was killed instantly and suffered no pain' ... James' eyes flickered. Well, he supposed a sniper's

ullet in the side of the head was about as instantaneous as you
ould get. He looked again at the photograph; Sydney hand-
ome, Sydney smiling, Sydney running toward him across the
awns at Longhirst, roaring through the gates of Ford in that
ackety car ...

He replaced everything neatly in the envelope again. He
ished he could cry. He knew the pain behind his eyes was a
acklog of tears, an accumulation of misery and grief. He was
lad now that Marguerite had died when she did. He wouldn't
ave wanted her to have suffered like this. Marguerite, Drever,
ydney — all gone ... He passed a hand wearily across his
yes. He didn't think he could bear any more.

Outside the door Arthur hovered uncertainly. He couldn't
ake up his mind whether or not to go in. He sensed that his
ather wanted to be alone but it seemed so churlish to go off
ithout saying a word, not to offer some sort of comfort.
erhaps he'd give him another five minutes and then go in.

He paced up and down, nervously smoothing his hair. He
as wearing uniform, camouflage as he called it for he didn't
onsider himself properly in uniform at all. It was all rather a
ham, pretending he was doing something important. It didn't
eel right though, being at home, being in England when men
ere still dying by the hundred in France. Thank God, it might
e all over soon, if the big push on the Somme came off. His
rows drew together. His face assumed that queer ponderous
ook. Of course, he was better now although he felt that whilst
he war went on, he'd never be quite right. All the time it was
oing on and he still had to think about it, make the effort not
o think about it ... It still disturbed him, knowing what was
oing on. He didn't always fully take it in. There was still that
art of his mind that resisted knowing.

In the same way he hadn't quite taken it in about Sydney
et. He still couldn't believe that his half brother was dead.
ven now, he kept vaguely thinking that there'd been some
istake, that it was just another example of War Office bung-
ing. He felt guilty of course — for not having been there, for
ot having taken an equal risk, for being secretly relieved,
lmost pleased ... He halted in his pacing. Sydney was dead.
ydney wasn't ever coming home. After all he wouldn't have to
isten to all those heroic stories, he wouldn't have to feel guilty,

humiliated. He resumed his pacing, suddenly ashamed. How could he think like that when he knew what their father must be suffering? Two sons in as many years . . . Father was going to need him now. His face took on a resolute look. He must pull himself together for Father's sake. It would make all the difference, to feel needed, for someone to be relying on him instead of always the other way round.

He made up his mind and rapped decisively on the door. His father was sitting slumped at his desk. He turned his head and before Arthur could speak, before Arthur could say all those strong comforting things, he waved his hand in a dismissive gesture.

'Not now, Arthur. Please. Not now.'

November 11th, 1918 — London

It was over. After four years, three months and seven days, Germany had surrendered and hostilities had officially ceased at the eleventh hour of the eleventh day of the eleventh month — and ever since the bells of London had rung out with a fearful clamour. The noise was beginning to get on Arthur's nerves, the tumultuous, discordant, hysterical clanging carrying on far into the night.

He was dressing for dinner — a family celebration to mark the end of the war. That jarred a bit too. How could you celebrate the loss of millions of lives? How could you justify such an outrage? It was over. That's all everyone kept saying, as if suddenly they need not think about it any more, as if it could really be forgotten. Perhaps in time it could, in ten or twenty years' time when the grass had grown over No Man's Land and every other man you met didn't have some fearful disability. They'd all be just statistics then, meaningless names on war memorials; numbered files in the War Office vaults; the fifty thousand dead at Neuve Chapelle, sixty thousand just on the first day of the Somme. He knew all the figures off by heart for he had followed the last years of the war with fanatical devotion. Even if he had not taken part physically he had done so in mind and spirit. He knew every victory, every defeat — Loos, the Somme, Passchendaele — as if by dwelling upon the horror, by subjecting himself mentally to what others had suffered physically, he might in some way atone for his failure. He'd never been able to come to terms with that, that he'd survived when so many others hadn't. Nobody had ever said anything, of course, though they must have wondered why an apparently healthy young officer wasn't doing his duty in France. But how did you explain shell shock? How did you explain fear of light and movement and noise? How did you put a nightmare into words? But it was over now. They'd all be coming home. He'd have to face men who'd once been his subordinates and who were now his superiors in rank and prestige; Hugh Liddell and Willie Mackay had both made Lieutenant Colonel. Both had been awarded the Military Cross and Liddell was up for a D.S.O. He saw suddenly that things were going to be even worse. From now on, every club, every dinner party would be crowded with heroes, all full of tales of glory. And what would he say? What tales of courage and daring would he have to tell?

He turned his head as his wife came into the room. 'You look lovely, my dear,' he said and meant it.

Gina smiled at him. 'You look rather dashing yourself, Arthur.'

He smiled painfully and glanced at himself in the mirror. In full regimentals he didn't look so bad. He was still thin but not emaciated as he had been before. He looked old though, older than a man of thirty-eight. His eyes had a permanently vague expression and his shoulders had the beginnings of a stoop.

'Gina,' he called out to her sharply in a voice of pain. 'Do we have to go downstairs? I don't think you know that I'm really up to it ...'

'Of course you're up to it, Arthur,' Gina spoke to him lovingly, soothingly, as if she spoke to a child. 'It's over, Arthur. You must stop thinking about it. It's all over, my dear. Don't you understand?'

Arthur nodded and smiled his vague and poignant smile. Somehow he didn't think it would ever be over for him.

In the adjoining room James muttered irritably, fiddling with his tie. It never seemed to go right when he did it himself. 'Oh for God's sake,' he shouted, pulling it out for the fourth time.

'Father, aren't you ready yet? We're all downstairs waiting.' Margot came toward him, laughing as she saw his furious face. 'Oh honestly, Father. Give it to me. I've told you before. The secret is not to do it in the mirror.'

James subjected himself meekly to his daughter's hands. 'I suppose the earnest Mr Edward King will be coming tonight?'

She smiled. 'Why do you always sound so disapproving when you know perfectly well you're dying to get me married off?'

'No, I'm not — although, yes, I suppose I'd like to see you settled — happy, you know.'

'I am happy, Father,' Margot said firmly. 'It's purely a male concept that a woman can't be happy unless she's married with ten children. I'm lucky enough not to have to marry unless I want to. A great many women aren't. Their only hope of financial security is to marry the first man that asks them.'

'Oh, for goodness sake, Margot. You're not going to start all that business again?'

'Father, I've never stopped it. Four years of war haven't made the slightest difference to my views. If anything the war has made the Women's Movement more determined to press for their rights. If we are responsible enough to make bombs and drive ambulances then we're responsible enough to vote.'

'I'm not arguing about that. I just don't think you go the right way about it. This militancy only puts people's back up and I just don't want you involved in that sort of thing.'

She laughed. 'It's all right, darling. I'm not going to chain myself to the railings or throw myself under a horse. My methods are more subtle ...' She leant toward him and kissed his cheek, 'Like persuading my dear Papa to have a word with his influential friends, to try and get them on our side.'

'I have tried,' said James. 'It didn't do any good.'

'Well, you weren't trying hard enough then. I've never met anyone you couldn't persuade yet.'

James smiled ruefully. He'd never really been able to refuse Margot anything. 'All right, my dear. I'll try.'

They went downstairs. Instinctively James' eyes went to Arthur's face to see how he was bearing up. He looked distinctly seedy still though perhaps now it was over he'd buck up a bit. And Gina, she looked pale. It must be a strain having o prop Arthur up. He admired her for that and admitted now that he'd misjudged her. Gina was a brave and sensible woman. Between them they'd have Arthur on his feet.

Margot came up to him. 'Father, dear. Will you go and talk o Vere? She's feeling a bit out of things, I think.'

'Yes, of course,' James smiled above a mild exasperation. Vere always felt out of things and he sometimes wondered why Margot bothered to drag her about. He looked across to where he girl sat. Really, she looked a mess. Her face was quite naked, without powder or rouge. She wore her hair in a rather untidy chignon. And her frock didn't suit her. She had no idea of style at all. All her movements were clumsy and without grace. He went toward her and as soon as she saw him she stumbled to her feet dropping her bag and gloves, which he dutifully retrieved.

'I'm sorry. How clumsy ...' She fixed him with wide apprehensive eyes and he knew instinctively that she was afraid of men. At least, she was afraid of him.

Then he forgot about Vere. Arthur had raised his glass. 'A toast,' he announced in an emotional voice. 'To peace. To the end of the war to end all wars.'

They drew together in a small intimate group. James raised his glass. 'To absent friends.'

June and July, 1919
— Northumberland

Lieutenant Colonel Hugh Joicey, D.S.O. and Greek Military Cross, surveyed the heaving mass of dancers with an expression of polite boredom. He wasn't really sure that he wanted to be here. The artificial brightness made his head ache and the jostling crowd, all talking too much, laughing too much, projected an air of raucous gaiety that grated on his nerves. It was going to take some getting used to, civilian life. He didn't even feel at ease in mufti yet. It seemed strange not to hear the clink of spurs as he walked, not to feel the high collar of the Hussars' coat chafing his throat. But then everything was different, everyone was changed. The England that he remembered didn't exist anymore. He wasn't sure that he cared for the one that had taken its place.

He sighed inaudibly. It was a month since he'd resigned his commission and he'd felt like a fish out of water ever since. He hadn't the faintest idea what he was going to do. He didn't even know what he could do. He'd been a soldier for nearly all of his life and his qualifications weren't numerous, at least not the sort that people wanted these days. He was only really at home on the back of a horse. He rather hoped, when things got back to normal, to be able to take over the running of the estates. Going into the firm was the only other alternative and none of them could even be certain that there was a future in that. The trade was in chaos, still crippled by government control, and now the threat of nationalization hanging over its head. Everything seemed to depend on the outcome of a government enquiry which had begun as far back as January and still debated even now.

He glanced down as a small hand slipped through his arm. 'What's up, Hugh?' Margot smiled at him. 'You don't look as if you're enjoying yourself.'

'No,' he answered slowly. 'I'm not sure that I am. This enormous crush and yet there seems to be hardly anyone I know.'

'Yes, it's awful, isn't it? That's when it hits you, I think, at parties like this. You realize then all the faces that are missing, faces that you aren't going to see again.' She was silent for a moment then said cheerfully. 'Still, on the credit side, there's a huge surplus of women. You'll be able to take your pick.'

Hugh smiled half-heartedly and she squeezed his arm. She was terribly fond of Hugh, more than she'd ever been of Sydney or Drever. But then all women were. Hugh had an inborn reverence for women and treated them all, old or young, as if they were royalty. And he listened. So few men ever listened to a woman seriously. As far as Margot was concerned it was his greatest asset.

They stood for a moment on the edge of the floor. Their father glided past, a plump and bejewelled dowager in his arms. 'He looks tired,' said Hugh. 'Do you think this nationalization business is getting him down?'

'Not a bit of it. That's probably just what he needs. There's nothing Father likes more than a good fight. And actually, he's

382

looking much better than he did. I was desperately worried about him at one point, when Sydney was killed and we had that awful business with Arthur. He just seemed to shut himself off from everything. Still, he's bucked up enormously since you've been back. In fact, we all have. You're good for us, Hugh.'

They smiled at each other. Then Margot said, 'You're going to miss the army, aren't you, Hugh? It's difficult to think of you doing anything else.'

Hugh grinned wryly. 'I'm not sure yet that I can do anything else.' He looked regretful. 'I think it's India I'm going to miss more than the army. I'd begun to think of it as home, you know.'

'Yes, I know. There's so many things to get used to.'

They were silent for a moment. 'I was sorry to hear about Everard,' Hugh said suddenly. 'You were rather fond of him, weren't you.'

'Yes. Yes, I was,' Margot looked sad. 'Apart from anything else it seems such a waste ... Still,' she smiled brightly, 'life goes on, doesn't it? Well, at least for men it does,' she added provocatively. 'For women it seems to be standing still.'

Hugh pulled a face. 'Don't tell me you're still banging that drum, Margot.'

'Why not? I thought you sympathized, Hugh?'

'I do, but I don't think you should try and force things. Women will get the vote in time. It's just a question of being patient.'

'We've been patient, Hugh, but still nobody is taking us seriously. It's the injustice of the whole system, Hugh, when you think that an illiterate labourer can vote but I cannot ...' She broke off. 'Hugh, you're not listening. What are you staring at?'

'I'm sorry. That was rude of me. I was just wondering who that lovely creature was talking to Harry Percy — that dark haired girl in the silvery frock?'

Margot followed his eyes and gave a wry exclamation. 'Goodness, Hugh. You do like a challenge. That's Joan Lambton, the Earl of Durham's niece.'

Hugh glanced at her, frowning. 'What is that supposed to mean?'

'Oh, Hugh, don't tell me you didn't know. Father and the Lambtons have been mortal enemies for years.'

Of course Margot exaggerated, she always did. Arthur's version was not quite so dramatic. They weren't enemies exactly but neither were they friends. They were, as Arthur quaintly put it, just socially estranged. It was an old story, years old, something to do with their father's takeover of the Lambton Collieries; that was all that any of them knew. It wasn't enough to put Hugh off, in fact, nothing attracted him more than the prospect of opposition. And he wasn't the sort of man that changed his mind easily. People never grew on Hugh, he either loved them or hated them instantly. Not that he had any great experience of women, at least not women like Joan Lambton. He'd never been in one place long enough to form any attachment but always at the back of his mind he'd had a vague picture of the sort of woman he would marry. That hazy picture had suddenly taken on a definite shape; small, slim, delicately boned; eyes as clear and blue as a summer sea; hair with the colour and sheen of raw silk. Oh, yes, he was quite certain after just one glance that he wanted to marry Joan Lambton.

He saw her again quite soon, at Newcastle Races. Up until then it had been a disappointing day. He'd had a winner in the first race but that was all. Neither he nor the horses seemed to be on their form. Hugh smiled ruefully as a complete outsider romped home at staggering odds. It was that sort of day; hot favourites not even making the frame; old hacks coming in at fifty-to-one. He moved away from the rails, head and shoulders above a sea of oddly assorted hats. Nobody seemed to bother to dress now except for Ascot and he felt rather out of place in his morning suit and grey top hat. He glanced around him. His father and Arthur were somewhere about ... Then he saw her, standing just feet away from him, her head bent thoughtfully over an open race card, a swirl of ostrich feathers obscuring her cheek.

'Hello,' he said, smiling. 'Are you having any luck?'

She looked up at him, startled, 'I'm sorry ...'

'I must apologize,' he said quickly, 'for my rather unconventional approach, Miss Lambton, but I always think it rather

384

illy to walk past people you know perfectly well just because ou haven't been formally introduced.' He held out his hand. I'm Hugh Joicey. You probably know my sister, Margot.'

'Oh yes. Yes, of course I do,' she smiled at him uncertainly, a little flustered. 'How do you do, Mr Joicey ... although it's Colonel Joicey, isn't it?'

He smiled. 'It was. I'm out of the army now.'

'Oh, yes, I see,' She stared down at the race card and he saw the soft colour sweep over her face. He smiled. She wasn't at all like he'd imagined, rather cool and aloof. She had a child-like naivete that enchanted him even more. She looked incredibly young and he wondered how old she was. He was suddenly very conscious of his thirty-eight years. He opened his mouth to speak when a loud arrogant voice suddenly cut him off.

'Oh, there you are, Joan. I've been looking for you everywhere ...' Johnny Lambton broke off as he saw Hugh. 'Oh hello, Joicey. Heard you were back. Packed the army in for good now, I understand?'

'Yes, that's right.'

'Best thing. Nobody wants to know about the army these days.' He took his sister's arm. 'You'll excuse us, won't you? We've a horse running in the next race and my father always insists that we cheer it on.'

Joan held out her hand. 'Well, goodbye, Colonel Joicey. I expect we shall meet again soon.'

'Yes, I'm sure we shall.' Hugh smiled. He was going to make quite sure that they did.

James stared bleakly at the mountain of paper that littered his desk — the Sankey Report: the death warrant of the coal industry, the end of a lifetime's ambition, with its recommendation that the coal industry be taken out of the hands of private enterprise and be placed under the permanent control of the state.

'I think it's disgraceful,' said Arthur feelingly, 'that a man can be deprived of his property and livelihood merely on the whim of the state. It's so blatantly dishonest. Government control of the industry was meant to be a purely temporary measure. As I see it, the government have done well out of it and are now refusing to hand it back.' He looked at his father.

'What on earth are we going to do? What if they just take everything over and don't even pay out compensation?'

'They won't,' said James shortly. 'They wouldn't go that far.'

'But that's what some of the union leaders want. That's what they did in Russia.'

'This is England, not Russia. We haven't got a Communist government yet. It hasn't even happened yet, Arthur. The report merely recommends that it does.'

'It's the same thing isn't it? The Government gave its word that it would abide by the decision of the commission.'

'Lloyd George gave his word,' James replied cynically. 'Lloyd George would say anything to get out of a tight corner. If he hadn't come up with something to placate the unions, he'd have had an all-out strike on his hands. It's up to the coal-owners to force him into an equally tight corner.'

He pushed back his chair and went to stand beneath old James' portrait. He looked up into the cynical sneering face. My God, the old boy would be turning in his grave. He was suffering from a sense of shock himself. And he should have seen it coming; control of the mines for the duration of the war had just been the first and fatal step. It naturally followed that the unions would pull out all the stops to prevent them being handed back. But that the government should actually countenance it, that a man like Lloyd George could bind himself to the outcome of a flimsy and circumstantial report . . . No, he hadn't expected that. He gnawed at his lip. What the hell was that crafty old buzzard up to? He could follow his strategy in as much as the enquiry had put off the threatened miners' strike and had kept the union quiet throughout the general election at the end of 1918. But that was all history now. It certainly wasn't public opinion he was courting with almost a complete term of office to run. He could be certain of being Prime Minister for at least another four years, albeit of another coalition. No, there was something else, something that he'd missed . . . He looked to the future and wondered how aware the Prime Minister was that their current prosperity was to be short lived. He gave it a year, before the 'Make Germany Pay' policy began to take effect, before reparation coal killed their export markets stone dead. He winced at the thought of

ungling government officials attempting to steer the industry
through such hazardous seas. He couldn't allow it to happen,
he couldn't allow his dream to be just swept away. He turned
back into the room and smiled at his son. 'Don't worry, Arthur,
we're not beaten yet. We haven't even started to fight.'

'My lord ...' David Lloyd George welcomed James with an
affable smile. He was a small man of vaguely Bohemian
appearance, his hair carefully dishevelled and a little too long.
A heavy moustache concealed a full and sensuous upper lip.

James shook hands. 'It's good of you to see me at such short
notice, Prime Minister.'

'Not at all. Not at all.' Lloyd George drew him on into the
room. 'Do you know Bob Smillie? President of the Miners'
Federation of Great Britain. I thought it important that he
should hear what you have to say.'

James shook hands briefly, slightly taken aback by the union
man's unexpected presence. They hadn't met before but he
instantly recognized the type; an ardent Socialist, burning with
Bolshevik ideas and revolutionary zeal. He would use words
like 'bourgeois' and 'proletariat'. Then the three men sat down
in a general atmosphere of suspicion and distrust. James didn't
trust Lloyd George, Lloyd George didn't trust him and the
union man trusted neither of them.

'Well then, my lord. I think both Mr Smillie and I have an
idea why you're here — though quite frankly I would have
thought it a little late in the day. It seems to me that any pleas
in mitigation of sentence might have been better said whilst the
commission was in session rather than after it had delivered its
verdict.'

James smiled. 'I was under the impression that the committee's verdict, as you put it, was merely a recommendation. I
wasn't aware that it had already become a fact in law. I
remember you saying, Prime Minister, before this business
began, that nationalization wasn't a religion to be followed
blindly as an act of faith. You stated quite clearly that the aim
of the commission was to show whether state ownership of the
coal industry was a viable business proposition. In my opinion
it hasn't done so. It has merely shown that nationalization
would be of benefit to the miners — but we didn't need an

enquiry to tell us that.'

It was Smillie who answered him. 'It proved that the present system under private enterprise is extravagant and wasteful that the owners are reluctant to modernize and improve.'

'You think so, Mr Smillie?' James smiled at him unpleasantly. 'Did you know that my company was the first in the north to use coal cutting machines and face conveyors? And that within three weeks I had a strike on my hands. I was told by the Federation representative that machines degraded the dignity of labour apart from being able to do the work of two men, therefore rendering fifty per cent of the workforce redundant. Mechanization means safety and increased production, but it also means an overall reduction of the labour force which in turn means trouble with the unions. Can you wonder that some owners are reluctant to take it up?'

'That may have been so,' Smillie admitted. 'These things take time to win acceptance, I agree. But you would not deny that the combination of a large number of pits under a single management is a more economical proposition. In fact, as the owner of the largest and most successful colliery company in Britain, you have proved that to be true yourself.'

'Large combines, yes — but not so large as nationalization would entail, the entire industry ruled by faceless Whitehall bureaucrats, subject to the whim and fancy of whatever government happened to be in power. The industry would end up as a bone between two dogs. Its policies would be formulated by politicans and civil servants who've never been near a pit in their life.'

'Well, that might be preferable to the policies formulated by some owners, which always seem to be to cut the men's pay.'

James looked at the union man coldly. 'I have never advocated low wages, Mr Smillie, as I have never advocated that men be paid according to the selling price of coal which none of us can control. Greater production is the answer which every man can control. High output equals cheap coal which means that we can compete on equal terms with the rest of the world. That is plain economics, Mr Smillie, not, as the Federation seem to believe, a cheap trick to boost the owners' profits. It occurs to me sometimes, Mr Smillie, that you might do more for the men you pretend to represent if your negoti tions were not always clouded with prejudice and suspicion.'

'If we are suspicious, then it's only past experience that has made us so. We've learned not to expect honest treatment from capitalists and profiteers.'

'So what you're really saying is that this is a class war, that pay and conditions are secondary to the removal of the capitalist class, that however decent an employer may be, he must go, merely because he is master. Is that your dream, Mr Smillie? The setting up here of a Bolshevik state, where all men are masters — or is it that all men are servants? That point in your philosophy always confuses me. But there will always be masters, Mr Smillie. There will always be clever men, ambitious men. Inevitably they rise to the top like the scum on a pot. Even if you get what you want, the state will be just as much a master as I am. The industry will still have to show a profit unless it is to be subsidised like a charity by the tax-payer.'

'And it will show a profit once the men realize they are working for themselves. Perhaps not the vast amounts that the owners demand. Did you know, my lord, that in 1916 alone, the Exchequer took three million pounds out of the industry?'

'And how much did it put back?' James argued. 'How much did it spend on new machinery and equipment? How much on the opening up and exploration of new seams? Perhaps it's the government rather than the owners that should be accused of profiteering, of exploiting a wartime market desperate for coal, of pushing prices to astronomical levels. As far as I can see, all the state has done in the three years of its control is to exploit both the owners and the men. It's taken everything out and put nothing back. It's plundered all the most profitable faces, working the thick and more accessible seams, taking the coal from where it can most easily be got.' His eyes fastened coldly on the silent figure of Lloyd George. 'For a Welshman your knowledge of coal is abysmal, Prime Minister. And yet I assume you know something about money, about the principle of supply and demand? Because very soon, you know, there isn't going to be any demand. At the moment you've got a captive market. Everyone wants British coal and at any price. But what's going to happen when the French and Belgian pits get back on their feet, when reparations start to bite and

Europe is flooded with free German coal? Twenty million ton a year to France alone. Who's going to want our coal then?'

Lloyd George shifted uneasily in his seat. 'We shall naturall fall back on our former markets ...'

'What markets? By limiting exports to protect hom consumption you've already allowed the Americans to snap u our Canadian trade ...'

'My lord, I wonder, considering the gloomy picture yo paint of the industry's future, that you are so keen to ge control of it back.'

'I am a rich man, Prime Minister. Even if you closed up m collieries tomorrow, I should still be a rich man. I am also a old man and probably I won't survive another ten years. But want the coal industry to survive long after me and it will no do so in the hands of politicans and union men. It's a ris business; sometimes it means pouring thousands of pounds int a hole in the ground and never seeing a penny of it again Would the state be in a position to speculate so freely wit what, after all, is public money? Who would take the risks Who would make the decisions? Who would bear th responsibility if they were the wrong decisions? The industr would stagnate, it would go under at the first major crisis. If is to survive into better times then it must be handed back t the men who know it best, who have the most to lose shoul they fail.'

'And the most to gain if they succeed,' put in Smillie.

James turned to look at him. 'And you would have nothin to gain? The men would have nothing to gain from a health and thriving industry?'

'We will have that under the state.'

James smiled. 'You are convinced, are you not, that th state will make a better master than me — and yet you are sti haggling after six months over a thirty per cent advance.' He turned toward Lloyd George. 'Why don't you give it to them Prime Minister? Why don't you give it to them out of th massive profits the industry is supposed to have made?'

Lloyd George's eyelids flickered briefly. He answered midly 'I'm sure you appreciate it's not as simple as that.'

'I don't see the difficulty,' James countered swiftly. 'Indus trial coal is making a profit of nineteen shillings a ton and th owners receive less than two shillings of that. Surely there is surplus enough to meet Mr Smillie's demands?'

'Forgive me, my lord,' the Prime Minister's soft voice took on a sudden edge. 'But I was under the impression that you were here to discuss nationalization, not to assist Mr Smillie in his negotiations.'

James inclined his head. 'My apologies, Prime Minister. I was just demonstrating to the President that he'd have just as much difficulty extracting money from the state as he maintains he does from the owners.'

Lloyd George made no reply and James stared thoughtfully at his impassive face. For this devious, voluble and self opinionated man to remain so consistently silent under attack was suspicious in itself. 'You know, Prime Minister,' he said at last. 'I get the impression that you're not particularly concerned to bring about a settlement at all. I think, in fact, that you are playing for time. Whilst Mr Smillie extolls the virtues of state ownership, he has quite forgotten about pressing for his thirty per cent demand, and in the same way, so intent am I on demonstrating to Mr Smillie the folly of his ideas, it quite slips my mind that the state is still in control of my collieries. I believe it's called playing both ends against the middle. Presumably you think that if you keep us talking long enough, negotiating long enough, then we'll all get fed up and go away. But I shall not go away, Prime Minister. I shall fight the government and the unions and the men themselves to win back control of my collieries. But I shall fight openly and honestly. With me at least the Federation know where they stand. I wonder if they'll know so well how they stand with you.'

November, 1919 — Ford Castle

James eased his chair a little closer to the fire. He felt cold and irritable and out of sorts. November always took him like that. He hated the short damp days and the long dark nights. The one made his bones ache, the others his heart. He still remembered, even after getting on for forty years. The memories so easily came rushing back.

He sighed and looked at his watch. Amazing how sometimes the time seemed to drag. The trouble was he had nothing really urgent to occupy his mind now the scare of nationalization was over. He'd won, of course, or rather the coalowners had won — at least they'd won that particular battle if not the war. And sometimes he wasn't even sure about that. He'd never been convinced, at the bottom of him, that Lloyd George had ever intended to nationalize. It had been something of a red herring, a bribe to the union, a threat to the owners, a diversionary tactic to take their minds off the real issues. Therefore, he hadn't been surprised when in August, Lloyd George had rejected the Sankey Report, even less so when he had extended government control of the industry for another year. Obviously, he meant to get what he could, while he could. Business was still booming, steam and bunker coal selling at an unprecedented hundred and sixty shillings at ton. And very nice too, he thought bitterly. All of the profit and none of the responsibility. Between them, the unions and the government meant to bleed the industry dry.

He leant forward and prodded restlessly at the fire. He wondered how he would fill the afternoon. He supposed he could work on his speech for the Newcastle Chamber of Commerce. That was all he seemed to do these days, make speeches, open bazaars, sign his name to cheques for a host of charities. He leant back in his chair and stared broodingly round the vast chilly room into which ugly radiators pulsed an inadequate heat. It wasn't the same since the army had been here. Ford was too large for him now, a great vaulted barn in which they were outnumbered by the servants ten to one. He supposed the long and the short of it was that he was lonely. Sometimes he felt like an old fossil washed up on a foreign shore. Everything was different; cars instead of carriages, paper money, women who didn't even look like women any more, with cropped hair and fringes and dresses like sacks which showed their knees. Every function he went to there were fewer faces that he recognized, fewer people who had lived through his times. Yes, he often felt isolated, out of touch with the modern world. Of course, he had Margot and the boys, but even they seemed to live separate lives. Arthur had his family, Margot's head was always full of this suffrage business. And Hugh ... He glanced at his daughter, 'What's Hugh up to today? He must have gone out early.'

'Yes. He's out cubbing with the Milvain.'

James pursed his lips. 'He's seeing a lot of the Lambton girl, isn't he?'

'Well, he's bound to, isn't he?' Margot said evasively. 'Seeing as they're virtually neighbours and attend the same social events, I should have thought it rather difficult to avoid her.'

'That's not what I mean. You know that's not what I mean.' He gave the fire a vicious prod. 'Is it serious, do you think?'

'I don't know, Father. Hugh hasn't told me anything. You know how secretive Hugh can be when he likes.'

'He isn't usually with you. You've always been close. If he confided in anyone it would be you.'

'Well, he hasn't — and even if he had I shouldn't tell you about it. If you want to know you'll have to ask him yourself.'

James scowled, knowing perfectly well that she knew what was going on. My God, it was too ironic. Of all the women he could have picked it had to be a Lambton. Just the thought of it roused all manner of unpleasant memories: Jack Lambton's high and sneering voice — 'Well, I suppose with your background you think you know these things ...' It still rankled even after all these years. Other men would have forgotten it, taken it in their stride. It would have been outweighed by the years of wealth and success. But he hadn't forgotten, and looking back, he could see that every action of his life had been a subconcious vindication of that memory. And nothing had changed. People like the Lambtons didn't change. They'd insult Hugh as readily as they'd insulted him ... He gnawed at his lip. He'd have to do something about it before it got out of hand though how you dictated to a man like Hugh he didn't know. But if he didn't, then the Lambtons would. He couldn't see them welcoming Hugh as a son-in-law. They usually set their sights far higher than that. The eldest daughter Violet had married the Earl of Ellesmere, the other girl Lillian, Earl Home ...

He got abruptly to his feet. He really couldn't stand all this sitting around thinking. 'I think I'll go along to the library, if you don't mind. I have some letters to write.'

'Yes, all right, Father,' Margot smiled at him over the top of her book. 'We'll have tea in there if you like.'

The library was his refuge and he felt strangely calmed once inside the large quiet room. He glanced around him, smiling faintly; high backed winged chairs — cocoons of privacy; rows of leather bound books gleaming from behind polished glass. And the smell: dry dust, tobacco, parchment and ink, as if the presence of scholarly and erudite men had lingered on in the pages of their books.

He poured himself a whisky though normally he did not drink before six o'clock. Then he spun round quickly as he heard a sound and caught Vere on her way to the door. 'For God's sake, girl — what do you think you're doing creeping about like that?'

She stood transfixed, staring at him like a cornered rabbit. He saw her stricken eyes fill with tears.

'Look, I'm sorry,' he said awkwardly. 'I didn't mean to be so sharp. You startled me, that's all.'

'I'm sorry. I thought ... You see, I realized that you didn't know I was here and I know how annoying it is when you think you're alone to suddenly find that you're not ...' She gabbled on, twisting her handerchief between nervous fingers.

'Oh, sit down, Vere, for goodness sake. Here, have a drink. You look as if it might do you good.'

She subsided meekly onto the edge of a chair and he thrust a glass of sherry into her hand. My God, he thought, she looks dreadful; her clothes drab and unfashionable, her hair a mess, her face naked of everything except a miserable expression. Pretty eyes though, soft and warm. And her hands were small and delicately shaped. He couldn't abide women with ugly hands.

She sipped at the sherry as if it were hemlock. 'I'm sorry to be a nuisance,' she said at last. 'You must get rather tired of me always being here.'

'Don't you get rather tired of being here yourself? It must be rather dull for you sometimes?'

'Oh, but it isn't,' she protested. 'I love it here. And anyway, I suppose I'm a dull person really. I've never liked doing the things that other people call fun.'

'What do you like doing then?'

'Oh, reading, walking, things like that.'

'Aren't you keen on this Women's Rights stuff then?'

'Well, not really, you know — at least I don't feel so strongly about it as Margot does. It's probably right that women like Margot should be allowed to vote but I'm not sure that someone like me would use it wisely. You know how you either take to people or not? Well, I should probably vote for the candidate with the nice blue eyes rather than the one with the untidy moustache.'

He laughed aloud, rich merry laughter that echoed round the room. 'Oh, Vere! What an absolutely priceless remark.'

She smiled back at him tentatively and he thought suddenly that she was rather sweet. 'Smiling suits you,' he said. 'You should do it more often.'

'So should you,' she said. 'You've been unhappy for far too long.' She regarded him steadily. 'That's the trouble with men — they can't share their grief as women do. They just keep everything locked up inside themselves until it turns bitter and sour.'

He looked at her strangely, wondering why he didn't resent what he would normally have considered an invasion of his privacy. 'Do you think I'm bitter and sour, then?'

'Sometimes. It's so very easy, isn't it, to make sorrow a way of life. And yet don't you think that the finest way to honour the dead is to continue to care about the living?'

He frowned. 'I'm not sure what you mean?'

She flushed. 'I mean that you're so intent on remembering the sons that you've lost that sometimes you forget about the ones that are still living.' She averted her eyes from his suddenly hostile gaze. 'It was Arthur I was thinking about rather than Hugh. Hugh is like you. He's strong and resilient; he'll shake life by the throat until it gives in. But people like Arthur and I don't have that kind of strength. We're pessimists, defeatists, always expecting the worst. And because we do expect it, the worst always happens, and then we blame ourselves. We always feel that when things go wrong it must be our fault ...' She broke off. 'I'm sorry. I've made you angry, saying all this. It's the sherry, I suppose. I'm not usually so outspoken. You must think me unforgiveably rude.'

He stared at her for a long time. Then suddenly he smiled.

'No, I don't. And you're quite right. Everything you say is perfectly true. I'm just surprised I suppose, to hear it from you.'

Vere gave her shy and nervous laugh. 'I suppose I'm a little surprised myself. Usually I only say the things that people expect me to say.' She shrugged. 'Perhaps it's the war. It seems more acceptable now to speak one's mind, to question other people's standards. I find that quite frightening sometimes. Suddenly there doesn't seem to be any restraint. All the things that once mattered don't matter any more.'

James was silent though he was deeply affected by all that she had said. Reluctantly he stirred himself. 'I must get on, I'm afraid. I have some rather pressing letters to write ...'

'Oh, yes. Well, I'll leave you alone ...'

'No. Please stay. Finish your book.' He smiled at her. 'I can work quite well with you here.'

He went to the desk and took out paper and envelopes; Dear Sir, he wrote. I feel I must call into question your article of the 10th instant ...

The rasp of his pen over the paper was the only sound in the room and several times he looked across at the small dark woman curled in the chair. He smiled quietly to himself. For some reason he felt easier than he had done for years.

April 17th, 1920 — Northumberland

Hugh gentled the big bay up onto the bare summit of the hill. They'd had a good run: out from Ford across Bar Moor then dropping down by Roughting Linn to skirt the dark pine woods east of Fenton. He lifted his face to the pale April sun. The wind was cold, bracing yet sweet. Winter had at last begun to relinquish its grip and though the hills and high moorland were still streaked with snow, the thawed meadows by the Till were tentatively green. An expression of pure contentment swept over his face. A year ago this view would have meant nothing to him. Now he knew it like the back of his hand. He knew every farm and cottage, every wood and hill; he knew where the trout rose and salmon leapt, the haunts of deer and grouse and partridge. It was a strange feeling, the pull of the land, the sense of suddenly belonging, as if after years of exile he had at last come home. And all so easily and effortlessly, that restless urge suddenly quenched. And he was in love, gloriously, exhilaratingly, possessively in love. Today he was going to ask Joan Lambton to marry him.

He spurred the horse forward, plunging recklessly down the slope. He was in Lambton territory now — enemy territory, for that was how he had come to think of it. It had been a strange courtship, often together but always as part of a crowd. Probably he hadn't seen her more than half a dozen times alone. And he still wasn't sure how he stood with the Lambtons. They treated him politely but warily and kept him at arm's length. He had the impression that they were biding their time, waiting to see how things turned out. Perhaps they hoped, like his father did, that if they didn't interfere, the affair would come to nothing. His mouth set in a resolute line. The Lambtons could be forgiven for thinking that but his father should have known him better.

He halted in the little clearing where they always met. As always he was there long before her. He dismounted and lit a nervous cigarette. Through the trees he could see the walls of Fenton House, the single high turret thrusting up over the parkland. Joan called it her Ivory Tower, her refuge from an unpleasant world. A look of tenderness transformed his face. He thought suddenly how different they were. Joan was so shy and sensitive whereas he ...

He flung away his cigarette, sensing her approach and walked back along the path till he should see her. She was on foot and bareheaded, two fat spaniels panting at her heels. Her face lit when she saw him and she broke into an eager run. His heart lurched. He always waited for that look, the soft colour sweeping her face, the curving of her mouth into its uncertain smile.

'You look cold,' he said, slipping his arm around her. 'Are you?'

'No, not really — though it's quite chilly once you're out of the sun. I suppose I should have gone upstairs for a warmer coat but I didn't want to risk ...' Her voice tailed away and Hugh's eyes darkened. He knew how it distressed her, meeting like this. She was so open and honest. She couldn't bear deceit.

They didn't talk about it much, the unspoken disapproval of her family and his. It was the only cloud on an otherwise perfect horizon.

They walked in silence, the dogs running ahead, damp muzzles questing the ground. There wasn't any real need to speak. They were used to communicating with just their eyes, with the clinging of their hands as he helped her over a stile, the little ripples of breathless laughter as they raced down a bank.

They entered the wood. It was dim and still, shot with ripples of dusty sunlight; banks of primroses and violet gave of a sweet heady scent. He took her hand and their fingers twined lovingly together. There was between them a feeling of quiet joy. Then like a schoolboy he picked violets for her and tried unsuccessfully to pin them in her hair. She buried her face in the small shy blooms. She looked up at him smiling. 'Whenever I smell violets I shall think of you.'

'Only then?' He gave her a look of mock reproach. 'I would have hoped you thought of me more than that. I think of you all the time.'

'And what do you think?'

The mocking smile faded from his mouth. 'That you're beautiful and gentle and sensitive and kind — and that even if you were not I should still love you.' He took her hands. 'Marry me, Joan. I care for you so very much.'

Then she was in his arms. 'Oh Hugh, darling Hugh.' She lifted her radiant face to his. 'Oh yes, yes, I'll marry you ...' Then her face clouded and she drew away from him. 'But is it going to be as easy as that?'

'I win, I think, my dear.' James flung Vere a triumphant look and laid down a pair and three kings.

Vere sighed. 'I'm not very good, am I?' She said ruefully. 'I can never remember what cards are out.'

James smiled. 'That's why I enjoy playing against you. I can always win.'

'Is that so important to you then? Winning, I mean.'

'Isn't it important to everyone?'

She considered this thoughtfully. 'No, I don't think so. It's not important to me.'

'What is important to you then?'

Vere shrugged. 'People, I suppose. I'm not really sure now. Things seemed to have changed so much.'

James glanced at her. It was strange how much he'd come to value her company, how at ease they were together. He rather liked her simple and old fashioned clothes, the stubborn way she defied modern fashions. She reminded him of a world that was gone, a world of feminine women and courteous men, of waltzes and polkas, long dresses and long hair. He remarked, smiling, 'You should marry, you know, Vere.'

She blushed. 'That's rather difficult when nobody has asked you.'

'Well, they won't, will they, if you hide yourself away up here. You should be going to parties and dances, meeting handsome young men.'

'I don't like parties and dances all that much. For that matter, I don't like young men either. They always make me feel so awkward.'

'What sort of men do you like then?'

She looked away from his direct gaze. 'I don't know. I've never thought about it.'

'Well, you should think about it. You're full of love and kindness, Vere. It seems great pity to waste it.'

He turned his head as Hugh came into the room. 'I'm sorry to butt in, Father, but do you think I could have a word?' He glanced at Vere. 'It's rather private. I'm afraid.'

'Oh yes, of course . . .' Vere flushed deeply and rose abruptly to her feet. 'I'll just go and see what's happening to tea.'

She almost ran from the room and James frowned. 'That was a bit tactless, wasn't it, Hugh? I don't like Vere treated as an outsider.'

'Yes, I'm sorry.' Hugh looked desperate. 'But I really needed to speak to you alone.'

'All right. What's on your mind?'

Hugh sat down. 'Look, Father, I'll come straight to the point. I want to marry Joan Lambton.'

James was silent for a moment then he said. 'And does Joan Lambton want to marry you?'

'Yes, she does. I asked her this morning and she said yes.'

'What seems to be the problem, then? You're of age, Hugh.

You don't need my consent.'

Hugh sprang to his feet. 'You know perfectly well what th
problem is, Father. This feud, this vendetta ... If there's goin
to be any awkwardness about my marrying Joan then I thin]
I've a right to know why.'

'Haven't you guessed why, Hugh?' James' voice was harsh
'Hasn't it dawned on you that as far as the Lambtons are
concerned we're not up to scratch? We're what is known a
nouveau riche, only three generations removed from pitmen.'

'Oh, that's rot, Father — and you know it. People just don'
think like that any more.'

'People like the Lambtons do,' James observed grimly
'They're very sensitive about their pedigrees.'

'I don't believe that,' said Hugh calmly. 'In case you've
forgotten, Joan is a Lambton and my pedigree doesn't seem to
worry her.' He stared at James' set face. 'Oh come on, Father
There's more to it than that. I shan't leave it alone till I fine
out.'

James sighed inwardly. 'Yes, all right, there's more to it than
that, a great deal more, very little of which you'll probabl)
understand.'

'Well, try me,' said Hugh.

James shrugged. 'Well, I'm not sure that there's any simple
explanation. The Lambtons were our business rivals for twenty
years and it was a fight for survival in those days. I usually
won, that's all, and I kept on winning until in the end I bough
them out. Probably they don't think I fought fairly.'

'And did you?'

'Everything's fair in business, Hugh. I just fought harder
that's all and with different weapons.' He was silent for a
moment then he went on. 'You don't believe me when I say it':
all about snobbery and class, but that's where it has its roots, ir
bigotry and ignorance, in the contempt of the aristocracy for
the working class. That's where Jack Lambton went wrong. He
didn't take me seriously. He thought I was a nobody, in fact he
said so publicly once. I never forgave him for that, for hi
ignorance, his contempt. I promised myself that one day I'c
prove that I wasn't just as good as he was but better.' He
smiled thinly. 'So from then on, every time Jack Lambton
looked over his shoulder I was there. Every opportunity to take

unities; I made myself the most efficient and successful coal-owner in the north until in the end I was able to buy him out and turn his failure into my success. And I let him know what I had done. I let him know that I had deliberately set out to ruin him.' He stared down at his hands. 'So there it is, Hugh. Now you know what it's about. It isn't you their hostility is directed against. It's me.' He looked at Hugh. 'I don't suppose you understand that, do you?'

Hugh shook his head. 'I can understand how you felt perhaps about the Earl of Durham but he's just one man, Father. What about the others? What have Joan or Joan's father ever done to you?'

'They're Lambtons,' James said bitterly. 'They're all the same.'

'My God, Father,' Hugh burst out. 'We've just fought a war because people thought like that. Millions of men died just because they were English or German or French.'

James was silent. For a long time he was silent. Then at last he said, 'It'll be all right, Hugh. I'll make sure it is. You'll marry Joan Lambton and live happily every after.' He gave a painful half smile. He'd sacrificed a great many people on the altar of his pride but Hugh wasn't going to be one of them.

It wasn't going to be the easiest thing he'd ever done. Backing down had never been his strong point yet he knew it was up to him to make the first move, to make some gesture of reconciliation. But sitting in the back of the Wolseley as it swept through the gates of Fenton House, he was seized by doubts. Here he was going cap in hand to a Lambton, making up to a man he hardly knew. He tried to recall to mind what he knew about Freddy Lambton. A familiar face in some ways, seen at a distance across a room, in the steward's enclosure at race meetings. He'd heard he was a quiet man, a private man — hopefully then an understanding man, a forgiving man ... He set his teeth. He was doing this for Hugh, he reminded himself as he was admitted into the spacious hall. A footman relieved him of his hat and gloves. He heard himself announced. His name seemed to ring like a challenge round the walls.

Freddy Lambton greeted him stiffly. James noticed that he

did not offer his hand. He studied him covertly. He was like his brother the Earl in looks and colouring, but there the resemblance ended. He saw now that the impression of aloof condescension masked a sensitive nature. He knew just by looking at him that he was painfully shy. His eyes were kind, though and his face was lined in such a way as to show that he often smiled. His voice was soft and hesitant, and listening to it James had the impression that he had perhaps stammered in his youth.

'May I offer you some refreshment, my lord?'

'Thank you, no. It's a little early for me.'

'Well, won't you sit down. We may as well be comfortable.'

James cleared his throat. 'Perhaps you have some idea of why I am here?'

Lambton smiled thinly. 'I presume it concerns my daughter and your son.'

'Yes. Perhaps you already know? It seems that they wish to marry.'

Lambton's expression grew cold. 'No,' he said stonily. 'I didn't know.'

'I must assume from your tone that you do not approve?'

Lambton flushed. 'You can hardly expect me to welcome the idea of my daughter marrying the son of a man whose name has caused such distress to my family.'

'Not always without cause, if I may say so, Mr Lambton.'

'Well, one can always find reasons. I dare say in your own mind you can justify the things you have done. Is that why you came here? To justify yourself?'

'No.' James controlled himself with an effort. 'I came here to say that my quarrel, if you can call it that, is solely with your brother, the Earl. It is of a personal nature and was never meant to involve you or your family.'

'My brother is also my family, my lord. What offends him must necessarily offend me.'

James rose to his feet. 'I'm sorry to have wasted your time Mr Lambton. I came here because I thought the happiness of two young people was more important than the grudges and squabbles of two old men. You, obviously, do not agree.'

Lambton stared at him, then quietly he said, 'Sit down, my lord. Perhaps we should begin again.' He got up and went toward a table where there was a decanter and glasses. Are you sure you won't join me? I have a fine Amontillado of which I'm rather proud. It hasn't been possible to get anything decent until just recently.'

James murmured his acceptance and resumed his seat. He glanced round the room; a pleasant room, quietly informal, a room usually inhabited by dogs and people. There seemed to be photographs everywhere; girls in white debutante's frocks, young men in striped blazers. One in particular caught his eye, a smiling young man in army uniform. Lambton followed his gaze, 'My son Geoffrey,' he said. 'He was killed just three weeks after the war began.' A look of pain crossed his amiable face. 'He was a fine boy — but then they were all fine boys, weren't they?' He handed James his glass. 'I understand you lost a boy yourself.'

'Yes,' said James shortly. 'My son Sydney ...'

Lambton nodded. 'Yes, it does make everything seem trivial, doesn't it? As you say, the grudges and squabbles of two old men.' He sipped at the sherry. 'May we speak frankly, my lord? I feel that we shan't get anywhere unless we do. Despite appearances to the contrary, I am grateful for you coming here. I'm ashamed to say that I wouldn't have had the courage to make the gesture myself.' He came and sat opposite James. 'But there is still my brother. My daughter Joan is still his niece. Does this offer of truce, if I may call it that, also extend to him? It's a question of family, you see,' he added as James hesitated. 'As the quarrel between you involved us all, so then must any reconciliation.' He went on as James remained silent. 'This is difficult for me to say without appearing disloyal but I know that my brother can be a difficult man. But he is also an unhappy man, a lonely man and has been for some years ... What I'm trying to say is that if it is a victory you are looking for then you have already won. There is nothing to be gained by pursuing it further.'

James said slowly, 'And if I were to make this gesture, how would the Earl react?'

'With relief, I should imagine after all these years. Yes, I think, like me, he will be glad to make an end.' He held out his glass and smiled shyly. 'Shall we drink a toast, my lord, to my daughter and your son? To Hugh and Joan.'

403

The two men touched the rims of their glasses together and Lambton murmured, half to himself, 'From forth the fatal lions of these two foes ... Shakespeare,' he said in answer to James' quizzical look. 'It's quotation from Romeo and Juliet, happily not appropriate now.'

February, 1921 — Newcastle

In the plush inner sanctum of the Association offices, six men sat in silence. It was a queer sort of silence, Arthur thought, not really a silence at all, more a suspension of movement and sound, as if they were all holding their breath. He glanced at the faces of the men either side of him: Austen Kirkup, Managing Director of the Lambton and Hetton group; Hugh Taylor and John Straker; Charles Carr, agent of the Londonderry Collieries and Lord Gainsford of Pease and Partners. It was Gainsford who had dropped the latest bombshell; the Government's decision to decontrol four months early and return the industry to private control. A year ago, six months even, all of them would have welcomed the news, when British coal was a commodity that could still be sold, before Europe and half the world had shut them out. But not now, whilst the industry was still reeling from the effects of the trade's collapse, whilst they were still trying to make some order out of the chaos. It had all been so sudden. Overnight it seemed the export market had collapsed. Prices had halved, quartered, falling in just weeks from a hundred and sixty to forty shillings a ton. Coal was costing more to produce than it could be sold for. In the last week eleven Durham collieries had closed. A hundred others were working short time or laid in.

Arthur moved his head in a mute gesture of despair. This was the third meeting he had attended this week, and before that, over the last two months, he had sat, often late into the night, arguing, negotiating, making proposals and counter proposals, desperately seeking a way out of the crisis. This was the final blow, for the Government to abandon them at such a time.

'Well, what now?' Austen Kirkup broke the deadly silence. 'Where do we go from here?'

'Down, my dear Austen,' said Hugh Taylor cynically. 'In the circumstances, that's the only direction possible. Without the Government to subsidise the men's rate of pay, the industry's had it as far as I can see.'

'But what's happened?' said Arthur. 'What's brought all this on. We were promised Government support until August.'

'My dear Arthur,' said Gainsford. 'It's a case of the rats deserting the proverbial sinking ship. The Government has been subsidising the industry since the beginning of the year to the tune of five million pounds a month. They've just had enough that's all.'

'But can they do that?' demanded Straker. 'Can they abandon their responsibilities just like that?'

'Governments can do anything they like,' snapped Gainsford. 'It's perfectly obvious they're getting out whilst the going's good. Like the unions, they're perfectly happy to take a share of our profits but they don't want anything to do with our losses. Between them they've bled the industry dry and now they're handing us back the skin and bones.' He paused to select a hand-made cigarette from a handsome gold case. 'It's going to mean trouble with the men of course. There's nothing left for it now but for us to demand that they take a cut in pay. I propose that we seek a reduction of at least thirty per cent ...'

Arthur blanched. 'But that would take the men's wages below pre-war level ...'

'I might point out that our profits are already below pre-war level. In fact, at the moment, we are not making any profits at all but a loss of over four shillings a ton. It's a question of hard economic fact.'

'But the Federation won't stand for it,' protested Arthur. 'It's more money they're looking for, not less.'

'Then they must complain to the Government,' said Gainsford irritably. 'They're the ones that made all the money during the war.

'In the meantime, I suggest that we take such steps as we can to protect ourselves. Decontrol is scheduled for the end of March. That gives us a breathing space of just under six weeks. We must use it to build up what stocks we can. I propose a circular be issued to all members to that effect, warning them to prepare for a lengthy stoppage and instructing them to issue

405

notices to all grades of men, terminating their contracts as from the end of March. Then providing that they agree to our terms ...'

'And if they don't,' interrupted Arthur. 'If they don't agree? What do we do then?'

Gainsford's hard face cracked into a smile. 'Then we lock them out, my dear Arthur. It's as simple as that.'

On the 24th March, the Mines Decontrol Bill was passed by Parliament and the prospect of a lock-out seemed almost certain. Negotiations still went on — between union and Government, Government and employer, but with only two days to go before the notices expired, no agreement had been reached. Arthur blamed the union; he blamed the Government, both seemed equally intransigent. And in a way he blamed himself. He felt very strongly that he hadn't done enough to avoid the coming confrontation. He spoke about it to his father. He was convinced that if only he could speak to the men directly, if he could just put their case, explain the simple facts, that wages had to be governed by the industry's ability to pay ...

James smiled. 'It wouldn't be possible, Arthur, I'm afraid — and even if it were they wouldn't listen. This isn't just about pay, you know. It's a political fight. It's not really money they're after.'

'What are they after then?' cried Arthur passionately. 'More pits laid idle? More men out of work? I just can't see the sense of it. The men are simply destroying themselves, condemning themselves to weeks of starvation and misery, and if they don't allow pumping and safety men to work on, there won't even be any jobs to go back to. I just don't see the point of it all. Surely they must know they can't possibly win.'

'No, they don't, Arthur. They think that the Government is going to step in at the last minute and renew the subsidy, or better still, it'll take over the mines again for good. They see the state as their saviour. They don't understand yet that the state is the people and that governments are merely men. Oh yes, they think they're going to win. They can't believe that Saint Lloyd George is going to abandon them in their hour of need. And besides, they don't intend to stand and fight alone

hey're banking on the transport and railway unions to give
ıem support. That way they think they're going to force the
ʳovernment to concede.'

'And how do you know that they won't?'

'Because I know governments. I know politicans — in case
ou had forgotten I used to be one. Lloyd George has changed
ıs position completely. He's as determined now to avoid
ᵉsponsibility for the industry as once he was to take it on. I
ıappen to know for a fact that he's making contingency plans
ɔr a national strike. An Emergency Powers Bill has already
ʲeen drafted. He'll bring troops into the coalfields if necessary.'

Arthur grew pale.' But surely if this were explained to the
ıen? If they knew from the outset that it was futile? They're
ot fools, Father ...'

'No, they're not fools, Arthur, but with pitmen it isn't
ılways just the need to win that's important. It's the need to
ıght. They've always been fighters, even against impossible
ɔdds. They've always been angry men, full of a bitterness and
ıatred that's rooted in their past. And we'll never be able to
ᵉparate them from that past. Even if we conceded to their every
ᵉmand they'd still think of us as slavedrivers and oppressors,
ʰey'll still always want to fight us ... And all the harder now
ınce they know what they're fighting for. The war gave them
. taste of power, you see. They know now that it's not just
ımployers they can hold to ransom, but governments, even the
ᵉry people themselves.' He gave a slow bitter smile. 'So you
ᵉe, Arthur, in a way, we've already lost. They won't ever give
ıp. Oh yes, they're going to lose this battle and probably a
ıundred more. They'll be defeated time and time again but
ʰey'll still come out fighting. And in the end, you know, they'll
ᵛin. Not in my lifetime I hope, but yes, in the end they'll get
ᵛhat they want. The state will take over the entire industry.'

'And what will happen to us?'

'We'll be paid off, pensioned off ...' He smiled. 'But not yet,
ırthur. Not quite yet. It'll have to wait until the industry's on
ʳs feet again and God knows when that will be.'

The next day Arthur drove down to Durham. At Lambton B
ıe sat in his car and watched the last of the coals come rattling
ɔutbye. At four o'clock the men came up and queued for their
ɔay. They seemed to Arthur unbelievably cheerful. It was a

shock to hear their laughter as they dispersed into the gre
drizzle of the afternoon. Gradually it grew quiet, the pulle
wheels at last were still. More men came out; deputie:
overmen — the pit manager was the last. Then the gates wer
slammed shut and chain laid across them. The lock-out ha
begun.

It was like the war all over again: the two sides solid
entrenched to resist, the government, supposedly impartial, i
between. Negotiations went on. Concessions were wrung from
both sides like blood. The owners offered more talks; th
Government, under threat of a general strike, offered
temporary subsidy. The Federation, confident of the suppo
of the two other big unions, stubbornly turned down both
Then on the 12th April, just hours before the national stoppag
was to begin, the transport and railway unions withdrew the
support. The miners were left to fight alone.

And fight they did, all through April and May, though the
adversaries now were hunger and want. Arthur took it a
badly, as if he, in some way were responsible. He took again
going out. With Morpeth and Ashington just miles away h
couldn't avoid seeing what was going on; the death-like exhau
tion that hung over the streets, the pinched and hungry face
He did what he could. He gave money discreetly. He se:
produce from Longhirst to keep the soup kitchens going. H
insisted that the men of his own collieries continued to receiv
their free coal. But it wasn't enough and as the dreary da:
passed it preyed increasingly on his mind. He began to fe
more and more wretched, overcome by terrible feelings of gui
— guilt over the men's suffering, more guilt because by tryir
to alleviate it he undermined the owners' efforts to bring th
lock-out to an end. He became difficult and moody ar
quarrelled with his father and Hugh for the first time in his lif
It sickened him sometimes, how little they seemed to car
Preparations were still going ahead for Hugh's wedding
July. They were talking about champagne and sturgeon, salmc
and caviare whilst thousands of their workers were starving .
And Gina wasn't any help. She didn't agree with his views
any case and she felt she had grievances of her own. She w
jealous of course. Even Arthur recognised that. Hugh and Joa

vere getting all the attention and after their marriage they
vere to live at Etal Manor. Gina had always coveted Etal.

'Why couldn't we have had Etal?' she complained to Arthur.

'Because it wouldn't be practical. Hugh needs to be near
Ford for the running of the estates. I need to be near the
ollieries. Anyway, Longhirst is our home.'

'It doesn't have to be,' argued Gina. 'We could live at Ford.
t seems ridiculous, your father and Margot living there alone.'

'I told you, I need to be near to Newcastle for the running of
he firm.'

Gina laughed. 'Well, I wouldn't mind that if you really did
un the firm. But it's still your father who makes all the
lecisions.'

Arthur coloured. 'Only because that suits us both.'

'Well, it would suit him wouldn't it? He's never been able to
give anything up ...'

'For God's sake, Gina,' Arthur snapped. 'What's the matter
with you lately.'

Gina stood up. 'I'll tell you what's the matter, Arthur. I'm
ired of everyone taking advantage of you. You always seem to
be content to be second best. You always let people have their
own way. You seem to forget that you're the eldest son, that
you are to inherit the title. And yet it's Hugh who has all the
nfluence. It's Hugh who's up there at Ford being lord of the
manor. Hugh wants Etal so Hugh gets Etal. You're not even
consulted.'

'I didn't need to be consulted,' Arthur said. 'Father knows I
don't want to leave Longhirst.'

Gina looked sulky. 'I don't see why not. You're going to
have to leave one day. When your father dies, we'll have to live
at Ford — or are you going to let Hugh have that as well?'

Arthur had said nothing. It was all getting too much for him.
He began to feel as he had during the war, frightened and
nadequate and helpless. And then on the 1st of July, just three
weeks before Hugh's wedding, just when he felt his nerves
couldn't take any more, the terrible struggle came to an end.
The miners were beaten. After twelve bitter weeks of misery
and starvation, at last they had given in. But it wasn't the end.
The fight would go on in their hearts and minds and looking
round at the hatred and desolation on their faces, Arthur knew

that someone, someday would have to pay for this. He felt instinctively that it would be him.

Christmas, 1922 — Northumberland

James stood at the window and watched the carol singers depart. He was always moved by children singing, the clear sweet sound of innocent youth conjured up briefly the vanished magic of childhood. They came every year. It was a ritual now: Good King Wenceslaus and Silent Night, then into the house for hot mince pies and a glass of punch, for the children there was ginger beer. Then Edward, the second footman would appear disguised as Santa Claus and distribute the customary gifts; bags of fruit and sweets and nuts for the children, bottles of sherry and port for the grown-ups. He smiled faintly, remembering the sometimes spartan Christmases of his youth, when an apple and an orange and a secondhand book had been received with excitement and delight. Things were different now. Children were different, they attached more importance to material things. The thought made him glance toward the mountain of parcels, all conscientiously wrapped by himself: rather unimaginatively, pearls for his eighteen year old grandaughter Norah; a silver bangle for Sylvia, just fifteen. Angela being the youngest he had rather spoilt and there were several gaily wrapped parcels for her. And for Jimmy, sixteen, mad on horses, there was a silver handled riding crop engraved with his crest. Then for Hugh there was a collection of stud books, a set of pretty cameos for Joan. For Arthur and Gina he had chosen a fine silver epergne and for Margot, jewels of course, a sapphire and diamond necklace. Vere had been more difficult. She would have been embarrassed by anything too extravagant and he had reluctantly confined himself to a finely bound edition of Byron's poems and then when this had seemed a little too impersonal, had added a simple gold filigree brooch.

He turned away, smiling, feeling rather like a benevolent Santa Claus. He remembered when the children had been young ... He sighed faintly. At his age he supposed that was what Christmas was all about, looking back, reminiscing.

410

inking about people you normally never thought of at all. It as a little sad really; friends, family, people who'd once been aportant in his life, dwindled down to the exchange of a card ace a year. He glanced toward the mantel where a half dozen ards had pride of place, selected from the hundreds that had een sent to him. The pert robin on a log was from his sister olly and the brood of nieces and nephews he hardly ever saw. he religious scene was from Hannah, his brother Jacob's idow; the winter landscape from one of Rosandra's girls. The eld in full cry was from his cousins at Blenkinsopp; the repro- action of a Rubens, all naked infants and goitrous virgins, was om William James' errant son Jimmy. They grew fewer every ear and the faces of the people who'd sent them ever harder to call. He probably wouldn't know Hannah if she walked in on im now. She must be getting on for eighty now ...

That brought a rueful twist to his lips, remembering that he asn't so far off himself, Seventy-five this April coming. He lanced at himself sharply in the pier mirror that reflected the oom. He supposed he wasn't so very decrepit. He'd always aade a point of keeping himself trim. He smoothed a hand own over his waist, looking for signs of a paunch ... Then he und himself flushing. He wasn't usually vain. He wasn't sually so conscious of his age.

He went downstairs and into the Labyrinth Room where the amily were gathered. Joan came up to him and slipped a hand arough his arm. 'We've saved some punch for you but I'm fraid it's rather cold. Would you prefer to try one of Norah's ocktails?'

'No, I would not,' said James feelingly. 'I'll just have a sherry, think.'

Then Gina said, 'Margot and Vere haven't arrived yet. I sent tevens with the car at five o'clock but he's just telephoned rom the station to say that they're not on the train.'

'I expect they've missed it,' said Hugh. 'You know what Margot's like. Or perhaps they couldn't get on the fast train. Everything's a terrible crush at this time of year.'

James frowned. 'But surely she would have telephoned if she as going to be late?'

'Probably she couldn't find anywhere to telephone from.' Iugh smiled at his father's worried expression. 'She's all right,

411

Father. Edward and Vere are with her, you know. They've ju[st] missed the train that's all.'

James nodded. 'Yes, of course.' He looked at Gina. 'Wh[at] time is the next train due?'

'Eight o'clock. I told Stevens to wait. Shall I have dinner p[ut] back or what?'

'No. No. We'll carry on.'

He went in to dinner but his appetite was spoilt. He push[ed] pheasant and truffles around on his plate and tried to mak[e] interesting conversation. But he couldn't keep his eyes from h[er] empty place. He began to be irritated. It was really to bad [of] her to let them down like this, to keep Stevens hanging abo[ut] half the night in the cold. He should have insisted that sh[e] come up earlier in the week. It was ridiculous leaving it to th[e] last minute like this. She might have known that the trai[n] would be all over the place. Tomorrow there wouldn't be any [at] all. His expression grew stern. It was time she married and ha[d] a family. He'd have a word with Edward when he eventual[ly] turned up. It was time that young man pinned her down.

Then just as he was thinking of telephoning the statio[n] again, the glare of headlights swept into the drive. He flun[g] down his napkin and strode into the hall as Margot bur[st] through the door, laughing.

'Father, I'm sorry. We're terribly late, but we missed th[e] train and had to catch the next one which stopped at almo[st] every station.'

'You could have telephoned,' he said crossly.

'But there wasn't time, you see. If we'd looked for a tel[e-] phone we'd have missed that train as well ...'

She came toward him, chattering continuously and he wa[s] suddenly aware of Vere standing hunched and silent by th[e] door. 'Where's Edward?' he asked. 'I though[t] he was coming ..[.]'

'Well, he was,' said Margot quickly. 'But something croppe[d] up at the very last minute ...' She broke off and put her han[d] over her mouth to stifle a spasm of coughing and James felt th[e] hair on the back of his neck stand up. The gesture was familia[r] horribly so, but he couldn't remember ...

Margot smiled up at him weakly. 'I don't think I'm up t[o] very much tonight. Would you mind if I went straight up t[o] bed. It's been a wretched journey and I'm rather fagged ...'

James stared at her. My God, she looked awful; her eyes red rimmed, burning and feverish; two spots of high colour staining her thin pallid cheeks. 'Yes, of course, my dear, if that's how you feel.'

Margot smiled with an effort and squeezed his arm. 'I'm sorry to spoil things. I'll be all right tomorrow. I just need some sleep, that's all.' Then she walked past him. He heard her dry intimate cough as she went up the stairs.

He looked at Vere and knew quite definitely then that something was wrong. Beneath the thin veil of powder Vere's face was all blotched. She looked as if she had been crying. 'What's so, Vere? What's the matter? Have Margot and Edward quarrelled?'

She avoided his eyes. 'No — yes — well, something like that.' Then she glared at him defiantly. 'I really can't talk about it. You'll have to ask Margot. Now please excuse me. I must see if there's anything she wants.'

He stood looking after her, frowning and perplexed. Then he turned and made his way back to the dining room. He halted suddenly, his hand extended toward the door and he remained in that rather foolish frozen position for some minutes. It had come to him suddenly the circumstances in which he had seen that gesture before. His father's skeletal hand clamped over his mouth, blood seeping through his fingers, spilling out over his chin, in the final stages of the disease that had killed him.

Hugh knocked quietly upon his sister's bedroom door and after a minute's silence called out softly, 'It's me, Margot. Can I come in?'

Margot turned away from the window and stared at the door, then she crossed the room and slipped quickly back into the bed. She picked up a book, pretending to read. 'Yes, come in, Hugh,' she called out casually.

'I've brought you a nightcap,' he said cheerfully. 'Hot brandy and milk. I thought it might help you to sleep.'

Margot smiled at him weakly. 'Thank you, Hugh. That's kind of you. I am having trouble getting off.'

'Yes, I know. I saw your light when I let the dogs out for their run.' He sat down on the edge of the bed and took her hands. 'What's up, old girl? Want to tell me about it. Had a tiff with Edward, is that it?'

'No, no — nothing like that.' She gave a shaky laugh. 'As a matter of fact, Edward has asked me to marry him.'

'Oh Margot,' Hugh kissed her. 'I'm delighted for you. Edward's a thoroughly decent chap.'

Margot smiled. 'Yes, he is, isn't he?' The smile faltered. 'That's why I had to turn him down.'

Hugh looked a bit blank. 'I'm sorry, I'm not with you, old girl.'

'I had to, Hugh.' She drew a long shuddering breath. 'I've got consumption, Hugh. Tuberculosis to use the modern term.'

He received the news as he would have received an unexpected physical blow. His shoulders sagged, his body seemed to crumple, there was a sickening nausea in the pit of his stomach. For a long time he couldn't speak, for though he was a man of tremendous physical courage who could have faced a firing squad without wincing, a child in distress, a woman in tears reduced him to a trembling coward. At last he whispered, 'Isn't there anything they can do?'

She saw his distress and tried to appear cheerful. 'I'm not sure really. It depends, apparently, on how bad the lesion on my lung is. The specialist I spoke to appeared quite hopeful. He said that with fresh air and rest and healthy diet ... Of course, I shall have to go away. There's a place, a sanitorium somewhere near Aberdeen — clear mountain air and that sort of thing ...' Her voice tailed away and she took out a hanky and blew her nose. 'Oh, Hugh, that will be the worst thing, having to leave here, having to leave you and Father. What am I going to tell him, Hugh. He's had so much to bear already ...'

'I'm not sure that you'll have to tell him anything,' Hugh said grimly. 'I think he knows, at least he suspects. His face when he came back after seeing you ...' He shook his head. 'I can't quite explain how he looked — sort of bruised almost, as if he'd just had a bad beating.'

Then he took her hands. 'Don't worry about Father. He'll survive. He's a tough old bird really. It's you we have to worry about.' He smiled at her reassuringly. 'It's going to be all right, Margot. You're going to get better, I know you are.' He leaned forward and kissed her hot dry cheek. 'Now you must get some rest. Colonel's orders.'

Obediently she lay down. 'Stay with me, Hugh, until I'm asleep.' Then she smiled as the clock on the mantel struck the hour. 'Twelve o'clock. It's Christmas Day. Merry Christmas, Hugh.'

Hugh attempted to smile, swallowing against the tears that welled up in his throat. 'Merry Christmas, dearest Margot,' he whispered.

April 23rd, 1924 — Aberdeen

The overnight train pulled slowly out of Aberdeen, plunging almost immediately over the wide estuary of the Dee, diminished by the vast landscape of sea and sky and blue granite mountains.

James rose to his feet and pulled down the blind. Familiarity with the view had blunted his appreciation. Every week for the past year he had made the gruelling two hundred mile journey; five hours cooped up in a plush mahogany and brass box; five hours of fruitless speculation, alternating between wild hope and abject despair. Perhaps this time the doctors would be able to tell him there had been some improvement — or perhaps they would tell him there was no hope at all. Usually they were noncommittal, telling him nothing. They spoke grandly about lesions and pulminary tissue and tubercular nodes. They counselled patience and hope and faith.

He closed his eyes. The journey back was always worse, after the misery of seeing her; his daughter, his child, a thin, frail creature crushed by a mountain of blankets. The room was always cold, white and sterile, icy like a tomb, the windows flung open to the clear healing air. And he would sit beside her bed, talking, smiling, holding her small hot dry hands and remembering with anguish all the other times he had sat helplessly by and watched a woman that he loved slowly dying.

He always left about four; she was always tired by then. With Vere he would drive the fifteen miles to Aberdeen and they would have tea in the rather bleak hotel where she kept a suite of rooms. An expression of tenderness softened his face. He was immensely grateful to Vere for that. It eased him a great deal to know that Margot had somebody at hand.

He picked up a newspaper and opened it out, though there was nothing in it that interested him. Nothing interested him now. He read the financial page purely out of habit and followed the antics in the political arena with the half hearted interest of a paid critic forced to watch a second rate revue. It was pure vaudeville. Two general elections in as many years and the certainty of a third before Christmas. Lloyd George was out, the Liberals were out. The Labour party were top of the bill now, with the vain and eloquent Ramsey MacDonald playing the leading man. It would be a short run though. It was only MacDonald that was holding the act together. Supporting cast were a rabble of idealistic Bolsheviks and raw trade unionists, desperately juggling with policies they didn't understand. He'd give them another six months. By the end of the year they'd have been forced out of office. A general election would let the Tories in. Bonar Law and Baldwin were already waiting quietly in the wings, an experienced and polished professional act. They knew what the people wanted.

Then he laid his paper aside and checked his watch. Five minutes to seven. Just time to wash and freshen himself before making his way to the dining car. It was his habit always to take the first sitting. And habit seemed to govern all of his actions now; the same table, the same order, it never varied. Soup and a Dover sole, lightly grilled, cheese and dry biscuits, a half bottle of Sauterne, a single cup of bitter black coffee. Now and then he would glance around him. The dining car was full tonight; men with sleeked back glistening hair, women with smiling red lips. And everybody seemed to be with somebody else. He was suddenly aware of being on his own. Occasionally he found himself under similar scrutiny. Looking up he would catch the odd curious glance, a look — did he imagine it — of sympathy. He smiled wryly to himself, wondering what they saw. Not a giant of industry as the papers liked to describe him, not a man who in his time had swayed governments and kings. No. What they saw was a sad old man sitting on his own, for that, in reality was all that he was — a sad old man, a lonely old man ...

He went back to his compartment and laid down fully clothed upon the made up bunk. He dozed fitfully until the attendant rapped upon the compartment door and announced they were fifteen minutes outside of Berwick.

The next day he went down to Newcastle with Arthur. There were some papers to be signed for at last he had agreed for the Joicey Collieries to be amalgamated with the main Lambton and Hetton group. For three hours he sat in a stuffy and overheated office. He signed countless documents. He approved plans for linking up the lower seams at Lumley, for deepening the shaft at Herrington. He looked at balance sheets and tonnage rates, projections for the future as to profit and loss. The market was sliding again. The brief coal boom of the past year, due to German economic collapse, was gradually levelling out. Even so, the figures were impressive; output touching the five million mark at a profit of one and seven-pence per ton. And finally, he relinquished his long hold on the Joicey Collieries and saw it swallowed up by the giant he had made. From now on they were to be known as the Lambton, Hetton and Joicey Collieries and taken together with his possessions in other parts of the globe, it made him what he had always desired to be, the largest single coalowner in the world.

He insisted on returning home that night, though Arthur pressed him to stay at Longhirst. It was a tiresome journey, driving over mostly rough and badly surfaced roads and as they reached open country it began to rain. Arthur was quiet, but then he always was. Even after all these years one could never be quite sure what he was thinking. He was better of course, a hundred times improved on the end of the war but there was still that underlying nervousness in his manner, that deep tragic sensitivity to pain. He turned to look at him though he could only see his face dimly in the dark interior of the car.

'Penny for them, Arthur,' he said with a smile.

Arthur stirred. 'Oh,' he said, 'I was just thinking about Jimmy, wondering, you know, how he was getting on ... and rather wishing that he hadn't chosen to go into the army.'

'Why not?' enquired James. 'He's gone into a good regiment — Hugh's regiment.'

'Yes, I know ...' Arthur hesitated. 'But it means, doesn't it, that he'll be away a lot? You know we never saw Hugh from one year to the next.' He forced a smile. 'I shall miss him so much, that's all. With Gina and the three girls I'm rather overwhelmed with females. Jimmy rather helped to even it out ...' Arthur's voice tailed off, dropping down to a dispirited note. He didn't really know now why he bothered to pretend. Why not say outright that he hadn't wanted his only son to go into the army because in his mind he equated the army with war and war with death and pain. He turned his head to stare from the window. The car rushed headlong through the night. Rain spattered the glass; white rain seen in the glare of the headlights; darkness arching solidly overhead. Strange how he always felt so much safer in the dark, more able to be himself, more able to express sensibly his sometimes painful and confused thoughts. The dim confines of the car were encouraging too. It had the air of a church confessional. Darkness. Secrecy. They could not be seen, they could not be overhead. He spoke suddenly, expressing a thought that was constantly on his mind. 'Margot's going to die, isn't she, Father?'

From the corner of his eye he saw the agonised movement of his father's head. His voice, drained and stifled answered after a while. 'I don't know, Arthur. We'll have to wait and see. They're discovering new things all the time.'

'But not in time for Margot, Father. You're just deluding yourself, thinking that she's going to get well. You're just hoping when you know that there isn't any hope. It's so futile to keep pretending that everything's going to be all right. And you're only doing it, you know, to protect yourself. It isn't Margot who's clinging so desperately to her life, it's you, because you can't face up to the fact that they're not going to cure her, that all these new treatments you insist upon are only prolonging the misery of her life ...'

'That's not true,' James cried. 'You don't know what you're talking about, Arthur. You see giving in as the answer to everything.'

Arthur flinched but he answered steadily. 'I've never seen the point of struggling against the inevitable and death is inevitable, don't you agree?'

James shook his head. 'I wish you'd talk about something else, Arthur. You're getting a morbid fixation about death.'

Arthur smiled. 'Yes, I suppose I am in a way. Probably

418

because it's the only thing I'm really certain about — that one day I'm going to die. I'm not afraid of it though. Quite the contrary, in fact. I suppose that's the great difference between us, Father. For you life has always been something to be fought and conquered whereas for me it's always been something to be endured.' He gave a harsh laugh. 'Ridiculous, isn't it? To be afraid of life rather than death?'

'Oh, I don't know, Arthur. We all feel a bit like that at times.'

Arthur smiled. 'I can't imagine you being afraid of life, Father.'

'No,' said James. 'Not afraid of it, perhaps. But tired, you know. Just very very tired.'

It was late when James eventually got back to Ford. He paused in the hallway, checking his watch against the long case clock. Exactly one minute to twelve.

Then Jessop came out of the drawing room. He said in his quiet deferential voice. 'Excuse me, my lord. But Miss Bertie's here. She arrived about twenty minutes ago. She's waiting for you in the library.'

James stood very still. Besides him the Tompion long-case clock began to chime, deep mournful notes, like the tolling of a bell.

'Will you be requiring anything else tonight, my lord? I have put whisky and soda on the library table ...'

'No. No, thank you Jessop. That'll be all ...'

He walked slowly toward the library door. He felt faintly dizzy, short of breath. Keep calm, he thought. Everything's all right. That's not why she's here. Oh God, dear God, don't let that be why she's here ...

She was standing by the fire, her head bowed down, staring into the flames.

'Vere?' He called out to her in a quiet desperate voice and after a moment she turned her head and looked at him. Nothing needed to be said. The anguish in her face was a visible thing.

He came slowly into the room and sat down very carefully in his usual chair. His face was quite expressionless, as if fixed by some deep inner despair that numbed all outward feeling. He thought suddenly of Marguerite; Marguerite and the three children she had lovingly borne him, all dead, all vanished, as if they had never really existed at all. Forty years of his life wiped out just like that, as if they had never been. He sat for a long time in rigid silence then eventually he asked, 'Were you with her?'

'Yes. I was with her — right until the end.' She knelt beside him and took his hand. 'She didn't suffer, James. There was no pain.'

He nodded dumbly. He wished he could cry. There would have been such intense relief in tears.

They sat together for a long time in silence, then Vere said quietly 'James. Can I stay?'

He roused himself with an effort. 'Yes, of course. I'll get Mrs Stevens to make up your bed ...'

'No, I didn't mean that — not just overnight. I meant, can I stay here at Ford, all the time?' She scrubbed at her face with a damp handkerchief. 'I haven't really got anywhere else to go — at least nowhere that I want to go. You've all been part of my life for so long.'

'And we'll still be part of it,' James said kindly. 'You know that you can come here whenever you like.'

'Yes, well, people always say that, don't they. Like friends who go abroad and promise they'll write. And they do for a while until it becomes a bore.' She stared up at him miserably. 'I wouldn't be a nuisance, you know. I could make myself useful. I can type a bit and I'm good at arranging things. You'll need someone to see to things ...'

'Vere ...' he leant down and took her hands. 'Nothing would please me more than to have you here — but it wouldn't be fair, it wouldn't be any life for you ...'

'Oh, James,' she pulled her hands away in an exasperated gesture. 'Don't you know? Don't you understand. I want to be with you.'

He stared at her. 'Well, that's kind of you, Vere ...'

'You still don't understand, do you?' She choked back a sob. 'I care for you, James. I have since I was fifteen years old.'

He found it difficult to speak, to even look at her. 'Vere, my dear girl. You don't know what you're saying. Don't you know I'm nearly twice your age.'

'That doesn't matter. I don't care about that.'

He shook his head. 'It wouldn't be fair, Vere. I have to be honest — I couldn't ever marry you, you know.'

'I don't care about that either. As long as I can be with you.'

He was tempted, Oh dear God, he was tempted. This dear sweet girl was offering him the precious gift of love. How sad that it should have taken him all of his life to realize its value. He put out a hand and stroked her hair. 'You know I'm almost selfish enough to let you make that sacrifice.'

She caught at his hand. 'But it wouldn't be a sacrifice, don't you see? The sacrifice would be having to leave you.'

He leant back in his chair and closed his eyes. He was too tired to fight her, too tired and too lonely and too desolate. 'Stay then, Vere,' he said softly. 'Oh yes, please stay, my dear.'

November 21st, 1936 — Ford Castle

It was a special day — he knew immediately upon rising that it was a special day; not just Hugh's fifty-fifth birthday, the day, so long ago now, when Elizabeth had begun her brief, vain battle for life. Today was more than that, grey and silent, full of strange ghostly echoes that drifted in his mind. He went and stood by the window, moving stiffly and slowly, weighed down by the burden of his ninety years. It was still a source of irritation: the mind could live for ever, but inevitably, in the end, the body failed.

The room was hot, oppressively so, and he pushed open the window to let in the air. He surveyed, without interest, the dead November landscape. There was a strange acrid smell on the damp static air, like ashes too long upon the hearth.

He turned back into the room and sat down by the fire. *'Sit yersel' down, Mr James, and hev a bit warm. Whatever else we divvn't hev, we allus hev a champion fire.'*

He frowned, wondering why he should suddenly think of old Matt. It happened quite often now, this sudden, inexplicable turning of his mind toward the distant past. He heard their voices; old friends, old enemies. Things said long ago would suddenly come into his mind.

He looked at his watch. Vere would be here soon. They always took their coffee together at eleven o'clock. His faded eyes softened. Dearest Vere. What a comfort she had been to him these past twelve years. Theirs had been a very special relationship, without passion or desire; undemanding, uncomplicated, asking no more of him than he'd been able to give. It was Vere who had done all the giving; affection, companionship, loyalty and trust. He always thought it strange that only toward the end of his life had he found real peace and contentment with a woman. If he had any regrets, it was only that he hadn't married her, although it was for her sake that he hadn't. It stuck in his mind, a foolish superstition — women who married him seemed to have tragic lives.

He opened his paper. The front page was occupied by the abdication crisis; pictures of the king and Mrs Simpson; a romantic appeal from Churchill to allow a morganatic marriage to go ahead, countered by a lengthy speech from Baldwin, backed by the moral rectitude of the Church. The King must choose — the Crown or Mrs Simpson; Duty or Love. James smiled wryly, thinking as he often did, how times had changed. He couldn't help looking back to the Victorian era in which he'd grown up. My God, the old girl would be turning in her grave at the thought of her great grandson wishing to marry a twice divorced woman and an American at that.

He turned to less controversial issues though it seemed that these hadn't changed much in the last ten years; unemployment, strikes, financial crisis, long winded speeches by naive politicians promising a new prosperity. It was a long time coming, at least it was here in the north. Here they seemed to have reverted to almost Dickensian standards. It was still Bleak House rather than Great Expectations; an industrial wilderness of closed collieries and shipyards, empty factories; grey ghostly towns populated by grey ghostly men who hadn't had a job in years. Looking back, it seemed to him that ever since the Armistice they had blundered inevitably toward disaster. Of course, in retrospect it was always easy to see the mistakes. The 1921 lock-out had been a mistake, the grievances and bitterness left to fester for five years until they'd erupted into the General Strike of 1926. That had been a bad year; the pits closed down for seven long months and a disastrous run on the pound, everyone rushing to turn sterling into dollars. And nearer home, the collapse of Armstrong-Whitworth, the closure of Newburn Steelworks; their own engineering works shut down after sixty years. Their collieries had survived, but only just. For the last four years they had made a thirty thousand pound loss.

And the politicians did nothing except open their mouths and talk. To be fair, there was nothing else they could really do. It all came down to economics in the end, and he'd always held to the theory that the real heart of government was in the City, that the real sources of power were the banks. Over the years he'd lost count of the governments who'd collapsed because they couldn't do their sums. And he'd seen a few come and go: Tory, Labour, Coalition, National — and not one of them had done any lasting good. The Liberals were finished. They'd been bleeding to death since 1916 but not until 1931 had they laid out the corpse. It had been a straight choice then, Right or Left, Tory or Labour. It had been no choice at all for him and three years ago he had crossed the floor of the Lords. He was a fully fledged Tory now.

He turned the page and gave the obituaries a cursory glance. It was strange not to see a name that he knew. He'd worn mourning so often in the last ten years that he'd begun to think of himself as the president of a rather exclusive club with a rapidly declining membership: old Hannah in 1926: in 1928 and 29, within four months of each other, his old enemy Jack Lambton and his brother Freddy. And again in 1929, on a bright morning in May, he'd put it on for his grandson Jimmy, killed by a fall from a horse at Folkestone races, three weeks before his twenty-first birthday. He blinked as the page blurred under his eyes. He could never think of Jimmy without pain — and the even greater anguish perhaps, of seeing Arthur retreat back into his silent and solitary world.

He read on, struggling now with the small fine print. A photograph caught his eye; Chamberlain shaking hands with Adolf Hitler. He stared thoughtfully at Germany's new leader — a ridiculous little man with his lank forelock and Charlie Chaplin moustache, laughable almost, till you looked at his eyes. His own eyesight might be failing but he could still recognize a maniac when he saw one. Chamberlain — all of them — they were wasting their time. No peace pact or arms agreement would stop this man, no amount of mealy talk or placating gestures would prevent him riding roughshod over anyone who stood in his way. There were already sinister rumours creeping out of Europe. People were talking about a Fascist takeover, a world trembling under Nazi rule. Even if you discounted half of them there was still cause for alarm. To him, a man who'd had his ear to the ground for nearly a century the vibrations were unmistakeable. There would be war — war or a peace under German domination. Inevitably, in the end, that would be the choice.

He sighed inwardly. He couldn't help thinking about the future, although he realized that it would be none of his concern. Another war was inevitable, nationalization as well. He couldn't see Arthur coping with either. He still worried about Arthur, his growing instability, his inability to face life. Hugh was all right. Hugh had never given him a moment's concern, except when he'd been abroad in the army, and of course, when he'd married the Lambton girl. But despite his misgivings, that had turned out all right. Hugh and Joan were happy in a way that he'd never been. And they'd given him two bonny grandsons, David and Michael. That was a comfort, to know that Hugh and his boys would carry on. But Arthur, poor Arthur. What would happen to Arthur when he was gone? When he was gone! When he was dead! Why did he keep thinking about that? Probably because at his age death was the only certainty left. And yet the thought didn't disturb him as once it had. He had no conscious wish to die, but his appetite for life was jaded. He felt, sometimes, like a professional voyeur, always looking on but never joining in. But then he'd seen all that he wanted to see, he'd done all there was to do. He heard a voice. '*How much do you want out of life, young James?*' He heard his answer, 'Everything. Everything I can get.' Well, he'd had everything, everything he'd wanted and a great deal that he had not. Ambition and love — these had been satisfied; sorrow and grief had been endured. There was nothing left now but the inevitable physical and mental deterioration, the hope that he would exit with reasonable dignity.

Then another voice; William James. '*That's going to be a bit of a poser, James. To be faced in the end with something that can't be bribed or bought off or taken over.*'

Death. The ultimate takeover bid. James smiled. Yes, he liked that. Putting it like that robbed it of its mystery and error. That was a language he could understand. He hoped that when it came he would give in with good grace. He'd fought it off long enough. When he thought about it, he'd had the most amazing run.

Then he laid his newspaper aside and stared absently into the flames. The warmth and stillness of the room made him drowsy. It was difficult to keep his thoughts from slipping away into the past. He imagined he heard laughter, the rustle of long skirts, a woman bending over him, softly kissing his cheek. Elizabeth? Was it Elizabeth? Or perhaps Marguerite ...? He opened his eyes, but there was nobody there, at least nobody that he could see. But he was aware somehow that he was not alone, that the room with its flickering diminishing light was crowded with vivid memories. Then all at once, he became aware of the beating of his heart, its slow, unhurried, dragging pace. A feeling of wonderful languor swept over him, a draining away of all energy and strength. And he knew suddenly that today had been a special day because today was his last. This was the place then, and this was the time — and what better place than his own fireside, what better time than now with the ghosts of the past softly calling him. His hand slipped down from the arm of the chair. He smiled faintly and closed his eyes.

EPILOGUE

July 24th, 1940
— Ford, Northumberland

It was going to be a glorious day; another scorcher, Arthur thought as he came down from the house, his gun beneath his arm and Butler, the old Labrador at his heels. It was early, just a little after eight. He always like to get out early, before the sun reached its peak and shrivelled him up. And at this time of day he could always be sure of bagging a rabbit or two. They were always a pest just now.

He stood for a moment, lifting his face to the light sun. It was an old man's face, spent and drained, and his eyes, shadowed and pouched by sleepless nights, seemed a long way back in his head. Then he walked quickly down the little path that led to the church. Just inside the gate, in the shadow of the yew trees, two tall stone crosses looked out over the hills. He paused by the first. At the foot of the plinth an arrangement of carnations wilted in a marble vase. That was Vere. Every week she put flowers on his father's grave; carnations, stocks, whatever was about — not roses though. His father had never cared for roses.

He walked round the grave. All four sides of the plinth bore engraved plaques. He read them again even though he knew them off be heart: *In Proud and loving memory of Sydney James Drever Joicey, Killed in action 20th March, 1916; In affectionate memory of Drever Joicey ... of Marguerite de Fontaine Drever Joicey ...* Even his own mother was commemorated here; *In loving memory of Elizabeth Amy ...*'

He turned away and stood before the second cross, where his son lay buried, where he himelf would be buried one day. He visualized the inscription; James Arthur, Second Baron Joicey, born 1st May, 1880, died ... He smiled bitterly. In some ways he hoped it wouldn't be long. He moved away. It wasn't really good for him to keep coming here, to allow himself to keep brooding about Jimmy. It was only since his father had died that he'd begun to make a fetish of it. Without his father he felt no stability. He felt he'd lost the only constant thing in his life. If he thought about it, he'd lost everything, really. Even Gina was lost to him, wrapped up in her own bitterness and grief. His pale sad eyes filled with tears — Jimmy, his dearest Jimmy, his beloved son ... It had been the finish of him really. He's always felt that whatever else he had failed at, he had managed to produce a wonderful son. He'd been so proud of Jimmy; handsome, confident, clever and amusing ... Oh yes, Jimmy had always been able to make him laugh. And now all the laughter was gone. Jimmy was dead, crushed by his own horse and he still didn't know why. If he could have just known the reason, if he could have just know why — Christ, he hadn't even begun to live ... He brushed a hand across his eyes. There was no consolation, even in prayer — and besides, he wasn't even convinced now that there was a God, and even if there was, he didn't know that he could communicate with a God that preyed on innocent young men and left thieves and murderers to prosper.

He lifted his eyes and stared out blankly toward the hills; brassy fields, scorched trees, a sky like a sheet of solid blue glass. No visible signs of the war yet, though there was talk of organizing a force for home defence. Would it ever come to that? German jackboots trampling over his land. They said that it wouldn't but then they'd said that Hitler wouldn't invade Poland either. A muscle in his cheek began to twitch. He'd heard some terrible things, rumours of labour camps, persecution of Jews, whole nations living under a reign of Nazi terror. They'd said it couldn't happen again, that the last war had been the war to end all wars. And yet here they were, just twenty-five years on; the same foe, the same battleground, the same disregard for human life, blundering in with the same muddled optimism. And they hadn't even learnt from their past. They'd been caught on the hop, just like the last time, not enough ships or aircraft, not even enough weapons. He thought bitterly about the fiasco at Dunkirk, thousands of men left on the beaches to die. In a month France had been over-run. Paris was occupied. Holland and Belgium had given in ...

He began to sweat, beads of moisture dripped from his moustache. They said it couldn't happen again and yet it was happening; the monster of war gobbling up their youth, their future. His future was gone. Perhaps he should be thankful that Jimmy hadn't lived to endure it, but there were still Hugh's two boys, David and Michael. Michael was too young, though if the war went on he wouldn't be. But they'd already got David. David was in the Guards, David would soon be fighting ... He licked his lips. He must do something to stop it, though he didn't know what. Everything was going wrong, slipping out of control. The collieries were under state supervision again, and he knew this time they wouldn't get them back. The government were bound to nationalize as soon as the war was over. He thought of his father, how he had fought. He wouldn't be able to fight like that. He wouldn't be able to keep them off, and sometimes he felt that he really couldn't face it, he just couldn't stand the crushing responsibility ...

Then he looked up at the sound of aircraft overhead; two small specks, buzzing like flies. For a long time he stared at them. He didn't know how long, it might have been minutes or hours. The sun dazzled him. There was a pain in his neck from constantly looking up, a strange blankness suddenly descended upon his mind. He turned back toward the house, turning at the last moment into the little beech wood. He had some vague idea in his mind of seeking cover. The wood was dark, shut in by dense whispering leaves. What were they saying? Were they talking to him? Talking about him? He stared at the trees, marching in rows like camouflaged troops. He thought of the war, not this war, though he wasn't sure in his mind that the two weren't the same. He thought about death, the sound and fury of bursting shells, fire and flames consuming him. Then he thought about life, how useless and painful his own really was. Pain that was past. Pain that was yet to come. And in between the awful agony of expectation, wondering where the next blow would come from, cringing, waiting for it to fall ...

Then he started suddenly as a young rabbit scuttled across his path. It froze at the sight of him, transfixed with fear, staring at him in helpless terror. Arthur stared back, round frightened eye meeting round frightened eye. Then he put up his gun. The creature was in his sights. He saw how its muscles

429

twitched and rippled under its sleek grey fur. Grey, like the Bosch uniforms; grey like Flanders mud ... And yes, he could hear the gunfire now, a dull and distant roaring in his ears, but getting closer all the time. They were coming for him. He knew with terrifying certainty that it was him they wanted. They were going to take him back to the trenches. He wouldn't be able to escape this time ... Then slowly he smiled. But he could. Of course he could. Why hadn't he thought of it before? He lowered the gun — and quite calmly and deliberately, he turned it upon himself.

Two miles away at Etal, Hugh Joicey turned his head at the sound of the distant shot. Arthur out rabbiting, he thought to himself, though of course, these days you could never be sure of anything. He turned back to watch his fifteen year old son Michael finish saddling his horse. The sun touched and gilded the boy's fair hair. He whistled softly and tunelessly as he worked, and though there was no physical resemblance at all, Hugh was suddenly reminded of his own father. Suddenly he felt the old man's presence acutely. It was unnerving. He almost expected to see him walk round from the house ... Slowly the sensation passed, but it left in its wake a curious feeling of well being. He felt suddenly optimistic and strangely light hearted, as if, quite unexpectedly, the future was settled and assured.

'Ready, then, Mike?' He held the horse's head whilst his son mounted. Then together they rode out of Etal and took the road for Ford. Hugh glanced up at the brilliant, cloudless sky. It was going to be a glorious day.

GLOSSARY

FTER DAMP — Toxic mixture of gases found in mines after explosions.

IRWAYS — Underground passage along which the current of air travels.

ANK — Above ground. The surface.

ARRIER — Breadth of coal left against an adjoining pit for security against water or gas.

LACK DAMP — Asphyxiating gas high in carbon dioxide. Also called choke damp or stythe.

ORD AND WALL — Method of working coal by driving headings into the seam to form coal pillars.

ROKEN WORKING — Removal of coal pillars left for roof support.

AGE — Iron framework for raising and lowering men and tubs of coal in a shaft.

OWNCAST — Shaft by which air enters the pit.

ACE — The actual coal wall where coal is being got.

ATHOM — A measure of six feet.

IREDAMP — Inflammable non-poisonous gas occluded from coal.

LAT — Station where putters take the full tubs.

OAF or GOB — Worked out portion of the mine from where the coal has been extracted.

EWER — A man who works the coal.

EADGEAR — The head frame of a mine shaft.

EAPSTEAD — All the surface structure around the shaft.

NBYE — In the workings, away from the shaft

NTAKE — Airway along which fresh air is taken into the pit.

UD — Portion of a pillar being worked away.

IBBLE — A square wooden or iron tub.

IRVING — Cutting. A wedge shaped excavation made by the hewer in the lower part of the seam.

AID IN — A pit that has closed for an indefinite period.

ONGWALL — A system of working where the whole of the coal is extracted in a single operation.

NSETTER — Men who put full tubs in and take empty ones out at the shaft bottom.

UTBYE — Toward the shaft.

VERMAN — Person having charge of pit under direction of viewer or under-viewer.

ACK WALLS — Walls or pillars built up of waste stone.

ILLAR — Mass of coal left for roof support.

ULLEYS — The wheels placed above the pit over which ropes for drawing coal are passed.

PUTTER — Usually boys, who bring full tubs from hewers to the flats.

RIDE — To ascend the shaft.

RISE — Upward inclination of coal seam.

ROLLEY WAY — Underground haulage road.

ROYALTY — The minerals below the ground and the right of working them

SCORE — Standard number of tubs of coal upon which hewers and putters prices are based.

SCREEN — Frame for sorting and grading coals.

SEAM — A bed of coal.

SET — A train of tubs.

SLIDING SCALE — A scale agreed between owners and men by which wages are regulated according to the selling price of coal.

STAITH — Coal depot for shipment of coal.

STAPLE — A small shaft sunk upwards or downwards between two seams.

STOPPING — An underground wall or door built to conduct air further into the pit.

STYTHE — Black damp or choke damp. Sometimes used as a general term for gas.

THILL — Floor of a seam of coal.

TUBBING — Wood or metal lining of shaft wall to hold back water.

UPCAST — The shaft by which used air is discharged from the pit.

VIEWER — Manager of the pit.

WAYLEAVE — A rent charged for transporting coals across another royalty

WINDING ENGINE — Engine which raises and lowers the cage.

WORKINGS — Underground excavations from which coal has, or is being worked.